Speak

"In Valen's solid seventh novel featuring St. Paul homicide detective John Santana (after 2015's *The Darkness Hunter*), Santana looks into the stabbing murder of Kim Austin, an accident investigator for the National Transportation Board, whose body was found buried in a cave along the Mississippi River . . . The trail eventually takes the dogged detective to Colombia, where he confronts *el Lobo*, a contract killer, in a dramatic showdown . . ."
— *Publisher's Weekly*

"Valen slips in a lot of red herrings that keep the reader guessing. In the middle of the plot is beautiful, flirty Reyna Tran, one of the most intriguing characters to walk onto a page in a while. Is she friend or foe, would-be lover or killer? She's unreadable and that makes a lot of fun for readers. Almost as chilling as the murders in *Speak for the Dead* is what Santana learns about the terrors of spoofing, a way for bad guys to hack into and take over phones, airplane navigation systems and other devices. You'll start to look at your cellphone in a new way. As usual, Valen conveys a sense of place, from the damp chill of the river caves to the beauty of nature along the St. Croix River."
— St. Paul *Pioneer Press*

The Darkness Hunter

"[A] taut story full of mystery and tension . . . with a pertinent message interwoven into a thrilling plot."
— *Reader's Favorite*

Death's Way

"The tightly wound story moves at a fast pace, with each chapter ending on a cliffhanger so that the audience will want to keep reading . . . this novel represents a gripping offering from an award-winning author."

— *Foreword Reviews*

Bone Shadows

Midwest Independent Publishers' Association 2012
Best Mystery of The Year

"*Bone Shadows* is guaranteed to hold readers' attention until the last page . . . Valen's highly moral Santana character is golden . . ."

— *Library Journal*

Bad Weeds Never Die

"The latest John Santana police procedural is an excellent investigative thriller . . ."

— *Midwest Book Review*

"Christopher Valen's third novel, *Bad Weeds Never Die*, continues the story of John Santana, a homicide detective in St. Paul, Minn., who was introduced in *White Tombs*, and whose story was continued in *The Black Minute*. The three novels are all great police procedural stories . . . I have thoroughly enjoyed reading Valen's novels . . ."

— *Bismarck Tribune*

The Black Minute

"Santana—an appealing series lead, strong and intelligent . . . Readers who enjoyed *White Tombs* will settle easily into this one; on the other hand, it works fine as a stand-alone, and fans of well-plotted mysteries with a regional flair . . . should be encouraged to give this one a look."

—*Booklist*

"[A]s in *White Tombs*, Valen writes well about St. Paul and surrounding areas. He gives just enough sense of place to make you feel like you're there, but he never loses track of his story's fast pacing. And he does a super job of keeping the suspense going as the action reaches a crescendo . . ."

—St. Paul *Pioneer Press*

White Tombs

"Valen's debut police procedural provides enough plot twists to keep readers engrossed and paints a clear picture of the Hispanic community in St. Paul."

—*Library Journal*

"*White Tombs* is a superb police procedural starring a fascinating lead detective. Santana is a wonderful new addition to the subgenre."

—*Midwest Book Review*

The John Santana Novels

White Tombs

The Black Minute

Bad Weeds Never Die

Bone Shadows

Death's Way

The Darkness Hunter

Speak for the Dead

Also By Christopher Valen

All the Fields

City of Stones

For Jennifer Adkins

Many thanks for always making my books better

The Price of
LIFE

A John Santana Novel

Christopher Valen

Santa Rita Press
Tucson, Arizona

THE PRICE OF LIFE
Copyright © 2021 By Christopher Valen

SANTA RITA PRESS
1261 W. Camino Urbano
Green Valley, AZ 85622

Cover Design: Rebecca Treadway

Library of Congress Control Number: 2021916157
Valen, Christopher
THE PRICE OF LIFE: a novel / by Christopher Valen – 1st edition
ISBN: 978-1-7377471-0-9

Santa Rita Press/October 2021
Printed in the United States of America
10 9 8 7 6 5 4 3 2 1

The Price of
LIFE

by

Christopher Valen

"The price of anything is the amount of life you exchange for it."

—Henry David Thoreau

Chapter 1

Four years had passed since Madison Porter's body had been dumped in five-foot-high prairie grass in Pig's Eye Regional Park on the east side of St. Paul. Santana identified the shady spot where the young woman's body had been discovered by the torn strips of yellow crime scene tape still hanging around the trunks of three cottonwood trees. Embedded wheel tracks in the dirt and grass near the trees marked a trail where vehicles had repeatedly driven.

Before driving to the park, he'd reviewed the crime scene photos in the murder book and had stopped by the Property Room, where he checked out the sealed evidence box marked with Madison Porter's case number. The only names written on the sign-out sheet were the original two investigators who had rolled on the body call, Ellis Taylor and Darnell Robinson. Taylor had signed out the box again five months after the investigation began. With no solid leads or suspects since that time, the box had sat unopened, collecting dust.

Santana took a photo of the sign-out sheet and then cross-checked the contents of the box with the evidence list. Nothing was missing. Not satisfied with viewing the evidence list, he wanted to see the actual evidence first-hand, for the same reason that he'd come to the crime scene.

Now, as he stood in the park, he opened the three-ring binder and turned again to the section labeled Crime Scene Photos. He removed the photos from the plastic sleeve and set the binder in the tall grass at his feet. His jaw tightened as he studied the graphic photos once more, saw again what the perpetrator had done to her.

Madison Porter's pale face was turned upward. Her white T-shirt with the reflective red stripes across the chest had been

1

lifted up, exposing her breasts. Her red running trunks and underwear had been pulled down, displaying her genitalia. Her legs were spread open and her arms splayed above her head. Clutched in her hands were the handles of a long jump rope, the cord arcing above her head like a halo. Red rose petals sprinkled her hair and hands. Numerous petechiae congested her face, and a deep mark overlying her larynx encircled her neck, suggesting a thin, tough ligature, like a wire or cord, had been used. Forensics had found no prints on the jump rope or fibers on her neck and had determined that it wasn't used to strangle her.

The crime scene photo reminded Santana of a stanza in the poem *"El Dulce Milagro"* by Chilean poet Juana De Ibarbourou, which he'd been taught as a child.

What is this? Prodigy! My hands bloom,
Roses, roses, roses to my fingers grow.
My lover kissed my hands, and in them,
Oh grace! Roses sprouted like stars.

The scene triggered something else now, something from his distant past. But he couldn't unlock the subconscious gate in his mind, couldn't recall where he'd seen a similar image of the jump rope and rose petals before. Still the depiction lingered, like an amorphous cloud.

Santana's thoughts returned to the evidence box and list. Madison Porter's red running shorts, white shoes, cotton socks with the Nike emblem on the side, her T-shirt with the reflective red stripes, underpants, and sport bra had all been accounted for, as well as the gold chain and locket she'd worn. Inside the locket was a picture of her mother. The jump rope had been in the box along with samples of the rose petals found at the crime scene. Though stored in a dry, dark place inside the evidence box, the petals had begun turning brown.

When Santana decided to reopen the investigation into Madison Porter's unsolved murder, he'd pinned her yearbook photo to the wall above his desk in the Homicide and Robbery Unit. Looking at the photo evoked, for him, the promises and the life that had lain ahead.

Now the photo gave him purpose and a new mission.

He would always remember her face, the brunette hair, crescent-shaped hazel eyes, smooth jawline, and slim nose. In the photo she'd worn braces and had a touch of acne on her milky skin. At 5' 8" tall she had the thin, gawky look of a shy teenager. But Santana knew that teenage awkwardness was often a stage before beauty blossomed. He could tell that once the braces came off and the teenage acne cleared up, the sixteen-year-old girl would have grown into a beautiful woman.

Someone had taken it all from her.

Glancing at the crime scene photo again, Santana noted the slight break in the furrow at the back of her neck, where a hand had grasped the ligature and tightened it at this point. The ligature mark initially would have had a yellow-parchment-like appearance. But the furrow had turned dark brown by the time her body was discovered. Cause of death was listed as ligature strangulation.

Santana knew that physical evidence could often explain what had occurred at a crime scene, but it didn't always tell you everything you needed to know to accurately reconstruct the events of a crime. And the crime scene didn't always put the weapon in the hands of the offender, particularly in this case where there was no ligature, DNA, or other physical evidence found.

A gust of wind scattered papers in the small dirt and gravel parking lot. The lot was more of a turnaround off Fish Hatchery Road, which led to the Minnesota Nature Store warehouse and a large, fenced-in area that held an assortment of state vehicles.

The road dead-ended at the northernmost part of the park, a small triangle of space that included an archery range with six targets, two picnic tables, an outhouse, and a small storage shed that looked like a large dollhouse. But to reach the park's prairie and a 500-acre lake, visitors had to cross sets of train tracks or find the unmarked dirt lot miles to the south. Except for state natural resource officials, few people crossed from one side of the park to the other.

Santana sensed the solitude and the park's isolation. Few people even knew it was a park and even fewer visited it. Forty-five years ago it was a landfill called the Pig's Eye Dump, the largest Superfund site in the state.

Santana had wondered about the name when he first lived in the city. He'd forgotten who'd told him that before St. Paul was established, it was called "Pig's Eye" after the nickname of a Frenchman who was blind in one eye. The Frenchman had built a shack and operated a tavern near Fountain Cave along the Mississippi River, becoming the first inhabitant of what would eventually become the capital city of St. Paul.

Several feet of organic soil had been dumped on top of the landfill and its worst contamination excavated after the turn of the millennium. No solid structures could be built here. There were no immediate residential neighbors, only barge traffic along the river and train yards.

Picking up the murder book, Santana squared the edges of the photos and placed them in the plastic sleeve once more. Then he flipped back to the Chronological Record of the investigation in the beginning of the murder book.

All homicide investigations contained a chronological record of events that documented the investigation and provided information needed for any future investigation. The chrono referenced where in the murder book a report or notes could be found. Each entry provided a description of the detective's actions, what was investigated, and what might need to be further investigated at a later time.

As per department policy, Ellis Taylor and Darnell Robinson had recorded the date and time of each entry, as well as the name of the detective who authored the entry. Done well, any

4

detective reading the chrono should have a clear picture of how the investigation had progressed.

It was evident that Ellis Taylor had completed much of the paperwork. This wasn't unusual as one partner often exhibited better writing skills. Though English wasn't his first language, Santana had lived in the US since fleeing Colombia at the age of sixteen and was fluent in both Spanish and English. Still, given a choice, he'd rather his partner complete the reports. As he was often lead detective now, he could assign the task to his younger partner, as more experienced detectives had once assigned the task to him. But he had no partner on this case. He'd have to write all the reports. That could slow or stall the momentum of the case, which was why, he knew, he shouldn't be working cold cases alone.

He also knew that in reopening a cold case file, he'd have to determine, at least in his own mind, if Taylor and Robinson had conducted a thorough investigation. From what he'd read so far in the murder book, he thought they had. Known throughout the department as "The Blues Brothers" because of their love of blues music and lengthy partnership, they were experienced detectives.

Unless a suspect confessed or was caught committing a crime, there were only two courses a detective could follow in pursuit of a resolution and eventual conviction. He or she either follows a chain of evidence to the suspect, or the detective begins with a suspect in mind and follows the evidence back to the crime.

In the first twenty-four hours Ellis Taylor and Darnell Robinson had collected the evidence, made death notification to the mother, and interviewed the hiker who had veered off the path to investigate a foul odor and had come across the decomposing body. Santana wondered for a time if the hiker was the perpetrator.

Some perps liked getting close to cops, liked helping out. Made them feel better about what they had done. Cops called it the Good Samaritan complex. But Santana saw nothing in Ellis Taylor's notes that indicated either detective suspected the hiker of murdering Madison Porter.

Information about the murder had been released to the press, but specific details of the crime scene, such as the jump rope and rose petals, had been purposely omitted to eliminate publicity seekers who confessed to the crime. Only the perpetrator would know those details.

Because relatives or acquaintances kill the majority of homicide victims, Santana knew that the identity of the victim was the starting point of any investigation. The victim's identity, along with her background and character, indicated possible suspects.

Over the course of the following weeks, Taylor and Robinson had traced Madison Porter's movements, personal habits, and daily-life routines. The detectives ran routine computer checks on the residents living in the vicinity of her neighborhood. They studied her cellphone records and interviewed and re-interviewed all family members and known friends and associates.

They hit a wall.

No one they talked to had a clue as to why someone would want to kill Madison Porter. This led the two detectives in the direction of a random attack, indicating a crime of opportunity and a possible sexual predator. Madison Porter had just been in the wrong place at the wrong time.

But this crime scene wasn't the kill site. Taylor and Robinson had come to the same conclusion after they found one of Madison Porter's running shoes in Battle Creek Park, a two-mile, three-minute drive. Her body had been transported here after the murder.

Five months in, the two detectives were still at a dead end. With each passing day, the probability of clearing the case was weighed against the need for them to work other cases and help shoulder the Homicide and Robbery caseload.

Then, six months after Madison Porter's murder, Ellis Taylor had been shot and killed during a robbery attempt at an ATM while off-duty. A year after his partner's death, Darnell Robinson had retired from the department.

The case went cold.

Santana closed the murder book when he heard the rumble of thunder. Dark clouds overhead cut the last cords of sunlight, leaving him enveloped in shadow. Heat lightning pulsed like a beating heart in the black clouds along the horizon. He could feel the barometer dropping and smell sulfur and distant rain.

Santana was reminded of the Colombian saying he'd learned as a child. *Entre cielo y tierra no hay nada oculto.* Between heaven and earth there is nothing hidden.

Whatever it took, he would find justice for Madison Porter.

Chapter 2

Martin Lozano and his wife, Benita, were the first US distributors for the CJNG, Cartel de Jalisco Nueva Generación, in the Twin Cities. Four years ago the Mexican cartel had sent two high-level members to set up stash houses and front businesses in the Twin Cities. Martin had used his connections within the Latino community to dispense large quantities of nearly pure crystal meth that had been smuggled into the Midwest. The Mexican crystal meth that he and his wife sold now was much better than the old homemade shake-and-bake meth.

The CJNG recruited Americans with Hispanic backgrounds it could trust to move meth, those with clean records and a good job, people who blended seamlessly into the local community without arousing suspicion, couples like Martin and Benita, who had deep roots in the Mexican-American and Latino communities, rather than a cartel member unfamiliar with American law, culture, and language.

Before setting up the new larger distribution network, scores of individual dealers had sold smaller amounts of meth to Asians, blacks, Latinos, outlaw motorcycle gangs, and white trash. Now the CJNG relied on residents like the Lozanos to deal its meth to users. Few knew that they were living a double life in the drug trade. Martin worked forty hours a week managing his auto dealership. He paid taxes and he and his wife had citizenship. His hardworking front was exactly what the cartel bosses wanted. It was a symbiotic relationship that allowed the drug business to thrive.

The Lozanos lived in a large Tudor in the Desnoyer Park neighborhood overlooking the Mississippi River, near the Town and Country Club in St. Paul. They furnished the house with expensive items they'd obtained by bartering with their drug-addicted customers who would give up anything for meth: jet skis, snowmobiles, silverware and china, jewelry and clothes. With four bedrooms and five baths, and nearly 5,000 square feet, they had plenty of room for a family when the time came.

Their supply chain began in Mexico, where the CJNG hid drugs on trucks shipping furniture and produce into the US. The meth was then transferred to individual cars. One vehicle a month arrived at Martin's auto dealership in St. Paul, where he would unload the meth and distribute the drugs to corner slingers in other counties and in Midwest states, taking his cut in the process.

It was a slick operation—until Martin found himself staring down the barrel of a gun.

*   *   *

Martin, Benita, and a young escort named Ana Soriano sat with their backs pressed against the headboard in the Lozanos' master bedroom, their legs stretched out in front of them, a sheet pulled up to their chins, their eyes wide, their faces masks of fear. The heavy scent of perfume and sex hung in the air.

Joel Ryker held his Glock on them and chuckled to himself. "Well, isn't this a treat," he said. "Always wanted a *ménage à trois*, but my ex wouldn't go for it." He shook his head as though he couldn't understand her reluctance. "She had zero sense of humor, so we split."

He tossed an empty canvas backpack on the floor near the far wall. "The money," he said.

Martin glanced at the canvas bag. No way he was losing his money to some two-bit rip-off artist. "What money?"

"The drug money in the wall safe."

"You are mistaken," Martin said, forcing a smile. "There is no wall safe. No drugs."

Keeping the gun leveled at the three of them, Ryker side-stepped across the room, yanked a painting of Frida Kahlo off the far wall, and tossed it on the floor.

"This safe," he said. He motioned with the gun. "Get up and get dressed."

"And if I don't?"

"I'll kill you and your wife and your girlfriend."

"Then you would not get the money."

"And then you and your two pin cushions would be dead. Your choice."

Martin weighed his options, knowing full well that there was no good option, just a less bad one. Finally, he settled on, "You know whose money this is?"

Ryker smiled. "Yeah. It's mine—now." He motioned with the gun again.

Martin got out of bed. Put on a pair of underwear, dark slacks, and a white shirt, which he took his time buttoning, maybe hoping he'd come up with an alternative before handing over the money. Then he walked to the safe.

Ryker held his aim on Martin while he looked at the two women still in bed. "Get up," he said.

The young woman on his right slid out of bed and reached for her black panties and the black dress slung over the back of a cushioned chair. No hurry. No embarrassment. Like she was used to being naked in front of men.

Beautiful, Ryker thought, black waist-length hair, a little short, but best body he'd ever seen.

Benita hesitated, her hands still clutching the sheet under her chin. Ryker nodded and waved the gun at her.

She got out of bed and let the sheet fall from her hand as she reached for her clothes on an armchair beside the bed.

When the safe clicked open, Ryker could see the multiple stacks of bills.

"In the sack," Ryker said. "Now."

Martin shrugged his shoulders and picked up the back-pack. As he turned his back to Ryker, he reached farther into the safe and yanked out a Ruger.

He was quick—but not quick enough.

Ryker fired twice.

Martin crumpled, the Ruger tumbling from his hand and sliding away from him.

Benita looked at her dying husband on the floor and then at Ryker, her eyes growing wide with surprise as he pointed the barrel at her and fired again.

The round hit her in the head, scattering brain and skull fragments. Blood spattered on the bed and the wall behind her. She fell face first onto the hardwood floor.

Ears ringing, heart hammering in her chest, Ana Soriano sank to her knees and clasped her hands in prayer. The pungent smell of nitroglycerin, sawdust, and graphite from the gunpowder hung in the air.

Ryker stepped forward. Pressed the gun barrel against her head.

"*Morenita, mi virgen de Guadalupe, ayúdame, por favor,*" she whispered.

"The Virgin of Guadalupe isn't going to help you, sweetheart. What's your name?"

"Ana."

"Okay, Ana. The money. In the backpack," Ryker said in a calm but firm voice.

Ana peered up at him, a questioning look on her face.

Ryker saw the haunted look in her blue eyes, as if she'd seen more than she should have in her young life.

Then, understanding his meaning, Ana nodded. Fighting a rising panic, she scrambled to her feet and hurriedly stuffed the stacks of money in the backpack. Holding a corner of the backpack toward Ryker, she bowed her head and began praying again for help from the virgin of Guadalupe.

"Tell me why I shouldn't kill you," Ryker said.

Ana paused a moment, unsure if he was kidding or serious. "Because I won't talk," she said quickly.

Ryker smiled. "Anyone in your situation would say that. But I think you mean it. Your accent isn't Mexican American. You illegal?"

She nodded and suppressed a shiver.

"Hooking to make some money, or maybe a high-class escort," Ryker said. "Not some street ho." He paused a moment before continuing. "I don't think you'll talk. You might want to consider leaving before the cops show up and send your cute little ass back across the border."

He slung the backpack over his shoulder and holstered his Glock. Heading for the front door, he said, "Today's your lucky day, *señorita*. Maybe I'll come see you some time."

In that split second Ana Soriano knew her life could change forever. Knew that she would never get this opportunity again. She dove for the Ruger Martin Lozano had dropped. Holding it unsteadily in one hand, she aimed the barrel at Ryker's back.

When he reached the door, she said, "Not your lucky day, *hijo de puta.*"

Ryker turned, his expression switching suddenly from brazenness to shock. "Made a mistake trusting you, huh?"

"Leave the money and go."

Ryker shook his head. "No way, *señorita.*"

He stepped toward her.

"Don't!" she yelled.

"Easy now," Ryker said, stopping and raising his hands in surrender. "You don't want to shoot me."

"Then drop the bag and go. Now!"

Ryker shrugged. "Sure."

He let the backpack slip off his shoulders and fall toward the floor, his eyes still locked on Ana. When he saw her gaze shift to the backpack, he went for his Glock.

Ana heard a shot as she closed her eyes and jerked the trigger. The roar of the gun was deafening, the powerful recoil as palm numbing as a shot of Novocain.

Blood streaked the wall as Ryker slammed into it and slid to a sitting position.

With her eyes closed, Ana continued firing till the slide locked open on an empty chamber.

Smoke drifted upward from the barrel, like a spirit leaving a corpse.

Chapter 3

After leaving Pig's Eye Regional Park, Santana drove to Darnell Robinson's home. The retired detective lived in a Craftsman in the Highwood Hills neighborhood on St. Paul's East Side.

Santana parked along the curb behind a U-Haul trailer attached to a late-model black Ford-150 pickup. Raindrops splattered on the windshield as Santana got out of his unmarked, hurried up the sidewalk and onto the porch, and rang the doorbell.

"John Santana," Robinson said in a surprised tone as he swung open the front door. "How the hell are you?"

"I'm good, Darnell."

"Come on in," he said, holding open the screen door.

When Santana entered, he saw that the living room was bare of furniture save for two fabric club chairs. Moving boxes were stacked in the corners.

"Sold the house and moving up to my cabin in a couple days," Robinson said. "Now that the wife has passed, figure I might as well take advantage of the place."

"Hadn't heard about Regina's death," Santana said. "Sorry for your loss."

He'd met Robinson's wife, Regina, at a few SPPD functions over the years though he hadn't known her well. He did remember that she was born in Figueres, a small city close to the French border in Catalonia, Spain. She'd left Spain in her early teens when her parents had moved to the States, where she'd learned the English language. She spoke Spanish reasonably well, though she'd grown up primarily speaking Catalan.

"Stroke," Robinson said. "Pretty unexpected, like a lot of things in life." He let out a long breath and gazed at the room as if he half expected to see his wife standing there. He looked at Santana again. "But you gotta move on."

"Best that you do."

"Yeah." Robinson shrugged his big shoulders. "What choice do you have?" He gestured toward one of the chairs. "Get you a beer or are you on the clock?"

"Officially, yes."

"Another time then."

As Santana sat down, he heard rain hammering the roof and a rumble of thunder.

Robinson eased himself into the second chair.

He wore a white tank top and jeans. Like his former partner, Robinson was a 6'4" former college basketball player who had stayed in shape. His smooth dark skin made him appear at least ten years younger. He had an 82nd Airborne tattoo on his upper right arm.

"You're looking good," Santana said.

"Blacks don't crack," he said with a chuckle.

"How's retirement?"

"Always thought getting old would take longer." He grinned. "Thought I'd be looking for something to do, but I'm busier now than when I was with the department. How 'bout you? Heard you retired."

"Took a leave. I'm back now."

"Good to know," he said. "Department needs guys like you." Robinson was quiet for a time before he said, "You didn't stop by to talk about my retirement."

"Madison Porter."

"Ah," Robinson said with a knowing nod.

"I'm working cold cases. Thought I'd give this one a look."

"Wish Ellis and I could've cracked it. Got any leads?" Curiosity was now evident in his voice.

"A little early," Santana said.

"Yeah. Takes time to get your head around everything."

"You have a cell number where I can reach you?"

"Sure thing," he said, rattling off the number.

Santana added the number to his contact list on his personal cellphone. Then he said, "I was hoping you might have something that wasn't in the murder book."

Robinson paused before responding. "Like what?"

"A hunch. Maybe something you considered but couldn't prove."

"Nah," Robinson said. "Wish I did. Toughest cases to prove are the random ones. Ellis and I pretty much agreed that it went down that way. But you can't let a case eat you up."

"How so?"

"I've had a lot of time to think about my years on the force, John, particularly the years I spent in Homicide. Got to know quite a few homicide detectives over the years. Came to realize there were two types."

"Tell me."

"First type finishes one case and moves on to the next without letting the darkness get to them. The second type uses it as motivator to bring the perp to justice no matter what the cost. Always pegged you as the second type."

"Maybe so."

"No doubt about it. Problem is, John, you carry all that shit with you from case to case. You know how it can go. Sometimes the burden becomes too much, and a cop swallows his gun or drinks himself to death."

"What type was Ellis Taylor?" Santana asked

"Couldn't let the ugliness roll off his back. Don't take me wrong. Ellis was a good cop. I really miss the guy. But I think the darkness was getting to him."

"And you?"

"I used to hit the sauce pretty hard. Now I fish, hunt. Take lots of walks in the woods near my cabin. I've lost weight and enjoy an occasional cocktail."

"Good to hear you let it all go."

Robinson offered a half smile and a pause before he said, "Not all of it."

*   *   *

Madison Porter's older sister, Ashley, was a loan officer at Elysium Bank, located on the main floor of a ten-story office building in downtown St. Paul. Ellis Taylor had been shot and killed while withdrawing money from an ATM at the bank.

Santana was well aware of the phrase "Shit Happens" — and it did. Far too often it was bad shit that he had to deal with in Homicide and Robbery. But he never ascribed to the belief that everything in the universe was the result of fate, or God's work.

He'd lost his faith in his teens with the accidental death of his father at the hands of a drunk driver and with the murder of his mother. So no, he thought, God didn't have a hand in all of this. Coincidences existed. Coincidences were real. Saying they weren't stopped inquiry. Santana chose to keep an open mind and to seek the path of investigation.

A large computer monitor took up most of the space on the cherry-wood desk that sat in front of a small matching bookshelf in Ashley Porter's office. On either side of the bookshelf were a framed degree in economics from the University of Minnesota and a Certified Regulatory Compliance Manager license.

Ashley Porter stood up behind the desk and offered a ringless hand and cursory smile. She had the same features as her younger sister, Madison, but her eyes were light brown and her pale skin was dusted with light brown freckles. Her strawberry blond hair was cut in a short fringe style with a low, loose ponytail, giving her a chic, French look. The expression on her face was as blank as the whiteboard on the opposite wall.

"Please, sit down, Detective," she said, gesturing at one of the two cushioned chairs in front of the desk.

She wasted no time once he was seated. "You said on the phone that you were looking into my sister's murder."

"That's right." Santana retrieved a pen and spiral notebook from an inner pocket in his sport coat. He never trusted detectives who wrote in pencil.

"Why now?" she asked.

"Not sure I understand your question."

"It's been four years since Maddie's death, Detective. Do you finally have a suspect?"

"Not at this time."

She pursed her lips and shook her head in frustration. "Then why are you here?"

"I need to get up to speed on the case. One way of doing that is to interview the friends and family of the victim."

"Our mother passed away two years after Maddie's death. You can attribute that to Maddie's murder as well. Mom never got over it."

Santana had learned from the follow-up reports that Madison Porter's mother had contracted cancer shortly after her daughter's murder and had died two years ago. He had no children of his own, but experience had taught him that there was nothing worse than telling a mother she'd lost a child. Those anguished cries had forever scarred his memory. But while working cold cases offered additional challenges, Santana was relieved that he wouldn't be facing a traumatic death notification or a mother set on revenge.

"What about your father?" Santana asked.

"He might as well be dead as far as I'm concerned."

From the Investigative Summary report Santana had learned that Madison Porter had moved with her mother and 19-year-old-sister, Ashley, from Indiana to Minnesota after their parents' divorce and a year before Madison's death. Their mother, who had grown up in St. Paul, had accepted a job as a management assistant for Ecolab.

Ellis Taylor had flown to Indiana to interview the father during the original investigation. Taylor had concluded that Ryan Porter was not the perpetrator. Santana had found nothing in the reports as to why Madison was estranged from her father and wanted to explore the issue further.

"You don't get along with your father?"

She gave him a contemptuous smile. "My father was a likeable, friendly guy—when he wasn't drunk."

"Did he always drink?"

She shook her head. "The heavy drinking started after the Indiana plant where he worked for twenty years closed down and moved its production to Mexico. Madison began jogging shortly after that. Kind of surprised me since she was always more into her studies than sports. But it got her out of the house, away from our parents' constant arguing."

"What about you?"

"I played some basketball and lacrosse in high school."

"I meant how did you cope with your father's drinking and your parents' arguing?"

"I left for Indiana University. Dropped out after two years and moved here to live with my mother and sister."

"What do you remember about the night Madison was murdered?"

Santana chose to refer to long-ago victims by first names only. It was part of an effort to forge personal connections, rather than think of the victims as case numbers.

"You already have all that information, Detective."

"Technically, yes. But in my experience, I've found that over time, people sometimes remember things."

"They also try to forget things." She paused. "What makes you any different than the two detectives who tried and failed to solve my sister's murder four years ago?"

19

"I'm a set of fresh eyes. And I'm good at what I do."

"Better than the previous detectives?"

Santana saw the skepticism and the challenge in her eyes.

"Give me a chance to find out."

She exhaled a heavy breath and gave a reluctant nod.

"Was there anything unusual or different you remember about that evening, Ms. Porter?"

"No. It was pretty much the same."

"You were home all evening."

"Yes." She held her eyes on Santana for a moment. Then she closed them as if to deflect the ugly memory before she spoke.

"My sister liked to run before sunset. Every summer evening between eight and nine o'clock, after the temperature had fallen, she'd run." Her voice was flat, emotionless, like someone in a trance. "I remember it was about eight p.m. July sixteenth. Maddie waved good-bye to my mother and headed for a run in Battle Creek Park, near our home. When she didn't return by eleven p.m., my mother called 911." She opened her eyes suddenly and glared at Santana. "But the police did nothing."

Because Madison was in the age group with one of the highest runaway rates, Santana knew her disappearance was viewed by the department as a possible runaway situation and handled as a routine missing-persons case, despite the mother's protests that her daughter hadn't run away.

Battle Creek Park closed thirty minutes after sunset, around nine thirty p.m. in mid-July. According to Ellis Taylor's notes, Madison had told her mother she would be home before dark, a requirement her mother had insisted upon. Three weeks later, her decomposing body was found among the tall grass in Pig's Eye Regional Park.

Santana was familiar with the Battle Creek neighborhood. The homes were mostly older but well-maintained one-and-a-half-story rectangular bungalows with steep-pitched gabled roofs.

He'd once investigated the death of a young call girl who'd been murdered in Battle Creek Park.

"Was Madison dating anyone?"

"My mother thought she was too young to date."

"Were you dating?"

She leaned back as if to create distance from the conversation. "What does my dating life have to do with my sister's murder?"

"Maybe nothing."

"But you still want to know."

"I do."

"I was dating Derek Shelton."

Santana had found nothing in the Investigative Summary report indicating that Robinson or Taylor had interviewed Ashley Porter's boyfriend. Santana considered it an oversight, though he wondered if Ashley had denied having a boyfriend at the time in order to spare him from the investigation.

"Did Mr. Shelton know your sister?"

"Of course."

"How long did you two date?"

"We're still dating."

"Congratulations."

When Ashley Porter offered no response, Santana continued. "I understand you work as a compliance officer here at Elysium."

She nodded.

"What exactly does a compliance officer do?"

"We oversee accounting, investment, and lending operations at the bank to make sure that we're in compliance with federal, state and local laws. We also monitor new financial regulation and keep everyone apprised of recent updates."

"You said 'we,' Ms. Porter. So there's more than one compliance officer at the bank."

"Several, including our chief compliance officer."

"And who would that be?"

She hesitated a moment before replying. "Derek Shelton."

"Your boyfriend."

"Significant other," she said with a half smile.

Santana peered at the questions he'd written down in his notebook before saying, "You were the last person your sister spoke to before her death. What did you talk about on that last night?"

"I don't remember specifically."

"Did your sister seem anxious or concerned about anything the last time you spoke with her?"

"No," she said, her eyes not quite meeting his.

As an experienced homicide detective, Santana believed that everyone had secrets they kept from family members and close friends. He had secrets of his own.

There was a knock on the office door and then it swung open.

"Hope I'm not interrupting," the man said, knowing full well that he was.

"Derek, this is Detective Santana from the St. Paul Police Department," Ashley Porter said.

Derek Shelton had dark brown eyes and the burly build of a weightlifter. He came forward with a big, reassuring smile and a thick outstretched hand. "Nice to meet you, Detective Santana."

Santana stood and shook his hand.

Shelton had a firm handshake and the exuberant, self-assured personality of a used car salesman. His dark blue suit fit small and tight across his broad shoulders.

"You're here about Madison Porter's murder," Shelton said.

Santana looked at Ashley Porter.

"I told Derek that you were coming," she said.

Santana pointed to the chair beside his. "Saves me a trip."

Shelton appeared surprised and remained standing. "I don't know anything about her death."

Though his tone was casual, Santana heard the defensiveness behind the words.

"But you were dating her sister," Santana said.

Shelton's eyes narrowed with suspicion and then brightened again, as though a dark cloud was moving past the sun. "Was it three years ago that she was murdered?"

"Four," Ashley Porter said, glancing at him.

"Okay," he said, focusing on Santana. "So, it was four years ago."

"Do you recall where you were and what you were doing the night she died?" Santana asked.

"I couldn't tell you exactly what I had for breakfast a week ago." He spread his hands. "How am I supposed to remember what I was doing that particular evening?"

"Because that evening *was* particular, Mr. Shelton. It was the evening your girlfriend's sister went missing and was later found murdered. Most people would remember an evening like that."

He held up his hands in defense. "Wish I could help. But I'm sure Ashley will do all she can to help you." He shot her a thin smile and headed for the door.

"One more question, Mr. Shelton," Santana said, stopping him in his tracks.

Shelton turned, an expectant look on his face.

"Ellis Taylor, one of the two detectives originally assigned to investigate Madison Porter's murder, was shot to death six months after her murder."

"I'm sorry to hear that," Shelton said.

"You don't recall the shooting?"

"No," he said. "Why would I?"

"Because it took place at the ATM outside this bank, Mr. Shelton."

Shelton's eyelids fluttered in discomfort for a split second. "Oh, right," he said, with a tight-lipped smile. "I do remember that shooting. Did they ever catch the, how do you say it in your parlance, the *perpetrator*?"

Having been trained in facial recognition, Santana had noticed Derek Shelton's micro-expression of discomfort and his tight-lipped smile. Both were indications of a concealed emotion, most likely deceit in this instance. People often got emotional when they lied, especially when the stakes were high. Maybe Shelton feared getting caught or felt guilt or shame for lying about Taylor's murder. Or maybe Shelton liked the thought of successfully lying to others, especially those in positions of authority.

"No," Santana said. "We haven't caught the perpetrator. At least not yet."

Shelton nodded and opened the office door. Before stepping out he said, "Everyone at the bank hopes that you find Madison's killer. The perpetrator who killed the cop as well."

He closed the door behind him as he left.

Santana removed a business card from his badge wallet and set it on Ashley Porter's desktop. "Feel free to call me if you remember anything else."

She glanced at the card but didn't pick it up.

Chapter 4

Two whiteboards hung side-by-side on a wall in the St. Paul Police Department's Homicide and Robbery Unit located on the second floor of the James Griffin building. The building was connected to the Ramsey County Law Enforcement Center, which also housed the Ramsey County Sheriff's Department.

One of the whiteboards listed the current homicides detectives were working and the various stages of investigation. The second whiteboard listed ten cold cases previous detectives assigned to the cold case unit thought they had a chance of solving, if new information came forward.

Santana glanced at the boards as he headed for Janet Kendrick's office. Kendrick was the SPPD's Senior Homicide Commander. Pete Romano, the former homicide commander, was now Deputy Chief of Operations, which oversaw the Western, Central, and Eastern Patrol Districts, along with City-Wide Services.

Janet Kendrick was considered a fair-minded, by-the-book cop. But outside of an occasional "Hello," or a nod in passing over the years, she was more of a stranger than a colleague to Santana. Before his return to the SPPD he had reviewed her background, as much out of curiosity as preparation. In her ten years with the department she'd worked Narcotics and Vice, Homicide and Robbery, and Internal Affairs.

It was her most recent position in IA that concerned Santana. Officers who worked in, or came out of, IA were viewed with suspicion by their colleagues—and often with good reason. Still, he was willing to give Kendrick the benefit of the doubt. Until proven otherwise, he didn't believe, as some detectives did, that IA existed only to hem them up for something stupid or for an honest mistake.

Christopher Valen

As Senior Commander of the Internal Affairs Unit, Kendrick had reported directly to the Chief of Police. The two Investigative Sergeants working under her were supposedly chosen because of their integrity, fairness, excellent work record, investigative ability, and common sense. In Santana's experience not all who were chosen for IA exhibited these characteristics.

Santana hoped that Janet Kendrick was the exception.

As he entered her office she was leaning forward in her chair, staring at a sheet of paper. With her left elbow on the desk and her left hand fisted under her chin, she reminded Santana of Rodin's *The Thinker*, the sculpture that depicted Dante reflecting on his *Divine Comedy*, the epic poem about heaven, hell, and the fate of all humankind.

A yellow brick sat on the corner of her desk. Kendrick had completed a ten-week professional course of study at the FBI National Academy. Enrollees had to be nominated by their agency heads because of demonstrated leadership qualities.

During the graduation ceremony Kendrick had received the Yellow Brick Road award. The award was the culmination of a fitness challenge that included a 6.1-mile run through a hilly, wooded trail that was built by Marines. Enrollees had to climb over walls, run through creeks, jump through simulated windows, scale rock faces with ropes, crawl under barbed wire in muddy water, and maneuver across a cargo net. If they completed the endurance test, they received an actual yellow brick to memorialize their achievement.

"Good to have you back in the fold," Kendrick said.

She pushed her straight black hair behind her ears as Santana sat down. She wore it parted in the middle and blunt cut just above her shoulders.

He wasn't certain yet that it was "good" to be back after six months of R&R, much of it spent with his sister, Natalia, who lived and worked in Spain. He had taken an approved leave from the department, not knowing if he would ever return. As

26

per department policy, employees granted leaves of absence of thirty days or more had to turn in their badge, handgun, and ID card to the SPPD's Human Resources and Inspection units prior to taking a leave. Now Santana once again felt the familiar weight of his Glock and his badge, and the responsibility and power that came with each.

"I hope you're happy working in the Cold Case unit."

What there is of it, Santana thought. But rather than start out on the wrong foot with Kendrick, he said, "I assumed I'd be working with my partner again."

"In your absence, Kacie Hawkins was assigned another partner. That pairing seems to be working out quite well. Besides, it's my understanding that you've had a history of going your own way."

Santana started to protest, but Kendrick held up a hand in a stopping gesture. "Let me finish. You're a fine homicide detective. Although some in the department haven't always agreed with your methods, the results can't be denied. For that reason, I thought you would be happy working alone on cold cases that need solving."

"There are over one hundred cold cases," Santana said. "We need more than one person."

"I have full confidence in you getting the job done, Detective."

"Why not apply for another federal grant?"

A $260,000 federal grant that once funded the Cold Case unit had run out. Santana was curious as to why Kendrick hadn't reapplied. There were always federal monies available if you were willing to look—and were willing to take the time to write the grant.

"Would you like to write the grant, Detective?"

"Not really."

"Well, then, it's up to you. It's my understanding that before the grant money ran out, ten cases were turned over to Homicide and Robbery to be investigated."

"That's right."

"Have you selected a case that has promise?"

Santana explained that he had chosen Madison Porter's case. "I've gone through the murder book, looked at the crime scene. I've talked with the sister."

"Any DNA?"

Santana shook his head.

"Any fingerprints?"

"No. But we might be able to link the murder weapon through the unique configuration of the ligature—if we had it."

"Any new leads at all?"

Santana knew that when it came to investigating cold cases, new evidence primarily came from DNA, fingerprints, or ballistics. Without one or more hits from these databases, typically a cold case binder would be returned to the shelf.

"Afraid not," he said.

"Then why waste what little resources we have on the Porter case?" Kendrick asked.

"First of all, I don't consider this case a waste of time."

"You know what I meant, Detective."

Santana wasn't sure what she meant, but he decided not to press the issue.

"When I worked Homicide," Kendrick continued, "I built connections with the families, as I'm sure you have. And in my current position I continue to hear from family members and relatives in unsolved cases. They're still struggling to understand their loss. I try to provide them with updates, but if nothing is happening . . ." Kendrick ended the thought with a helpless shrug.

Santana's heart went out to the families of the victims. No detective ever joined the department to ignore a murder. Cases turn cold for good reasons. But getting to the bottom of a case that was four years old without additional staff and evidence would be difficult—but not impossible.

"We have a sixteen-year-old young woman who was brutally murdered," he said. "We have no justice and no closure for the remaining family members. And we have somebody out there that committed this crime."

Kendrick nodded as though she understood. "I'm sorry we don't have more resources to offer you. I know you'll give this case—every case—your best."

Santana hoped his best was good enough. As he stood to leave, her desk phone rang. He was halfway to the door when she called out to him.

He turned back.

Kendrick held up an index finger, indicating he should wait. She listened for a moment, wrote something on a piece of paper, and then said, "Thanks, Ray."

Santana figured the "Ray" she was speaking to was probably Ray Bainbridge, the on-duty watch commander.

Kendrick's eyes ticked up at him as she hung up the phone. "There's been a shooting. Three DBs." She held out a piece of paper. "Here's the address in Desnoyer Park."

"What about Madison Porter?"

"She's waited four years. She'll have to wait a little longer."

Chapter 5

Santana saw the flashing red, blue, and yellow from the LED light bars on the two black-and-whites parked beside the curb in front of a large Tudor with its half-timbers and stucco-clad exterior. A white crime scene van owned by the SPPD's Forensic Services Unit and a refrigerated morgue trailer belonging to the Ramsey County Medical Examiner's office were angle-parked on either side of the squads. A dark blue Mercedes sedan was parked in front of one of the double garage doors. A Dodge Ram pickup was parked in front of the other garage door. Media vans from the local TV stations lurked at the corner of the next block. Reporters thronged behind a boundary of crime scene tape strung around the oak trees in the yard.

Santana's thoughts were still fixated on Madison Porter's murder, though he knew he needed to shift his focus. He was upset that Kendrick had pulled him off the cold case just as he was gaining forward momentum, but he understood that the department had more current homicides than they could handle.

Santana showed his badge to the heavyset African-American officer holding a clipboard with the Crime Scene Attendance Log. His nametag ID'd him as EDWARDS.

"Who was first on the scene?" Santana asked him.

Edwards made a hitchhiking motion toward a second officer manning the front door.

"You clear the house?"

"Sure did." He hesitated.

"And?"

"Lotta drugs in the back bedroom. Looks like a stash house."

Santana nodded. Then he signed the log and slipped under the tape.

Ignoring the TV cameras and the media questions shouted at him from a crowd of reporters, Santana climbed a wide set of five brick steps that angled left from the concrete driveway and then followed a flat brick pathway leading to a stone arch over the entrance.

The second officer stationed at the front door had a buzz cut and the face of a teenager. His nametag identified him as COPELAND.

"Who found the bodies?" Santana asked.

"Maintenance man named Gordon Grant came to replace the shower head in the master bedroom upstairs," the officer said, reading from his notepad. "Front door was partially open. Found the bodies in the master bedroom. Called the station."

The maintenance man's name sounded familiar, but Santana couldn't place where he'd heard it before. "Where's Grant now?"

"On the back patio."

"Tell him to stay there," Santana said.

"Copy that."

"Either of you officers turn off any lights or open any doors or windows?"

"No, sir."

"Touch the bodies?"

Copeland shook his head.

"How about Grant?"

"Said he didn't touch anything but the door handle. Found the bodies upstairs and called 911 on his cell."

"Is there a back door into the house?"

"Yes, sir."

"Make sure it's locked. I want everyone coming in the front door."

"You got it."

"You run the plates on the Mercedes and pickup in the driveway?"

"I did. Mercedes belongs to a Martin Lozano listed at this address. Pickup is registered to a Joel Ryker."

As Santana gloved up, Copeland said, "Edwards tell you about the drugs in the back bedroom?"

"He did."

Santana pressed each foot into the Bootie Box the Forensic Services Unit had left on the doorstep and walked through the half-open door into a high-ceilinged entryway. A curving stairway led to the upstairs master bedroom and the bloody smell of copper and rusted iron.

Santana squatted in front of the body slumped against the wall beside the bedroom door. The man's chin rested on his chest. His head rocked to one side. He appeared to be in his mid-thirties. He had long blond hair, a mustache and goatee. He wore an olive-drab field jacket over a black T-shirt, jeans, and black combat boots. A Glock 19 rested in a belt holster on the right side of his waist. The pooled blood beside the body was smeared, as if something had been dragged through it.

Santana saw Tony Novak, manager of the FSU, bent at his knees dusting fingerprint powder onto a nightstand next to the king-size bed. Novak wore a full-length open-back gown, disposable vinyl gloves, and booties over his shoes. Novak managed seven sworn officers, including one police sergeant and two civilian criminalists with natural science backgrounds. One of the female criminalists, dressed in protective clothing, was photographing the scene. Another was videotaping it.

Novak's mustache and short curly hair were both gray, and as he tilted his head forward to look down, Santana could see the small, round bald spot on the crown of his head. Because of the bald spot, he was affectionately known as "Monk" around the department. Since his days as an amateur middleweight, he had added a few pounds to his stocky frame. Outside of his former partner, Kacie Hawkins, Novak was Santana's closest friend on the department.

Intent on dusting for prints, Novak didn't notice Santana as he counted five shots in the wall, one entry wound in the man's right shoulder, another entry wound in the man's right hip, and one entry wound in the man's head. The blood spatter and smear on the door suggested he'd been standing when shot and had slid down into a sitting position. The tapered end of the elongated stains pointed in the direction in which the droplets were traveling when they hit the wall, indicating the angle of impact. Aware that every crime scene was three-dimensional, Santana peered up at the ceiling, but he saw no additional blood spatter.

To his left, a second body lay face down on the floor near the headboard. A headshot had blown away a chunk of her skull as the bullet passed through it and embedded itself in the wall to the left of the bed.

The medical examiner, Reiko Tanabe, was leaning over the woman's body. Tanabe, like Novak, wore a similar gown, booties, and gloves. Because she wore her long dark hair tied up and covered with a hairnet, he could see the birthmark just below her right ear. The *café au lait* mark was small and light brown in color.

A third body lay on its belly to his right near the blood-spattered far wall and under an open wall safe. Santana noted the two exit wounds in the man's back and a Sig Sauer P238 subcompact and one shell casing near his hand.

A Ruger LCP .380 with its breech locked back lay on the floor in front of him. Like the Sig Sauer, the Ruger was a lightweight, compact gun that could be easily concealed in a pocket —or a safe. Ten shell casings were scattered on the floor near the Ruger. Noting the length of each casing, Santana determined that three 9x19mm casings had been fired from the Glock. Seven 9x17mm casings had been fired from the Ruger.

One shot had been fired from the Sig Sauer.

Tony Novak would use bright strings and lasers for accurate bullet trajectory reconstruction. But based on the guns involved, the number of shell casings, the bloodstain patterns, and the position of the bodies, Santana had already visualized how the shooting had gone down—and what essential puzzle piece was still missing.

Reiko Tanabe, her brow furrowed with concentration, was testing the woman's body for rigor mortis by feeling the smaller face and neck muscles, where rigor began about two hours after death. She then worked her way down to the arms and legs. Santana knew that unless temperatures were extreme, a body became completely stiff approximately eight to twelve hours after death. Bodies remained rigid for approximately eighteen hours before the process began to reverse itself in the same order—small muscles first, followed by the larger ones, moving from head to toe.

"What's your estimate of TOD, Reiko?" Santana asked.

"Rectal temp is eighty-three point six degrees," she said. "Given that the room temperature is steady, I'm assuming this victim lost one point five degrees per hour. Extremities are stiff. Lividity is fixed. Bodies haven't been moved. All things considered, that would make time of death between ten and twelve hours ago."

Hearing Santana's voice, Novak got to his feet. "John," he said with a nod and a smile. Then, with a sweep of an arm indicating the crime scene, he added, "Welcome back."

"Any ID's on the vics?"

"Guy near the wall safe is Martin Lozano. The woman is his wife, Benita."

"What about the guy against the wall?"

"No wallet, no ID, no cellphone, no money. *Nada.*"

"Uniform outside told me the Ram pickup in the driveway belonged to a Joel Ryker. Might be the guy against the wall."

"I'll send his prints through MAFIN and NGI."

Novak was referring to the Midwest Automated Fingerprint Identification Network, a regional database of finger and palm prints from Minnesota, North Dakota, and South Dakota. Searches could be conducted at the state or national level through access to the FBI's Next Generation Identification (NGI) system. The biometric system had replaced the Integrated Automated Fingerprint Identification System (IAFIS) and contained fingerprint, palm print, iris, and facial recognition. Both MAFIN and NGI contained a file of unknown prints left at crime scenes, which were continually compared to known prints.

Santana looked around the room one more time, at the fireplace in the corner, at the California king-size bed, the sheets splattered with blood, the bullet holes in the walls, the open wall safe to his right, at each of the bodies and the shell casings scattered on the dark oak floor. Putting the scenario together.

"You have a theory, John?" Novak asked.

Santana nodded. "The blond guy by the door fired three shots from his Glock, two into Martin Lozano and one head-shot into his wife."

"How did the blond guy get off three shots with his gun in his holster and a bullet in his head?"

Santana nodded and pointed to the woman's body. "Hard to shoot a Ruger—or any gun, for that matter—when you're missing a chunk of your skull."

"So what's your theory?"

"You check the rounds in the Glock 19?"

"Eleven in the magazine and one in the chamber. Fifteen total when you count the three shell casings on the floor."

"The Ruger LCP holds six in the mag and one in the chamber," Santana said. "Total of seven shell casings on the floor. The Sig Sauer holds seven .380 rounds as well. One shell casing on the floor." Santana gestured toward the blond guy by the door. "The blood smear on the floor beside the body. Something was dragged through it."

"Wanna guess what?"

"Possibly some kind of bag or backpack."

Novak cocked his head. "So where is it?"

"Someone else was here, Tony. Someone who fired seven shots at the DB slumped against the wall, someone who took something valuable out of the safe. See if you can get some prints off the Ruger, the safe, and GSR on the three guns."

"Will do."

Santana walked to one of the nightstands beside the bed. A cellphone lay next to the lamp. The screen was dark, so he wasn't sure if the phone was turned on. It needed to be turned off and batteries removed, if possible, to preserve cell tower location information and call logs. If it couldn't be turned off, then it had to be placed in a Faraday bag or antistatic packaging. Plastic could convey static electricity or allow a buildup of condensation or humidity.

"Make sure you get this cellphone, Tony."

Novak gave him a thumbs-up.

Santana then drew a sketch of the scene in his spiral notebook and conducted a sweep of the house. He was relying on the homicide scene exception to conduct a warrantless search of the premises. Without knowing why the murders were committed, or who did it, he was unable to specify exactly what he wanted to seize or where he wanted to search with enough detail to support the issuance of a warrant.

The house was clean and furnished in southwest décor: leather and suede rustic furniture, brightly colored woven rugs, rope baskets, and pottery. Expensive-looking china filled a large glass door cabinet in the dining room.

In a back bedroom that had no furniture, Santana gave a low whistle. Quart-sized bags packed tightly with crystal meth were stacked along the wall. He estimated over one hundred bags.

A small pill press sat on a six-foot-long collapsible table. The press had a flywheel, feeding hopper, drive gear, and pulley system. On the table beside the pill press were boxes of cornstarch, powdered lactose, sodium aminobenzoate, talc, and stearic acid, a waxy, white powder obtained from palm oil, commonly used as a thickening agent to harden candles and soap products. Bottles of 100-count 5mg white methamphetamine hydrochloride tablets, also known as Desoxyn, were stacked neatly in a small cardboard box. Placing the raw materials in the cone-shaped hopper and turning the flywheel could run the machine by hand if someone wanted to make a few tablets ready to be bottled. Plugging in the electric cord and letting it run on its own could make a larger batch.

An Apple laptop computer sat on a table desk without drawers. Santana knew that opening a computer file would change that file. And the computer would record the time and date the file was accessed. If he started opening files, there would be no way to tell for sure that he hadn't changed anything. Lawyers could contest the validity of the evidence when the case went to court. Instead, after he'd obtained a search warrant, Santana would notify Lynn Pierce, the department's computer forensics specialist, to take an in-depth look at the hard drive and history, and at any cellphones. Pierce would only work from copies of files while searching for evidence. The original system would remain preserved and intact.

Santana shut the bedroom door and pressed a crime scene sticker between the door and the jamb to make sure no one entered till Narco/Vice could be notified. Then he exited the front door, dropping the latex gloves and booties in a container, before heading to the backyard to speak to the maintenance man.

"Mr. Grant," he said, approaching the man sitting in a lawn chair at a round table under the shade of a tall oak tree. "I'm Detective John Santana." Santana badged him.

The lanky man with shaggy sun-bleached hair, sunglasses, and dark tan made no reply. He wore jeans, work boots, and a strap undershirt that showed off his muscular arms. He had big-knuckled hands and the Roman numeral III, surrounded by stars, tattooed on his right forearm, a logo for the Three Percenters, a far-right militia movement and paramilitary group. Santana made Grant for mid-to-late thirties.

He sat down opposite Grant in another lawn chair and placed his cellphone on the table. "I'm going to record our interview, Mr. Grant."

Grant eyed the iPhone but said nothing, apparently aware that Santana didn't need permission to record their interview.

"I got nothin' to hide," he said.

"Mind removing the sunglasses, Mr. Grant?"

"What for?" He said it in a questioning tone rather than a defiant one.

So I can read your eyes, Santana thought. But he said, "It's like wearing a hat inside a building. It isn't polite, especially when talking to a cop."

Grant hiked his shoulders, removed the aviator Ray-Bans, and tucked them into his T-shirt. He narrowed his close-set eyes and offered a lopsided smile as if to say, "How's that?"

"Better."

Once Santana started to record, he identified himself and Grant and gave the time, date, and location of the interview.

"I understand you discovered the bodies," Santana said.

"But I never touched anything. Never actually went into the room once I saw the bodies."

"You were here to repair the shower?"

"To change the shower head and repair a leaky pipe in the basement."

"You've done work for the Lozanos before?"

He shook his head.

"You know how they got your name?"

"Maybe Google. Maybe a neighbor. I do quite a bit of work around here."

"Self-employed then."

"Not exactly."

"What does that mean?"

"I take care of maintenance for James McGowan. He owns a lot of properties in town."

Santana was familiar with McGowan's name, as were many citizens of the city. "How many properties do you take care of?"

"Twenty-five."

"Must keep you busy."

"Sure does."

"Did you know the Lozanos before they moved in?"

"Nope. But it just goes to show you can't trust spics. Something I'm sure you're familiar with in your job, Detective Santana." He offered a knowing smile, as if he'd shared a secret. "Hey," he said with a chuckle, "no offense meant."

Santana held his eyes on Grant for a moment till he looked away.

"Know where the slur 'spic' comes from, Mr. Grant?"

Grant kept his eyes averted as he shook his head.

"Comes from Panama. What Americans working on the canal called the Panamanian laborers who pronounced the word speak as spik, like in, No spik d' English. Funny, huh?"

Grant shrugged.

Santana let him think about it for a while before he said, "Anyone else living here?"

"Well, if there was someone else here, I don't know about it."

"Were you aware the Lozanos were operating a meth stash house, Mr. Grant?"

His nostrils flared with indignation. "Course not."

"Ever been arrested?"

"I know you're gonna check later, so, yeah. I got arrested for criminal sexual contact in the fifth degree. It was a bogus charge."

Like they all are, Santana thought.

"Said she was eighteen. How the hell was I supposed to know she was only fifteen?"

"Consent by the complainant is not a defense," Santana said.

"Tell me about it."

"You serve time?"

"Hey, it's a gross misdemeanor. Judge stayed the one-year sentence. I paid a three-thousand-dollar fine and went to treatment. Got *cured*. Court should've sent that lying little bitch to jail for setting me up."

Santana handed him a business card. "Here's my number in case you think of anything else. I'll need a phone number where you can be reached."

Grant gave Santana his area code and then snickered.

"Something funny, Mr. Grant?"

"My phone number. Three two eight, six three two eight."

"Afraid I don't get the joke."

"Numbers spell the words EAT MEAT. Easy to remember, huh?"

When Santana returned to the living room, Gina Luttrell, the SPPD district supervisor, was standing over the blond man's body that lay slumped against the door. Her short dark hair complemented her narrow face and slim body. She wore a light blue pants suit. Her gold shield hung from a lanyard around her neck.

"Real mess," Santana said.

Luttrell turned to face him. "More than a mess, John." She gestured at the body. "Name is Joel Ryker. He was a DEA agent."

Chapter 6

Santana had six uniformed officers canvass the neighborhood, asking residents if they'd heard or seen anything unusual in the past twenty-four hours, but they all came up empty. Given the distances between the houses and the relative seclusion of the Lozanos' home, Santana wasn't surprised.

Like most homicide detectives, he dreaded death notifications. He found the whole experience stressful and emotionally draining. And it never got any easier. Given how his parents had died, he knew what the victim's surviving family members had to endure. As per SPPD policy, death notification was done in person, always in pairs, and never over the phone unless there was absolutely no other choice.

Because Joel Ryker's wife, Julie, lived in Dallas, Texas—and the SPPD wouldn't fly him there—Santana was left with no choice but to conduct the death notification over the phone.

The problem with having third parties involved in death notification after a homicide was that a spouse or family member might say or do something during notification that could change the course of the investigation. That one piece of vital information might not mean anything to those not directly involved in the investigation, but to Santana the entire case might hinge on that one piece of information. It was why he preferred to handle notification within the bubble of people directly involved in the case.

The DEA agreed to send an agent friend of Joel Ryker's to the house, along with a Dallas PD police chaplain and a female patrol officer who had been trained in death notification procedures. Santana requested that they all be present at the house when he made the phone call.

When he'd informed a family member of a loved one's death, he'd seen varied reactions, from tears, to grief and rage, to outright denial, to complete silence, sometimes all in the same notification.

Julie Ryker seemed to take the news of her husband's death as an unemotional inevitability.

"You said he was shot."

"Yes."

"Was he working on a case?"

"I believe so."

"Do you have a suspect?"

"Not at this time."

She went quiet for a moment before speaking again. "Working for the DEA was a dangerous job. Joel and I both knew it."

"I'm sorry for your loss, Mrs. Ryker."

"We've been separated for over a year now. Haven't spoken in months. I own two women's clothing shops and am busy opening a third. I'm not flying up there to ID Joel's body."

Not sure how to respond, Santana moved on. "Did you and your husband have any children, Mrs. Ryker?"

"I never wanted children for this very reason," she said, her voice laced with anger. "No child should lose a father because he chose to surround himself with drug dealers and gangbangers. That's what you call them, Detective, don't you? Gangbangers."

"Yes, we do."

She let out a hard laugh. "You know, my husband was *banging* that whore partner he worked with. She can ID his body since she's had her hands all over it."

"The DEA has my contact information," Santana said, moving quickly to another subject. "In case you have any questions."

"Well, isn't that sweet of you," she said, disconnecting the phone.

Santana cleared the uncomfortable conversation from his mind by typing up warrants for Martin Lozano's cellphone and

Joel Ryker's apartment and emailed them to a judge. While he waited for the warrants to be signed, he searched for Martin and Benita Lozanos' immediate family or relatives in the city, but could locate neither family nor relatives living in the cities or in Minnesota. He'd have to find a neighbor or co-worker to ID the bodies.

An hour later, armed with the warrant, he headed for Joel Ryker's Lowertown apartment located in the Custom House along Kellogg Boulevard in downtown St. Paul. The tall art deco building across the street from the Union Depot transportation hub had functioned as the city of Saint Paul's main post office for seventy-nine years before being renovated for luxury apartments.

Santana was searching for evidence related to Ryker's murder. He showed the building manager the search warrant, gave him a copy, and was let in.

Ryker's apartment had quartz countertops, dark plank flooring, ten-foot ceilings, oversize windows with roller blinds —and not much furniture. The kitchen smelled strongly of bacon from an unwashed frying pan in the sink. Six black dahlias stood in a terra cotta vase on the kitchen counter.

More burgundy than black, as the name suggested, the dahlia was a beautiful, large flower native to Colombia, Mexico, and Central America. Flowers were supposed to be colorful and cheerful, but the black dahlia was often associated with darkness, mourning, and death. The flowers also represented betrayal.

A folded "Thank You" card stood like a small tent next to the vase.

Thanks for the quickie. Love the new pad.
Here's a little gift to brighten up the place.
See if you can keep them alive.
> Love,
> B—

Santana started with the monthly billing statements stacked on the kitchen table. It didn't take long to see that the bills from Xcel Energy, AT&T, Cabela's Sporting Goods, Bank of America, Capital One, and Chase Bank were all overdue, the credit cards by nearly three months. AT&T and Xcel Energy were threatening to cut off service if they didn't receive a minimum payment. Ryker had large balances on all three of the credit cards, many for cash advances. The payment book from Chase Bank for his Dodge Ram pickup revealed that he was also two months behind on his truck payments.

Santana knew that DEA Special Agents earned approximately $40,000 to $70,000 a year. After four years of service, GS-13 level agents could earn around $93,000.

He wondered what Joel Ryker had been spending his salary on.

Chapter 7

In her nightmares Ana Soriano sits atop a freight car with nothing to hold onto, hears the screeching of the metallic wheels, the deafening sound of the train's couplings striking against one another, feels the hot, humid air pressing against her as the train rolls through the poorest towns and past dilapidated houses. She smells the stench of garbage and the body odor of the fourteen-year-old Honduran boy sitting next to her. Having lost a leg falling from the train in his first attempt at reaching the Mexican/US border, he is trying again.

Despite her struggles to stay awake, Ana falls asleep, topples off the train and lands hard on the tracks. Sharp wheels bear down on her like a butcher knife about to slice meat. Heart pounding, palms sweating, she jerks awake, stifling the scream in her throat, wondering if the nightmare is not only a remembrance of the past but also a foretelling of the future.

Now, Ana stood outside the bungalow that her friend, Christine Hammond, rented. The pack she'd taken from the Lozanos, stained with blood and filled with money, was strapped to her back. Sweat dampened the blouse and jeans she'd stolen from Benita Lozano's closet. Thankfully, the Mexican woman was about the same size. Ana couldn't imagine walking this far in the evening dress and heels she'd worn to the Lozanos. She'd stuffed her dress and heels into the backpack and taken a pair of flats along with the clothes.

She'd taken a taxi to the Lozanos' house last night, but chose not to call one this morning. If any of the neighbors saw the taxi, the police could get the description and follow the trail to her apartment.

The long walk to her apartment and then to her friend's place hadn't erased the bloody images from her mind's eye, though it had slowed her pounding heart rate and stopped her trembling hands. Suddenly feeling sick to her stomach, she stood beside a thick oak and threw up in a sewer grate along the curb.

She used a Kleenex from her purse to wipe her mouth as she leaned against the tree.

She wasn't sure how much was in the backpack, but she knew it was enough to start a new life, to get out of the life she was living. Her horoscope had predicted she would soon come into wealth.

It hadn't predicted how she would attain it.

Her mother had told her once that because she was born under the astrological sign of Taurus, one of the most powerful signs of the zodiac, she was like the bull among the stars, stubborn, determined, and tenacious, never taking no for an answer. Always adventurous, Ana knew what she wanted, just not how to get it.

Two years ago, at the age of fifteen, she'd left her mother and younger sister in the shantytown surrounding the capital city of San Salvador, fleeing from the Mara Salvatrucha, or MS-13, and their rivals, the Barrio-18, the gangs that had threatened her life.

Ana's older brother, Marco, a quiet, studious teenager, had been forced to join the MS-13, knowing that if he refused Ana would be gang raped. Marco spent a year in the gang before the *Sombra Negra* captured him. The *Sombra Negra*, or Black Shadow, was a vigilante death squad composed mostly of police and military personnel that hunted the MS-13.

The police found Marco's body in a creek with his hands tied behind his back. His genitalia and tongue had been cut off before a bullet cored out the back of his head. A sign placed beside his body read, *"La Sombra Negra ha llegado a San Salvador."* The Sombra Negra has arrived to San Salvador. *"Es hora de que las MS ratas se vayan."* It is time for the MS-13 rats to leave.

Ana had ridden *el tren de la muerte*, the death train, also known as *la bestia*, the beast, or *el tren de los desconocidos*, the train of the unknowns, from the town of Tapachula in the Mexican state of Chiapas on the southern border of Guatemala and Mexico, to the US border in Nogales, Mexico.

Once in Customs and Border Patrol custody she was placed in a detention center, commonly known as the *hielera*, or the "icebox." She soon learned that the name derived not just from being in ICE custody, but because the center was constantly blasted with gelid air, like a freezer designed to kill germs and keep the "foreign meat" from going bad.

A friendly female CBP agent took her name, birth date, home country, and fingerprints for a background check. Because Ana feared returning to El Salvador, a US Citizenship and Immigration Services asylum officer gave her a "credible fear" interview. The heavy-set man with the slick black hair and ruddy complexion leered at her the whole time. His teeth were yellow and his breath smelled of garlic. He said his name was Raúl Torres, and he asked her where she was planning on staying—if he granted her a court appearance.

Like the majority of Salvadorans of Spanish ancestry in her country, Ana had Mediterranean features: olive skin and dark hair, but her eyes were cerulean blue. She was three inches taller than the average 5'3" Salvadoran female. Mature for her age, she knew by the way men looked at her that she was pretty and that they would offer to do things for her without her asking.

Raúl told her he had a sister in Nogales, Arizona. Courts were backlogged and her hearing before a judge might take years. ICE could place her in the Intensive Supervision Appearance Program, or ISAP, monitored by a private contractor. One Wednesday a month—she never knew which one—she would receive an automated call on her cellphone asking her to repeat five numbers and register her voice. If she didn't answer or call back within minutes, ICE agents would come looking for her.

Ana agreed to join the program and to live with Raúl's sister, Luciana, until her hearing before a judge.

The pink ramshackle single-family house near an elementary school had a chain-link fenced-in dirt yard and carport garage. Ana slept in a small bedroom in back, the heavy smell of garlic, chili, and onion seemingly baked into the walls and bedspread. While welcoming at first, by the end of the first month, Luciana complained that Ana needed to make money, though it was illegal for her to work.

"The judges look the other way," Luciana assured her. "No worry."

The woman looked like a female version of her younger brother, the many wrinkles in her ruddy face a testament to a hard life and aging body.

Raúl came to visit once a week, always sitting close to Ana on the couch and always looking at her as a rat would a piece of cheese.

Three months into her stay, after an enchilada dinner, Ana could not stay awake. She lay down on her bed, the room spinning before her eyes. The next few days, or weeks, she was never sure which, were a haze. She thought she'd been in a van at some point, the radio turned loudly to a Latino station, and in a series of houses with uncomfortable beds, where she and other young Latina women were forced to have sex. Whenever she would wake, groggy and dizzy, images swimming in front of her eyes, she would be fed a small meal, drugged, and the ordeal would begin again.

Ana was terrified, but her survival instinct kicked in. She quickly learned to do what she was told to avoid beatings.

One day a lean Mexican man named Chico Caldera came to the house where Ana was held prisoner. He had a small mouth with a curvy upper lip and dark, empty eyes that were close-set and heavy-lidded. He wore a black sport coat over a white T-shirt, tight jeans, a pair of Nike running shoes, and a thick gold chain around his neck. Chico took Ana to a photo studio, where she had her picture taken. Then he drove her to a Victoria's Secret store and bought her skimpy lingerie.

She remembered looking around the store, wondering if she could run away and disappear. But she didn't know anyone in the US or even where she was. Then she looked at Chico again and saw that he was concealing a gun under his sport coat. He stared at her with dead eyes and made a gesture that warned her not to try anything.

Later that day he drove her to a house where she was forced to perform more sex acts with American men who spoke little Spanish and used body language and intimidation to get their meaning across. But what confused and frightened Ana the most was the man with the police badge. She wasn't sure if it was real, or if this man was like so many of the policemen in El Salvador, men who were as corrupt and as violent as the gang members spreading terror and spilling blood throughout the country, men who used influence and power to terrify and control the poor and defenseless.

Chico told her that she owed him $20,000 and that she would pay off the debt $100 at a time by serving men. She felt sure she would die before she ever served two hundred men.

Over the following weeks she was driven to different brothels, apartment buildings, and hotels, rarely staying in the same place for more than three days, and never knowing where she was or where she was going.

The brothels were older houses in and out of the city, which she realized was St. Paul when she saw a sign on the interstate. She wasn't sure where St. Paul was till a young girl from Honduras told her they were in Minnesota.

Ample supplies of cocaine, crystal meth, and weed were laid out on the tables inside the houses. Chico encouraged her to sample the drugs to keep her compliant and high. But she stuck to the weed, beer, and whiskey, after seeing how cocaine and meth scrambled the brains of the girls who used it. At least, she thought, the weed and alcohol helped make it all bearable. She stayed away from the tap water because she was unaware that the water in the US was safe to drink.

Twenty-four hours a day, she would sit around with other girls, completely naked, waiting for customers to come in. If no one came she would occasionally sleep, though never in a bed.

At least once a month, Chico would drive her to downtown hotels, where she would be escorted through the staff entrance rather than through the lobby, and taken up to the rooms in the freight elevator.

There were times she thought of making a break for it when she came out of a room, but Chico was always waiting for her in the corridor. He would show her to the next room and the next. Forty-five minutes in each room, Chico always waiting on the other side of the door.

Because she was compliant, Chico didn't beat her, but the customers were often violent. She was forced to have sex with white, black, and Latino men. Some were old and some were young university students.

She had no possessions besides the clothes on her back. She had no money, no credit cards, and no ID, so she didn't need a pocketbook or purse. She had carried a small Spanish to English dictionary with her from El Salvador, but it had been lost along the way. Her thoughts were constantly on escape, but the opportunities were few and far between.

Soon Ana grew numb, unable to cry. Overwhelmed with sadness and anger. She went through the motions, did what she was told, and tried hard to survive. Those girls who resisted or refused sex were beaten. The gun, the knife, and the baseball bat were fixtures in her nightmarish world.

Physically, she was growing weak. She was given small amounts of rice and black beans and tortillas for nearly every meal. The constant threat of violence and the need to stay alert was exhausting.

Then one night Chico brought her a beautiful long-sleeve black dress, a black lace bra and panties, and a pair of black high heels, all in her size, and told her to take a hot shower and to put everything on. An older Mexican woman Ana had never met before washed and styled her hair and applied makeup and lipstick. Looking in the mirror, Ana could not believe she was the same woman she'd been two hours ago. Chico fed her a wonderfully tender steak and a baked potato for dinner. Wearing a black suit and shiny black shoes, his dark hair washed and combed, his face freshly shaved, Chico blindfolded her and drove her to a house in the city. Before removing her blindfold, he warned her that the men she was about to meet were very wealthy and influential and would treat her well.

They sat in his car for a few minutes while he took a phone call.

Ana had lost track of days and time, but she could see a full moon in the sky and the red, orange, and yellow leaves taking their last breaths as they died and fell from the trees. A light breeze scattered them across the lawns and asphalt and blew them onto the hood of the car, leaving a heavy scent of decay and wood smoke in the cool air.

When Chico finished his phone call he said in Spanish, "Before we go inside, remember what I told you, Ana."

"Or what?" she answered in their native language.

He slid the gun out of his waist holster and rested it on his thigh, his hand wrapped around the grip. "I'll kill you."

Smiling, Ana reached slowly for Chico's gun hand.

He pulled back and raised the weapon, pointing it directly at her face. "What are you doing?"

"It's okay," she said, her smile still sculpted on her face like that of a statue. Gently taking hold of Chico's forearm, she moved it toward her till she felt the cold, hard barrel pressed against her forehead.

"Do it," she said.

"What?"

"Do it. Kill me."

Chico tried to pull his arm back but she held it fast.

"*Por favor,*" she pleaded.

"*Eres una perra loca,*" Chico said, wresting his arm and the gun away from her.

"I am not crazy," she said. "I am ready to die."

"Listen to me," he said, raising his voice. "You do what I tell you. And if you do what they tell you in there," he added, waving the gun at a large house behind him, "you can have a new life."

"Who are *they*?"

"You will soon see. You are one of the fortunate ones."

Ana laughed. She could not remember the last time that she'd laughed, but this laugh was filled with disbelief, anguish, and pain.

Chico holstered his gun and looked at her for a time without speaking. "I can turn this car around now. Take you back to the house. Take your fancy clothes, everything, if that's what you want. Or you can do what I tell you and maybe change your life. Up to you."

As Chico escorted her into what looked like a mansion, and up a long set of stairs to a thick, elegantly carved heavy door, he reminded her once more of his threat. Then he turned her over to two elegantly dressed, attractive women Ana guessed were a few years older than her. They didn't offer their names or where they were from, but they both spoke fluent Spanish. Based on their accent, Ana guessed the women were from Mexico, perhaps Mexico City.

She stepped inside the room, and one of the two women closed the door behind her. With its parquet floors, crystal chandelier, and marble fireplace, the large room had an Old-World feel. Ana felt like she'd stepped back in time.

The two Mexican women explained to Ana that she was brought here this evening to observe. Nothing else was expected of her. She was to remain seated in one of the comfortable chairs placed around the living room. If she would like champagne or anything else to drink, she merely had to ask and one of the women would get it for her. Drugs were strictly prohibited.

There were twenty or so men and women at the party that night. All the men wore strange-looking masks that covered their face and hid their age. No one else spoke to Ana or interacted with her. The men and women offered only a nod if their eyes connected with hers. All the women were stunning in expensive dresses and gold and silver jewelry. They laughed often and seemed genuinely interested in the conversations, hanging on every word, leaning in close, exposing their necks by tilting their heads to one side, affectionately touching the man's arm and back, a knee pressed against his thigh, a display of sensuality in their smiles.

Ana sipped a glass of champagne, which she found awfully sweet tasting. She listened to string music playing in the background and the hum of conversations and words that were foreign to her. She did understand as the evening progressed, and the men and women began leaving together, that the women were prostitutes. What wasn't clear to her was how the women were able to leave with the men. She saw no bodyguards or security, no one threatening the women with guns or other weapons. The women seemed free to come and go as they pleased.

Later that evening, after a second glass of champagne, Ana felt sleepy and asked one of the two Mexican women if she could lie down.

She awoke the next morning in a large room with a comfortable bed, tucked under a soft, thick comforter, the silk sheets scented like a pine forest. The sun streamed through half-open blinds and dappled the black and white furniture and contemporary paintings on the walls of fragmented bodies in erotic positions.

In the mirror attached to the canopied bed overhead, she could see that her hair had been washed and combed. It smelled like coconuts and splayed on the pillow under her head like black satin.

The elegant-looking woman sitting on the edge of the bed was in her mid-thirties with blond hair cut short, understated makeup expertly applied, and delicate hands with manicured crimson nails. She wore a black business suit, small diamond drop earrings, and a silver watch on her thin wrist.

"I'm Dominique Lejeune," the elegant woman said.

"Where am I?" Ana asked.

"Home," Lejeune said with a reassuring smile, her hazel eyes dancing with a welcoming light.

Chapter 8

Standing outside the door of Christine Hammond's apartment, Ana Soriano used her burner phone to call her friend.

"It's Ana," she said when Hammond answered. "I need your help."

"Where are you?" Hammond asked, her voice slow and thick as if she'd just woken up.

"At your door."

Ana waited till the latch turned. When the door swung open, she knew immediately that her friend was drugged rather than sleepy.

Hammond wore open-toed slippers, sweat pants, and a purple Minnesota Vikings sweatshirt. She wore no makeup. Her blond hair framed her heart-shaped face like limp straw and looked as though it hadn't been washed in days.

Hammond waved her in, leaning against the door's edge for support, her chestnut eyes tracking the bloodstained backpack slung over Ana's shoulder.

Ana sat on a well-worn couch in the small living room that smelled strongly of pot from the joint smoldering on the edge of an ashtray on the coffee table. Ana's eyes focused on a single, silver-framed photo sitting on a small, mostly empty bookshelf in a corner.

It was a photo taken a few years ago of Christine Hammond with a woman Ana knew was Hammond's mother. They were standing beside each other. Their hands were folded in front of them, fingers clenched together, staring blankly at the camera, their faces devoid of smiles and any sense of happiness and closeness.

Christine Hammond dropped on the couch beside Ana. Her eyes fixed on the backpack at Ana's feet.

"What's that?" she asked.

"Our freedom."

Hammond cocked her head. "Huh?"

Ana bent over and unzipped the backpack.

"Holy shit!" Hammond said, her eyes suddenly wide with shock and disbelief. "Where'd you get the money?"

Ana didn't know how much she should tell her, but figured for now, the less the better. "What's important is what we can do with it."

Hammond shook her head slightly. "I don't get it."

"This is our ticket out of the life," Ana said. "Our *freedom*."

"Why would you help me?"

"Because you helped me in the beginning. You've been a friend."

"But I'm not fucking men for money anymore."

Ana gave her a tight smile.

"I'm sorry," Hammond said. "That sounded harsh."

"It is what it is."

Hammond clasped Ana's hand. "Your situation is different than mine. You're not from here. You can't just walk away. I get that."

"I can walk away now," Ana said. "And there's enough here so that you can start a new life, too."

"How much is it?"

"I haven't had time to count it."

"I'd like to get off the drugs. Maybe get some treatment."

"However much you want, it's yours."

Hammond gestured toward the backpack. "Is that blood?"

Ana nodded.

"Whose?"

"The man I took it from."

Hammond sat quietly, her eyes fixed on a distant point. "What can I do?" she asked after a time, her gaze finding Ana again.

Chapter 9

The following morning Santana stood beside the ME, Reiko Tanabe, in the Ramsey County morgue, a one-story building just off University Avenue next to Regions Hospital. They were dressed in green scrubs and booties. Tanabe wore large latex gloves and a disposable plastic apron over the scrubs. Stiff white masks covered their mouths and noses. The temperature hovered just above freezing, and the room reeked of astringent cleaner, tissue preservative, and bodies on the verge of decomposition.

Tanabe had completed her external evaluation of Ryker's body. She'd started with the neck and worked her way downward to the chest, abdomen, pelvis and genitalia, as she spoke into a microphone connected to a digital recorder. This sequence allowed the blood to drain from Ryker's head, which she examined last.

Tanabe then used a scalpel to make a U-shaped incision that began at Ryker's left shoulder and continued under his nipples over to the right shoulder. The cut opened Ryker's skin as if the ME were unzipping a coat. She then turned the U into a Y by cutting downward below the sternum to the abdomen. With no heart beating, there was no pressure and very little blood. She called out the weight and measurement of each organ to her female attendant, who wrote them down on a sheet attached to the clipboard. She worked methodically, talking into the microphone as she removed each organ and then the bullet lodged in Ryker's shoulder and the one in his hip.

Santana went back to the counter and placed the bullets in an evidence envelope and initialed it, making sure he followed the chain of evidence by adding the date the items were collected, the case number, type of crime, victim or suspect's name, and a brief description of the items.

He then walked over to a second stainless steel table and looked at Martin Lozano's naked body. Lozano had balloon-like paper bags around his hands and feet to entrap any trace evidence. The entry openings in his shoulder and stomach where Ryker's bullets had struck him had drawn together after the bullets passed through the skin. Santana could see the distinct contusion rings around the entrance caused by the bullets scraping off the external layer of epithelial cells. The round contusion rings indicated Ryker's bullets had struck Lozano squarely, though no smudge ring was evident because the bullets had first passed through clothing.

Lozano had bled out from the stomach wound, but not right away. He'd had time to get to the safe and the Sig Sauer. Time enough to kill Joel Ryker.

It took awhile before Tanabe pulled out the .380 caliber bullet from Ryker's head.

"The bullet that killed him," she said, holding it up to the light with a set of forceps.

"Not the bullets in Ryker's hip and shoulder."

Tanabe shook her head. "Definitely not."

Santana took the two evidence envelopes containing the three bullets to Tony Novak in the SPPD's Forensic Services Unit. Then he headed for the chief's office.

* * *

Tim Branigan, the SPPD's Chief of Police, was seated in one of the three cushioned chairs surrounding a circular glass coffee table at the far end of his office when Santana entered. Branigan's tasseled loafers were shined, his dark blue slacks ironed with knife-edged creases, his burgundy tie perfectly knotted. The gold cuff links in his wrinkle-free white shirt glimmered in the sunlight seeping through the window blinds. He directed Santana to have a seat to his right.

Besides the ceremonial plaques, awards, and family photos on the office walls, Branigan had a life-sized sculpted raven on the corner of his desk. Supposedly, Branigan's surname came from a very famous Irish clan and meant the descendent of the son of the raven. But Santana had never asked Branigan about it.

The chief had the dark hair and eyes associated with the Black Irish and their Iberian ancestors, rather than the stereotypical fair hair, pale skin, and blue or green eyes. He'd been a respected detective while working in Fraud and Forgery and later in Homicide before becoming Deputy Chief of Major Crimes and more recently Chief of Police.

When Santana was seated, Branigan said, "We're waiting for Bobby Chacon to arrive. Should be here any time now."

"Who's Chacon?"

"Works for the DEA."

Santana figured the DEA would be part of the SPPD investigation because one of their agents had been shot and killed in the stash house. Having worked with DEA agents before, Santana wasn't looking forward to it.

"This has been a bloody year for the community," Branigan said, interrupting Santana's thoughts. "Particularly when we're known as America's most livable city."

"Who came up with that saying?"

Branigan swatted the question away as he would a bothersome fly. "Homicide rates are increasing. People are uptight. We've got to get a handle on this pattern of violence."

Branigan conveniently failed to mention that if the record pace of killings continued, the SPPD would be looking for a new chief. But if rumors about Branigan applying for a chief's job in another state were correct, they might be looking for a new chief anyway. Still, whether he stayed or left, Branigan needed to maintain "law and order."

Politicians and law enforcement officials were debating solutions to prevent future gun-related violence in the city. The

SPPD had advocated for more police officers and technology that would help them find the location of gunfire faster. But the mayor and city council hadn't agreed to a plan—or the money to fund it.

"Homicides ebb and flow," Santana said.

"Of course they do. But you know the majority of street killings are drug and gang related." Branigan exhaled a frustrated breath as if for emphasis.

Santana was aware that gang members used to have to get permission from the head banger to shoot somebody. It wasn't like that anymore. Frequently, gangbangers reacted impulsively to a slur or insult.

"I've had our Gun and Gang unit patrolling the streets after dark, responding to frequent shots-fired calls and assisting Homicide and Robbery with investigations. We've brought murder or manslaughter charges in half the killings this year, but we need to do better. That's why I requested help."

"From the DEA?" Santana said.

"The pace of the killings is burning out our detectives."

Since returning to active duty, Santana had heard talk that the Homicide and Robbery division might be divided into separate units. One unit assigned to cold cases, another for robberies and kidnappings, and a Violent Crimes Against Persons Unit dedicated to assaults and nonfatal shootings. Currently, homicide detectives were handling murder investigations alongside aggravated assaults, shootings, kidnappings, and robberies.

"Are the rumors about separating the unit true?" Santana asked.

"I won't deny it. Right now, crimes assigned to the Homicide Unit can't be properly investigated because of the increasing number of them. Detectives should be solely focused on death investigations. That's why I'm temporarily assigning several officers from the local FBI Safe Streets Task Force to help the Homicide and Special Investigations units. The FBI, ATF, US

Marshals, and DEA all plan to provide extra resources to the city."

"Not easy working with the feds, Chief."

"Get used to it," Branigan said.

Santana wondered if Branigan was setting him up for failure out of a perverse sense of revenge. He'd become aware of Branigan's infidelity when he worked a case involving the murder of a high-priced escort. Branigan and his wife were separated at the time. But had Branigan's dalliance become public, his climb up the SPPD ladder, along with his marriage, would have abruptly ended. Santana had never shared Branigan's secret with anyone besides his former partner, Kacie Hawkins. Nor had he used the knowledge of Branigan's infidelity for his own personal benefit. But he was not above using it whenever he needed resources or support on a case he was investigating.

"We had a five-year average murder closure rate of eighty-three percent," Branigan said. "Last year it was sixty-seven percent, and we had double the murders."

Santana knew that clearing a murder was harder than it used to be. As in many cities, a growing lack of trust between cops and minority communities had led to a lack of cooperation from eyewitnesses, making it difficult for detectives to solve homicides.

Instead of crimes of passion—the kind most often committed by someone close to the victim, which made solving the case easier—there were more random drive-by shootings now between loosely connected gang members and in communities where residents were reluctant to talk to police.

"Clearing a homicide doesn't mean that a prosecutor will get a conviction," Santana said.

"But arrests deliver a message. When clearance rates fall, so does community trust in the police. If families or friends of victims feel they can't rely on law enforcement to deliver justice, they might take the law into their own hands."

Santana remembered the case of Louis Domingo, a Sureños 13 gangbanger, who was shot and killed in a drive-by. It took Santana and his partner, Kacie Hawkins, months before they finally arrested the killer. In the meantime, Domingo's mother would often put a gun in her purse at night and make the short drive to the home of the man she believed had murdered her son. Parked across the street, she would sit for hours, watching from behind tinted windows as people entered and left the house, resisting the urge to use her weapon. Santana was thankful she hadn't shot the man she felt was responsible for her son's murder since the perp turned out to be someone else.

He was about to ask Branigan if he'd consider overriding Janet Kendrick's decision to partner Kacie Hawkins with Diana Lee when a tall woman marched into Branigan's office. She wore jeans, a black T-shirt under a denim jacket, and a pair of Blauer crush boots—a cross between a tactical boot and an athletic shoe.

Branigan raised his eyebrows. "Can I help you?"

"No," she said. "I'm here to help you. Name is Chacon. From the DEA."

"But I thought—"

"Yeah," she said, interrupting Branigan. "I get that a lot. It's B-O-B-B-I. And don't bother getting up."

Bobbi Chacon dropped her lean six-foot frame in a chair beside Tim Branigan and opposite Santana and crossed her long legs. Her brunette hair was slicked back in a bob, the blunt ends cut just above the neckline. Pomade gave her thick hair a wet, shiny appearance. Her tanned complexion suggested she'd recently been south, or out of the country, in a warm climate.

Branigan started to introduce Santana when Chacon cut him off. "I know who he is," she said, looking directly at Santana, her amber eyes lit like flames. "Mike Rios is a colleague and friend."

Santana had worked with Rios on the case involving high-priced escorts from Costa Rica, the same case in which Tim

Branigan had gotten entangled with an escort while separated from his wife, though Rios never knew of Branigan's involvement. As far as Santana was concerned, he had no ax to grind with Rios and vice versa. Chacon's edge was likely due to Joel Ryker's death. He'd take a partner's death hard, too, though he had lingering doubts about why and how Ryker was killed.

"Small world," Santana said.

Bobbi Chacon's eyes roamed over his face. "Yeah," she said sarcastically. "It is."

Branigan's face had turned ashen. He shot Santana a piercing glance. Santana wondered if Branigan thought Bobbi Chacon knew about his affair with the escort.

The chief cleared his throat and straightened his tie. "So much for introductions. Let's focus on the case at hand."

Bobbi Chacon's amber eyes reminded Santana of a cat's. They held his eyes for a moment before she spoke again. "Tell me about the shooting."

Santana had picked up the slight Southern accent in her voice, Texas, maybe? His gaze moved to Branigan.

"We need to share everything with the DEA," Branigan said.

"All right," Santana said. His eyes found hers again. "But first I want to know what Joel Ryker was doing in that stash house."

"Making a drug bust," she said.

"You know that for certain?"

Chacon's face twisted in anger. "I worked with Joel. What're you getting at?"

"Easy," Branigan cautioned. "We're all trying to figure out what happened."

"What were you two working on?" Santana asked, his voice level but firm.

She looked at Branigan and cocked her head in a question.

"Fair is fair," Branigan said. "You want us to work with you, you gotta work with us."

"The Mexican meth pipeline," she said.

"What about it?" Santana asked.

"Minnesota is a trans-shipment point for Mexican meth. City and suburban homes double as temporary storage for meth intended for customers across state lines."

"And you know this because?"

Chacon let out heavy sigh. "Larger amounts of the drug are being seized, and we've linked cells here to a high-level cartel boss in Mexico."

Santana fixed his gaze on her till her eyes slid off him. "What else aren't you telling us?"

She hesitated before responding, her eyes settling for a moment on each of them. "This is between the three of us."

Branigan and Santana both nodded in agreement.

"Early tomorrow morning we're raiding stash houses across the country. We've been investigating this particular Minnesota cell for nearly a year. Joel and I were supposed to raid the place tomorrow with the DEA team."

"Any ideas why Ryker went in early on his own?"

Chacon shook her head—slowly.

"How much meth did you find?" Branigan asked Santana.

"Narco/Vice pegged the stash at one hundred forty pounds. Street value is over a million dollars."

"You never answered my question about the shooting, Detective," Chacon said.

Santana wondered if she was holding something back, but he put his question aside for the time being and answered hers. "Forensics is still working out the details. But I think Ryker shot Martin and Benita Lozano."

"Which one of them shot Joel?"

"Neither."

Bobbi Chacon lifted her chin. "What?"

"I believe someone else was in that house at the time of the shooting. Whoever it was shot Ryker. They also took some cash, meth, or both from the house."

"What gave you that idea?"

"Forensics."

"So now what?" Branigan asked.

Bobbi Chacon forced a weak smile. "We all keep working together, like one happy family."

*　　*　　*

Santana was standing in front of the elevator on the sixth floor outside Branigan's office, using his SPPD cellphone to call James McGowan—the man who owned the properties where Gordon Grant worked as a maintenance man—when the elevator doors slid open and Rita Gamboni stepped out.

His heart skipped a beat.

"Hello, John," she said with a grin.

Santana disconnected the call and slid the cellphone into a pocket.

Rita stepped forward and gave him a hug as the elevator doors closed behind her.

Tall and fair-skinned, with white blond hair that touched her shoulders, she wore a blue pantsuit that matched her eyes.

Santana had dated Rita when they were partners, prior to her becoming the first woman homicide commander for the SPPD, before she took a job as the SPPD's liaison with the FBI, and later became an FBI agent.

"What are you doing here?" he asked.

"Catching up with old friends."

"I'll bet."

"I planned on calling you. Thought we might have dinner."

"What happened to the FBI?"

"Still in DC," she said.

"You know what I mean."

She patted him on the arm and started down the hallway. "We'll talk."

Chapter 10

The brick house Santana owned sat on two heavily wooded acres of birch and pine on a secluded bluff overlooking the St. Croix River, which formed a natural boundary between Minnesota and Wisconsin.

He unlocked the back door, turned off the security system, and unclipped his Kydex belt holster, which held the Glock 23 he carried.

As soon as he entered, his golden retriever, Gitana, came bounding toward him, her feathered tail wagging furiously, her mouth open in a wide smile. Her name, which meant Gypsy in English, suited her because Santana had adopted her after her original owner had been murdered. He squatted and let her lick his face as he stroked her shiny golden coat and gave her a hug.

Because of his odd work hours, a contractor had installed a dog door in a back wall. A computer chip in her collar activated the door that gave her access to an enclosed dog run Santana had constructed in the backyard. Another chip implanted under her skin held a number corresponding to the information in a pet locator's computer, which included her name and his address and phone number.

He refreshed her water bowl and watched as she lapped it up. He always fed her in the morning and could see that her food bowl was empty now. In a cupboard in the kitchen, where he kept her food and treats, he opened a bag of Premium Chicken Filets for dogs and gave her one. She took it gently in her mouth and ran into the living room and leapt on the couch, where she devoured it.

He went upstairs to the computer on his desk and clicked on the application for the security cameras mounted around the house, Gitana close at his heels. Four separate rectangular black-

and-white boxes appeared, representing the sides of the house. He entered his password for the CVR, Continuous Video Recording, and selected today's date. All recordings for each camera appeared. He saw nothing unusual as he quickly reviewed each short recording.

He then changed into a T-shirt and shorts, a black jogging suit with an orange Day-Glo stripe down the leg, and a pair of Nike running shoes. He strapped on a smaller Kydex kidney holster and filled it with a Glock 27 that he removed from a nightstand drawer. He always carried his compact Glock or the slightly larger SPPD standard issue Glock 23, not out of some distorted sense of masculinity, but because the Cali cartel had hunted him for years. The last of those who wanted him dead had been killed in an auto accident and the Cali cartel dismantled, but Santana believed in being prepared. Before leaving, he armed the security system and took Gitana out for a two-mile run.

She jogged beside him, the wind feathering her hair. He rarely kept her on a leash since she never ventured far and always seemed to have him in her sights. They ran together along the flat tar road that paralleled the St. Croix River, the sun low and red in the west, the air alive with the heavy scents of muddy river bottoms, algae-covered rocks, and schools of fish.

After the first mile, sweat had loosened his muscles, and Santana picked up the pace. Whenever he ran or worked out, he tried to clear his mind of any theories or feelings about a case or cases, but thoughts about the two cases he was currently working kept pulling at him like strong currents. Something he'd heard today troubled him, but the thought was like a distant sound he couldn't identify.

His thoughts switched to his encounter with Rita Gamboni. He'd been caught off-guard. Then again, he hadn't spoken to her recently. He wondered about the rumors that the chief, Tim Branigan, was about to retire. He wondered if she was seeking to return to the SPPD, which seemed like a downward career move for her. But then he figured she wasn't really happy working for the Bureau. Too much bureaucracy and ass kissing, far more than she'd dealt with working for the SPPD. He recalled being surprised when she'd taken the SPPD/FBI liaison position, and even more surprised when she'd become a full-time agent. Maybe she'd come to her senses. He wasn't sure how that decision would impact him.

After finishing his run, he went into the main level bedroom he'd converted into a workout room, where he completed three sets of bench presses and curls and hammered the heavy bag and speed bag till he was soaked in sweat and could barely lift his arms. He finished his workout with a hundred sit-ups before showering in the upstairs bathroom.

He slipped into a pair of blue jeans, deck shoes, and a black T-shirt with white lettering that Tony Novak, head of Forensic Services, had given him as a gift when Santana had taken a leave from the department. The lettering on the front read:

I'M A COP
TO SAVE TIME, ASSUME I KNOW EVERYTHING

Famished after skipping lunch, Santana ate a large *Bandeja Paisa* dinner consisting of grilled steak, fried pork rind, a chorizo sausage on a bed of white rice and beans, topped with a fried egg, and served with fried plantains.

Sitting on the living room couch after dinner with Madison Porter's murder book in his lap, Santana gazed at the mantel over the fireplace where he kept his father's favorite meerschaum pipe, one of the few mementos that he'd managed to take with him when he fled Colombia and the Cali cartel at the age of sixteen. The pipe reminded him of René Magritte's surrealistic painting *This Is Not a Pipe*, in which Magritte argued that the pipe in his painting was only a representation because you could not stuff it. If he'd written on the painting, "This is a pipe," he would've been lying.

Santana rested his head against the soft leather cushion and looked up at the beamed ceiling, and then at the painting above the fireplace of the *arriero* with his two mules carrying sacks of coffee down a dirt road in the mountains of Colombia. His childhood friend, Pablo Chaves, had done the painting. Santana had found it on a Colombian website. An artist friend had ordered it for him.

Gitana lay on the floor at his feet with her head on the large stuffed bunny Santana had recently purchased for her. Though her eyes were closed, he knew she was aware of his every movement.

He'd established a good life here, but he missed Colombia, missed the magic that Gabriel García Márquez had written about, the magic he'd never found here. Sometimes he felt unmoored, like a sailor adrift in a boat, fighting against a stiff wind that was blowing him toward a distant shore. He wondered now if he'd ever return permanently to his homeland.

He opened the murder book, which he had signed out of the property room, and reread the Chronological Record, the Crime Scene Log, and the Crime Report, as thoughts of Colombia faded like a dying light. Then he flipped several sections over on the three-ring binder till he came to the Miscellaneous Notes containing the detectives' canvassing notes.

As he carefully reread the section, a name he'd heard earlier today jumped out at him.

Gordon Grant.

The maintenance man who'd found the bodies in the stash house.

The thought kept pulling at him. Could this Gordon Grant be the same Gordon Grant whom Ellis Taylor and Darnell Robinson had questioned regarding Madison Porter's murder, the same Gordon Grant who had lived next door to her?

* * *

Dylan Walsh was dressed in his usual outfit: stonewashed jeans riding low on his thin waist, sandals, a light-blue T-shirt, and a long silk robe open at the waist. With his fine features, razor-cut dark hair, and pretty face, women often thought of him as an edgy-but-handsome leading man, the bad boy every woman wanted to reform.

Seated beside him on the couch was his current squeeze, Christine Hammond. She'd called him earlier and asked to come over on the pretense that she had something important to ask him. He suspected that she just wanted to get high on meth, but what the hell? She was good in bed, and he liked that she kept her mouth shut most of the time, unlike a lot of women who thought if they weren't constantly talking and *sharing*, something was wrong in the relationship.

"A friend of mine's in trouble," Hammond said.

"How is that my problem?"

"You have connections."

"So?"

"She's my friend. I told her you could help."

"What kind of trouble is she in?" Walsh asked.

"She needs to get out of the country."

"What the hell for?"

"She took someone's money."

"Did she rob a bank?"

"Not exactly."

"Then what?" Walsh asked.

"She really didn't tell me. But she'll pay you."

Walsh thought about it. Began connecting the dots. "How much money does she have?"

"I don't know. But it's a lot. And she'll give me some money, too. Help me get back on my feet."

"I like you better when you're off your feet," Walsh said.

"That's not funny, Dylan."

"Hey, try getting a sense of humor."

"I'm funny when I want to be."

"Yeah. Hilarious. So why does she want to help you?"

"I'm her friend."

"Right," Walsh said. "Never can have too many of them."

"So will you do it?"

"What's your friend's name?"

"She goes by Ana Luna."

"Tell you what. Have your friend, Ana, come talk to me."

Hammond smiled. "Thank you, honey." She leaned over and kissed his cheek.

He grabbed the back of her head and drew her toward his crotch. "Show me how much you appreciate it. And tell your friend to bring the money."

*   *   *

In a dream that night Santana falls into a deep, dark hole and lands in a river. The river is formed by the tears of a young woman in a Victorian dress crying on the riverbank. Santana cannot see her face, though he senses the young woman is Madison Porter.

Carried along by the current, struggling to stay afloat, he's suddenly swept out of the river and onto an abandoned, desolate landscape. A lone, melted pocket watch hangs on a leafless, dried-out tree branch, like a piece of laundry left out on the line to dry. A strange, undefined figure lies in the middle of the landscape, wearing a clocklike saddle. To his left Santana sees a clock covered in ants.

Santana sat up in bed, awakened by the transient, hazy light of false dawn as it broke along the horizon. The light seeping through the partially opened blinds on the sliding glass door bathed the room in an ambient yellow glow.

He opened the nightstand drawer and removed his latest dream journal. He'd always possessed the ability to vividly recall his dreams, having been taught as a child to trust his intuition and to interpret his dreams, to believe that hidden meanings inhabited the images created by his subconscious. He'd left all but one of his childhood journals in Colombia when he'd fled to the States at the age of sixteen, but he'd kept every one of them since.

Now, whenever he awoke from a vivid dream, he would write in his journal and then remind himself to look for the images and dream signs when he fell asleep again and was in a dream state. Both techniques often allowed him to actively participate in his dream environment while the dream was in progress. It also helped him understand the dark images and objects that had haunted his sleep since the age of sixteen. Writing about and describing the images he'd encountered in this latest dream allowed Santana to connect the real with the fantasy.

In his teens he'd read *The Surrealist Manifesto*, by the French poet and critic André Breton, which had greatly influenced his belief about the subconscious mind. Attaching more importance to waking events than to those occurring in dreams was antithetical to Breton. Surrealism, Breton believed, was a means of connecting conscious and unconscious realms of experience.

In studying Breton, Santana had become familiar with Sigmund Freud and Salvador Dalí. Freud believed dreams were coded messages from the subconscious. His psychological view that our fantasies shape our dreams and delusions became the central point for Dalí's Surrealist work. Dalí's Surrealist paintings were full of imagery that drew from Freudian symbolism, as well as his own subconscious. Santana had read that Dalí would often stand on his head until almost passing out in an attempted to tap into his subconscious.

The desert landscape with the melting watch on an empty branch, Santana recalled, were images from the famous Salvador Dalí painting *The Persistence of Memory*, a painting Santana had first seen in the Dalí Museum in Paris when he'd traveled as a boy to the city with his parents and younger sister.

Clocks in Dalí's works were always melting or distorted as a way of representing the subjectivity of time and the fading or melting away of childhood and adolescent memories. While keeping track of time during the day was relatively easy, keeping track of time while asleep was a different story. Like this morning, Santana had sometimes woken up and expected it to still be the middle of the night only to be surprised that it was already dawn.

He understood that the creature in the center of *The Persistence of Memory* represented a fading image that often appeared in dreams, where the dreamer couldn't pinpoint the creature's exact form and composition. The ants eating away the clock face were symbols Dalí often used in his paintings and represented decay and mortality.

As Santana sat looking at what he'd written in his journal, he remembered Madison Porter's crime scene. How it had triggered something from his distant past. As he stood in Pig's Eye Regional Park viewing the crime scene photos that day, he hadn't been able to unlock the subconscious gate in his mind that prevented him from recalling where he'd seen a similar image of the jump rope and rose petals before.

The Dalí imagery in his latest dream had helped him bridge the connection between his subconscious mind and Madison Porter's murder.

Madison Porter's murder scene was a depiction of Dalí's Alice in Wonderland sculpture. The long jump rope, the red rose petals sprinkled in her hair and hands.

He'd seen the sculpture as a child in the Dalí museum in Paris.

Chapter 11

Four Years Ago
Puerto Vallarta, Mexico

On a warm moonlit night a Lexus SUV with dark tinted windows pulled up in front of a fancy nightclub called La Leche. Expensive sedans and SUVs filled the parking lot. Splinters of lightning flashed on the distant horizon. Waves splashed against the shoreline across a blacktop road off the beach.

A young, handsome couple exited the Lexus followed by two muscular bodyguards. The driver tossed the keys to Eduardo "Eddie" Machado, one of the valets.

"Park around back," the driver said to Machado. "I don't want my ride scratched or dented."

Eddie recognized the handsome man who'd given him the keys and the order. He'd been vacationing at a resort in the area for the past few days. He was Rubén Oseguera Gonzáles, the son of Rubén Nemesio Oseguera Cervantes, or El Mencho, the leader of the Cartel Jalisco New Generation, or CJNG, the most violent cartel in all of Mexico.

Messing up the Lexus could cost Eddie his life.

"*Sí, señor*," Eddie said.

Rubén took the hand of his girlfriend, Paulina Correa, and led her up the steps, where two doormen pulled open the main doors.

Cumbia music exploded. Couples jammed the floor and danced between the tables.

A hostess in a tight fitting, low-cut dress escorted the couple to the lounge and a long candle-lit table covered with a white tablecloth. Six young, handsome, and well-dressed men and women were seated at the table. In front of each was a glass of Champagne. Two vacant chairs waited at the head of the table. A large white frosted cake with twenty-seven candles sat in the center of the table. HAPPY BIRTHDAY, RUBÉN was scripted in blue letters.

The men stood to greet the guest of honor.

Rubén moved around the table, shaking hands, kissing the ladies' cheeks, a confident young man, seemingly humbled by the celebration. But behind the smile he believed he was entitled to the adoration and attention.

Once he and Paulina were seated, each of the men rose from his chair and offered a toast and a birthday wish in Spanish.

Rubén thanked everyone and offered a toast of his own. *"A mis amigos y amigas."*

In a small parking lot behind the club used primarily by the help, Eddie Machado was enjoying a smoke break and admiring Rubén's luxury Lexus LX 570. With the suspension and brake upgrades and bulletproof armor and glass that could stop handguns, high-powered rifles, and explosives, like IEDs and DM-51 grenades, the Lexus was virtually impenetrable. Eddie had never driven anything like it before. Despite the upgrades and its heavy weight, he could tell it handled like a dream just with the short trip to the back of the club.

Eddie vowed that one day he'd own one.

As he finished his smoke, he glanced at his watch. Two thirty a.m. The club was open Thursdays through Saturdays from 11:00 p.m. to 6:00 a.m. Eddie liked the great tips, but the hours sucked. Plus, how was he supposed to enjoy himself when he had to work every Friday and Saturday night?

He was thinking about a new line of work as he rounded a corner at the front of the building when he caught something in his peripheral vision.

Two SUVs with dark tinted windows were parked along the road.

Funny, Eddie thought. Why park out there?

Then he saw the *sicarios* coming. Four of them, dressed all in black, balaclavas covering their faces, carrying AR-15s, bulletproof vests wrapped around their chests.

Shit! It's a hit!

Heart pounding, Eddie sprinted toward the front door. The two valets he worked with were each getting into cars as he ran past. Yanking the front door of the club open, Eddie yelled, "*Sicarios!*" to the doormen as if either of them could hear or understand him over the loud music.

Eddie ran like the young *fútbol* player he once was, weaving through the crowd as though he were racing down the field. As he burst into the lounge, one of Rubén's huge bodyguards grabbed him around the chest and held him, his gun barrel pressed against Eddie's head.

"*Sicarios!*" Eddie said. "Outside."

The *sicarios* burst through the front doors and fired rounds into the ceiling, scattering the crowd and sending women screaming and dancers stumbling over one another.

The bodyguard holding Eddie shoved him to one side, pivoted toward the open door of the lounge, and attempted to close it.

Like that's gonna help, Eddie thought, dropping to the floor.

Seconds later bullets were zinging through the walls and over Eddie's head, fragmenting glass and spraying liquor.

The bodyguard opened the door and blasted away till a hail of bullets cut him down.

The *sicarios* were pushing their way through the fleeing crowd now, searching for Rubén.

Panic had broken out in the lounge as the party guests scrambled for cover. All the men and—to Eddie's surprise—two of the women were armed with handguns and returned fire.

Eddie belly-crawled toward Rubén, who was hunkered down behind the heavy wooden table with his woman and handgun.

"*Señor.*"

Rubén's eyes were large and wild with fear. He pointed his gun at Eddie.

"Wait!" Eddie hollered, lifting his chest off the ground and raising his arms in the air. "I can get you out of here."

Rubén hesitated a moment, not sure he could trust Eddie. "How?"

Eddie gestured toward the back of the lounge.

Rubén nodded. "Paulina," he called, taking her hand. He pulled her close to him and yelled at Eddie. "Go!"

Eddie grabbed the dead bodyguard's gun as he ran past. Could he hit anything with it or actually kill someone? Maybe if his life depended on it—which it did.

The remaining bodyguard laid down cover fire as Eddie, Rubén, and Paulina stayed low and dashed toward the back of the building. A cacophony of deafening gunfire had erupted as the surviving security guards in the club opened up with their weapons. Innocent customers were caught in the crossfire.

In a narrow hallway off the lounge, Eddie led Rubén and Paulina to a roof access ladder.

"Why not the fire door?" Rubén said.

"Probably someone out back," Eddie said. He tucked the gun behind his belt and started up the ladder.

Rubén helped Paulina up and then followed.

Once they were all on the roof, Paulina crouched down as Eddie and Rubén peered over the parapet.

Two *sicarios* stood in the lot below, their AR-15s aimed at the back door, ready to kill anyone who came out.

"Now what?" Rubén said.

"I go down the side of the building," Eddie said.

"Not alone." Rubén pulled the gun out from behind Eddie's belt. "You ever fire one of these before?"

Eddie shook his head.

Rubén checked the action and handed it back to Eddie. "All you do is point and shoot."

Eddie followed Rubén and Paulina to the side of the building. Because of a tall, grassy embankment, it was only a ten-foot drop to the ground.

Eddie went over the parapet first. Rubén lowered Paulina into his arms and then jumped down beside them.

Eddie peered around the back corner of the building. The two *sicarios* had moved closer to the door as if expecting fleeing customers would be coming out soon. Their backs were turned toward Eddie and Rubén. Eddie could still hear the muffled gunshots and screams inside the club as the gun battle continued.

Rubén put an index finger vertically to his lips, indicating silence. Then he stepped out from cover and, with Eddie to his right, moved slowly toward the two *sicarios*.

They were within eight feet when one of the sicarios turned his head. His eyes widened in surprise as he raised his weapon.

Rubén shot him in the face.

As the second *sicario* raised his weapon and turned to fire, Rubén pulled the trigger again.

Nothing.

Jammed!

The *sicario* smiled. Then he saw Eddie's gun.

Eddie shot him in the chest.

Rubén looked at Eddie. "*Gracias.*" He took Eddie's gun away, walked over to the unconscious *sicario*, and shot him in the head.

Eddie realized that a bulletproof vest had stopped his bullet.

"Paulina," Rubén called.

She ran to him in her bare feet, her high-heeled shoes in her hand.

The three of them made it to the Lexus. Ten minutes later they were safely away from the carnage, roaring along the highway. Paulina, his *buchona*, was seated in the passenger seat beside Rubén, looking pretty *tranquillo*, Eddie thought, after what they'd been through.

Buchonas, or the girlfriends of cartel members in Mexico, all had the same look. Long black hair, expensive jewelry and clothes, and full lips—often with the help of plastic surgery—and the unlimited supply of money provided to them by their boyfriends.

Grateful that he hadn't actually killed anyone, Eddie was still processing how easily and unemotionally Rubén had shot the unconscious *sicario*. Eddie had been shocked and surprised when the bullet from his gun had actually hit the target. He hadn't had time to process what had happened. How lucky he was to still be alive.

"Who were they?" Paula asked.

"*Hijos de puta* from the Nueva Plaza Cartel," Rubén said.

The hit ordered by the sons of bitches from the Nueva Plaza Cartel, as Rubén had called them, made sense to Eddie now. El Mencho had ordered the murder of high-ranking CJNG member Carlos Enrique Sánchez, alias El Cholo, after Sánchez had murdered a CJNG financial operator nicknamed El Colombiano. The murder attempt on Sánchez had failed, and he'd retaliated by co-founding the Nueva Plaza Cartel and targeting El Mencho for assassination.

Supported by the Sinaloa Cartel, the CJNG's arch enemy, the Nueva Plaza Cartel controlled the western part of Guadalajara and the towns of Tlaquepaque, Tonalá, Tlajomulco, and El Salto to the southeast of the city, but had not yet reached downtown Guadalajara—though cartel members lived in some of the most exclusive residential zones in the city. Lacking the military-grade weaponry that the CJNG had and not advanced enough for drug production or international trafficking, their criminal enterprises were confined to street dealing, auto part theft, and phone extortion.

Now Sánchez and his cartel had raised the stakes by going after El Mencho's son, Rubén.

Venganza. Payback.

Day in the life of a cartel member, Eddie thought.

Rubén looked in the rearview mirror. "What is your name, *señor*?"

"Eduardo. But friends call me Eddie."

"You saved my life," Rubén said. "I will call you anything you want."

"*Gracias*," Eddie said.

Paulina turned in her seat and smiled at him. Her eye shadow had run and her makeup was smeared, but she still looked good.

Eddie wondered if he'd ever have a woman with beauty and guts like her.

He leaned back in the comfortable leather seat and released the receding tension in his body with a long breath. The ride was so smooth and quiet, he hardly felt like they were moving. He could get used to this kind of luxury in life.

"How would you like to come and work for me?" Rubén asked. "My father and I could use a guy like you. A man with a big future."

Eddie wondered if El Cholo would be targeting him now, too?

"I could be a problem, *señor*."

Rubén chuckled. "Always remember this, Eddie. It is not a real problem if money can solve it."

Chapter 12

On Friday morning Santana located a CRI named Luis Garcia. Luis was working at a construction site along Johnson Parkway in St. Paul. He'd once been a member of the Latin Kings, but had gone straight after helping Santana solve a murder case involving forged visas. Santana had looked out for Luis's mother while he served a short stint at the Minnesota Correctional Facility in Faribault for his involvement in the scam. Luis was what Santana and the department considered a Confidential Reliable Informant. The department used a number of CIs for information. But CRIs like Luis had proven their reliability over time and were better compensated for the information they provided. Santana had spoken to him on the phone yesterday.

Workers were just arriving at the construction site, lunch boxes and thermoses in hand, when Santana parked his unmarked squad and got out. The rain had quit, but he could still smell the ozone in the air and feel the thick humidity that raised beads of condensation on his skin and caused his shirt to cling to him like a wet rag.

Luis, dressed in a white sleeveless T-shirt, blue jeans, and heavy work boots, was seated on a curb, looking at his iPhone. He was a muscular young man in his early twenties, about five feet seven inches tall. He had a flat nose and darker complexion in keeping with his Mixtec Mexican heritage. Gone was the thick silver chain around his neck and the five-pointed crown tattooed on his right forearm, a symbol of the Latin King Nation.

"Hey, Santana," he said with a wide smile. He stood, stuffed his phone in a front pocket of his jeans, and stuck out a hand.

Santana shook it.

Luis gestured for Santana to follow as he walked along the grassy bank toward a construction trailer.

"You talked to Angelina Torres lately?" Luis asked.

Angelina Torres had also been part of the previous case.

"I haven't," Santana said.

"She's working for CLUES now."

CLUES stood for *Comunidades Latinas Unidas En Servicio,* a non-profit organization that provided a variety of resources for Latinos in St. Paul.

"If you see her, tell her I said, 'Hi.'"

"Better you told her yourself," Luis said.

Santana couldn't disagree.

They stopped at the back of the trailer, but Luis's right foot kept tapping to the beat of some inner rhythm, a symptom of his hyperactivity.

"You still taking your meds, Luis?"

"Hard to concentrate without them."

"What do you take?"

"Desoxyn. Why?"

"The drug might be related to a case I'm working."

Garcia thought about it for a time. Then he said, "Word on the street is two gringos brought a large shipment of meth into town last night from Tucson."

"Names?"

"Jamal Washburn and Dean Moody. Bad dudes. Rather shoot than talk."

"Got a location?"

Garcia handed him a slip of paper. "On the West Side."

"Appreciate the tip, Luis."

"You think the shipment is related to the Desoxyn black market?"

"Could be," Santana said. "Give your mother my regards."

"I will. Hey, Santana . . ."

Santana waited.

"Watch your back, *amigo.*"

*   *   *

Using the computer in his unmarked, Santana logged into SPPD's VPN, or Virtual Private Network, using his unique log-in and password, and then into the state of Minnesota Department of Vehicle Registration database, searching for driver's license records and photos for Jamal Washburn and Dean Moody. Then he logged into NCIC, the National Crime Information Center, looking for current wants and warrants on the two men. They were clean.

When Santana's cellphone rang, he recognized the number from the Forensic Unit.

"What's up, Tony?"

"The only set of prints we found on the Sig Sauer in the stash house belonged to Martin Lozano. We captured two sets of prints from the Ruger. One set belonged to Lozano. Ran the other set of prints on the Ruger through NGI and MAFIN. Those prints matched a young woman named Ana Soriano from El Salvador," Novak said. "She was fingerprinted and photographed at the border two years ago."

Santana wondered why she hadn't taken the Ruger with her. Then again, the gun was empty and, as an immigrant, she might not have been aware that she'd left her fingerprints on the gun. But why not take the loaded Sig Sauer?

"Anything on her from MAFIN?" Santana asked.

"Nothing. I'll text you a photo."

"Thanks, Tony. What about GSR?" Santana asked, refer-ring to gunshot residue.

"On Ryker's hand and on Martin Lozano's."

"Then Martin Lozano fired the Sig Sauer."

"That's my conclusion. I also matched his fingerprints with the prints I found on the Sig Sauer cartridge casing."

Novak routinely examined cartridge casings for fingerprints since the act of loading the ammunition into the magazine or chamber often left recoverable impressions. Santana knew that fingerprints could survive the firing process, though obtaining prints from the casings recovered from the scene wasn't always a forgone conclusion.

"Good work, Tony. How about the .380 caliber bullet the ME removed from Ryker's brain?"

"I fired three test rounds from the Sig Sauer into the water tank."

Santana understood how important it was that Novak fired no more than three rounds into the water tank for comparison purposes because the microscopic striations in a gun barrel changed every three to five shots. A smart defense attorney in a case Santana once investigated had created reasonable doubt with a jury by showing how this occurred.

"I compared the striations on the Sig Sauer with the test bullets and the bullet from Ryker's brain," Novak continued. "All three characteristics matched."

Santana knew that lands and grooves, the caliber of the bullet, and the rifling twist—the three characteristics Novak had referenced—could all be tied directly to the type of barrel that was used to fire the bullet.

Santana wasn't sure what Ana Soriano was doing in Martin and Benita Lozanos' house, but convincing Bobbi Chacon and the DEA that Soriano wasn't responsible for Joel Ryker's murder might not remove the target on her back. The only way to find out what she knew about the shooting was to keep her alive till he could locate her.

Despite the plain mug shot that Tony Novak texted him, Santana could see that Ana Soriano was darkly beautiful. She had straight jet-black hair that hung down her back and the high cheekbones of a model.

"Do me a favor, Tony. Keep Ana Soriano's name between you and me for the time being."

"You got it."

"Anything else?"

"How you doin,' John?"

"I'm doin'."

"Wife and I want to have you over soon."

"Look forward to it."

"You take care."

"Thanks for the info, Tony."

After disconnecting, Santana called Gordon Grant's cell-phone number but got no answer. He decided to drive to Gordon Grant's house in Battle Creek on the off chance Grant might be home.

Grant's small one-story house was set back from the street and surrounded by a five-foot-high wooden fence. Santana entered through an unlocked gate and knocked on the front door. He waited for a short time and then knocked again but got no response.

Standing on the front steps looking over the fence toward Madison Porter's house, Santana wondered what the odds were that Gordon Grant would live next door to a young girl who had been murdered four years ago. In the interview statement Darnell Robinson had included in the murder book, Gordon Grant had said that he hadn't heard or seen anything unusual on the night of Madison Porter's murder. Taylor and Robinson had subsequently excluded Grant from the suspect list.

Santana walked counterclockwise around the house, hoping to get a glimpse inside through the shades and blinds covering the windows. At the last window he came to along the back of the house, Santana noticed that a corner of the shade had been torn away.

He cupped his hands and peered through the glass. He could see a partially made bed and then a nightstand beside it, closest to the window. Four colored photos were taped to the wall above the nightstand. Santana squinted but couldn't see the photos clearly.

He returned to his unmarked squad and retrieved a set of Bushnell binoculars.

Back at the window again, he held the binoculars vertically and looked through one lens with his right eye as he would a telescope.

He could see now that the man in each of the four photos was Gordon Grant. The females in each photo were different, but they all looked young.

One of them was Madison Porter.

Chapter 13

Four Years Ago
Puerto Vallarta, Mexico

The morning after the nightclub shooting, twenty-year-old Eddie Machado boarded a school bus with thirty other men. All were in their late teens and early twenties. Tall and slender, with a narrow face and dark brown eyes, Eddie Machado moved with the grace of an athlete. Exceptionally skilled as a child, he'd hoped to play professional soccer one day, but after his parents died in a factory fire when he was twelve, and his relatives refused to take him in, he became one of the thousands of "Rat Kids" who lived in the parks and sewers in Mexico City.

He washed windshields at stoplights, performed acrobatics and juggling, sold his body to perverts. Whatever it took to make a dollar. Whatever it took to survive.

To deaden the pain he sniffed toluene, a colorless, flammable liquid used to make paint thinners, glue, and disinfectants. The kids in the encampment where he lived called it *activo*. He sniffed it through a bottle or a soaked rag known as a *mona*. Toluene induced a drunken feeling, suppressed the cold and hunger, and deadened the pain in his soul. It also blunted his inhibitions and dulled the nightmarish memories.

Through it all, his motto was NEVER TRUST ANYONE.

At nineteen Eddie drifted to Guadalajara, where he got a job at La Rojo de Jose Cuervo loading cases of tequila from the factory onto trucks. He soon grew tired of the hard labor and low pay while local cartel members earned riches and respect that bordered on fear.

Shortly after quitting his job at the tequila factory, he'd landed the valet job at the La Leche nightclub. Six months later, Eddie's lucky shot had saved Rubén Oseguera Gonzáles' life and forever changed the course of his.

When Rubén had offered Eddie a job, he thought he'd be driving a luxury ride and body guarding Rubén, especially after Rubén had lost two of his primo bodyguards in the nightclub gunfight. But Rubén had told Eddie security didn't work that way. Eddie needed to train and to learn skills that would keep him, and most importantly Rubén and El Mencho, alive. The job would pay Eddie 3,500 pesos, or about $180, per week. All expenses, including training, would be covered.

Not exactly enough *dinero* to buy a ride or a woman like Rubén had.

Before the school bus left the city, the driver, a large man with a pit-bull face, scraggly beard, and black hair slicked back on his head, stood beside the driver's seat, a thick hand wrapped around the stanchion attached to the metal modesty shield. Speaking in a gravelly voice, he gave them all a choice. Get off the bus now if they wanted, no questions asked. Because once the bus left the city, the only way out was in a body bag.

Eddie thought the man was kidding. It was hard to tell because his flat eyes were impossible to read. Eddie looked at the lanky teen in the seat across the aisle from him. He had introduced himself when they were waiting for the bus. His name was Juan.

The Indian with the shoulder-length black hair sitting in the seat in front of Juan said in Spanish, "We are training to be security guards."

"You are," the large man said. "But from this day forward, your life belongs to the Cartel de Jalisco Nueva Generación."

Half the men scurried off the bus.

Eddie, Juan, and the Indian stayed.

Eddie's justification was simple. Many of the police and government officials he'd known were as corrupt as those they called criminals. He'd dealt with people who'd tried to take advantage of him ever since he was twelve. Eddie figured he knew the risk he was taking.

He would soon learn how wrong he was.

In the pine-covered mountains surrounding the city of Talpa de Allende, two dozen men dressed in camo and armed with assault rifles met the bus at a gated camp enclosed by an eight-foot fence topped with razor wire. Inside the camp Eddie saw multiple tents, two sets of barracks, a mess hall, guard towers, and a cabin where he assumed the camp commander lived.

The armed men took all cellphones and stripped the recruits. They were then hosed down with water and ordered, one by one, to grab the terminals of a car battery sitting on a long folding table. If any man had a GPS device hidden inside him, it would burn.

The strong shock caused Juan and some of the other men to scream.

Eddie had no hidden GPS, but he knew arguing would get him nowhere. He gritted his teeth, gripped the terminals, and made no sound as electricity jolted through him.

Like Eddie, the Indian made no sound.

The large man who had driven the bus, the one the other trainers called Bautista, told the recruits they would have to pass yet another test before the training began.

Eddie wondered if this test, too, would involve pain, and he set his teeth as he and the recruits followed Bautista to the far side of the clearing. A dozen trainers with the steely demeanor of drill sergeants stood in a tight row, waiting. As the recruits lined up in front of them, the trainers separated, revealing a naked corpse face up in the grass.

One trainer held out a machete to Juan, the first recruit in line. "Dismember the body," he ordered.

Juan froze. Then his head jerked toward Eddie beside him, his frightened eyes boring into Eddie's. Panic etched his face.

"Do not look to the others for courage," the trainer cautioned.

Juan faced the instructor and grasped the machete in his trembling hand.

The trainer waited.

Juan stood stiffly in his tracks, staring down at the bloodied body at his feet.

The only sound Eddie heard was the sound of Juan's deep, heavy breaths.

"Quit whining like a woman," the trainer said. "Do what you are told."

Juan hesitated. With tears running down his cheeks, he dropped the machete in the pine needles at his feet. He looked at the trainer once more and slowly shook his head. "*No. No puedo.*"

Bautista walked up behind Juan and shot him in the back of the head.

Eddie's body jerked at the sound of the gunshot. He watched in horror as Juan's body collapsed to the ground.

"Now there are two bodies to dismember," Bautista said, looking at Eddie, a sinister smile slashing his broad face.

Eddie stared into the dark empty spaces that were Bautista's eyes. He'd seen similar eyes more times than he could count. Seen them in those who preyed on him. Seen them again in the nightmares that haunted his sleep.

Pointing at the first corpse, Bautista said, "Cut off his head." He said it calmly and without emotion, as if ordering a meal at a restaurant.

Eddie's throat tightened. He could barely breathe.

"Did you not hear me?" Bautista said, raising the barrel of the gun. "Pick up the machete," he repeated.

Eddie's stomach churned. He realized now that Bautista and the other trainers wanted to strip him of everything that was human.

All the recruits stood motionless, stunned looks glazing their eyes—except for the Indian, who stepped forward, picked up the machete, and did as ordered.

Bautista laughed. "*Sí, señor*. It is not difficult for a *Cholo*, a real man."

The Indian held out the machete for Eddie and gave him an encouraging nod.

Eddie knew the Indian, for whatever reason, was trying to help him. Save him, really. To survive, Eddie needed to stay the course.

He gripped the machete tightly in his hands. He considered cutting off Bautista's head instead. But the large man seemed to know what he was thinking.

Bautista stepped back, a crooked smile carving his face, and pointed the handgun at Eddie again. The trainers with the assault rifles did the same.

Standing over Juan's body, Eddie knew that if he refused to follow Bautista's order, he, too, would be shot and dismembered. For a moment he wondered if giving up his life would be the best option. An only child, he'd been alone in the world for eight years, struggling to survive, and for what end? His future, he thought, was as bleak as the clouds settling over the mountains. But at least he had a future, as dark and uncertain as it was.

He bent down, laid the blade over Juan's throat, closed his eyes, and imagined he was taking the trophy head of a white-tailed deer, as he'd done as a young boy on hunts with his father.

When Eddie finished, he rose to his feet, his hands and shirt spotted with blood, unable to make eye contact with Juan's body. He held out the bloody machete to Bautista, who ordered him to hand it to the nearest recruit.

No one else resisted.

Afterwards the recruits packed the remaining body parts in plastic bags. Trainers hauled the bags away.

"This is the first rule you must learn," Bautista said to the recruits. "Repeat after me. If there is no body, there is no crime to investigate."

The men repeated in unison.

"Louder," Bautista ordered.

They all repeated the phrase again.

"Good," Bautista said, clapping his hands together like a *fútbol* coach encouraging his team.

That night as Eddie lay on his cot in a barracks-like structure in the woods, the Indian told him his name was Yuma Rivera. Born of a Mexican father and Chiricahua Apache mother, Yuma Rivera grew up on the Mescalero Apache Reservation in Mescalero, New Mexico, where many of the Chiricahua Apaches lived after being transferred from the Fort Sill Oklahoma Reservation in the 19th century.

Eddie had suspected that Yuma was not a Mexican Indian, given that he was over six feet tall, unlike many of the shorter Indians of Mexico and South America.

Like tumbleweed blowing across barren hardpan, Yuma had been drifting through life since leaving the reservation at the age of twenty-two. He'd been working as a hunting guide when Rubén Jr., El Mencho's son, and a few of his friends paid Yuma to guide them into the mountains to hunt mule deer and bighorn sheep. After the successful hunt, Rubén Jr. offered him a job as a security guard.

Bautista had given Yuma the nickname of *Cholo* and had laughed like a fool when he'd said it.

Having lived in Arizona for eight years after he was born —and before his parents had migrated to Mexico—Eddie understood that in the Southwest *Cholo* was a term of affection. He'd heard women call their boyfriends that on occasion, as in he was her "*Cholo*," her man.

Yuma said that he'd often called his woman his *Chola*. But *Cholo* could mean a gangsta or homey, Eddie knew. The Spanish in Latin America also used it as a derogatory term for mixed-blood *castas*.

Later that night, as Eddie slept fitfully on his cot, he dreamt of Los Dias de los Muertos, the Day of the Dead, a time for remembering friends, family, and ancestors. In his dream his mother was telling him about the Mexican tradition of three deaths.

The first death is when the body ceases to function, when our hearts no longer beat, when our gaze becomes dark, when the space we now occupy is empty.

The second death is when our body is lowered into the grave.

The third and final death is that moment in the future when there is no one left alive to remember us. The last time someone speaks our name.

Eddie felt a large hand clasped tightly over his mouth, and he woke with a start. As he struggled, he saw Yuma Rivera's face in the dim light.

Yuma put a finger to his lips as a warning to remain quiet.

Eddie quit struggling and nodded.

Yuma released his hand. "I am leaving. Come with me."

Eddie shook his head.

"This life is not for us."

"It is all I have, Yuma."

"No," Yuma said. "If you stay, you will have nothing. Not even your soul. These men will take it all."

Eddie considered Yuma's offer. But fleeing into the forested mountains was a dead man's quest. "Sorry, Yuma."

"*Adios, amigo.*"

As Yuma turned to leave, Eddie grabbed his arm. "Bautista will come after you."

"No," Yuma said. "He will not."

With that he was gone like a puff of smoke.

The next morning trainers found Bautista's head on a wooden spike outside his tent. There was no sign of Yuma.

A new commander arrived the following day, and for the next six months Eddie and the remaining recruits trained like soldiers in the mountains of southern Mexico, the specter of death always hanging over them.

They did calisthenics every morning and ran with heavy packs in the afternoons. The remainders of the days were devoted to martial arts and hand-to-hand training, instructions on how to build car bombs, IEDs, and how to use C-4 without blowing yourself up.

Trainers taught him how to throw grenades and use grenade launchers. He learned how to shoot AK-47s, Uzis, and the Belgian-made FN-7 handgun, often called the Five-seveN. It was used by military and police forces all over the world, including the US Secret Service. Eddie learned that the Five-seveN was a favorite of the cartel because of its lightweight polymer shell, twenty-round magazine, and the small-caliber, high-velocity cartridge that could penetrate body armor. He could fieldstrip and reassemble a Five-seveN in fifteen seconds.

One of the recruits failed to do it in the allotted time of twenty seconds. The new commander shot him. In a real confrontation, he explained, the recruit could put everyone in danger.

Any recruit who ran afoul of the instructors was strung up from trees and used for target practice.

Knowing he might die for failing to follow orders was all the incentive Eddie needed to do the unthinkable. At least that's how he justified it.

In the months that followed, Eddie became a skilled, battle-tested assassin. But behind every decision and every inhuman act was a truth he could not escape. He had chosen this life. It was what he thought he wanted.

After completing—and surviving—the training, Eddie and the five remaining recruits left the camp in the bus they had arrived in. Their destination was the compound of Rubén Nemesio Oseguera Cervantes—El Mencho—the most feared drug kingpin in the world.

Chapter 14

Bobbi Chacon sat in an uncomfortable chair at the far end of a long table in a large conference room at the DEA administration building in downtown Minneapolis. There were thirty plus people in the room from an alphabet soup of law enforcement agencies. Some were seated around the table; some stood along the back wall.

She was the only woman in the room.

Tacked up on the wall to her left was a large map of Minnesota studded with pins, indicating suspected stash-house locations around the state.

United States DEA Omaha Division Special Agent in Charge Scott Weston stood stiffly in front of a lectern. With his short blond hair, his blue suit and tie, and button-down, freshly pressed white shirt, Weston fit his ex-military and by-the-book reputation. An Apple laptop computer sat open on the lectern. A pull-down screen behind him covered most of the wall.

"Before we get into the PowerPoint presentation and the main purpose of our meeting today," he said, pausing till the chatter died down, "I'd like to acknowledge the passing of one of our own, Special Agent Joel Ryker. Agent Ryker was tragically gunned down in a senseless killing yesterday, while investigating a stash house in St. Paul. He was able to take two known meth dealers down with him, but a possible third dealer escaped. We believe that person is responsible for Agent Ryker's death. We are working in conjunction with the St. Paul Police Department to bring this person to justice."

Bobbi Chacon knew what *she* meant by "justice," but she wasn't sure if Weston meant the same.

"Our condolences go out to Joel's family and friends," Weston continued, "and to his partner, who's with us today, Bobbi Chacon."

Everyone turned to look at her, offering nods and pats on the back. A few agents mumbled, "We'll get the son-of-a-bitch," or words to that effect.

She felt the heat of embarrassment in her face and averted her eyes by looking down.

"Agent Ryker's body will be shipped back to his family in Texas once the SPPD releases it."

Weston paused, giving time for agents to vent and to process Ryker's death before asking if there were any questions. When no one responded, he said, "All right, then."

He pushed the space bar on the computer, and the first slide in his PowerPoint presentation appeared on the screen.

"In recent years, Minnesota has emerged as an important hub for Mexican drug cartels trafficking meth in the Upper Midwest," Weston said. "It's a key source of much of the meth flowing into neighboring states. We anticipated that the change in the Midwestern field division would produce more effective investigations on methamphetamine, heroin, fentanyl, and prescription opioid trafficking, all of which have a significant impact on the region. Our anticipation of this increasing traffic has proved accurate. Together with our partners at the state and local level, we combined to seize almost fifteen hundred pounds of meth in Minnesota last year—the highest total ever recovered. Congratulations to all those involved."

A round of applause ensued.

Bobbi Chacon had quickly tuned out Weston's opening presentation. She'd heard enough of them in her seven years with the DEA. She'd cut her teeth working homicides in Dallas before joining the DEA and her first post in the El Paso Division, where the real action was. She hadn't been excited about her transfer to the Miami Division four years later and even less so on her recent transfer to fucking Minneapolis two months ago.

At least it was summer now, or what passed for summer, here. She just couldn't wait for that first snowfall. Yippee! She'd never lived in the shit before and was hoping like hell she'd be out of here before the first flakes fell in September. Or was it October or November?

She looked at the next slide in Weston's PowerPoint presentation, which showed a pie chart listing the major cartels operating in Mexico.

"We're currently listing six Mexican criminal organizations as having significant trafficking impact on the United States: Sinaloa, Cartel Jalisco New Generation, Beltran-Leyva, Juarez, Gulf, and the Zetas. Most of the cartels have splintered into competing factions in recent years. As of today only Sinaloa and Jalisco meet the traditional definition of cohesive organizations with a large footprint.

"Sinaloa, formerly led by Joaquín 'El Chapo' Guzmán, who is now serving a life sentence at the Colorado Supermax—"

Another round of applause, accompanied by backslaps and cheers, interrupted Weston's presentation.

He managed a smile and continued. "Sinaloa is based out of the Pacific coast state of the same name but still has a presence in much of the country, sometimes aided by local proxies.

"Jalisco, based in Guadalajara, is Mexico's fastest rising cartel, aggressively expansionist and not shying away from brazen, brutal tactics. CJNG wants to control the entire drug market and doesn't care how many they have to kill to reach that goal.

"The cartel runs brothels in Mexico, often forcing teens and women into sexual slavery. It also operates a tequila label, casinos, two shopping centers, a medical clinic, real estate companies, and a Pacific Ocean resort frequented by Americans.

"Adults and children are forced to work in their meth labs hidden in the jungle. Entire families who resist have been slaughtered. The cartel also recruits spies in the Mexican government and police to keep its leaders out of jail and avoid drug busts. Those who refuse bribes are threatened or killed.

"They're led by Rubén Nemesio Oseguera Cervantes, alias El Mencho. We consider him and his cartel to be one of the five most dangerous transnational criminal organizations on the face of the Earth.

"He typically travels in a convoy, surrounding himself with dozens of well-trained mercenaries armed with military-grade weapons that can rip through tanks, even aircraft.

"He doesn't make a lot of mistakes. There's a ten-million-dollar reward for his capture. Any of you want to collect, please raise your hand."

Chacon shook her head at the lame joke as a smattering of hands went up, followed by a few ass-kissing laughs, breaking the somber mood in the room.

Weston continued with a pleased smile still plastered on his face. "Jalisco is present in at least twenty-four of Mexico's thirty-two states. They're fighting Sinaloa from Tijuana to Zacatecas, to Quintana Roo, which includes Cancún and other popular Caribbean resorts.

"It's fighting Gulf and Zetas splinters in Veracruz, along the Gulf of Mexico, and in Guerrero and Michoacán, against local groups like Los Viagras. They began as a self-defense force before becoming involved in the production and distribution of meth. And no, they're not trafficking Viagra."

Another burst of laughter.

Men, Chacon thought. They never grew tired of their boyish locker room bullshit. But she had to admit Weston was on a roll. Maybe *he* was taking Viagra.

"Sinaloa is also in conflict with Juarez remnants and proxies in the border area of the northern states of Chihuahua and Sonora. Sinaloa is also said to be supporting some local groups in their fights against Jalisco. Zetas and Gulf offshoots are disputing control of the eastern part of Mexico's border with Texas, including the Gulf coast state of Tamaulipas, a key smuggling corridor. Jalisco has also made a play there, including in Reynosa, across from McAllen, Texas. It's a free-for-all. We don't see a single figure emerging to control the plaza, or territory, anytime soon.

"The violence is the worst it's been since the drug war began years ago, and assassins called *sicarios* are responsible for a disproportionate share of murders nationwide. Despite all the infighting, the Mexican cartels continue to export significant quantities of heroin, cocaine, methamphetamine, fentanyl, and marijuana to US markets. The majority of precursor chemicals are still coming from China. Meth and fentanyl offer the largest profit margins."

Weston paused a moment as his eyes roved over the faces standing and seated around the table. "Our job here, right now, is to hit El Mencho and the CJNG where it hurts—in the pocketbook. CJNG members are using relatives or friends who left Mexico for the US to find jobs. They're expanding into small communities far beyond border towns and major hubs."

"Smaller towns equal smaller police forces," one agent said.

"Exactly. Big cities have big police departments, as well as DEA, FBI, and Homeland Security Investigations. So we're going to hit El Mencho and his operations hard. Each of you has been assigned a team that will raid one of the stash houses on the map to your left. Your team leader will answer any questions you have."

Bobbi Chacon was surprised. She hadn't been assigned to a team or given any information about her assignment.

"We'll be dividing up into those teams in a moment to discuss the assignments with your team leader," Weston continued. "Regardless of what's happening with the new leadership in Mexico, the DEA will be doing our part to cripple and ultimately dismantle the cartels. All right," he said. "Let's get ready to rumble."

As the men sought out their team leaders and began forming groups, Bobbi Chacon went to the front of the room to talk with Scott Weston.

"Sir," she said, staring down at the 5'8" Weston. "What's going on?"

"Ah, yes, Agent Chacon." Weston took a deep breath and exhaled slowly. "I didn't assign you a team."

"Say again?"

"You're working with the SPPD. I'd like us to take over the murder investigation, but with the large-scale drug raids going on now, I don't have the manpower. Team members have been briefed on their roles, and I'm not going to change the teams now."

"Dammit, sir—"

Weston held up a hand. "I've gone against department protocol and allowed you to work your partner's murder. If you're unhappy with your assignment, perhaps you should take some time to process and to grieve."

"I don't need to, sir."

"That's your prerogative, Agent Chacon. But the decision is made. You can accept your current assignment, or I can put you on leave. Take it or leave it."

Chapter 15

It took Dylan Walsh a few seconds before he realized someone was knocking on his front door. Then the knocking grew louder. A voice said, "Open up, Walsh!"

Dylan thought it was the police. Heart pounding, mind suddenly racing, he stared at the drugs and assorted paraphernalia on the coffee table and wondered if he had time to flush everything down the toilet.

"It's Jamal Washburn," the voice said.

Dylan couldn't connect the name with a face through his coke-induced fog. He took a couple deep breaths to calm his nerves and to slow his heartbeat before it blew a hole in his chest. Then, swaying like a reed in a stiff breeze, he got up from the couch and shambled barefoot toward the front door, as though he were walking on a slippery sidewalk.

He peered through the peephole and then unlatched the multiple locks and swung the door open, leaning on the doorknob to keep his balance, narrowing his gray eyes as he stared at the two men in front of him, giving his best impression of a no-nonsense badass.

The two guys weren't impressed.

The thin black guy had sunken cheeks, beady eyes, a big Afro, and a Van Dyke beard. He wore baggy jeans, Adidas, and a black T-shirt with a picture of Malcolm X on the front. Stitched beneath the picture were the words Freedom—Justice —Equality, and beneath the three words in larger print was the motto: BY ANY MEANS NECESSARY. He held a small tote bag in one hand.

The other guy had a thick pale face and a white chinstrap beard that matched his short-on-the-sides haircut. Small liver spots dotted his pale skin. He wore sunglasses, a white T-shirt, cream-colored Levis, and white Reebok sneakers that added to his ghostly appearance.

Albino, Dylan thought.

"We need to talk," the black guy said.

Dylan couldn't place the face, but he figured the black dude was Jamal Washburn.

The two men stepped around Dylan and strolled into the apartment as if he wasn't there.

Dylan glanced behind him at Christine Hammond sitting on the living room couch, shrugged, and closed the door behind him.

"Place smells like a damn nail salon," Jamal Washburn said to no one in particular.

A small lamp on a side table beside the sectional cast a dim light on Hammond. Barefoot, in cutoff jean shorts and a halter top, her thick blond hair piled atop her head. Her eyes were glued to a big-screen television monitor showing the '60s cult film *Easy Rider*. Peter Fonda was stuffing dollar bills into a plastic tube hidden inside the Stars and Stripes–clad fuel tank of his Harley Chopper to the Steppenwolf tune "The Pusher."

On the end table beside her was a small square of charred aluminum foil. The two men watched as Hammond leaned over and picked up a piece of crack cocaine from a small pile in a candy dish. Dropping the crack on a clean place on the foil, she picked up a lighter and the barrel of a ballpoint pen she used as a straw. The crack sizzled as she heated the bottom of the foil and chased the smoke across it, taking a long hit through the pen barrel. She held the smoke as long as she could before releasing a cloud that smelled like the odor of burnt rubber and nail polish remover. Then her eyes glazed over, her face slackened, and her head fell back against the couch cushion.

"Great movie," Dylan said, pointing to the TV screen. "Ever see it?"

"Get rid of the woman," the albino said.

Dylan gave him his best hard-ass stare. "Who're you?"

"This is Dean Moody," Washburn said, like he was Moody's mouthpiece.

Dylan cocked his head at Washburn. "I recognize you now. We did some business awhile back."

"Why we're here," Washburn said. He looked Dylan over. "Lost some weight, huh. Been tweakin' on the Jenny Crank diet?"

Waving an index finger in the air, Dylan said, "One second."

He walked over to the coffee table in front of the sectional, bent over, and snorted a line of coke from a mirror on the table. "That's better," he said, slapping his hands on his thighs. Then he straightened up, wobbled a bit, and regained his balance. "She's no problem," he said with a dismissive wave toward Hammond. "Follow me."

Dylan led Washburn and Moody into the kitchen. "Want something to drink?" he asked, opening the refrigerator and removing a bottle of Corona.

Moody sat down at the table without responding.

Washburn sat across from him. "Got anything besides the suds?"

"Wine?" Dylan said.

"Shit, man," Washburn said with a disappointed shake of his head.

Dylan popped the cap with an opener and drank a mouthful of beer. Leaning his rear end against the counter, he said, "What can I do for you boys?"

Washburn unzipped the tote bag and pulled out a cellophane-wrapped package and dropped it on the table. "Got one hundred thirty-five of these in the panels of the car we drove up here from Tucson."

Dylan's eyes grew large as he swallowed a mouthful of beer and stared at the packaged meth. Regaining his composure, he did a quick mental calculation of the one hundred thirty-five packages. "Street value on that's over three hundred thousand."

Washburn gave him a half-smile. "Supposed to deliver it to Lozano, but he dead. Wife, too."

Blood drained from Walsh's face. "You killed 'em?"

"Someone else did."

"Who?"

"You been livin' under a rock?"

Dylan gestured toward the living room. "Been off the grid lately."

"Havin' some chemsex, huh?" Washburn said with a grin, his large white teeth shining like polished ivory.

Dylan shrugged. "When did it happen?"

"We stopped by Lozano's dealership to unload the shipment. Manager said Lozano was shot two days ago. Crime scene tape was still up when we drove by his crib."

"I don't believe it," Dylan said, swallowing a swig of beer.

"You callin' us liars?"

Dylan raised his hands in surrender. "Just a figure of speech. You know, like I'm surprised." He chugged the rest of his beer, wiped his mouth on the sleeve of his robe, and tossed the empty bottle into a wastebasket half full of empty TV dinner cartons. He burped and said, "I had nothin' to do with it."

"Did we say that?" Washburn said, looking at Moody.

"Don't think so," Moody said.

Washburn shifted his gaze to Dylan. "But now that you brought it up."

Dylan swallowed dryly. "Hell, I didn't even know they were dead."

Washburn held Dylan's eyes for a moment before he pulled an iPhone out of his pocket. "Take a look at this from two days ago."

He placed the phone on the table, turned the screen toward Dylan, and clicked on a YouTube link.

An airbrushed anchorman intoned, "Even as St. Paul's police chief seeks to reassure residents, the city was rocked today by the discovery of three new shooting victims. All three were pronounced dead at the scene."

A photogenic and equally serious anchorwoman continued. "At approximately three thirty p.m. today, officers were called to a house in the fashionable Desnoyer Park neighborhood on a report that three people had apparently been shot in what appeared to be a failed drug deal. Neighbors gathered at the scene watched as three bodies were wheeled out on gurneys covered by white sheets. Two of the victims were identified as Martin and Benita Lozano. The third victim has yet to be identified. Police suspect an unidentified fourth person may have fled the scene.

"The shootings were discovered not long after St. Paul Police Chief Tim Branigan gave back-to-back media interviews in which he sought to calm a city plagued by gun violence. "The record number of homicides isn't what keeps me up at night,' Chief Branigan said. 'It's the thought of another family being torn apart by gun violence. Violent crimes are often concentrated in high poverty areas and are tragically unpredictable. More than half the city's homicides have been gang-related.'"

The anchorman said, "Let's go to our reporter on the scene, Kelly Quinn."

Washburn picked up his phone and looked at Dylan. "Latest news says the unidentified dead-ass was a DEA agent."

"DEA!" Walsh yelped. "Holy shit!"

"Now that you know we ain't yankin' your chain, we gotta be paid for our trouble," Washburn said, leaning back in the chair.

"How's that my problem?"

"You part of Lozano's network."

"Yeah . . .?" Dylan said, not sure where the conversation was going and not liking it.

Moody removed his sunglasses and set them on the table. The blood vessels behind the irises of his translucent blue eyes gave them a pinkish appearance. "So we give you the meth and you give us our money," he said. His voice sounded as if he had sandpaper in his throat. "We usually get a grand apiece for our trouble. But since this whole operation has been a cluster-fuck, we'll each take five. Right, Jamal?"

Washburn nodded. "And a percent of the sales when you sell the crank. We ain't greedy. We'll take fifty percent."

Dylan cocked his head and then shook it slowly as if he couldn't understand what he'd just heard. "Hey, I'm just a small time dealer," he said, trying to keep the whine out of his voice and not having much success. "I don't have the Lozanos' connections."

"Well," Washburn said, "those connections are gonna come lookin' to you for their crank now that the Lozanos takin' a dirt nap. Maybe some of that drug money they kept in their safe."

"I don't have the money," Dylan protested.

"And you don't know who got it, either," Washburn said. "Do you?"

Dylan shook his head. His thoughts concentrated on the conversation he'd had with Christine about her friend Ana Luna, who suddenly wanted to get out of the country and could pay for it.

"'Cause if you did know who had the money, you'd tell us, right?" Washburn said.

"Absolutely."

Washburn grinned. "Good. We understand each other. Now, we gonna need a place to stay while you sell the crank." He winked at Moody. "Maybe have us some of that chemsex with your little ho, too?"

Dylan was about to object but then thought better of it. Pissing off these two stupid psychos was a bad move. No telling what they'd do. As he peered at the tote bag on the floor, a new thought struck him. "How 'bout we make it a sixty/forty split? After all, I have to do all the work."

"How 'bout you shove that idea up your lily white ass?" Washburn said. Turning to Moody he said, "No offense meant."

"None taken," Moody said.

"You push your luck," Washburn said to Dylan, "you disappear and we take it all."

"You got that right," Moody added with a sinister smile.

"Look, guys, we got a dead DEA agent and a possible unidentified fourth person at the scene. I guarantee you, the police and DEA are going scorched earth till they find that person." Dylan waved a hand at the meth on the table. "This stuff is too hot to handle. Best get rid of it."

Washburn chuckled. "Oh, we gonna get rid of it, Dylan. And you gonna help us."

Moody lifted up his shirt, slid the Springfield XD .45 ACP out of his waistband, and laid it on the kitchen table. His eyes jittered from side to side.

"We clear on that?" Washburn said.

Dylan attempted a smile. "Crystal."

"Good. Maybe I'll take one of those suds now."

"Sure, Jamal," Dylan said. "Anything you say."

*   *   *

From the back seat of the taxi in the parking lot, Ana Soriano had checked the address Christine Hammond had written on a sheet a paper and had watched the two men enter Dylan Walsh's home. Hammond had told her to come over with the money today and that Dylan would help her.

But now Ana had second thoughts.

She didn't like the look of the two men, their relaxed, ambling gait as they swaggered up to the apartment. She'd heard about the "gangster glide" and was sure she'd just witnessed it. No way she was going into the house now, especially with all the money in the new backpack she'd purchased on the seat beside her.

She told the taxi driver to leave quickly and to take her back to Hammond's apartment.

Chapter 16

Nogales, Mexico

Nogales, Mexico, is located on the northern border of the Mexican state of Sonora, across the US-Mexico border from Nogales, Arizona. The first drug tunnel in the nation was discovered near an old abandoned church in Nogales, Arizona, in 1995. Since then more than 110 drug tunnels have been found along the Arizona border.

Despite territorial inroads by the Cartel Jalisco Nueva Generación, the Sinaloa Cartel, operating primarily out of the city of Culiacán, controlled the plaza encompassing the Mexican states of Sinaloa, Durango, Chihuahua, and Sonora.

Eddie Machado knew this as he exited the Cessna parked on a small dirt airstrip outside Nogales, Mexico, and climbed into a waiting taxi. He wouldn't risk riding in a shiny, expensive "probable cause car" or SUV that let everyone in the city know that he was a cartel member. Might as well put a SHOOT ME sign on his back.

Vanity and greed often got the best of the *patróns*. Eddie had seen it before. Juan Guzmán, better known as El Chapo, was the latest to fall. DEA and government task forces loved seeing Guzmán's prized possessions getting trailered off to auction as he sat behind bars. As if it wasn't bad enough watching in cuffs as your life's work got seized, but to then see DEA agents hauling away your prized Ferrari was enough to make a grown man cry.

But El Mencho was different.

In the four years Eddie had worked for him, El Mencho had not fallen into the predictable pattern of expensive homes, cars, jewelry, and his own weed and blow, which had led to the downfall of so many *patróns* before him. Even though he was worth more than a billion dollars, El Mencho didn't flash his wealth like others known for buying marbled mansions and racing through the streets of Guadalajara and Mexico City in Lamborghinis and Ferraris. Rather, he spent time on ranches in the mountains of Jalisco riding horses and racing motorbikes. His only indulgence was betting on bullfights and cockfights. Eddie had once seen him lose $100,000 on a single bet.

Eddie believed discipline was the key to El Mencho's success. His *patrón* drank no alcohol and took no drugs. He exercised daily, keeping in fugitive shape, which enabled him to avoid capture by moving constantly and remaining on the run for days in the rugged Sierra Madre Mountains of Jalisco, Michoacán and Colima. Rarely seen, El Mencho stayed in remote, heavily fortified compounds, making it harder for police to breach security.

Eddie hadn't succumbed to temptations either, though he enjoyed an occasional shot of tequila and a good woman, preferably one with a big caboose and chest. El Mencho had noticed this discipline. He also knew that Eddie had saved Rubén's life and had rewarded him for it—though Eddie had paid a high price.

Expanding operations meant cleaning out the competition, not just other cartels, but also local criminals—thieves, rapists, small-time drug dealers and snitches, anyone who drew police scrutiny. He and the other *sicarios* hunted and killed rival cartel members and were killed themselves, sometimes by their own trainers for disobeying orders or showing hesitation.

Murder was rarely for sport. Eddie investigated the complaints against intended victims. Once confirmed, he warned them to stop, mostly to keep them from drawing too much attention from the authorities. If they didn't, he planned the killings methodically, carrying them out only with permission from above.

In the beginning he followed a code. He didn't recruit children for the cartel, and he wouldn't harm women or *campesinos*, if he could avoid it. But organized crime was rarely orderly, especially among cartels. Eddie *did* kill women and innocent peasants, mostly in firefights with rival cartels or with Mexican police. For all the talk of honoring a code, Eddie soon came to realize it was just talk. Business always came first.

Of all the people he'd killed, only one haunted him.

He'd met Isabella while shopping at a boot store in Guadalajara. Her waist-length, shiny black hair and her eyes that were the color of the Caribbean Sea immediately drew him to her.

"You are looking for a pair of western boots," she said in Spanish, her smile melting his defenses.

He'd always been shy around young women, even the hookers El Mencho offered to his *sicarios*. Now he had trouble getting the words out of his mouth.

He nodded.

"Follow me," she said. Taking him gently by the hand, she led him to a long rack near the back of the store filled with leather, snakeskin, and alligator western boots and the shorter shaft ropers with a square, short heel and round toe.

There was nothing sexual as she looked him over, an index finger tapping her sensual mouth in thought, but Eddie's body was humming as if he'd been struck by a jolt of electricity.

"I believe you would like the western style."

"*Sí*," he mumbled.

"Do you ride much?"

"No," he said.

She concentrated her gaze on the rack of boots for a time before making a decision.

"Here," she said, picking out a pair of dusty brown leather boots with a fancy stitched pattern on the shaft that matched the color of her eyes. "The wider toe and square heel make them better for standing up rather than sitting in the saddle."

As she held the boots out to him, he saw no ring on her finger.

"If I buy the boots, will you go out with me?" he blurted.

When she didn't reply immediately, Eddie felt the heat of embarrassment in his face.

"I am sorry," he said.

"Don't be," she said, her smile warm and genuine. "I will go out with you whether you buy the boots or not."

Eddie bought the boots.

Two months later, he convinced Isabella to fly with him to Puerto Vallarta. She was reluctant at first, but he was able to convince her with a promise of a stay at a beautiful beachfront resort—and that they'd be alone together.

Isabella told her mother that she was going to Puerto Vallarta to visit her cousin. The cousin swore on the Virgin Mary that she would never reveal Isabella's true destination.

Eddie and Isabella took the forty-five-minute flight from Guadalajara and then a forty-minute ride in a small, covered boat to a palm-thatched, elegant cabin on stilts located on a private, secluded beach. The room had three walls. The fourth was open and facing the ocean. At night it could be closed with blinds. The bed could be covered with mosquito netting. From the first day Eddie felt like he'd traveled to a distant island separated from the rest of the world.

He'd never been with a young woman like Isabella, and he was nervous. He knew she was a virgin, and it would be her first time, but Eddie felt like it was his as well. The hookers he'd been with had shown him how to please a woman, but had never shown him how to love one.

The memory of that first time with Isabella would always be burned into his memory. The warmness of the evening, the moonless sky sprinkled with stars, the sound of the waves washing against the shore, the wonderful fragrance of *huele de noche*, or night-blooming jasmine, the vanilla scent of her perfume. But the image Eddie would most remember was Isabella's face in that moment when they became one. Her eyes were closed, her lips parted, and then she looked up at him suddenly, her azure eyes gazing at him as if she were looking into his soul. Then she took his face in her hands and kissed him deeply.

One month later, Isabella discovered Eddie worked for El Mencho. Eddie had told her that he worked security but not that he worked for a cartel. She would not tell him who'd told her, but when he confronted her, the look of terror on her face, her body language, twisted his heart in a knot. He knew in that moment that the innocence they'd felt together was gone. He'd lost her. The ache in his heart that day when she vowed never to see him again was a feeling he hadn't experienced since the death of his parents. A feeling he planned never to experience again.

Two months later El Mencho sent Eddie to eliminate a man the *patrón* said was snitching to the local police. When Eddie arrived, he found Isabella with the young man he soon learned was her brother. He'd been the one who'd told her Eddie was a *sicario*.

After Eddie bound them both, he called El Mencho. He wanted to let Isabella go. She didn't belong to a rival cartel and wasn't a snitch. There was no need to kill her. But El Mencho said no. Any witness was a liability. She would just be *daños colaterales*, or collateral damage, a common excuse used by the cartels when innocent civilians were killed.

Eddie took her brother to another room and shot him first. Isabella's anguished scream at the sound of the gunshot tore at his heart.

Silent tears streaked her cheeks as Eddie stood over her. He told her to look away. She refused. She would not give him the satisfaction.

"You will have to look into my eyes when you kill me," she said.

It was Eddie who looked away as tears welled in his eyes. He said he was sorry before putting a bullet in her head. Eddie broke down then, cried like a baby, cried like he never had be-fore—and would never cry again.

Isabella's death lived on in his nightmares. Her anguished scream when he'd shot her brother still lingered in the darkest hours like the forlorn cry of a lone coyote. Eddie often saw her face—and her eyes. She was the only one who had ever looked at him that way.

Sometimes now, in the dark, the spirit of his mother quietly kneels beside his bed, whispering over him as he sleeps.

"Stop working for the cartel, *mi hijo*."

But Eddie knew her pleas could not save him.

He'd grown numb to killing, hunting for targets without emotion, like a wild animal seeking its next meal. Life mattered even less to him, his own included.

He was told to kill members of his own team by lieutenants who worried they were growing too influential or undisciplined. He killed so many that he almost never recruited people within his circle.

When Mexican security forces killed the head of the CJNG's assassin network, Heriberto Acevedo Cárdenas, alias "El Gringo," Eddie moved up the ladder. He was now one of CJNG's top *sicarios*, which was why he'd flown in from Guadalajara on one of El Mencho's private planes and landed on a small, private airstrip outside Nogales, Mexico.

Eddie had trained for nearly two years before El Mencho allowed him to make his first trip across the Mexican border into El Paso. He hadn't spoken much English since his childhood in the States, but he understood the language whose rules made little sense. Now, a US passport, a conceal and carry permit, and an Arizona driver's license identified him as Eddie Lopez. He carried five thousand US dollars in a money belt and a Belgian-made FN-7 in a waistband holster.

Eddie was on his way to Minnesota to collect the half-million dollars that had gone missing from a stash house—and to seek payback on those who had stolen it. But before he could collect the money, he needed to safely cross the border.

The taxi drove him through the downtown area of bars, hotels, restaurants, and curio stores selling handicrafts, leather art, handmade flowers, and clothes for the thousands of tourists looking for a good deal, or for those visiting the numerous pharmacies and dental offices that catered to Americans by charging half to a third of the price for the same prescriptions and services found in the States.

Along with the tourists, large clusters of haggard asylum seekers crowded the city, causing a huge backup at the border crossing. For most asylum-seekers their gateway to the American dream had become a nightmare.

Drones were being used, and US military specialists had been dispatched to help the Customs and Border Patrol monitor video and sensors planted underground that activated when migrants passed, relaying information to CBP agents in the field.

The latest security measures had made it more difficult— but not impossible—for Eddie to safely cross the border.

The taxi traveled through the Plaza de Benito Juárez and past a statue called the *Monument to Ignorance*, where a naked man representing the Mexican people was fighting with a winged creature representing ignorance.

Eddie could see the border fence out the backseat window, an ugly wall of vertical steel rods fifteen to eighteen feet high, set four inches apart in a deep bed of concrete. A rusty ribbon covered on top by coiled razor wire stretched up and down dusty hills and streets, cutting one city into two and jutting into the desert for a few miles east and west. He gave a shit about politics, but he thought the wall was another "Monument to Ignorance," given there were ways around it. Coyotes smuggling illegals were already cutting through border fencing with power tools.

Not to mention tunnels.

The taxi dropped Eddie at a small warehouse sixty yards from the border. He adjusted the strap on the satchel that he wore diagonally across his body, the bag hanging on his opposite hip, rather than hanging directly down from his shoulder, leaving his gun hand free. Then he headed for the warehouse door.

The animosity between the CJNG and the Sinaloa cartel and the fight to be the number one cartel in the world was well documented. Rented through third-party buyers as a produce-processing facility, the building concealed a tunnel the CJNG had secretly built right under the noses of the Sinaloa cartel.

Seated on an old beer barrel inside the warehouse, Tito Palomas, a muscular man with a thin white scar carved in his left cheek and a tight-fitting T-shirt and jeans, stood as Eddie entered and shoved a handgun down behind his belt. Tito was on El Mencho's payroll. Eddie had met him in Jalisco a few years ago and hadn't seen him since.

"Hey, *muchacho*," Palomas said, speaking in Spanish. They gave each other a dap handshake. "Happy you made it, man."

"I will be happy once I am safely on the US side," Eddie said.

"*No hay problema.* Follow me."

The underground passage began inside a small office, where Tito moved a large metal desk and tapped on a tile beneath it with the end of a flashlight he'd snatched from the desktop.

From inside the tunnel, a thick-shouldered man with Dumbo ears pushed aside a tile slab cutout, revealing a narrow mineshaft with a ladder leading to the floor ten feet below.

"*Esto es*, Victor," Tito said.

Victor climbed out and nodded at Eddie but didn't speak. Instead he gestured with an open hand for Eddie and Tito to proceed down the ladder.

Tito looked at Eddie with a grin. "I hope you are not claustrophobic, *amigo*."

Eddie shook his head. "I once lived in the sewers of Mexico City." Sometimes, he thought, I still smell the stink on my body.

"The tunnel is not as filthy as a sewer," Tito said.

"You smuggle many people through here?"

Tito grinned and shook his head. "Drugs are worth more than people, *amigo*, and drugs don't talk. If a person was smuggled through a tunnel, word could get out and the tunnel could be discovered. That is a huge loss of time and money."

"Yet you are taking me through it."

Tito shrugged. "You are a *sicario* for our cartel." He pointed with an index finger. "*Vamos*." He started down the ten-foot ladder. Eddie followed. Victor closed the tile over the opening and came down the ladder after them.

The air smelled like wet dirt and felt damp against Eddie's skin as he descended. When they reached the bottom, he saw that the five-foot-high by three-foot-wide passageway to his left was lit by a string of 60-watt bulbs dangling from the ceiling.

El Mencho had begun digging tunnels that required a smaller investment because of the high risk of being discovered by DEA and CBP agents, or by their arch-enemy, the Sinaloa cartel. Recently, CBP agents had discovered a half-mile long tunnel along the California-Mexico border. The tunnel included railing and ventilation systems, lighting, and a large elevator.

This tunnel was nothing like that.

"Careful as you walk," Tito cautioned, his voice sounding like a dull echo.

"How far to the other side?" Eddie asked.

"Not far," Tito said.

Victor took the lead, gesturing for Eddie to follow. As Victor leaned forward and headed down the tunnel, Eddie saw the bulge of a handgun tucked in his back waistband under his T-shirt.

It wasn't unusual for Tito and Victor to be carrying handguns. Eddie would be surprised if they weren't. Still, a little voice his head, some primitive instinct, reminded him to "Trust no one." He motioned a polite *after you* to Tito.

Tito gave him a crooked smile and shrugged his shoulders, brushing against Eddie as he stepped around him in the narrow space.

Eddie's right hand adjusted the FN-7 in the waist holster under his guayabera shirt before starting down the passageway. Then he ducked his head and walked slowly forward behind Tito.

As he moved down the tunnel, Eddie noticed he was breathing harder in the thinner air. Though the smell was different—better actually—it still reminded him of his days living in the streets and sewers of Mexico City, and how far he'd come since those terrible days when he had to sell his body just to survive. No one cared about him then, but he'd never felt sorry for himself.

Now the cartel was his family. Working as a *sicario* gave him a sense of purpose, a reason for being. Those who weren't involved with the cartel would call him a murderer, someone who should be shunned and either sent to prison for the rest of his life or put to death. Eddie understood this, though he would argue that he'd never killed anyone who didn't deserve to die— except Isabella. Not much of an excuse. But the only one he had.

Eddie could see Tito four feet in front of him and glimpses of Victor ten feet ahead. His thighs were beginning to burn from walking in a crouch, but then he saw Victor straighten up and grab the rungs of a ladder attached to a wall up ahead. Ten yards more and he was standing in a small circular exit shaft, watching Victor and Tito ascend. Eddie stepped on the first rung and climbed.

Daylight filled the shaft as Victor pushed open a trap door above and climbed out of the tunnel; Tito followed.

When Eddie reached the opening and stepped out and onto a cement floor, Victor and Tito stood three feet away. Tito pointed a Beretta PX4 Storm at Eddie's chest. "Take his gun and the satchel," he said to Victor.

Eddie didn't resist as Victor stepped forward, took the satchel and lifted Eddie's shirt. Sliding the FN-7 out of its holster, he handed it to Tito.

"*Lo siento, amigo,*" Tito said.

Eddie stared at him. "*El verdadero mal tiene una cara que conoces y una voz en la que confías.*" True Evil has a face you know and a voice you trust.

"It is night's twin," Tito replied.

"How much are they paying you to kill me?" Eddie asked, referring to the Sinaloa cartel.

Tito laughed. "We are not going to kill you."

"What then?"

"We are turning you over to the CBP."

Eddie thought about it for a time but couldn't come up with a reason. "Why?"

"They will offer you a reduced sentence for information on the CJNG. You will talk."

Eddie suddenly saw the logic of it. "This information will weaken El Mencho."

"Of course," Tito said with a grin.

And strengthen the Sinaloa cartel, Eddie thought.

"Maybe I won't talk," he said.

"And maybe you will spend the rest of your life in a prison cell." Tito gestured with the gun barrel toward a heavy-looking wooden chair in the middle of the floor. "Have a seat, *amigo.*"

Eddie hesitated when he saw the restraining straps attached to the chair's arms and legs, and Victor standing beside it.

Tito's stance shifted slightly, legs farther apart. "Or maybe I will shoot you dead right here," he said.

Eddie had faced death before and had come to terms with it. His pulse wasn't racing. He wasn't perspiring. He'd understood for years now, long before he'd become a *sicario,* that he would die a violent death at a young age.

Still, he wasn't suicidal. He wasn't dead yet. There was always a chance that he would get out of this alive—if he used his head.

The gun and the distance between them gave Tito confidence. Eddie knew that overconfidence could quickly lead to mistakes.

Eddie walked slowly to the chair and sat down. He placed his forearms on the arms of the chair and his ankles against its legs. Make strapping him in look easy, he thought.

Tito nodded at Victor.

As Victor carelessly stepped in front of the chair to secure Eddie's ankles and hands, Eddie grabbed him by the front of his shirt with his left hand and pulled him forward and off-balance, while simultaneously reaching with his right hand for the gun tucked in the back of Victor's pants.

"Hey!" Tito called. He fired three quick shots. All of them hit Victor in the back.

Protected by Victor's body, Eddie yanked the Beretta out of Victor's waistband and fired one shot that punched in Tito's face.

Chapter 17

That same afternoon Santana left a voicemail for James McGowan asking if he'd return Santana's call. As he disconnected, his phone rang.

"What's happening, Santana?" Bobbi Chacon said.

"Thought you were involved in the DEA drug raids that were taking place this morning." The raid Joel Ryker had jumped the gun on and gotten himself killed, Santana thought.

"My supervisor stood me down. The prick. Said I was still too amped up about Joel's murder."

"Aren't you?"

"If it'd been your partner, wouldn't you be?"

"I would."

"Any other intel?"

"Not yet."

The line went silent for a time. "Something in your voice," she said at last. "Something's up."

"Pure conjecture."

"Come on, Santana."

He considered hanging up and then had a change of heart. If he tried cutting out the DEA, he could lose control of the case. He needed to keep Chacon close.

"A tip on a meth shipment," he said.

"I want in."

Santana knew he had little choice.

"You're supposed to be working with the DEA," she said as a reminder. "I call your commander or chief, what do you think they'll say?"

"That supposed to scare me?"

"Okay. I heard you're a tough guy, Santana. You go your own way and all that bullshit. My partner's dead. I need to find out who's responsible. If the roles were reversed, tell me you wouldn't be hounding my ass."

"Guess I would."

She didn't reply, though he could hear her breathing through the line.

"Two guys named Jamal Washburn and Dean Moody drove a large meth shipment into town last night from Tucson," he said. "Ever hear of them?"

"No. How do you know about Washburn and Moody?"

"A CRI."

"You know where Washburn and Moody are?"

"I've got a possible address."

"You have a search warrant?"

"Doubt I can convince a judge for probable cause. Washburn and Moody could be anywhere in the city."

"If they heard about the shooting at the stash house or drove by there and saw the crime scene tape, they're lying low."

"Could've heard about the DEA raids this morning as well."

"You'll need backup," she said.

"You need to chill out."

"I'm as cold as ice."

She had more fire than ice in her voice, Santana thought.

"Meet me at the Ramsey County Morgue first. I need someone to ID Ryker's body."

"Get another agent," she said. "I don't want to see him like that."

Santana understood. "All right."

Chacon stayed quiet for a time before she said, "His wife wouldn't do it?"

"Didn't want to make the trip up here from Dallas."

"Figures," she said. "What a bitch."

*   *   *

The West Side of St. Paul got its name not because it sits west of St. Paul, but because the Mississippi bends from its north-south direction to an east-west bearing, placing the West Side left of the river. Populated by a large Mexican community, it was the only St. Paul neighborhood on the other side of the Mississippi.

Dylan Walsh lived in an apartment complex on East Wood, a dead-end street near the Torre de San Miguel. The renamed bell tower in honor of the Mexican community was all that remained of the demolished St. Michael's Catholic Church.

Santana parked at the corner of Livingston and East Wood as clouds darkened the afternoon sky. The temperature had fallen ten degrees with the approaching thunderstorm, though the air remained heavy with humidity. June was usually the rainiest month in Minnesota, and this year had been no exception.

While he waited for Bobbi Chacon to arrive, Santana scoped the area behind Dylan Walsh's apartment with his Bushnell binoculars.

The complex looked more like attached townhomes than apartments. Walsh's ground-floor apartment had a deck that faced east toward the backyard. A thick grove of trees lined the far side of the street where no cars were parked. Venetian blinds covered the sliding door off the deck. The unfenced yard allowed access to the deck and the sliding glass door. Santana saw no dog dishes or leashes. Then again, maybe Dylan Walsh kept Fido's dog dishes and leash inside.

Ten minutes after he'd arrived, Bobbi Chacon slid into the passenger seat beside him. "Anything?"

Santana shook his head and peeled his eyes away from the binoculars. Her outfit was similar to the one she'd worn when he'd first met her in the chief's office—blue jeans, Blauer boots, and a black, sleeveless pullover, minus the jacket. Her arms were tanned and her deltoids notched with muscle.

"What're you looking at?"

"Sorry. Didn't mean to stare."

"What?" she urged.

"You don't have any tattoos. At least none that I can see."

"I don't have any tattoos for the same reason you don't put a bumper sticker on a Ferrari."

"Point taken," he said.

"How 'bout you?"

"No tattoos. Same reason."

"Yeah. I figured," she said, looking out the windshield, a half-smile on her face.

He handed her copies of the mug shots he'd run on Washburn and Moody. "No wants and warrants, but between the two of them they've got rap sheets for drug possession and trafficking, burglary, and assault."

Chacon nodded. "Couple of choirboys."

Santana peered through the binoculars again. "I'd like to get a front view of the apartment, but I'd have to stand out in the open. Good news is that East Wood is a dead-end, so there's no way out using a vehicle."

"We could sit here the rest of the day and not see them," Chacon said. "Or maybe they're not in there at all."

Santana set the binoculars in his lap and started the unmarked. "Let's drive through the parking lot. See if there's a vehicle with an Arizona plate."

He turned left and then turned left again into an asphalt lot off East Wood that was located south of the apartments. They cruised along the outside aisle closest to the street, Santana's eyes scanning the plates. Then they worked their way back along the inside aisle closest to the buildings, giving Chacon the best view of the cars and their plates through the passenger-side window.

They were nearly back to the lot entrance when she said, "Stop."

Santana hit the brake and leaned forward to look around her. She sat back in the seat to give him a better view.

"Arizona plate," he said.

"Odds are . . ."

He looked at her and nodded.

The late-model black Toyota Highlander was parked with the front end facing out, ready for a quick getaway if the need ever arose.

Santana shifted his unmarked to PARK and got out.

"What're you doing?" Chacon asked

"Slowing them down if they decide to run."

He went to the rear of the Highlander, squatted down, and let air out of the right rear tire. Then he got back into the unmarked.

"What if it isn't their car?" she said.

"I'm guessing it is. We'll get a dog out here, pick up the drug scent."

"Hope no one saw you and called police," she said as Santana shifted into gear.

He let the wisecrack slide as he drove out to the street and stopped along the curb three lots away from Dylan Walsh's apartment.

"I'll knock on the front door. You watch the back," Chacon said.

Santana figured if Washburn and Moody were in the apartment and decided to run, they'd come out the back way off the deck.

"Sounds like a plan," he said.

Before getting out of the car, they drew their weapons and pulled back the slides to make sure his Glock 23 and her more concealable Glock 19 had a round in the chamber.

Chacon holstered her Glock 19 and lifted her left pants leg, revealing a Glock 26 tucked into a small black ankle holster just above her boot.

She peered at him and grinned. "Gun is like a tube of lipstick," she said.

Santana had used an ankle holster on occasion and knew it was best to carry it on your inside ankle on the non-dominant side. But ankle carry holsters tended to attract dirt and dust, which could cause the gun to malfunction. Also, time would not be his friend should he find himself in a life-or-death situation. Drawing from the ankle took more time than drawing from the shoulder or waist. To be really fast and accurate at ankle carry took hours of practice.

Bobbi Chacon snapped off the retention strap, pulled the Glock 26, and racked the slide. "Never can have too much firepower," she said.

"You have a vest in your ride," he said, "better put it on."

She slid the gun into the ankle holster and fastened the retention strap.

Holstering his Glock 23 as they exited the unmarked, they each went to their car trunks and pulled out their EVC, or External Vest Carrier, which made the standard tactical body armor vest look more like a shirt. The vests were designed not only for protection, but also to decrease an aggressive, over-militarized appearance that might escalate a situation.

Santana handed her an extra two-way. "Radio me when you're about to knock on the front door."

She nodded and headed for the front of the building while he cut in toward the back under a dome of black clouds. He moved quickly across the yards, past a pair of thick evergreens, before stopping at the corner of the apartment to the left of the deck, out of view in case someone parted the blinds and looked out, but in a position to confront anyone coming out the sliding glass door.

"I'm about to knock," Chacon radioed.

"Copy that," Santana said, glancing at his watch. He was too far away to hear any conversation, but he figured if either Washburn or Moody were inside and decided to run, it would happen soon after Chacon knocked.

Two minutes later the glass door off the deck slid open and Bobbi Chacon stepped out. Dean Moody, wearing a pair of sunglasses, was directly behind her with a semi-automatic pressed against her back. Jamal Washburn appeared right behind Moody. He held a semi-auto down along his right leg as his head swiveled left to right and back again, searching for any trouble.

Santana drew his Glock and moved quickly back along the wall, staying out of sight, knowing that they'd have to come by him to get to their ride in the parking lot. He assumed that Chacon had told the two men she was alone.

He kept moving around the far corner of the neighboring apartment and hunkered down behind the two tall evergreens, which offered good cover. He scanned the area, looking for any civilians who might be in danger. Seeing no one, he considered calling for backup but nixed the idea, figuring Washburn and Moody would pass directly in front of the evergreens as they walked toward the lot and would hear him talking. As lightning flashed and thunder rumbled in the near distance, Santana formulated a plan.

"Move it," Moody said to Chacon. "I ain't gettin' soaked."

He heard their footsteps pass by in the grass. First Chacon and Moody, then Washburn a few feet behind.

Santana scooted left toward the outer edge of the two evergreens, where he had a clear view of the three of them ten yards ahead.

The wind picked up as a bolt of lightning zigzagged across the sky.

Santana timed his move toward Washburn as a giant clap of thunder rattled the sky. He came quickly up behind him and wrapped his left forearm around Washburn's neck as he stuck the barrel of his Glock into the man's back.

"Drop the gun," Santana whispered in his ear.

Washburn let the gun fall from his hand.

"Moody!" Santana shouted.

Moody spun toward him, his gun held steady, ready to fire.

"Don't shoot!" Washburn yelled, raising his hands in a defensive move.

Behind Moody now, Bobbi Chacon dropped to one knee and drew the Glock 26 from the ankle holster as if she'd done it a thousand times. Springing to her feet, she pressed the barrel in the back of Moody's head.

"Drop it, asshole," she said in a voice laden with threat.

Chapter 18

Santana Mirandized Jamal Washburn and Dean Moody and then placed them in separate holding cells at the Law Enforcement Center, pending the formal booking process. Separating the two men prevented them from communicating or fabricating a story. They could be held in the cells for up to two hours. And since the holding cells were for short-term detention, requests for phone calls to attorneys weren't honored until after completion of the booking and identification process.

Santana knew he couldn't fudge the time because watch commanders made periodic checks of the holding cells during their tours of duty to ensure that the two-hour rule was observed. The checks were noted in their daily log report to the chief. Santana figured two hours would give forensics time to search the Toyota Highlander.

According to Dylan Walsh, whom Santana had questioned at the scene, he'd invited Bobbi Chacon into the apartment on orders from Moody, who'd hidden behind the door till Chacon entered. Walsh had insisted he had no part in the attempted kidnapping and then had lawyered up. Washburn and Moody had said nothing since their arrest.

Christine Hammond had been transported by ambulance to Regions Hospital for examination. Santana and Chacon had tried to question her at Walsh's apartment, but she was heavily under the influence of meth and/or coke and was unresponsive.

The SPPD impound lot was located next to a metal recycling plant in a large industrial area on Barge Channel Road on St. Paul's West Side. The Toyota Highlander had been taken inside the fence to a small secure building with a double-wide garage door, where it was offloaded from a flatbed truck.

By the time Santana arrived, forensic techs had already stripped the Toyota. One hundred thirty-four packages of meth-amphetamine had been found inside the gas tank, spare tire, and quarter panels of the vehicle. An additional package had been found inside the apartment. Santana now had leverage on Washburn, Moody, and Dylan Walsh.

Bobbi Chacon was waiting at Santana's desk in the vacant Homicide and Robbery Unit when he returned. It was late on a Friday afternoon and most of the day watch detectives had checked out. He told her what the techs had found in the Toyota.

"These guys are going down big time," Chacon said.

"And I'm taking them down."

She responded with a glare. "What about me?"

Santana shook his head. "You're not involved in this."

"Whatta you mean I'm not involved? Moody had a gun in my back. And what about the missing shooter at the Lozanos' house? I want him for Ryker's murder."

Santana could see Chacon was still jacked up on adrena-line—as he was—from the bust. But he wasn't about to let her interrogate Washburn or Moody. Still, he had to keep her close. As long as the two of them were working together on the Ryker murder, the DEA most likely wouldn't bigfoot the case by taking it over and cutting him out. The feds always were given priority, especially when it involved the murder of one of their agents. Santana wasn't sure Janet Kendrick would back him when it came to the feds.

"Give me a minute," he said, stepping away from the desk.

When he was out of earshot, Santana dialed a number on his cellphone and spoke quietly for two minutes with the man on the other end of the call. Then he came back to his desk and handed Bobbi Chacon his cellphone.

"What?" she said.

"Someone wants to talk to you."

She hesitated a moment before placing the phone next to her ear. "Hello?"

"Agent Chacon."

She immediately recognized the voice. "Yes, sir."

Scott Weston said, "What the hell is going on? Detective Santana told me that you nearly got yourself kidnapped."

Chacon glowered at Santana, who stood beside his desk, one arm draped casually over the top of the cubicle. "You asshole," she said.

"Pardon me?" Weston said.

"I wasn't talking to you, sir," Chacon said quickly.

"Now you listen to me, Agent Chacon. I need to see you in my office right now. I want a full report. Am I making myself clear?"

"Yes, sir."

Weston broke off the connection.

Chacon stared at the phone for a few seconds before handing it back to Santana. "Thanks for watching my back," she said.

"The only way we're shutting down this cell and finding the perp who murdered your partner is to let me do my job."

"Yeah. Like I didn't help you take down Washburn and Moody."

"You're lucky it worked out the way it did."

"If you'd gone in that apartment alone, where would you be now, Santana?"

He didn't reply.

"Pushing up fuckin' daisies. That's where." She stood and brushed past him, heading for the elevator and exit.

Santana didn't blame Chacon for being angry, but he didn't want her messing things up with an adrenaline-driven approach.

He glanced at the clock on the wall. He could use Minnesota's 36-hour rule to hold Washburn and Moody. The clock didn't start ticking till midnight on the day they were arrested.

Sundays and holidays weren't counted. That gave him till noon on Monday when they had to be brought before a judge.

It was well into the evening before Santana completed the paperwork that went along with the arrest and booking of Washburn and Moody on possession of a controlled substance, suspicion of kidnapping, and assault with a deadly weapon.

Drained from the long day and the receding adrenaline rush, Santana wished he could head home. But he wanted to take a crack at Jamal Washburn first. He thought Washburn might roll over on Moody, especially when he heard the charges against him.

Santana took the walkway on the second floor from the Homicide and Robbery Unit to the Adult Detention Center. Minnesota state statute required that the Ramsey County Sheriff's Office operate the 500-bed ADC, commonly referred to as the Ramsey County Jail. The ADC housed individuals being held for probation or supervised release violations, immigration and customs enforcement, and those like Washburn and Moody who were arrested and waiting court disposition.

A deputy brought Jamal Washburn into the interview room and sat him in a chair across the table from Santana.

Santana identified the two occupants in the room and announced the date and time, even though this information would be printed on the lower frame of the video recording of the session.

"I ain't talkin' to no one 'cept my lawyer," Washburn said as he slumped in the chair, his hands handcuffed, his eyes moving from Santana to the walls and then back again.

Santana opened the file folder on the table and scanned the document in front of him. "I see you're twenty-four years old, Jamal."

"So?"

Santana looked at him. "Well, you can call your lawyer—if that's what you really want. But you should know we found one hundred pounds—that's over forty-five thousand grams—

of meth in the Toyota you and Moody were driving. Anything over fifty grams in this state is an aggravated controlled substance crime in the first degree. You're looking at thirty years just for the drug charge alone. Add in another twenty years for assault with a deadly weapon and another seven for attempted kidnapping. That's fifty-seven years in charges. Even if you served half that time, you'd be in your fifties before you saw the light of day again."

Washburn tilted his head as if trying to understand. "Moody took the DEA agent hostage. Not me."

"Come on, Jamal. You were with him. You had a gun." Santana glanced at the pages in the file once more. Then he said, "Two years ago you were convicted of fourth-degree burglary. You needed one more year before you could legally own or possess a firearm. Now you're looking at even more time behind bars."

It took awhile for Washburn to process what Santana had told him. Finally, he spoke again. "What you want, Santana?"

"Information."

"And if I give you what you want?"

"I talk to the DA. Tell him how you cooperated."

"You gonna guarantee me a reduced sentence?"

"You know I can't do that."

He scoffed. "I give you what you want, but I get nothin'."

"Nothing but a long prison stretch. I can guarantee you that."

"I ain't a snitch."

"Tell that to your future cellmate." Santana stood up to leave.

"Hold on, Detective."

Santana faced him. "Don't waste my time."

"I got plenty of that."

"But I don't."

Washburn gestured toward the empty chair.

Santana sat. "Start from the beginning. How'd you get involved?"

"Dean Moody was my cellmate when I went down for the burglary beef. We got released about the same time. Hooked up. He had this job lined up."

"Transporting meth from Arizona."

"Yeah. Dean had this contact in Tucson. Said the meth came from one of them cartels in Mexico. All we had to do was drive to Tucson and pick it up."

"From the CJNG."

"What's that?"

"The Jalisco New Generation Cartel."

Washburn shrugged. "We met with some beaners."

"You were supposed to bring the shipment to the Lozanos."

"Yeah. But when we went to the car dealership to unload the shipment, we heard they were dead. So Dean said we should bring it to Walsh."

"He's a secondary distributor."

"Uh-huh."

"This the first trip you've made to Tucson, Jamal?"

"Yeah. Dean done it before. Learned the tricks so he don't get stopped on the highways while ridin' dirty."

"You know a woman named Ana Soriano?"

"Never heard of her," Washburn said.

"You sure?"

"Hell, yes."

"What about the girl with Walsh? Christine Hammond."

"What about her?"

Santana stood. "We're done here."

"Wait a minute," Washburn said.

"I don't need stupid, Jamal. I need answers. Tell me about the girl."

"Okay, man."

Santana sat.

"Walsh likes hookers."

"This girl doesn't look like someone off the street."

"Not yet, maybe," Washburn said. "But she headed in that direction."

"Thanks for the character reference. What else you got?"

"Walsh told me 'bout this place in town once. I ain't never been there myself."

"What place?"

"High class hookers. Lots of bling and fat cats."

"Where's the place? East Side, West Side, where?"

Washburn's face twisted in thought.

"Come on, Jamal."

"I tryin,' man. Somethin' like church."

"Church Street?" Santana knew there was a Church Street in Minneapolis near the University of Minnesota.

Washburn shook his head. "It's a hill."

"Church Hill?"

"Nah. Cat, maybe."

"What the hell is cat hill?"

"Cat Hill. That's it," he said with a grin.

Santana thought about it. "You mean Cathedral Hill?"

"Yeah," Washburn said, stabbing an index finger at him. "Cat drawl Hill."

Santana wasn't sure if the Cathedral Hill connection was a lead or a waste of time. He hadn't gotten much out of Washburn. But he figured if he took a run at Moody, he'd probably get less.

He stood. "You think of anything else, Jamal, you let me know."

"What about my deal?"

"I'll talk with the DA. Just keep your head down in the meantime."

Chapter 19

Nogales, Arizona

Customs and Border Patrol agent Danny Valdez held his Recon III thermal imaging binoculars on a section of the steel fence separating Nogales, Arizona, from its Mexican sister city. The thermal binoculars allowed him to see up to seven miles across the desert.

The fence was part of the 262-mile stretch of border in the Tucson sector that he and his fellow CBP agents covered. Two hundred twelve miles had synthetic barriers. Mountains and canyons provided natural barriers in the remainder of the harsh sand and scrub of the Sonoran desert landscape.

Though the June sky was clear and the temperature in the upper 90s, a slight breeze and the low humidity kept his green ball cap and short-sleeve green shirt and cargo pants from getting soaked with sweat.

Danny could see the hand marks on the fence where migrants had slid down. If they made it into town, they'd try to blend in with the local population, but rips in their clothing and rust left on their hands from climbing the fence often gave them away.

He scoped the desert floor, littered with backpacks, jackets, and empty water jugs, the thickets and drainage gullies where migrants hid, and the abandoned houses and downtown warehouses where smuggling tunnels were dug.

Switching his view through the binoculars to the sunbaked hilltops, he searched for vantage points where camouflaged cartel lookouts used encrypted radio transmissions to direct both human and drug smugglers. Then he scanned the high bluff on the Mexican side where the Sinaloa cartel kept a house called the "Castle," which was manned by lookouts. Because most of Mexico's Nogales loomed higher than Arizona's, Danny was at a geological disadvantage.

For the last few days he'd been observing a warehouse on the Mexican side near the border wall. Now he saw a taxi arrive and a man wearing a light blue guayabera shirt and jeans get out. The taxi pulled away while the man entered the building. Danny looked at his watch and noted the time.

He shifted his view to a small warehouse on the US side of the border. A silver Honda Accord drove into the dirt lot. Two men got out. The taller of the two unlocked the front door of the warehouse and both men went inside. Again, Danny noted the time. Then he got into his white 4x4 SUV with the green stripe and lettering.

Danny carried a Taser, knife, and handcuffs. The holster on his hip held the standard issue Heckler & Koch P2000 handgun chambered in .40 S&W. But Glock had recently been awarded a contract to supply agents with the newest generation of Glock pistols. Danny would soon be carrying a G19 or the new G47. Photos of his wife and two young daughters were clipped to the visor of his SUV. Danny always carried the photos with him regardless of what vehicle he was using.

Born in Mexico, the naturalized citizen and ex-Marine believed that when he put on the uniform he was a Border Patrol agent before anything else, regardless of his heritage or where he came from. He couldn't know the intentions of those who crossed the border illegally, whether they were immigrants seeking a better life, drug smugglers, or radicalized terrorists. He believed in and practiced an America-first, beware-of-all-threats brand of patriotism. He saw himself as an integral cog in the wheel that was the nation's first line of defense.

In his eight years working for the CBP, the thirty-two-year-old agent had seen the technological explosion of surveillance and rapid-response systems covering the entire sector: a digital fingerprinting system that provided instant responses from federal databases, fiber-optic scopes that allowed agents to peer into fuel tanks and through air-conditioning vents, drones, and the Z Backscatter Van in which a monitor showed a map of the area and displayed green dots whenever the radar detected movement. Based on the size of the dots, the operator could tell whether vehicle or foot traffic caused the movement.

A second monitor's real-time feed from a camera could pan and zoom as needed. If the operator spotted trouble, he could radio Danny and other agents to investigate and then either transmit GPS coordinates or guide them in by radio.

Danny had worked both primary and tactical border checkpoints, the first layer in a three-layer strategy that included line watch and roving patrol operations. Because tactical checkpoints were located along highways twenty-five to seventy-five miles inside the US border and were not well known on the Mexican side, he'd surprised smugglers and illegal immigrants who thought they'd left border security behind them.

The tactical checkpoints, the number and location of which changed daily, consisted of a few vehicles, portable water tanks, traffic cones and signs, and a mobile trailer. But in more remote areas Danny still relied on tracking and sign-cutting techniques he'd been taught as an agent. No person or animal could traverse ground without leaving a telltale sign.

He looked for kicked-over rocks, soil depressions, clothing fibers, and vegetation changes, as well as footprints and tire tracks. He could tell the size of a group, its speed and direction, and whether it included children.

Now he drove into Nogales on the US side, toward the warehouse where the two men had entered. He parked on a side street, near the border fence strung with razor wire, where he could observe the building without being seen.

He cracked the driver's-side window to let in some fresh air, but closed it again when the smell of urine and rotted garbage from the trash scattered along the curb became overwhelming.

Danny waited for thirty minutes before he saw the man in the light blue guayabera shirt and jeans come out of the warehouse and get into a black Toyota Camry that a young woman had left in the lot a few minutes ago. The same man who had walked into the ramshackle house on the other side of the border thirty-five minutes ago.

*   *   *

Eddie Machado saw the CBP agent's SUV in his rearview shortly after leaving Nogales, Arizona. He'd been directed to follow State Route 82 northeast through Patagonia and Sonoita till it intersected with SR 80 northwest of Tombstone. He'd take SR 80 to Interstate 10 toward Albuquerque if he made it through the Tombstone checkpoint, and if he could shake the agent on his tail.

He'd dropped Tito and Victor's bodies into the tunnel, along with their handguns. Then he'd called a Mexican contact and told him how he'd been double-crossed. The ride that Tito and Victor figured Eddie wouldn't need had been delivered to him before he left the warehouse. His FN-7, concealed carry permit, and the car's registration in the name of Eddie Lopez were tucked in the Toyota's glove compartment.

Eddie hadn't anticipated that Tito and Victor would sell him out to the Sinaloa cartel, or that a CBP agent would be following him so soon after leaving Nogales. He'd have to improvise on the fly, though the agent could be driving his regular route rather than tailing him. But instincts were everything in this business. They suggested he had a cop on his tail.

He had one advantage. CBP agents at checkpoints had legal authority that agents didn't have when patrolling areas away from the border. At fixed checkpoints agents could selectively refer motorists to a secondary inspection area for additional brief questioning, even if there was no reason to believe that the particular vehicle contained drugs or illegals. But CBP agents on roving patrol could stop a vehicle only if they had reasonable suspicion that the vehicle contained drugs or people who may be illegally in the United States—a higher threshold for stopping and questioning motorists than at checkpoints. Whether it was a roving patrol or a checkpoint, any search had to be supported by either consent or probable cause. Eddie figured the agent had no probable cause to stop him, and he sure as hell wouldn't consent to a search.

It was an hour-and-fifteen-minute drive from Nogales, Arizona, to Tombstone, Arizona, on SR-82, a lightly traveled two-lane asphalt highway. Eddie wondered if the agent would make his move soon or follow him all the way to Tombstone.

Ten minutes into the trip, as Eddie's Toyota snaked through a curve between bluffs and brown grasslands, he saw flashing red lights in his rearview. Eddie pulled into a turnout and killed the engine. Keeping his eyes on his rearview, he opened the glove compartment and removed the FN-7, settling it beside his right thigh on the front seat.

Eddie watched through the side view mirror as the agent got out of his SUV. He looked Mexican. Darker skin. Early thirties.

Eddie waited for the agent to approach the Toyota from the driver's side. But the agent surprised him as he crossed over between the two vehicles and approached from the passenger side.

Quickly grabbing his gun, Eddie slipped it in his waistband under his shirt.

The agent stopped behind the B-pillar of the Toyota and knuckled the passenger-side window till it slid down.

"Afternoon, sir."

"Afternoon," Eddie replied politely.

"License and registration, please."

"Is there a reason you pulled me over?"

The agent smiled and didn't reply.

Rather than push it, Eddie opened the glove compartment again, retrieved his license and registration, and handed them to the agent. As the agent leaned in, Eddie saw the name VAL-DEZ tagged on the uniform.

Agent Valdez peered briefly at the license, then at Eddie again. "Eddie Lopez."

"Yes."

"You live in Tucson."

"Yes."

"Where are you headed, Mr. Lopez?"

"Chicago," Eddie said. "To visit my mother."

"What were you doing in Nogales?"

"Business."

"What business is that?"

Eddie keyed up, tired of the questions. Valdez either knew something or thought he did. Either way, Eddie couldn't take the chance.

"Pharmaceuticals," he said.

The gun came up from under Eddie's shirt in a smooth motion. He saw Valdez's eyes widen with surprise as he stepped back and reached for his own weapon, just before the bullet hit him in the chest.

Eddie was out of the Toyota now, coming around the front, ready to put one in the agent's head, when Danny Valdez stumbled backward and rolled down a steep ravine, disappearing in the tall grass.

Eddie considered going after him. Then he heard a car coming from the opposite direction. He turned, walked back to his Camry, and got in.

The car slowed, the driver peering through his window at Eddie.

Eddie started the Toyota, focused his eyes straight ahead.
The car kept going.
Eddie slotted the gearshift into DRIVE and did the same.

Chapter 20

Heading toward his SUV in the LEC parking lot that evening, Santana heard Bobbi Chacon's voice call out. He turned and waited till she was close.

"Been waiting here long?"

Bobbi Chacon stopped in front of him. "I spoke with Weston and wrote up a report. But you owe me one, Santana."

He heard the slight edge of anger still in her voice. "Okay."

She stared off in the distance for a moment before looking at him again. "How 'bout I buy you a drink?"

"It's late."

"Not that late. And if I go back to the hotel now, I'll lie awake staring at the ceiling. You gonna sleep like a baby after what happened today?"

"Probably not."

"So?" she said with a shrug.

Santana knew what she was after and figured he owed her. "You know where Alary's is downtown?"

She shook her head. "I'll follow you." She walked away before he could change his mind.

*　　*　　*

Alary's was a sports bar decorated with police, fire, and sports memorabilia, and twenty-two flat-screen TVs. It had a sidewalk patio with chairs and umbrellas, and a bevy of young, pretty waitresses in tight T-shirts and short skirts. It was a meeting place for sports junkies, off-duty police officers and firefighters, attorneys, and city and state workers.

Al Baisi, who played for the Chicago Bears in the 1940s, partnered with Larry Lehner in 1949 to open Alary's Club Bar

(Al + Larry). Though both men had passed away, Alary's was still known as "St. Paul's original sports bar," and a staple of the historic Lowertown neighborhood on the edge of downtown. Originally the lower landing on the Mississippi River and first port of access to the Twin Cities, the sixteen-block warehouse and wholesaling district had become gentrified and now housed restaurants, condos, artists' lofts, the restored Union Depot, and the AAA St. Paul Saints baseball stadium.

Santana and Chacon had to wait fifteen minutes before a table cleared on a crowded Friday night.

"I'm starving," she said. "You hungry?"

"I am."

They looked over the menus for a time, got the waitress's attention, and both ordered a bacon cheeseburger with fries and a Blue Moon to wash it down.

"We did good today," Chacon said after the waitress had taken their orders.

"We did."

She gave him a crooked smile and locked eyes with his. "You must've braced Washburn, Moody, or both."

"Washburn."

"One I would've started with," she said, an expectant gleam in her amber eyes.

Santana waited.

"Gonna hold out on me?" she asked, tapping her fingers on the table.

"Washburn gave me the location of an escort service in St. Paul."

"What's that got to do with anything?"

"I don't know."

"Where in St. Paul?"

"In the Cathedral Hill neighborhood."

"Got an address?"

Santana shook his head.

"Well, what good is it?"

"Cathedral Hill isn't known for its escort services. I'll ask around. See what I can come up with."

"Should've let me have a crack at him," she said.

Santana ignored the comment. "What hotel you staying in?"

"The Residence Inn. It's an apartment hotel near the Xcel Energy Center."

"I know where it is."

"All the comforts of home," she said, each word dripping with sarcasm.

The waitress appeared with their Blue Moons.

"Cheers," Chacon said.

Santana preferred Sam Adams, but Alary's didn't serve it. Still, Santana let the Blue Moon sluice down his throat and quench his thirst.

"And home is?"

She told him about her stops in El Paso and Miami before landing in Minnesota.

"You grew up in Texas?"

"Mostly. My dad was in the Army. We moved around a lot."

"Parents still there?"

"Mother is."

She didn't offer any more about her father, and Santana didn't ask.

"Haven't lost all your accent," he said.

"You haven't either," she said. "You're from Colombia."

"You've done your homework."

"Straight A student when it comes to knowing my partners."

"We're not partners."

"Figure of speech, Detective."

"Never married?"

"Dangerous jobs and marriage usually don't work well," she said. "This career owns you."

Santana could relate to that. "Ever spend any time in Colombia with the DEA?"

She shook her head, drank another swallow of beer. "Mexico is the closest I've come."

"What's your impression?"

"It's about as transparent as a blackout curtain. I've been on a raid in Guadalajara trying to capture El Mencho. Though if anyone asks, I was never there."

"We have a saying in Colombia. *Mala yerba no muere.*"

"Bad weeds never die," she said with a nod.

"*Hablas español?*"

"*Mi español es bastante bueno, pero no creo que tenga mucho uso aquí.*"

"Your Spanish isn't bad. You don't have much of an accent. You'd be surprised at how much you can use it here in Minnesota. Especially on the West Side where we were today."

"I'd rather be back near the border where the real action is."

"Today wasn't enough for you?"

"I'm not an adrenaline junkie," she said.

Santana had his doubts.

"As far as the cartels go," Chacon said, "you need to erase that picture you have in your head of gem-studded pistols, gold chains, snakeskin boots, big belt buckles, and generally bad taste."

"Really."

"Yeah. The younger generation of drug smugglers doesn't look like your typical traffickers. Many have college degrees, and most keep low profiles."

The picture Santana had of cartels was indelibly etched in his mind and had been since the age of sixteen. Members of the Cali cartel had murdered his mother and attempted to kill him on numerous occasions. That picture would never change regardless of appearances. Cartel members might look different, might be more educated, but he believed they were even more ruthless now than the previous generations.

"I was part of the task force set up to track Joaquín Guzman, alias El Chapo," Chacon said. "Now that he's in prison, we've got El Mencho, and it's worse."

"How do you mean?"

"Killing was a necessary part of doing business for El Chapo. El Mencho is a real sadist even by narco standards. Loves the public spectacle. The way they torture and kill people. The sheer number of murders. Then filming the scenes with their iPhones. ISIS stuff. Nothing ever like it even in Mexico."

"Law of unintended consequences," Santana said.

She nodded. "Our government takes out Saddam Hussein in the Middle East. In steps ISIS. Even worse. Taking out El Chapo in Mexico opened the door for El Mencho."

"So he shouldn't have been taken down?"

"Not what I meant. It's just harder now. Only a handful of photos of him exist. Narco balladeers sing *narcocorridos* about his love of fast motorcycles and one-hundred-thousand-dollar cockfights. One of his nicknames is '*El Señor de los Gallos.*'"

"The Lord of the Roosters," Santana said.

"Yeah. He's a cipher. A ghost. His primary product is methamphetamine. Higher profit margins than cocaine or heroin. We figure he's worth in the neighborhood of twenty billion dollars. We've been focusing more of our attacks on the CJNG's financial infrastructure. Hit him in the pocketbook, where it hurts."

"Any idea where he is?"

"Likely hidden under a jungle canopy or in the mountains in rural areas of Jalisco, Colima, or his native Michoacán. Surrounded by layers of security guards who are paramilitary trained and heavily armed."

"We've got our share of opioids and prescription drug abuse here," Santana said. "But meth is number one."

"Poor man's cocaine. Was popular in the early two thousands before I began working for the DEA. Used to read the headlines about all those clandestine meth lab explosions. Then

Congress clamped down on the sale of nasal decongestant. Stories of meth made in makeshift labs, hotel bathtubs, or dimly lit trailers disappeared. But by then drug cartels had discovered a cheaper way to crank out a more potent version of meth. Key ingredients are shipped from China to super labs in southern Mexico and then manufactured to look like crystal shards."

"Ice," Santana said.

She nodded. "Befits its name."

Their waitress appeared with their burgers and fries. They both ordered a second Blue Moon.

Chacon finished her first glass and said, "Five years ago it would've taken more than a year in Minnesota to collect the amount of meth that Washburn and Moody had in their SUV in one load." Chacon chewed a bite of her burger and said, "What's the next move?"

"This isn't the only case I'm working."

"What's that mean?"

"Means I'm working more than one case."

She set her burger on the plate. "We're looking for a murderer here, Santana. A murderer who killed a DEA agent."

"There's more than one murderer in this city."

She leaned in closer. "I won't let this go."

Santana recalled the love note in Ryker's apartment signed B. "You and Ryker were more than partners."

She straightened in her chair, her eyes widening momentarily in surprise. "Where'd you get that idea? Because I care about what happened to Joel?"

It was feigned outrage. Empty words. Santana knew he'd struck a chord.

"Ryker was married."

"You're full of sanctimonious shit, Santana."

"It's an observation, not a condemnation."

"Could've fooled me," she said, eating another bite of her burger. She wiped her mouth on a napkin and said, "You've lost a partner before, you should know how it feels. How it hurts."

Santana figured she knew about it because his partner's murder had been well publicized in the media at the time. After his partner's death, he'd been teamed with Kacie Hawkins.

"I do know," he said, seeing the brutal image now in his mind of the deep knife wound in his former partner's stomach, realizing that it was too late to do anything, knowing that he would soon bleed out.

"Well, then . . ." she said, ending the thought with a hike of her shoulders. "I'd appreciate none of your holier-than-thou bullshit."

"Point taken. I'll keep you informed. But that goes both ways."

"Wanna clarify that?"

"You're holding out on me."

She let out a little laugh that sounded forced. "You *are* full of shit."

"The pill press in the stash house."

"What about it?"

"Seven pill dies, bags of meth and binding powder. I think the Lozanos were making Desoxyn pills and cutting ties with El Mencho. He wouldn't like that."

"It's a theory."

"If the Lozanos' house was on the DEA's list to be raided, why did Ryker go in early?"

"I don't know."

Santana had a second theory now. Ryker was after the money. Directly raising the possibility again with Chacon was like lighting a stick of dynamite. He came at it from a different direction.

"Why didn't Ryker have any ID on him when he went into the Lozanos' house?"

Chacon shrugged. Her feline eyes told a different story.

Chapter 21

It was ten p.m. when Eddie Machado walked into the gay nightclub in Albuquerque, New Mexico. A Gloria Gaynor song, "I Will Survive," blared from the speakers. The main room with the DJ was dimly lit and clouded with the heavy smell of cigarette smoke, but Eddie could see a wall of mirrors and pairs of men crowding the dance floor.

The back room was smaller and more intimate. There was a pool table and tables to sit around, where couples were talking.

Eddie's cartel contact in Mexico would have to arrange another way to cross back over the border once he'd retrieved the missing half-million dollars. He also needed a new ID.

He'd cleared the Tombstone checkpoint and driven the 425 miles to Albuquerque in just over six hours, his thoughts continually returning to the CBP agent who might've called in the license number of the Toyota Eddie was driving before being shot and tumbling down the embankment. Continuing to drive the Camry was too risky. Eddie needed another car. He couldn't chance renting one till he got a different ID.

He considered stopping at the Mescalero Apache Reservation in Mescalero, New Mexico, and asking if Yuma was there. Perhaps the Indian could help him as he'd once helped him before. But Eddie quickly dismissed the idea. He doubted Yuma had made it out of the Mexican mountains alive, and if he had, would he ever return to the reservation that he'd once chosen to leave?

At a Love's truck stop off I-40, Eddie had showered and shaved and then put on the white linen suit his handlers had packed and left in a garment bag in the trunk of the car. In a magazine rack in the lobby he'd picked up a copy of ABQ-Live magazine, where he'd found the club's address.

Leaning on the bar now, Eddie let his dark eyes rove around the large room, searching for a connection. Cher was belting out "Believe" through the speakers. From his experiences selling himself to men in Mexico City, Eddie knew it would only be a matter of time before someone hit on him.

Shortly, a man Eddie guessed was in his late twenties sidled up next to him, a bottle of Corona Extra in his hand. His sun-brown skin looked dark in the dim light, his blond hair tousled as if he combed it with his fingers. His eyes were bright green, his cheeks pooled with color. He wore a silk shirt open at the collar, western boots, tight jeans, and a leather belt with a wide silver and turquoise buckle.

"Mitch," he said, extending a hand.

"Eddie," Eddie said, shaking Mitch's hand.

"From Mexico?"

"Tucson. My parents were Mexican."

"Yeah. Got yourself an accent."

"You also have an accent," Eddie said.

"Guess everybody does," Mitch said with a gleaming smile. "I'm from Texas originally. Houston. Ever been there?"

Eddie shook his head.

"Here on business?"

"Passing through."

"What business you in?"

"Pharmaceuticals."

"I work for the county. Information analyst."

Eddie didn't bother asking what the job title meant. Instead he said, "You have family here in Albuquerque?"

"Family lives in and around Houston."

"Why live in Albuquerque?"

The skin twitched at the corner of Mitch's mouth as he stared at the dance floor. "Fell in love with a guy from here. Didn't work out. But I liked the area and my job. Decided to stay."

"And your . . . friend?"

"Last I heard, he's living with his partner in San Francisco."

"Too bad."

Mitch shrugged. "Buy you a drink?"

Eddie considered ordering a shot of tequila and then changed his mind. He had no time for small talk. He needed to be on his way. "I don't drink," he said.

"How 'bout a dance?"

"Don't dance either."

Mitch shook his head and gave a small laugh. "Sounds like you're in the wrong place, partner."

Eddie looked into the man's eyes. "Am I?"

*   *   *

Eddie followed Mitch's red Jeep Cherokee along Central Avenue, the old Route 66, past the University of New Mexico, vintage and retro motels and gas stations, foreign restaurants, neon signs, and colorful graffiti and wall murals, until the Jeep pulled into the driveway of a small, one-level adobe-style house in an area called Nob Hill.

Eddie exited his Toyota and headed for the front door behind Mitch, his eyes casing the quiet neighborhood, searching for anything out of the ordinary. The night air still held much of the afternoon heat and smelled of fresh tar and fried foods.

The front door led into a low-ceilinged living room. Mitch closed the curtains on the front window and told Alexa to play Kenny Chesney on his Amazon Echo.

"You like country music, Eddie?"

"Not particularly."

Mitch laughed. "Well, see if you like this. Be right back." He excused himself to use the bathroom.

As Mitch left the room, Eddie slipped on a pair of latex gloves, removed the FN-7 from the belt holster clipped to the back of his belt, and cranked up the music volume.

"A little loud, isn't it?" Mitch said, coming back into the room two minutes later.

Eddie walked to where Mitch stood frozen, his eyes wide at the sight of the gun pointed at him.

"This a robbery?" Mitch asked.

Sticking the gun barrel in Mitch's chest to muffle the sound, Eddie fired. Blood misted on his hand and suit coat as Mitch's body jerked and then crumpled to the floor.

Eddie holstered his gun, checked for a pulse, and turned down the music. Then he removed the Jeep's keys from Mitch's jean pocket, found the door leading to the garage, and opened the garage door.

Using a screwdriver he'd found in a toolbox on a work-bench, he removed the license plates on the Toyota he'd been driving and tossed the plates in the back of Mitch's Jeep Chero-kee. Then he backed the Jeep out and parked the Toyota in the garage, closing the garage door behind it. He carried Mitch's body to the Toyota and dropped it in the trunk. He wiped up the bloodstains on the floor with a wet towel and threw it in the washing machine. Turning out the lights, he left by the front door, locking it behind him.

Chapter 22

Santana rose early on Saturday morning, turned on the radio to some bluesy jazz, heated a cup of hot chocolate in the kitchen microwave, and went back upstairs and out the sliding glass door onto the wooden deck overlooking the river, Gitana by his side.

Resting his elbows on the railing, the cup held between both hands, he gazed at the transient light on the horizon and then at the hills silhouetted in the misty distance. A cold chill shivered across the river. Wispy threads of fog wrapped the brush along its banks. The air carried the earthy smell of sediment and decayed plants.

On the stereo radio Melody Gardot was singing "If You Love Me."

Santana saw the two fledglings in the large bald eagle nest high up in the dead oak along the riverbank. The parents returned to the nest each year. Now they were encouraging the fledglings to fly and hunt by limiting their food supply. Santana found it fascinating to watch the young eagles venture farther out on the limb every day and away from the safety of the nest.

Gitana pushed her head against him, indicating she wanted petting. He reached down and stroked her head, scratched gently behind her ears. She reminded him of a saying he'd once seen on a poster:

If you don't believe in unconditional love, then you've never had a dog.

He smiled at the thought.

Then he went for an early morning run with Gitana, finished a short but strenuous workout with weights and the heavy bag, and showered.

A light mist was falling outside the kitchen window as he prepared a *calentado,* or Colombian breakfast, of reheated rice and beans, a chorizo, and more hot chocolate. Tony Bennett and Alejandro Sanz were singing a duet entitled "Yesterday, I Heard the Rain." One of Santana's favorite composers, Armando Manzanero, had written the song, entitled *"Esta Tarde Vi Llover"* in Spanish.

As he ate, Santana read about the DEA raids in the St. Paul *Pioneer Press.*

"We've been planning the raids for six months," United States DEA Omaha Division Special Agent in Charge Scott Weston said. "Our primary goal is to dismantle the upper echelon of CJNG and to get closer to capturing its leader, one of the most wanted men in America. There's a $10 million reward for the arrest of Rubén Nemesio 'El Mencho' Oseguera.

"The CJNG cartel controls between one-third and two-thirds of the US drug market. El Mencho and his associates prey on the addicts, and they prey on small towns where they can act as bullies and infiltrate these small towns," Weston said. "They promise hope, and they deliver despair."

More than 600 people have been arrested during the operation in recent months, more than 15,000 kilos of meth was seized and nearly $20 million taken as search and arrest warrants were executed. About 250 were arrested Friday.

For the US, combating Mexico's fastest-growing and most violent gang is a top priority. Law enforcement officials believe the gang has infiltrated cities and towns all across the country.

Santana couldn't help wondering if Bobbi Chacon knew that Joel Ryker was planning on stealing the half-million from the Lozanos, and if she was somehow involved in the robbery that had all gone sideways with Ryker killed and the money vanished. Was Chacon interested in solving her partner's murder or getting her hands on the money? Maybe both? He needed to figure that out before he could trust her.

*   *   *

That afternoon Kacie Hawkins, Santana's former partner, came striding down the dock at the St. Croix Marina carrying a blue-and-white canvas tote bag in one hand and a wicker picnic basket with folded handles in the other. She wore large sunglasses, white sandals, and a blue-and-white-striped dress with a flared skirt and ribbon ties on the short sleeves. Perched on her head was a wide-brim straw sun hat with a wind lanyard. She spent much of her off-duty time working out, and her body looked as dark and hard as ebony.

Santana smiled to himself. She'd never been on his boat before and was clearly going for a maritime look.

He took the basket from her hand and helped her aboard his thirty-seven-foot Mainship named *Alibi*. She gave him a hug and stepped back, a big smile on her face. Gitana wagged her tail and pressed against her, looking for attention.

Kacie squatted and gently stroked Gitana's head. "How's my favorite girl?"

Gitana licked Kacie's nose.

She laughed, stood up, and surveyed her surroundings. "Quite a boat." Looking at Santana again, she said, "Where we going?"

"Thought we'd motor toward Prescott, Wisconsin."

"Sounds good to me."

Kacie helped him cast off. Once they were under way, she and Gitana came up to the flybridge and sat on the cushioned seats. She'd left her sun hat in the cabin. As the warm, intermittent breeze ruffled her hair, Santana could see that she'd added some dark blue highlights to her layered pixie cut.

The day was bright and breezy after the morning rain, warm for this early in the year, the flowers bursting with color, the water sprinkled with sunlight, the birds singing in the trees, the gulls keening as they flew over the water that smelled like schools of fish. The ordinary sights and the sounds almost soothed the shadows of his life.

They cruised south along the St. Croix between the high bluffs of Minnesota and Wisconsin, past Kinnickinnic State Park, where the Kinnickinnic River joined the St. Croix. The mouth of the Kinnickinnic River formed a sandy delta upon which boaters were picnicking and camping.

When they neared Prescott, Wisconsin, they anchored off-shore and sat at the dinette in the salon, eating grilled chicken, potato salad, and cherry pie. Santana remembered that it wasn't too long ago that he'd sat at the same table with Jordan Parrish, and he felt a familiar ache in his chest.

"You okay, John?" Kacie asked. She cocked her head as her brown eyes searched his face.

"I'm fine." He lifted his glass of Merlot. "To partners."

"Partners," she said, clinking her wine glass against his.

They sipped their wine. Then Santana asked, "How's it working out with Diana Lee?"

Diana Lee had transferred to Homicide and Robbery from the department's gang unit and was the only Hmong detective in the squad. She'd worked with two different homicide detectives before partnering with Kacie and had a solid reputation.

"Diana's fine. But I don't know why Kendrick decided the only two women in the unit had to work together. We were good partners, John."

"Maybe something will change in the near future," he said.

"I keep hoping."

Santana asked about the homicides she was working. She told him about a drive-by gang shooting and a robbery at a local liquor store.

When she'd finished, Santana told her about the Madison Porter cold case, giving her what he knew and didn't know, hoping she'd have some ideas.

"Not much to go on," Hawkins said, "though Gordon Grant piques my curiosity."

"Mine, too."

"Why keep a photo of Madison Porter in his house?"

"Why have one in the first place?" he said.

As he poured more wine in each of their glasses, Hawkins said, "How's it working out with Bobbi Chacon?"

"What'd you hear?"

"You two busted a couple of drug runners."

"She knows what she's doing," Santana said. "But she had a relationship with Joel Ryker."

"You mean like intimate?"

"Very. She wants the perp who killed him. Bad."

"As we both would if we were in her shoes."

"Yeah," he acknowledged.

"You be careful, John. Make sure she's got your back."

"I'm always careful."

Kacie laughed. "Sure you are."

"Well," he said with a smile, "most of the time."

Santana was a mentor to Hawkins, and he trusted her with his life. That bond couldn't be broken. He felt the same about Reiko Tanabe and Tony Novak. But Santana never trusted the brass. They had their own agendas and priorities, which usually involved covering their asses.

They were both quiet while finishing their lunches before Kacie said, "I didn't think you were coming back."

Her comment caught him off guard. "Why not?"

She looked out a portside window for a time before turning her gaze on Santana again. "After what you've been through, I thought maybe you'd had enough."

"What's enough?"

She shrugged. "That's the ultimate question, isn't it? So why *did* you come back?"

Santana thought about what she'd asked before responding. "I'm not sure, Kacie."

"That's not real encouraging."

"It's the truth."

She drank some wine, fiddled with the glass. "Remember what Wendell Hudson told you?"

Santana nodded as he recalled the words of a former partner, one of his earliest mentors in Homicide. Before cancer took his life, Hudson had encouraged Santana to *"Stay true to yourself. Do what you do best. What God put you on this earth to do."* Though Santana no longer believed in a higher power or an afterlife, he believed in Hudson's words.

"You always spoke about your sense of mission, of purpose," Hawkins said. "Is that no longer relevant?"

"Of course it is," he said, wondering if his job, his mission, was enough. "Maybe I need something more."

"Like what?"

"I wish I knew, Kacie. I really wish I knew."

Chapter 23

A small lamp on a side table beside the sectional in Dominique Lejeune's lavish mansion cast a dim light on the living room and the young auburn-haired woman seated there. Ana Soriano recognized her as one of the new women in the "After Dark Club." She wore jeans and a tight red pullover top that accentuated her large breasts. Her eyes were glued to a big screen television monitor showing the '60s French film *Breathless*, one of Dominique's favorites.

In the film Jean Paul Belmondo and Jean Seberg are walking down the Champs-Elysées in Paris. Seberg is selling copies of the New York *Herald Tribune*, and Belmondo, on the run after killing a cop, is trying to convince her to come to Rome with him. He buys a copy of the paper and then gives it back to her after discovering there is no horoscope foretelling his future.

"Go to the bedroom," Dominique said to the woman on the sectional. "I'll be in shortly."

The woman gave Ana a shy smile as she stood and walked out of the room.

Ana took her place on the sectional and set the new backpack at her feet. City lights shimmered in the glass of the double-hung windows.

Dominique sat beside her and muted the remote. Holding a cigarette in one hand, she looked Ana over. Always appearing as if she'd just stepped out of an issue of *Cosmopolitan*, Dominique was dressed in cigarette-leg white jeans, a pair of black patent leather sandals with four-inch stiletto heels, and a long-sleeved dark blue top with a mock neckline and flare cuffs. She wore a gold Rolex watch on her left wrist, gold-hooped earrings, and a simple matching gold bracelet that looked to be worth as much as the Rolex. Dominique reminded Ana of the French actress Jeanne Moreau.

"What's in the backpack?" she asked.

Ana bent down and unzipped the backpack, exposing the bricks of wrapped one-hundred-dollar bills.

Dominique's eyes grew large as she stared at the crisp bank-banded hundred-dollar bills. "A brick of hundred-dollar bills is one hundred thousand dollars. You've got five bricks there. That's five hundred thousand dollars."

A little less than that, Ana thought, since I gave Christine some money. She looked at Dominique but didn't reply.

Dominique let out a long breath. "Where'd you get it?"

"From drug sales."

"You're dealing?" she said, her face aghast.

"Martin and Benita Lozano were."

Dominique hesitated a moment. "You were there when they were killed?"

Ana nodded.

Blood drained from Dominique's face. "You killed them?"

"No. Someone else did."

"Who?"

"Someone who tried to steal this money. I don't know who he was. But he was white. Not Latino. Not some gangbanger or hophead either."

"How do you know this is drug money?"

"The man who tried to steal it said so."

"And what happened to him?"

"I shot him."

Startled, Dominique sat back and then shook her head slowly as if she couldn't understand what she'd just heard.

"You killed someone and then came here?" she said, her voice rising in alarm.

"I need your help."

"My God." Dominique took a long drag on her cigarette.

"You sent me to the Lozanos'."

"They were respected clients, like all the clients I've sent you to. Nothing more."

"Those respected clients were selling drugs."

Dominique took a last drag off her cigarette and crushed it in the ashtray on the coffee table. Then she stood and began pacing in front of the fireplace. "I can't protect you from the police."

"But you have to."

Dominique stopped and looked down at her. "And why is that?"

"Because I know everything about the club. About the important men involved, about the parties, the payoffs to police. Everything."

At first, Ana had balked at the idea of sleeping with more men. But Dominique had explained that her other option was deportation back to El Salvador, where gang rape from the MS-13 awaited her—and quite possibly death. Instead, she could make a great deal of money, some of which she could send back to her mother and sister in El Salvador. Dominique would make the arrangements. Ana decided she would not become some drug-addled, low-rent hooker on the streets.

Ana had no one to turn to, no one she knew in the US besides her one friend, Christine Hammond. She didn't trust the police. As far as she knew, they were involved in sex trafficking young women. Sometimes in this life you get shitty choices.

For the first six months Dominique had kept her away from the wealthy men who attended the elaborate parties. In that time she taught Ana how to dress, how to wear just the right amount of makeup, how to style her hair, what fork to use, how to hold a wine glass, how to make a man feel he was the most important person in the world. A tutor Dominique hired taught her French.

Ana shared a room with two other young women, one from Honduras and the other from Mexico. Though the two young women kept mostly to themselves, they helped make Ana's transition easier. Later, she'd met Christine Hammond at an After Dark Club party, and they'd become friends.

The parties in the mansion were restricted to twenty male guests. Men admitted to the After Dark Club were required to pass a strict vetting process that included headshots and were required to wear black tie at all parties. Phones were collected at the door. Before being given the green light, all men were invited to a Champagne reception where Dominique met with each one individually and gave her final stamp of approval. Membership fees ranged from $20,000 a year to a one-million-dollar lifetime option that included invitations to parties throughout the US.

"Be very careful who you threaten, Ana," Dominique said now. "You're talking about powerful men. They can do you great harm."

"Men have threatened me before. Evil men. Men much more ruthless than the men you are talking about."

Dominique's gaze turned inward, as if formulating her thoughts, before she focused on Ana again. "I took you in. Took care of you. Educated you. Taught you French. Taught you all that you know."

"I never wanted this for my life."

"Yet here you are. Asking for my help."

"You've made plenty of money off me," Ana said. "I've more than paid off whatever I cost you. You owe *me*."

Dominique sat down again, her knees touching Ana's, her expression softening. "It was always the plan to let you go when you were ready," she said. "That's the plan with all the girls. Once they've achieved financial stability, they leave this life behind and start anew." She smiled reassuringly as if it all made perfect sense.

"No one truly leaves this life behind," Ana said. "Ever. But I have financial stability now." She gestured at the backpack on the floor.

"No," Dominique said with a quick shake of her head. "That's not your money."

"The Lozanos are dead."

Dominique touched Ana lightly on the hand. "Don't be naïve. There are other players involved in this. There always are. Someone will come looking for that money, Ana. You should've left it there. Left it for the police to find."

A cold chill ran down Ana's spine. She'd acted on impulse. Now she'd have to deal with the consequences, whatever they were.

"I want you to help me get out of the country."

"Where will you go?"

"France. I'll live in France. And then I'll send for my mother and sister."

"That's impossible," Dominique said, reinforcing her words with the wave of a hand.

Ana looked into Dominique's eyes. "I remember you telling me when I first started working for you that nothing was impossible, that all our dreams could be realized."

"All of us have unmet dreams," Dominique said, her eyelids lowered, a melancholy expression on her face. "It's called life."

*   *   *

That evening, Santana took I-35W to James McGowan's home in Mendota Heights, a twelve-minute drive to the first-ring suburb southwest of St. Paul.

McGowan had grown up in the small town of Caledonia, Minnesota, the town named after the ancient Roman word for Scotland. His father owned a bank; his mother worked as an elementary teacher. An only child, McGowan had attended Macalester College in St. Paul, majoring in business. Upon graduation, he'd migrated to New York, where he took a job with a Wall

Street investment firm. Riding the technology wave, he soon became a multi-millionaire.

While living in New York, he'd met and married a young socialite. Known for their lavish parties and free spending, their extravagant lifestyle ended abruptly three years later when his wife died from an overdose of sleeping pills. Soon after, McGowan left New York and moved back to Minnesota, where he founded his own financial management firm. For tax advantages, he'd based his firm on the island of St. Thomas in the US Virgin Islands. The relocation acted as an offshore tax haven that reduced his federal income taxes by ninety percent while still being part of the US banking system.

When the economy collapsed in 2008, McGowan bought every foreclosed mortgage and closed business he could get his hands on. As the economy recovered, his wealth grew exponentially. Now one of Forbes' 400 richest men in the US, and a well-known philanthropist, McGowan was almost as famous for the opulent parties and insular social events at his large Mendota Heights estate as he was for his wealth. Still a bachelor, he'd been linked romantically to a number of celebrities and wealthy women.

An iron gate limited access to the long circular driveway that went up a slight hill to the house. But the gate was open and Santana could see a line of cars and limousines parked along both sides of the driveway. He considered leaving, but McGowan had not returned his phone calls. Santana wondered if McGowan was deliberately avoiding him, or if he thought Santana was an inconvenience that didn't register on his affluent radar. Either way, tonight might be the only opportunity Santana had to get some unfiltered answers to his questions.

He parked in the last spot along the right side of the driveway inside the gate and got out of his Ford SUV. He could hear soft music, laughter, and the hum of conversation coming from the back of the house. The moon was full, the black sky sprinkled with stars, the warm air sweet with the scent of freshly cut grass.

A muscular blond-headed man dressed in a white shirt, black vest, and black slacks approached Santana. Security, Santana thought.

"Good evening, sir," the man said with a bright smile. "Do you have your invitation?"

"As a matter of fact, I do." Santana showed him his gold shield.

The man's smile quickly faded.

"Nothing to concern you," Santana said. "I stopped by to speak with James McGowan."

"Of course. Just up the drive, Detective."

A long brick walkway led from the four-car garage to the backyard and a large flagstone patio strung with bulbs and Japanese lanterns. A stone fireplace and outdoor kitchen overlooked an Olympic-size pool and private pool house.

Knots of men in sport coats and women in cocktail dresses sipped champagne. Young women in short black dresses carrying trays of champagne glasses and *hors d' oeuvres* circulated amongst the guests. A red, white, and blue banner hung above a buffet table said JAMES MCGOWAN FOR SENATE!

Santana recognized some of the faces of the politicians, attorneys, and judges, who greeted each other with a level of laughter and camaraderie meant to portray a sense of close friendship and shared values, but driven primarily by political opportunism and entitlement.

One of the women carrying a tray offered Santana a flute of champagne as she passed.

"No, thanks," he said with a wave of his hand.

She smiled and headed toward a cluster of guests near the swimming pool, the lights glowing below its emerald surface.

From his spot on the patio Santana could look through the wall of glass and see the spiral staircase leading to the second floor, the formal dining room, the white oak floors and walnut woodwork.

The huge brick Tudor had smart-home features incorporated throughout. McGowan could use one of his iPads or smart-phones to check out the security cameras, fix the lighting, play music, or turn on one of the many TVs.

Facing in the opposite direction, down the slope of the perfectly cut lawn, Santana could see the rose garden near the back of the property, the dark ribbon that was the Mississippi River drifting by, and the glittering lights of the St. Paul skyline in the near distance.

"Proximity is power," a man's voice said.

Santana turned. The voice belonged to James McGowan.

"You mean close to the city," Santana said.

"Close enough." McGowan sipped champagne from the flute in his hand.

He was about six feet tall, deeply tanned, his salt-and-pepper hair expertly cut, his white teeth gleaming in the dim light. He wore a cream-colored sport coat, brown slacks, a lavender button-down shirt, and oxblood loafers. His smile was as relaxed as a cat on a cushion.

"Putting a name with a face is one of my rare talents," McGowan said with a disarming smile, "but I can't recall your name. Sorry."

Santana doubted that McGowan really believed his self-deprecating comment. "John Santana," he said. "I once worked security here at the house."

McGowan nodded, his brow furrowed. Then recognition lit his hazel eyes. "You're a police officer," he said with a satisfied smile, as if he'd solved a difficult puzzle.

"Detective," Santana said, showing McGowan his badge wallet.

McGowan stuck out his hand. "Well, thank you for coming. I appreciate your support."

Shaking McGowan's hand, Santana said, "Actually, I'm here on another matter."

"Oh," McGowan said, his silver eyebrows arching. "How can I be of help?"

"You own a number of properties in and around the city."

"Yes."

"A man named Gordon Grant handles maintenance for some of those properties."

"A few of my residential properties."

A man sidled up next to McGowan. "Who's your friend?" he asked, looking directly at Santana from behind a pair of flat, rectangular glasses.

"This is Detective John Santana from the St. Paul Police Department." Turning to Santana, McGowan said, "This is Hal Langford, my campaign manager."

Langford held out his hand and Santana shook it.

"The detective was asking me about an employee of mine, Gordon Grant," McGowan said.

"Is that so?" Langford said.

Santana nodded.

Langford had the large eyes, short chin, round face, and wide forehead of a baby. His salt-and-pepper hair matched McGowan's. Must've had the same barber, Santana thought, though the cut looked better on the candidate.

Santana focused his attention on McGowan once more. "How long have you known Grant?"

McGowan hesitated. Then he said, "What's this about, Detective?"

"Four years ago, a young woman named Madison Porter was murdered."

"Yes. I recall reading about that. Terrible." McGowan tilted his head as if he'd heard an unusual sound. "Is Grant a suspect in the woman's murder?"

"How long have you known him?" Santana asked, ignoring the question.

"I wouldn't say I *know* him."

"He works for you."

McGowan shrugged. "Many people work for me, Detective. I don't know them all. I'm not sure how long Gordon Grant has worked for me."

"Did you hire him?"

"I have a contract with a staffing agency. They do the hiring."

"Are you aware that Gordon Grant was once charged with sexual solicitation of an underage girl?"

McGowan's face paled.

"Of course he isn't," Hal Langford said.

McGowan's gaze shifted to Langford's face. "If the press gets ahold of this . . ." His voice trailed off as if the meaning was obvious.

Langford stepped forward, narrowing the space between himself and Santana. "Certainly you understand the implication, Detective."

"What I'm attempting to understand, Mr. Langford, is the relationship between Mr. McGowan and Gordon Grant."

"There is no relationship," Langford said, his eyes glancing sideways at McGowan. "Is there, James?"

McGowan shook his head but offered no verbal confirmation.

"Come, James," Langford said, gesturing toward the buffet table. "Lots of donors to thank."

"Sorry I couldn't be of more help," McGowan said, looking back over a shoulder as Hal Langford led him away.

Chapter 24

Lakewood Cemetery sits near the southeast shores of Lake Bde Maka Ska, the largest lake in Minneapolis. Santana parked along a paved road that wound its way through the 250-acre cemetery and 100,000-plus monuments, tombs, and grave markers. The morning sun was out in the hard blue sky above the trees, the grass a deep green from the June rains. A jogger ran along the road, a gaggle of geese trundled their way across the grass. A cool rain-washed breeze carried the scent of lilies and roses.

Modeled after the rural cemeteries of 19th-century France, Lakewood had a park-like feel despite its solemnity and silence. Many movers and shakers from Minnesota's past were buried here, but Santana was interested in only one gravesite.

Jordan Parrish's cremated remains had been placed in an urn and buried in a twelve-inch granite surround beneath a solid bronze marker in the Garden of Serenity, a picturesque land-scaped area located off the shore of Lakewood's eight-acre lake.

Santana squatted and placed the bouquet of a dozen red roses on the marker that read:

She walks in beauty like the night of cloudless climes and starry skies.

As Santana thought of the man who'd taken Jordan's life, a pang of anger as sharp as a knife's blade ripped through him.

Santana used to believe that people who committed horrible acts of violence were like everyone else—until the day they were not.

His years in homicide had taught him that the capacity for violence and aggression was embedded in all of us, if for no other reason than it was sometimes necessary for our survival. Even seemingly good people could be pushed to do something terrible in the pursuit of greed, sex, power, revenge, or survival.

But the men who'd taken his mother's life, and the man who'd taken Jordan's, had swum out of the bottom of the gene pool. He'd learned that those who committed violent acts *were* fundamentally different. Like the mass murderers and serial killers living among us, the psychopaths' and sociopaths' genetic makeup had been altered at a very early age, and no normal person could attempt to imagine what went on in their minds. Yet Santana needed to get inside their heads, not to understand them, but to stop them.

"It's from the Lord Byron poem," a deep voice said behind him.

Santana turned and saw Jordan's father, Tom Parrish. Not knowing what to say, he stood and simply nodded.

Tom Parrish was a heavy-set man with graying hair cut military style and brushed up stiffly on his scalp. He had a fire-plug for a neck and the wary brown eyes of a cop, which he was at one time. He wore a polo shirt, khakis, and a pair of scuffed brown oxford shoes. His stomach had shifted slightly over his belt, and a five o'clock shadow darkened his jowls. He held a bouquet of daisies in his hand.

"You familiar with the poem?" he asked.

Santana shook his head.

"It was my wife's idea. To put the quote on the marker, I mean."

"Jordan told me about her."

Tom Parrish looked off in the distance. "Seems Byron thought that physical appearance depends upon inner good-ness." He hesitated a moment before stepping around Santana and placing the bouquet of flowers beside the red roses. Then he stood facing Santana again. "You miss her?"

"I do."

Tom Parrish slipped his hands in his pants pockets as if he didn't know what to do with them. "I wanted to scatter her ashes in the river. She always liked the water. That's why she had her office in St. Anthony on Main."

"Good that she's here then. Near the water."

Tom Parrish looked down at Jordan's bronze marker for a time before his gaze returned to Santana. "Why are you here?"

Santana heard the growing anger in his voice. "I loved her."

"But you let her get involved in your case."

"I tried to talk her out of it."

Parrish blew out a breath as though releasing pent-up frustration. "You believe in heaven and hell?"

"I don't."

"Be easier, wouldn't it?"

"How so?"

"Asshole who killed her would be burning in hell."

"He went out the hard way."

Tom Parrish shook his head. "Not hard enough. Course it would've been easier had my only child not been murdered in the first place, huh? Maybe then I'd still be married and looking forward to seeing my grandchildren."

"Sorry, Tom. I didn't know."

"Now you do."

Santana lowered his eyes and turned to leave.

"Don't you dare forget her!" Parrish called after him.

Santana walked toward the parking lot, feeling as if he'd just been kicked in the gut. As he neared his SUV, he raised his eyes and saw a tall, slim, African-American man striding toward him.

"Kenny Coleman," the man said, flashing a Department of Treasury badge at him.

Santana glanced at the badge and then at the square-jawed face. He'd seen Coleman's face before on the news. That time he was wearing a Marine dress uniform instead of a nicely tailored sharkskin suit. He still had short hair and a worm-like two-inch-long scar at the corner of his left eyebrow, where a piece of shrapnel had nearly blinded him while he was serving in Iraq.

After he'd recovered from his wound, Coleman had mustered out of the Marines, taken a law degree from Harvard, and had gone to work as an agent for FinCEN, the Financial Crimes Enforcement Network, at the Treasury Department.

"Got a minute to talk, Detective?"

"Not really."

Coleman looked past Santana toward Jordan Parrish's bronze marker. "She was your girl, right?"

Santana locked eyes with him. "I read the *Pioneer Press* article on you and your war record. So maybe you do know something about loss."

Coleman slipped his large, manicured hands in his pants pockets as his brown eyes drifted past Santana and engaged the sunlight splashing through the foliage. "I know you can't make the whole world your enemy when you lose someone you love. You wanna talk about survivors' guilt, I got a couple dozen stories."

"But that's not why you're here."

"Nope. Besides, it isn't the same. Marines volunteer to play in traffic."

"What's on your mind?"

"Got a tip for you. Stop nosing around Elysium Bank."

Santana stared directly into Coleman's deceptively calm eyes. "And why is that?"

Coleman offered a lazy smile. "You look like a man who could use some friendly advice."

"My turn," Santana said. "I'm investigating the cold case murder of Madison Porter."

"We know that, Detective."

"I'm going to find out who killed her. And if that involves someone at the bank, then nothing you say or do will get in my way."

"Who said anyone at the bank killed her?"

"No one. But someone working there might know why she was killed and who killed her."

Santana clicked the keyless entry button on the door handle of his SUV and opened the door.

Coleman stood right behind him. "Feds and cops don't mix, Santana. Like oil and water. You oughta know that."

Santana slid into the front seat and started the SUV. "So stay out of my way," he said, slamming the door and driving off.

Chapter 25

Kenny Coleman's warning to stay away from the employees at the Elysium Bank only made Santana more curious. Whether it could lead him to the person who murdered Madison Porter was an open question. But if he wanted answers, he figured he knew where to start.

Ashley Porter lived in a corner condo on the top floor of a high rise called the Riverfront Flats near downtown St. Paul. Wearing a peach-colored sweater that nearly matched her strawberry blond hair, tight black jeans, and heeled sandals, she ushered Santana into the condo, where he sat opposite her on a U-shaped sectional sofa around a fireplace in the living room. Over Porter's shoulder, Santana could see the Mississippi River through the floor-to-ceiling windows.

He noted a man's jacket hanging over the back of a dining room chair.

"It's Sunday," she said. "Don't you take the day off?"

"Depends on the case I'm working," Santana said, taking out his notebook and pen.

She stared at him for a time, her eyes reflecting the pale light spilling through the windows. She wasn't wearing makeup, so Santana could see more of the light brown freckles dusting her pale skin.

"Unless you've solved Maddie's murder," she said, "this could've waited till tomorrow. She's been dead four years. Why the sudden rush?"

"A pretty cold response considering she was your sister."

"What do you know about Maddie?" she said, her eyes suddenly as hard as ceramic.

"I know that her sister would want to help me solve her murder."

"You think I don't?"

"I think you haven't told me everything you know."

"About what?"

"Let's start with the bank." Santana glanced at his notebook before continuing. "You're a compliance officer at the bank."

"That's right."

"You oversee accounting, investment, and lending operations."

"Yes. But what's this got to do with Maddie's murder?"

Not wanting to compromise a Treasury Department investigation, Santana phrased his next question carefully. "Is there any reason why the bank would be out of compliance?"

Her pale complexion reddened. He watched her struggle to formulate an answer. Footsteps sounded behind him. Turning, he saw Derek Shelton enter the room.

"Detective Santana," he said. "Nice to see you again." Shelton reached out a hand.

As Santana stood and shook hands, he noted the smell of sandalwood in Shelton's cologne and the man's damp graying hair, as if he'd recently shaved and showered.

"You two live together?" he asked.

"That a sin?" Shelton said with a grin.

Probably frowned upon by the bank, Santana thought. If they even knew.

"We've been together for four years now," Ashley Porter said.

"We don't need rings to recognize our relationship, right, babe?" Shelton said, glancing at her.

She acknowledged the statement with a half-hearted grin.

"So, what brings you here on a beautiful Sunday afternoon?" Shelton asked.

"What else but Maddie's murder," Ashley Porter said.

"Of course," Shelton said, gesturing for Santana to take a seat.

"Detective Santana wanted to know if I had noticed any compliance issues at the bank," Porter said.

"Compliance issues?" Shelton said, a confused look on his face as he sat down on the couch a few feet from Santana.

"If Ms. Porter here had found something, she'd report the issue to you, Mr. Shelton, wouldn't she?" Santana asked.

"She certainly would," he said, staring at his girlfriend.

Santana waited.

Uncomfortable with the silence, Shelton said, "Nothing to report. Right, babe?"

Ashley Porter offered a tight smile and a little nod.

*   *   *

Late that afternoon Santana sat at the picnic table in the sun-spangled shade in his backyard overlooking the St. Croix. The long yard sloped toward the river. High above the river, gulls glided on the updrafts of air currents, their pointed wings lit by the sun.

He tossed a Frisbee to Gitana just as his personal cellphone rang.

"Hello, Rita," he said, noting her name on the caller ID. "How are you?"

"Hungry. How about dinner? My house."

"Gitana would love to see you."

"How about you?"

"Me, too," he said

After a quick shower and shave, Santana put Gitana in his SUV and drove to Rita Gamboni's house.

When they arrived, Rita hugged him, held him tightly for a time while she whispered in his ear, "I'm glad you're safely home, John."

She always had felt good in his arms.

Rita stepped back and looked into his eyes, her smile genuine and happy. Then she hugged Gitana and led them through the house to the shaded patio near the pool. A redwood fence around the backyard gave her some privacy and kept the neighborhood children from falling into the pool.

Santana sat down in a comfortable padded chair and took a sip from the bottle of Sam Adams sitting on the table.

"You remembered," he said.

"Of course."

Gamboni sat down in a chair opposite him. She stroked Gitana's back and baby-talked her.

Santana swallowed a sip of Sam Adams. "You know she loves everyone."

Rita smiled. "But some more than others."

She drank from her own bottle of Sam Adams and then said, "You look good, John. Rested."

"Lots of time on the Barcelona beach."

Her gaze slid off him for a moment. "I never heard from you after you left for Spain. I thought you'd stay in touch."

"I should have."

She raised her eyebrows as though surprised by his response. "How is your sister, Natalia?"

"Safe now."

"No Colombian cartel members after the two of you?"

"Not anymore."

"Well, that's good news."

Santana flashed on the last assassin's death, and how close he'd come to his own death.

While they waited for the steaks to grill, they ate the Caesar salad she'd prepared.

"Working on anything interesting?" Rita asked.

Santana told her about the Madison Porter cold case and Joel Ryker's unsolved murder.

"How's it going with the DEA agent?"

"You heard about the DEA's interest."

"No secret," she said. She stood, opened the built-in grill, and used a set of tongs to turn over the steaks.

"Bobbi Chacon is abrasive as hell but can handle herself."

"It's an important case."

"They all are."

Rita closed the grill cover and sat down at the table again. "Branigan is moving on."

"I figured. Where?"

"It's not official yet, but he's headed for the chief's position in Twin Falls, Idaho."

"Blue heaven," Santana said, noting how retired cops, primarily from LA, referred to the state.

"Smaller town. Less crime. While he collects his SPPD pension."

"And you're applying for Branigan's position."

"No," she said, holding his eyes. "I've applied for the Deputy Chief of Major Crimes. That position is opening. Are you surprised?"

"That you weren't happy working for the feds and all their bureaucratic BS? No. But I am surprised that you'd come back here."

"This is my home, John. I grew up in St. Paul. I'm familiar with the department. You weren't aware that I rented my home when I left?"

He shook his head.

"My plan was always to return when the time was right."

"Budgets are tight. Crime is up. How is this the right time?"

Rita's gaze drifted toward the pool, and when her eyes came back to Santana's face, they were quiet with thought.

"It feels right."

"What about the current deputy chief?" he asked.

"He called and asked me to apply."

"So he doesn't want the job?"

"He'll be moving up to assistant chief."

"So the AC will take Branigan's position."

She nodded.

"You're awfully confident about your chances. There have to be other qualified applicants."

She smiled faintly and looked away for a second.

"The fix is in, huh?" he said.

Her eyes connected with his once more. "I'm good at what I do. I deserve the job."

Santana drank some beer as smoke seeped out of the grill, drifted in the air.

"Be careful, Rita."

"What do you mean?"

"The city is on edge. Bureaucrats are looking for a scapegoat. That's why Branigan is cutting bait. He doesn't want to take the fall. Neither does the AC."

"I can handle the council. And the men around me."

Santana chuckled. "I've always liked that about you."

Her face was lit with the evening sun's glow through the trees as she looked at him.

"Is that all you liked about me?"

Embarrassed, Santana finished what was left of his beer.

"Why did you break up with me, John?"

"You know why."

"No, I don't."

"You got promoted to Homicide Commander. You'd be my boss."

"That was a convenient excuse."

"You wanted children. I didn't."

"We could've worked around that."

"The Cali cartel was hunting me. I didn't want to put you in danger."

"I can take care of myself."

Santana blew out a frustrated breath. "What do you want me to say?"

"The truth."

Santana wrestled with his response for a time. "Okay. How about breaking up was a mistake?"

"I agree."

He let a few seconds pass before he said, "I'm still dealing with Jordan Parrish's death."

Rita nodded and leaned forward. Speaking in a soft voice that was almost a whisper, she said, "Grief is the cost of love, John."

Chapter 26

On Monday morning Santana called Regions Hospital to ask about Christine Hammond and was told that she'd been released. When he asked if the hospital had an address for Hammond, he was transferred to the clinical site manager. After giving his name and badge number, he learned that she'd gone to the Hazelden Betty Ford Treatment Center in Center City, Minnesota, about a forty-five-minute drive from St. Paul. He needed to talk with Hammond and would have to set aside some time to make the drive.

When he arrived at the Law Enforcement Center that morning, Santana stopped by the Computer/Digital Forensics Lab, located on the third floor of the Griffin Building, to see Lynn Pierce. Like the LEC adjacent to it, the lab required a key card for entry. Santana had met Lynn Pierce when he returned to the department, but this was the first time he would be working directly with her.

She'd attended night school at the University of Minnesota while working days as a patrol officer, eventually completing a BS degree in computer science and engineering. In her spare time she'd earned black belts in Taekwondo and in Brazilian Jiu-Jitsu.

She was seated in a chair in front of a gray metal desk, eating raw carrots and broccoli out of a Tupperware container and drinking from a bottle of sparkling water. She had shoulder-length raven hair and high cheekbones like her Mdewakanton Sioux ancestors. She took Santana's inventory as he entered.

The former head of the computer forensic lab was a jazz lover, but Santana could hear the low sound of classical music in the background now.

She offered a nod. "You got my phone message."

Santana pulled up a chair and sat beside her. "What've you got?"

Pierce wiped her mouth with a napkin. "You familiar with the TOR web browser?"

"I know TOR stands for The Onion Router," Santana said. "That's about as far as my knowledge goes."

She cocked her head as if she couldn't fathom his lack of understanding. Then she blew out a breath and said, "TOR wraps your data in multiple layers of encryption, like an onion. It uses thousands of relays to conceal a user's location and usage from any surveillance, making it nearly impossible for your activity to be traced back to you. The US Navy developed it to protect government intelligence communications. You simply download and install it, then connect to the Internet just like you would with any other browser."

"So how were the Lozanos using it?"

"They were selling Desoxyn on the dark nets. Most products were delivered through the mail using vacuum-sealed bags to escape detection. Know anything about Desoxyn?"

"Contains a small amount of meth," Santana said. "Often used to treat ADHD. They had a pill-making machine in their residence."

Santana felt sure now that the Lozanos were cutting ties with El Mencho and his meth operation and going into business for themselves, a dangerous proposition.

"There's something else," Pierce said, pointing to the computer screen. "Take a look."

She tapped a few keys and opened a website entitled "SEXTO."

On the screen Santana saw a young, topless blond girl standing with her arms tied behind her back. The rope securing her hands was connected to a tall wooden frame that held her upright. Her face was blurred to conceal her identity. The shadow of a man loomed in the background.

Beneath the photo an advertisement read:

Like Serena, all our girls are set for auctions only. If you wish, we can kidnap a specific target for your needs. The service will be rather expensive, especially for targets outside the US. All girls are checked for STDs and pure if the profile says so.

The advertisement for the upcoming auction included her breast size and weight. Serena's starting bid was set at $150,000.

Santana felt a knot in his stomach and heat in his face.

"Bottom feeders of the criminal world," Pierce said. She picked up a stress ball in the shape of a globe from her desktop and began squeezing it.

"And the Lozanos were into this?"

"Don't know if they ever purchased a young woman," Pierce said. "But they might've been considering it."

"Can you locate the server?" Santana asked.

"Besides the TOR browser, there are various types of encryption, things like compromised IP addresses that point to somewhere else. Makes it difficult or impossible to determine where someone is and who they are."

"So we're out of luck."

Pierce shook her head. "We have Martin Lozano's cellphone. The beauty of Apple products is that the company wants you to be able to browse your missed calls on multiple devices. That's why Apple uses iCloud to sync your data between all devices associated with the same Apple ID. As soon as you activate iCloud, your iPhone sends nearly everything to it—your text messages, your call history, your notes. Most users accept it or don't realize they're giving away a lot of personal information."

"How long is the call history stored?"

"Four months. You can manually delete a call, and it'll get deleted on iCloud's servers and all your devices."

Pierce held out a manila folder. "But handing out your call history to Apple has its downside." She smiled faintly. "I wrote up a summary report for Martin Lozano's iPhone and computer.

Everything you need is in there," she said. "Let me know if you have questions."

*   *   *

At his desk in the Homicide and Robbery Unit, Santana opened the manila folder that Lynn Pierce had given him. She'd first made a digital copy of Martin Lozano's computer hard drive in case she ever had to testify in court about anything she'd found in his computer. Once into the device, she was able to see much more than just the data on the drives. She'd examined the log files, which included Lozano's Google search history, photo galleries, online chats, and his deleted items. Besides the report on the SEXTO website, Santana found nothing incriminating in the computer information Pierce had provided. So he turned his attention to Pierce's reports about Martin Lozano's iPhone.

She'd viewed Lozano's call logs, photos, videos, texts, contacts, banking details, GPS location history, and emails, along with his third party apps like Facebook, WhatsApp, and Messenger, as well as his deleted content.

Going through a person's computer or iPhone, Santana thought, was like going through his mind.

He removed Martin Lozano's call list from the folder. Lynn Pierce had arranged the phone numbers in order from most frequently to least frequently called or received. Most of the phone numbers were in Lozano's contact list and included a personal or business name. As Santana worked his way through the numbers, his eyes stopped and focused on one of the businesses listed in the call record.

Elysium Bank.

The same bank where Ellis Taylor had been killed. The same bank where Madison Porter's sister Ashley worked, along with her boyfriend, Derek Shelton. The same bank that Kenny Coleman and the Treasury Department were looking into. Could the Lozanos be laundering money through the bank? Did Ashley Porter and Derek Shelton know about it? Were they involved in the scheme? Santana needed to talk to Kenny Coleman again. See if the agent would give up some information.

For now Santana focused his attention on the contact numbers that contained no information. He figured many were robo calls—but not all of them.

Using a reverse directory, he was able to pinpoint the source of most phone numbers. Unlike a standard telephone directory, where the user had individual details such as a name and address, a reverse telephone directory allowed him to search by a telephone number in order to retrieve the details.

As he scanned the list of phone numbers, one caught his attention. He wasn't sure why at first. Then he remembered. The numbers 328-6328 spelled EAT MEAT.

Gordon Grant had gotten a laugh out of it. Santana wasn't laughing now.

He counted fifteen calls between Grant and Martin Lozano over a three-month period. A lot of calls when Grant claimed all Lozano wanted was some plumbing fixed.

Santana's cellphone rang. He recognized the number. Bobbi Chacon.

No doubt wondering where he was and what he was doing to solve Joel Ryker's murder. He debated whether or not he wanted to speak to her. He knew she'd continue calling till he relented, so he answered after four rings.

"I haven't heard from you since Friday evening," she said, her voice sharp with anger.

"It's Monday."

"Yeah. So what?"

Leaving out the fact that he'd interviewed Ashley Porter and her boyfriend, Derek Shelton, on Sunday afternoon, he said, "So I wasn't working this weekend. Were you?"

"I've spent a lovely weekend sitting on my ass in my hotel room, waiting for a phone call from you."

"You aren't looking for a more permanent place to live?"

"Not if I can help it."

"If I had information, I'd let you know," Santana said.

"I'd like to believe that."

"So believe it."

Chacon went silent for a time before saying, "I'm going nuts sitting here."

"Take a walk. See the sights."

"Like that's gonna help."

"You never know."

"I'm not a tourist. My work is my . . ."

"Life?" Santana said.

"Yeah. It is. 'Bout the same for you, isn't it?"

Santana hated to admit she was right.

"You're working on that cold case, aren't you?"

"I am."

"We're supposed to be working together to solve Joel Ryker's murder."

"I can walk and chew gum at the same time."

"That's cute, Santana. You'd better call me the minute you have something."

"I will," he said, disconnecting.

Then he dialed Gordon Grant's number.

"Is this about the shooting again?" Grant asked.

"Something else."

Grant hesitated. "So what is it?"

"I'd rather speak to you in person, Mr. Grant. Are you at home?"

"Yes, but—"

"See you soon," Santana said, cutting off the call.

*   *   *

Bobbi Chacon was fuming. Santana was purposely avoiding her. She was sure of it. Working on that damn cold case. Well, she thought, she didn't need him to find out who'd killed Joel. She'd work the case alone. Fuck Santana.

She'd start at the Lozanos' house. Get a feel for the place where it all went down, where she'd lost her partner—and lover. Then she'd brace Dylan Walsh. So what if he'd lawyered up? She'd seen his kind before and knew just how to deal with him.

*　　*　　*

Eddie Machado was sitting in his SUV a few doors down from the Lozanos' house when a white Ford Mustang Shelby GT 350 parked along the opposite curb in front of the house. Eddie recognized the muscle car with the blue stripe running from the trunk, across the roof, hood, and grill because El Mencho had one with the same colors. Eddie had never driven it, but he'd seen it driven, heard the shriek that sounded more Ferrari than Ford, generated by the flat-crank V-8 engine that produced 526 of horsepower and 8,250 rpm.

Eddie watched as a woman got out of the Mustang and headed for Lozanos' front door.

A uniformed cop stood like a sentinel on the front stoop, his black-and-white parked directly in front of the Mustang. The strip of yellow crime scene tape across the door fluttered in the breeze.

Eddie couldn't see what was hanging from the lanyard around the woman's neck, but he guessed it was a badge when she held it up for the uniform to see.

The patrol officer wrote something on the clipboard in his hand, opened the front door, and held up the crime scene tape as she slid under it.

While Eddie waited for her to come out, he recalled the uneventful drive from Albuquerque to St. Paul. He'd rented a Hyundai Santa Fe after ditching Mitch's Jeep in Wichita. Tossed the license plates from the Toyota he'd used to cross the border into a dumpster. A contact in Wichita had provided him with a new ID. He was now Eduardo Alvarez, pharmaceutical salesman. He chuckled.

Periodically, Eddie had checked the *Albuquerque Journal* using Google, searching for information on Mitch the queer's death, but found nothing. Apparently, no one had discovered the body, which was good news. He doubted anyone could connect him to the murder, but he wanted to get back to Mexico as quickly as possible in case he figured wrong. That meant finding the missing half-million dollars the Lozanos owed El Mencho. Eddie had planned to burgle the house. See if he could find something that would lead him to the money. But the lady cop had given him another idea.

Twenty minutes later she reappeared and headed for the Mustang. When she drove off, Eddie followed.

Chapter 27

Santana entered Gordon Grant's yard through an unlocked gate in the five-foot-high wooden fence and knocked on the front door. Grant let him in and led him into a cramped living room containing a jumble of second-hand furniture and art. Stacks of magazines and newspapers filled three corners. A laptop computer sat on a small desk in the other corner. The house smelled of dust and age. If Grant weren't a hoarder, he'd soon be one, Santana thought.

Grant gestured for Santana to take a seat on the well-worn couch and then sat opposite him in an old rocking chair, his strap undershirt and jeans spotted with paint stains.

When Santana had his notebook and pen in hand he said, "You're a collector, Mr. Grant."

Grant scanned the room as if suddenly coming to the same realization. "Lots of cheap things at garage sales. Good things."

"You collect anything else?"

He cocked his head. "Like what?"

"I'm asking you."

Grant thought about it for a moment. "Well, I used to collect stamps and then coins. But I gave it up. Should've collected baseball cards. Many I had when I was a kid are worth a fortune now." He gave a regretful shake of his head.

"Lived here long?"

"Goin' on ten years. Nice neighborhood. 'Cept for the . . ."

"Murder," Santana said.

"Yeah."

"How well did you know the Porter family, Mr. Grant?"

"That what this is about?"

Santana nodded.

"You got the cold case now?"

"That's right. You know something about cold cases—or this case in particular?"

"All I know is what I seen on TV."

"But you knew the mother, Mrs. Porter."

"Not well."

Santana was tempted to ask Grant about the photo of Grant and Madison Porter he'd seen taped on the bedroom wall, but he didn't want Grant to know he'd observed it by peeking through a back window, or that he'd taken snapshots of the photo using his cellphone camera.

"What about Mrs. Porter's daughter, Madison?"

"I seen her around. Usually running. She'd wave. I'd wave back."

Santana wanted to search Grant's bedroom, get his hands on the photo, but he needed either a warrant or an excuse. He had no probable cause for a warrant, so he went with the next best option.

"Mind if I use your bathroom, Mr. Grant?"

Grant froze for a moment, his eyes focused inward.

"Mr. Grant?"

"Actually," he said, his eyes focusing on Santana again, "the toilet isn't working." He offered a false smile. "I've got a plumber coming out later today to repair it."

"You're a maintenance man but can't repair your own toilet?"

"I . . . ah . . . don't have the parts," he said with a crooked smile. "And I don't wanna take the time to buy 'em. Easier to have someone come out."

Santana knew it was a lie. But if Grant did have something to do with Madison Porter's murder, Santana had to play it by the book or risk having the case thrown out. He decided to squeeze Grant. See what came out.

"You ever take any photos of young girls?"

He shook his head. "Why would I do that?"

"I'm asking."

"Nah," he said, waving the question away as if swatting a pesky fly.

"Not even a photo of Madison Porter?"

Grant swallowed hard. "I don't think so."

"You don't think so."

"No," he said, shaking his head.

"So you're not sure if you took a photo of her or not."

Grant's thin lips curled in a lopsided grin. "Like I just said. Don't know why I would."

"I see."

"No, I don't think you do. A detective questioned me about the girl's murder four years ago."

"I know that," Santana said, wondering why Darnell Robinson and Ellis Taylor hadn't done a background check on Grant. They should've discovered he'd had a sex offense conviction. Santana recalled that Robinson had interviewed Grant and written the summary. Was it an oversight on his part or something else?

"Well, then you know I had nothing to do with the Porter girl's murder."

"And how do I know that?"

"Because I'm telling you," he said, his hands clenching and unclenching. "Are you accusing me of something?"

"Not yet."

Grant stood. "I think it's time you left."

Santana looked at his watch. "I've got plenty of time."

"I don't," Grant said.

"Sit down and tell me about your relationship with Martin Lozano."

"I don't have one."

"Yet you called Lozano fifteen times over a three-month period."

"What?" Grant's body had stiffened, and his eyes had a deer-in-the-headlights look.

"You heard me," Santana said.

Beads of sweat had broken out on Grant's forehead. He sank slowly into the rocking chair again.

Santana continued. "I'll bet if I got a warrant for Lozanos' call records prior to three months ago, your phone number would be on those as well." Santana flipped back a few pages in his notebook. "You told me before you'd only spoken to Lozano— let me make sure I have this correct," Santana said, studying the notebook page. "Yes, you said you'd talked to him only once about fixing a shower head and leaky pipe."

Grant sprang out of the chair and came at Santana.

Santana dropped the notebook but held onto the pen as he vaulted out of his chair and slipped the straight punch that Grant launched with his big, knuckled right hand. Clutching the pen tightly in his hand, Santana jabbed the point into the fleshy inner part of Grant's right arm just above the elbow and below the bicep.

Grant bellowed in pain and grabbed his right arm.

Keeping his head low and his chin tucked into his chest, Santana moved inside and hammered Grant's mid-section with a left/right combination. As the air rushed out of Grant, Santana stepped back and threw a short right uppercut that caught Grant flush on the chin.

The big man crashed against the computer desk behind him, his eyes rolling back in his head. A manila folder fell to the floor as Grant rolled off the desk and tumbled unconscious face first onto the carpet.

"Assaulting a police officer. Stupid move," Santana muttered as he shook the numbness out of his right hand. He removed the pair of handcuffs from the holder attached to the back of his belt, held them by the chain, and speedcuffed Grant by pressing the cuffs onto Grant's left and right wrist in one fast motion.

Once he'd double-locked the cuffs, he searched Grant for weapons and then squatted beside the five-by-seven photographs of bound and naked young women that had spilled out of the manila folder and now lay scattered on the floor beside Grant. The photos reminded Santana of the image of the young woman he'd seen on the SEXTO website and rekindled embers of anger smoldering in his gut. He wondered now if Gordon Grant had murdered Madison Porter and if evidence of her murder existed in the house.

Santana knew he needed a search warrant to collect any evidence. He also knew that as long as the big man remained unconscious, whatever he did now, Grant wouldn't know about it and couldn't testify against him in court. He decided to conduct a quick confirmatory search to determine if more evidence was present. If he found something related to the sexually explicit photos of sex-trafficked young women, then he'd seek a warrant to conduct a lawful search and *discover* the evidence needed to convict Gordon Grant.

After gloving up, Santana started his search in the master bedroom that smelled of sweat and body odor. Dirty clothes had been tossed in the corners and on the stained bedspread and sheets of the double bed.

Madison Porter's photograph was still taped to the wall above the headboard along with three other photos. One of those photos caught his attention. Where had he seen the blond hair and face before? Then it hit him. Christine Hammond. The blonde at Dylan Walsh's apartment the day he and Chacon took down Jamal Washburn and Dean Moody. She looked younger in the photo, but it was Hammond.

Santana found nothing of substance in the closet, but inside the nightstand drawer he discovered a stack of pornographic DVDs featuring old men with young girls and a pair of small keys.

Taking the keys from the drawer, Santana conducted a cursory search of the bathroom, a mostly empty guest bedroom, and the kitchen, where he noted a padlocked door.

One of the keys he'd found in the nightstand drawer worked on the padlock. He flipped back the hasp, opened the door, and flicked on the light switch attached to the wall just inside the door. Nothing.

Hello darkness.

Santana pulled a small Maglite flashlight from a coat pocket and held the light away from his body in an icepick grip so the beam of light wouldn't make him the target. Then he slipped his Glock out of the holster on his right hip and followed the beam down the set of wooden stairs into a musty, damp, pitch-black basement.

He played the beam across the concrete walls, the water heater, and the windows that had interior locks and aluminum foil over the glass. At the far end of the basement to his left, drywall panels had been nailed to studs, creating a small room with a wooden padlocked door that had no handle. Using the second key, he opened the padlock and the three-quarter-inch-thick plywood door.

In the beam of light Santana saw women's underwear, shoes, a video camera attached to a tripod, bondage cuffs, fetish ropes, and stacks of CDs and photo albums cluttering the floor, the single bed, and the soiled, bare mattress. Using a Sharpie, someone had scrawled, "My Mom and Dad love me" on the wall above the headboard.

Santana relocked the plywood door and went back upstairs, locking the basement door behind him. He returned the set of keys to the nightstand drawer and went into the living room, where Gordon Grant was regaining consciousness.

Santana got him off the floor and into the rocker, where he read him his rights off the card he kept in his badge wallet.

"Do you understand these rights as they have been read to you?"

"Yeah," Grant mumbled.

Santana then placed the photos of the naked young women back inside the manila folder and sat on the sofa across from Grant.

Holding the folder up in front of Grant, Santana said, "Tell me about the photos."

Grant sat silently with his lips pressed together, his eyes measuring Santana as if he were looking down a gun barrel.

"Who are the girls?" Santana asked again.

"How the hell would I know? I printed the photos off an Internet website. Somethin' wrong with that?"

"If they're underage."

Grant shook his head. "Don't look underage to me."

Santana placed the folder in his lap. He wanted to ask Grant about the leather wrist restraints and ropes, the women's clothes and shoes, the video camera and CDs in the basement room, but if he did, Grant would know he'd searched the place without a warrant. So Santana steered the conversation in a different direction.

Nodding at the computer, he said, "What do you suppose forensics will find on your hard drive, Grant?"

"Ain't nothin' wrong with lookin' at porn."

"But there is something wrong with sex trafficking."

"You've got no proof of that," he said, his voice rising.

"Not yet. But I'm sure I can add sex trafficking and murder to the charge of assaulting a police officer."

Grant's eyes grew wide. "Murder? What the hell you talking about?"

"Madison Porter."

"Shit," Grant said with a shake of his head. "I never killed that girl."

"I think we'll find evidence that she's been in this house. What do you think?"

Grant bit his bottom lip as if stifling a response.

Santana drove Gordon Grant to Regions Hospital to have the wound in his arm treated before booking him into the Ramsey County jail at the LEC. Then, using a search warrant template on his laptop, he filled in blanks about where he wanted to search and what he was looking for. It took him most of the afternoon to complete it and to get a signature from an administrative judge.

Together with the Forensic Services Unit, Santana collected evidence and DNA from Grant's house, including a package of what Santana suspected were roofies, one of the street names for Rohypnol, a common date rape drug.

Santana took the roofies to forensics and the computer, camera equipment, and the CDs from the locked room in the basement to Lynn Pierce and asked her to look at them as soon as possible.

*　　*　　*

Wearing a silk bathrobe, his eyes glazed, the skunky odor of weed emanating from the smoke drifting in the air behind him, Dylan Walsh held open his front door and squinted at Bobbi Chacon as if she were a strange object.

Chacon brushed past him.

"Hey," he said, turning to peer at her. "You can't come in here."

"Who's gonna stop me?" Chacon said, getting in his face.

Walsh stepped back, raised a hand in a stopping gesture. "Take it easy."

"Shut the door and open a window, for chrissake," Chacon said. "Smells like a cannabis dispensary in here."

Walsh followed her directive and then plopped down on the couch as if the effort had exhausted him.

Chacon stood on the other side of the coffee table from him with her arms crossed.

Walsh stared at the badge hanging from the lanyard around Chacon's neck. Then his eyes grew wide with recognition. "I remember you now. You're DEA."

"That's right. And we can add another drug charge to the previous charges."

"You're here to bust me?"

"Not if you play it straight."

"How so?"

"Tell me about Joel Ryker's murder," she said.

"Who's he?"

"Don't get cute."

"Talk to my lawyer," Walsh said with a dismissive wave.

Chacon looked from one side of the room to the other. "Don't see him here."

Walsh leaned back on the sofa. Clasped his hands behind his head. Casual. Unconcerned. "I don't have to tell you anything."

Chacon kicked the edge of the coffee table. Hard. It slammed against Walsh's shins.

"Ow!" he yelped, sitting up. He pushed the coffee table back a few inches and rubbed his shins with his hands. "That hurt."

Chacon bent over, grabbed the front of Walsh's bathrobe, scratching his cheek in the process, and looked him straight in the eyes. "Someone killed my partner, asshole. You know who did it. And you're gonna tell me, lawyer or no lawyer."

Walsh gently touched his cheek and then shook his head, the look of pain on his face suddenly dissolving into one of fear and recognition. "I don't know who killed your partner. I had nothin' to do with it. And I don't know what happened to the money either."

Chacon released him and straightened up, her hands fisted on her hips. "Who said anything about money?"

Walsh opened his mouth but said nothing.

"How'd you know about the money, Walsh, if you had nothing to do with Ryker's murder?"

"I . . . ah . . ."

"I'm losing patience."

Walsh spread his hands. "Washburn and Moody told me about it."

"What else did they tell you?"

"They wanted me to sell the meth they smuggled up from Tucson. Wanted to split the sales money."

"So you're a distributor for El Mencho."

"Sounds like some Mexican drug dealer."

"Not *some* Mexican drug dealer. *The* Mexican drug dealer."

"I worked for the Lozanos. Small time. Nothin' big. I don't ask where the meth comes from."

Chacon thought for a time. "Tell me about your girlfriend, the blonde that was here before."

"Christine isn't my girlfriend."

"Probably news to her," Chacon said.

"She's nobody."

"Wrong, Walsh. You're nobody."

He shrugged. "But my old man is somebody."

"That supposed to frighten me?"

"Oh, it will. Soon as I tell my lawyer about this."

Chacon kicked the coffee table again, the opposite edge slamming into Walsh's shins once more.

"Jesus!" he squealed.

"The blonde."

Rubbing his shins in pain, Walsh said. "She's nobod . . ." He stopped. "She's a hooker. High-class one. At least she was till she got on the meth."

"Who was her pimp?"

"She didn't have a pimp. She worked out of a service."

"Where?"

"Cathedral Hill," Walsh said.

Same place Santana had mentioned, she thought. "Not sure where that is. Got an address?"

"I don't know."

Chacon rested her boot on the edge of the table and leaned forward. "Want to think about that again, Walsh?"

"Maybe I've got the address around somewhere," he said, rubbing his shins.

Chapter 28

On Tuesday morning Lynn Pierce was waiting for Santana at the SPPD's forensic lab. Pierce had pulled up two chairs in front of a large computer screen. The evidence envelopes containing the CDs collected from Gordon Grant's basement were stacked beside it. The seals had been broken. Santana could see where he'd written his name and today's date on the envelopes.

Now that Pierce had broken the seals, she would have to indicate possession of the evidence on the chain of custody log, which was not unusual. Attorneys often opened evidence envelopes prior to presentation at trial for lab analysis and examination. As long as the officer who signed out the envelope resealed it and placed his or her mark and date on the seal after it was returned, the chain of custody would be maintained and withstand any legal challenge.

"Appreciate the quick turnaround," Santana said.

"No problem. I wanted you to see this."

She clicked on the CD. When it opened, Santana recognized the locked basement room with the single mattress—and the young blond woman lying naked on it.

Christine Hammond.

Her arms were stretched out behind her head, her wrists and ankles tied to the bedposts with leather straps. With her half-closed eyes, slack face, and mouth slightly open, Santana figured she'd been drugged.

"It's graphic," Pierce said, glancing at Santana.

"Play it," he said.

A naked, thick-bodied man with a black hood over his head appeared in the video. His back was turned to the camera. There were no birthmarks or tattoos on the man's backside and bare arms.

The man mounted Christine Hammond and entered her roughly as she cried out in pain.

Santana felt his jaw tighten, heard his teeth grinding. He recalled descending the stairs in Grant's house, enveloped in darkness.

"Are all the CDs like this?" he asked.

"The ones I've looked at."

"Are these men part of SEXTO?"

"I believe so."

"How do you know?"

"I've been working with Narco/Vice. They're working with the feds."

"Seems like everyone around here is," Santana said.

"The SEXTO investigation is part of Operation Predator. Feds are targeting sexual predators and traffickers. Talk to Gabe Thornton in Narco/Vice. He can fill in the details."

"Have you seen the faces of any of the men?"

"Sorry," she said with a shake of her head.

"Keep looking. We need to put a face with a name."

"Will do," Pierce said.

"How far do the CDs go back?"

"Five years."

"Can you pull the ones from four years ago?"

Pierce nodded and scanned her notes. "Only two from that time period," she said, pulling a CD out of an envelope. "What are we looking for?"

"A young woman named Madison Porter. She was murdered four years ago. Gordon Grant lived on the same block and knew the family."

"You think he's the perp who killed her?"

"He's my prime suspect."

Pierce slid a CD into the USB SuperDrive attached to her computer.

"She was killed on July sixteenth," Santana said. "Let's work backward from there."

What followed was a series of short vignettes like the one he'd seen with Christine Hammond. A naked man wearing only a black hood over his face would rape a young woman lying on a soiled mattress. The young woman in each scene was different. As far as Santana could tell, so were the men.

The video timestamps were about a month apart. Pierce had fast-forwarded through seven vignettes, but Madison Porter appeared in none of them.

*   *   *

Santana headed for the Narco/Vice Unit, where he found Gabe Thornton, the undercover narc Lynn Pierce had told him to see. Santana had never worked with him, but Thornton had a good reputation, high arrest stats, and a nose for solid information.

Thornton sat at his desk, hunched over an open file folder. His rolled-up sleeves revealed a sneaking tiger tattoo on his deeply tanned left forearm. A rubber band held his dark hair in a ponytail, and a thick, dark beard covered his cheeks.

His chocolate-colored eyes squinted in thought as he looked up and saw Santana standing in front of his cubicle. "Hey, Santana. What's up?"

"'SEXTO,'" Santana said.

Using the toe of one boot, Thornton pushed a straight-back chair out from the front of his desk toward Santana. "Have a seat."

Santana sat down.

"This related to something you're working on?" Thornton asked.

Santana nodded. "Arrested a guy yesterday named Gordon Grant. I believe he's a member."

Thornton's eyes lit with interest as he straightened up.

"Problem is, he's lawyered up," Santana said.

"Doesn't mean you can't take a run at him."

"I'll set it up with the DA. What do you have?"

Thornton thought for a moment before beginning. "A few months ago we arrested a small-time dealer and pedophile advocate named Timothy Ritter."

"Advocate?"

"Yeah. Ritter claims the emotional and psychological damage children suffer when they have sex with adults isn't caused by having sex with adults."

"So what's the cause?"

"All the outrage made by the police, social workers, and parents. Ritter says if pedophiles were just left alone to have sex with kids, everything would be fine. Children can consent to sexual relations. Thinks the law should be changed so the age of consent is ten years of age."

"You can't fix stupid," Santana said.

"Or insane," Thornton said.

"What does Ritter have to do with SEXTO?"

"He's one of the founders. Had more than a million images and videos of children and teens being sexually abused on his computer. Some of the most demented images I've ever seen." Thornton shook his head. "Man, I don't get why these sick fuckers are into this shit."

"How'd you get Ritter?"

"He tried to manipulate a mentally handicapped twelve-year-old girl into performing oral sex. We got a search warrant for his home. Found the DVDs and thumb drives containing thousands of images and videos depicting naked children and teens and adults sexually assaulting them. One of the recovered images displayed the name of a local high school girl. Ritter had changed his appearance and convinced her he was eighteen. He's actually thirty. They had sex at multiple locations over the course of a year. He took pictures and videos of their sexual activity, stored them on the electronic devices, and uploaded them onto the SEXTO website. She was fifteen years old at the time. We interviewed the girl, and she's agreed to testify against him."

Thornton opened a thermos on his desk and added fresh coffee to a mug with writing on the side that read:

**I don't know what I'd do without coffee.
I'm guessing 25 to life.**

Santana declined his offer of a cup.

Thornton said, "So the rule is that prospective SEXTO members have to create and share images and videos of adults molesting children and teens in order to join the group and to keep their membership. Members who didn't follow the rule were expelled. They communicated using aliases rather than their actual names. Timothy Ritter controlled membership."

"Know how many men are involved?"

Thornton sipped the steaming coffee and set the mug on the desktop. "At least thirty we've ID'd so far."

"Local?"

"Some are."

"I need the names."

"I'll email you a list."

"How'd they connect?"

"The way most of these sick bastards connect. Through the Internet, the Dark Web, porn sites."

Thornton drank more coffee and said, "What's Homicide's connection to Grant?"

"He might've murdered a teenager named Madison Porter. She was killed four years ago. I'm working her cold case."

"You gotta keep me in the loop on this, Santana."

"I will. One more question. What do you know about a high-class escort service in Cathedral Hill?"

Thornton thought about it for a time. Then he leaned back in his swivel chair and clasped his thick hands behind his head. "How'd you come by this information?"

Santana considered it an unusual question to ask, but he let it slide. "Low-level drug dealer I busted."

"Nice work," Thornton said with a crooked smile.

"And the escort service?"

"This related to the drug bust?"

"Could be. Why?"

"Woman who supposedly runs the service calls herself Dominique Lejeune."

"Supposedly?"

"We've never been able to prove anything."

"So what about Lejeune?"

"Real name is Carla Rossi. Busted a number of times for prostitution about ten years ago. Then she fell off the radar for seven or eight years. When she resurfaced, she'd changed her name and her location from a street corner to a mansion in Cathedral Hill."

"How did she go about that?"

"Somebody financed the operation and set her up."

"Any idea who?"

Thornton shook his head. "That place is strictly off limits."

"You must have an idea who's protecting the place."

"Yeah. Somebody way above my pay grade. That's as far as I'm taking it."

Santana stood. "Thanks for your help."

"Hey, Santana. One thing I learned diving into this shit over the years. Evil exists, even in places we least expect it."

"Believe me, I know."

* * *

That afternoon in an interview room at the LEC, Santana sat across the table from Gordon Grant and a defense attorney named Arthur Harrison. With his perfectly coiffed black hair, expensive suit, manicured nails, and pencil-thin mustache, Harrison looked every bit the part of a slick, high-priced attorney in one of St. Paul's most prestigious law firms.

Santana wondered how a maintenance man like Grant could afford him.

He pointed to an evidence envelope in front of him and locked eyes with Grant. "There's a CD in this envelope. We found a number of them in the basement room where you were video-taping and participating in raping young women."

"I never—"

Harrison held up his hand, stopping Grant in mid-sentence.

"My client is here as a courtesy, Detective," Harrison said with a false smile that showed off his bright white teeth. "He doesn't have to answer any questions."

Santana opened a second evidence envelope and removed the photos of Madison Porter and Christine Hammond. Sliding the photos to the middle of the table where Grant could see them, he said, "Tell me about these photos that were taped to the wall in your bedroom."

Harrison spoke before Grant could respond. "My client has nothing to say."

Santana opened a file folder and looked at Harrison and then at the first paper in the folder. "Receiving, recruiting, enticing, harboring, providing, or obtaining by any means an individual to aid in the prostitution of the individual" or "receiving profit or anything of value, knowing or having reason to know, it is derived from sex trafficking."

"I'm well aware of the Minnesota statute," Harrison said.

"You'd better be, because your client is looking at a long stretch and hard time, especially for child pornographers and molesters." Santana looked directly at Grant. "If this goes to trial, you're going down. You want a plea deal, you'd better start talking now, before charges are filed. And you're the prime suspect in the murder of Madison Porter."

"I don't know what the hell you're—"

Harrison put a hand on Grant's forearm in a stopping gesture.

Grant pulled his arm away. "I sure as hell didn't kill Madison Porter."

"Gordon," Harrison warned.

"What was Madison Porter's photo doing in your bedroom?" Santana asked.

"I take pictures of pretty girls."

"Just pictures?"

Grant shrugged.

"We also found roofies in your basement. Add the illegal drugs to the DA's charges."

Grant sat quietly for a few beats. Then he said, "What do you want to know?"

"I highly advise against you talking," Harrison said to Grant.

"I'm not gonna incriminate myself."

"Tell me about SEXTO," Santana said.

"It's a bunch of rich guys who get off watching homemade porn."

"Have to do better than that," Santana said.

"It's an online forum. Men contribute photos and videos."

"I know that."

"Then what the hell *do* you want to know?"

"Tell me about the young women who are sex trafficked."

"Don't have a clue about that," Grant said.

"What do you know about a group of men belonging to the After Dark Club?"

Grant rubbed his chin. "Rich guys with high-priced escorts. That's all I know."

"Was Martin Lozano a member?"

"Don't know."

Santana pulled out a second sheet of paper from the folder and pushed it across the table in front of Grant. Gabe Thornton had emailed him the list this morning. The men on the list had been arrested as part of Operation Predator.

"Did any of these men participate in the rapes of young women in your basement?" Santana asked.

Arthur Harrison placed a hand on top of the sheet and looked at Santana. "What's the DA's offer?"

"That's up to him. But I can guarantee you there won't be a plea deal without your client's cooperation."

"Not good enough, Detective." Harrison stood and picked up his briefcase. "We're done here."

Harrison knocked on the door. A sheriff's deputy opened it.

"Mr. Grant is ready to return to his cell."

Grant sat stiffly in his chair, staring at Santana.

"Gordon," Harrison said in a threatening voice. "I'll have you out soon on bail."

"Not likely," Santana said. Turning his attention to Arthur Harrison, he said, "Where did your client get the money to hire you, counselor?"

"I do a lot of pro bono work."

"For sex offenders?"

Harrison's complexion darkened. "Gordon," he said.

Grant got up and headed for the door.

"Think about it," Santana said to Grant. "Time is running out."

*   *   *

Early that evening while he was eating dinner at his house, Santana saw an article in the *Pioneer Press* about an art retrospective currently being held at a St. Paul gallery. Santana wasn't familiar with the featured artist or his work, but he was familiar with one of the volunteers quoted in the article.

Ashley Porter, Madison Porter's sister.

The gallery was located on the first floor of a large two-story Romanesque home on Fairmont Avenue. The home was originally owned by a prominent St. Paul architect and was listed in the National Register of Historic Places.

"We feature some of the best Minnesota and regional artists," Ashley Porter said.

They were standing in front of a collection of impasto paintings of brightly colored landscapes.

The aqua green, knee-length jacket dress she wore accented her strawberry blond hair.

"How long have you volunteered here?" Santana asked.

"About two years now." She glanced at her watch. "The gallery closes in thirty minutes, so we don't have much time."

"Perhaps we could meet afterward."

"I'm meeting Derek for a drink."

"Your 'significant other.'"

"Right," she said with a tight smile.

There were few people in the gallery and no one in close proximity.

"You have some new information about Maddie's death?" she asked.

"How well did you know Gordon Grant?"

Ashley Porter's mouth dropped open momentarily in surprise, but her complexion had turned ashen.

"Grant was your neighbor when your sister was murdered."

She lowered herself into a canvas-back chair against the wall, her eyes frozen on some distant point. "Yes. I remember."

Santana sat in the matching chair beside her.

She looked at him for a time, her eyes searching his face. "You think he killed Maddie?"

"He's a suspect."

"I never really *knew* him," she said. "And rarely saw him."

"Did your sister ever talk about Grant?"

"Not that I recall."

Santana looked at the notes he'd written in his notebook before asking the next question. "Are you familiar with the works of Salvador Dalí?"

"Vaguely. He's not one of my favorites. Why do you ask?"

Santana ignored the question. "Is Derek Shelton familiar with Dalí's work?"

She hesitated. "Well, I don't think so. You'd have to ask him."

"Does Derek ever volunteer here?"

"Oh, he's way too busy."

Doing what? Santana wondered.

Chapter 29

On Wednesday morning Santana went to see Karen Wong, a psychologist who'd recently moved her office into a townhome near downtown St. Paul, downsizing from a larger brownstone after the death of her husband. Besides her private practice, Wong treated SPPD officers who were involved in shootings, referred to her for mandatory counseling through the Employee Assistance Program.

It was how Santana had first come to know Wong.

The EAP was also available to anyone in the department who sought counseling for mental health issues, though the majority of police officers were reluctant to admit that they needed help or counseling. Much of the reluctance to seek counseling could be attributed to the macho culture that existed in all police departments. It didn't help that those seeking EAP counseling were derisively known throughout the department as "the rubber gun squad."

Clients used a separate entrance to Karen Wong's office.

"Nice to see you again, Detective Santana," she said as she held open the side door.

The voice belonged to an attractive Asian woman with a heart-shaped face and full black hair cut even with the nape of her neck. She wore it brushed across her forehead so that it drew attention to her large brown eyes. In her beige bouclé dress and Lurex threaded jacket, she projected a professional and elegant appearance.

Santana sat on the comfortable print sofa and set his briefcase in his lap, noting that she'd brought much of the Chinese furnishings from her previous office.

On one of the black-lacquer end tables stood a five-by-seven framed photograph of Karen Wong and her late husband,

George. He was Caucasian and was fifteen years older than his wife. Santana was out of the country at the time of George's death, but had online access to the two newspapers in town and had seen the announcement. Now he saw that Karen Wong still wore a large diamond on the third finger of her left hand.

She placed her ergonomically correct chair in such a way that the direction she and a client faced made an X with one another. Santana understood that the arrangement allowed a client to make eye contact with her and to easily look away when discussing a particularly difficult subject. There was no coffee table or psychological barrier between them, which allowed for open conversation. A large clock hung on the wall behind the sofa, allowing Karen Wong to see the time without looking at her watch.

"So," she said with an encouraging smile, "you wanted to talk to me about a case you're working."

"Yes. It's a cold case involving the murder of a sixteen-year-old girl."

"What was her name?"

"Madison Porter."

She nodded. "I remember reading about her murder in the newspaper. A very tragic case."

"We have a possible suspect in custody. Forensics found a picture of Madison in his bedroom, along with photos of bound young women on his computer from sex trafficking websites. He also had a film studio set up in a room in his basement, where he videotaped men having sex with underage girls. He made CDs and uploaded the videos to a website that trafficked in this porn."

"Were the women in the photos and CDs Madison Porter's age?"

"Look to be. Why?"

"We could be talking about ephebophilia."

"Never heard of it," Santana said.

"It's an attraction for older adolescents around fifteen to eighteen years old. Hebephilia is a sexual preference for children in early adolescence, between ages eleven and fourteen. Both are distinct from pedophilia, which is, as you know, a sexual preference for prepubescent children."

"However it's defined, there's no justification for the predators we're talking about."

"No, there isn't," she said. "But it does illustrate the full developmental cycle of child predators. They start with possession of child pornography. They next move to creating and distributing child pornography. Finally, they take the ultimate step to sexually assaulting and even trafficking children. Each act is a link in the chain of misery that is child sexual abuse."

"I'd like you to look at some crime scene photos," Santana said.

"Certainly."

He opened his briefcase and removed a photo. He hesitated, clutching the photo. "It's graphic."

Wong nodded and held out a small, delicate hand. "I've looked at some awful crime scenes."

Santana handed the photo to her. "Four years ago Madison Porter was strangled and placed in this position."

Wong peered at the photo for a moment, her brow furrowing in concentration, before looking at Santana again.

"I read nothing in the Investigators' Summary Reports indicating that the two detectives originally assigned to the case believed the crime scene was staged," Santana said. "But sometimes homicide investigators develop tunnel vision by focusing strictly on physical evidence."

She glanced at the photo once more. "You believe this scene was staged?"

"Are you familiar with the works of Salvador Dalí?"

"Yes," she said. Wong and her late husband were heavily involved in the Twin Cities art scene and were big donors.

Santana said, "Dalí was fascinated with the story of *Alice in Wonderland*. One of his works depicted a female figure in a long white dress with her arms raised and a rope in her hands. Dalí also created a sculpture in which Alice's silhouette was holding a skipping rope frozen in motion above her head while her hands and hair blossomed into roses. I believe whoever murdered Madison Porter deliberately posed her in this position."

"That suggests the perpetrator was aware of Dalí's art, or was, perhaps, a collector of it," Wong said.

"I agree. Any other insights you have?"

She thought about his question for a time before responding. "Cases involving strangulation have a high frequency of fantasy and psychosexual arousal," she said. "Strangulation also provides a hands-on power over life and death. The need for power and control often drives the perpetrator's fantasy in cases involving sexual posing of the victim's body."

"The sexual predators I've crossed paths with in my time in Homicide typically posed a body out of anger, retaliation, or to satisfy a perverse sexual fantasy."

"Yes," she said. "The act is like a weapon designed to punish and degrade the woman."

"There was no indication of bondage, mutilation, or insertion of objects based on the crime scene photos," Santana said. "And there was no evidence of sexual penetration in Madison Porter's autopsy report."

Wong nodded and considered Santana's response. "Posing is sometimes confused with staging a crime scene," she said. "Though the terms are similar, there are differences, as you're probably aware. Staging is when the perpetrator manipulates the scene as well as positioning the body to make it appear to be something it isn't."

"You think the perp staged the scene in order to misdirect the investigation?"

"It's possible. Instead of a sex-related murder, Madison Porter's murder could be about interpersonal violence. The posing could be an after-thought or a countermeasure intended to mislead investigators. The public has learned something about the actual process of criminal investigations by watching crime shows on television and in the movies."

"The 'CSI Effect,'" Santana said. "Perpetrators believe they have a better chance at misdirecting detectives during a death investigation."

She nodded. "Cases like this remind me of something Oscar Wilde once said."

"What's that?"

"'Everything in the world is about sex, except sex. Sex is about power.'"

*　　*　　*

As Santana left Karen Wong's house and walked toward his unmarked parked along the curb in the shade of a tall oak tree, he saw Treasury Agent Kenny Coleman leaning against the passenger-side door, munching on an apple. Dressed to the nines in a tan summer suit, Coleman grinned at him like they were old friends.

"Following me around?" Santana said as he approached.

"Just checking in."

"Didn't know we were working together."

"We're not," Coleman said, the grin fading like a dying light. "That's the problem."

"Is it now?"

Coleman nodded and bit into his apple. He chewed for a time and then said, "I asked you politely to stay away from Ashley Porter."

"This isn't Ashley Porter's residence."

"Neither was the art gallery last night. But you were there questioning her."

"She tell you that?"

"Doesn't matter if she did or didn't."

Coleman was good at hiding his emotions and any tells. But the way his gaze slid off Santana for a second suggested Ashley Porter had told Coleman about Santana's visit. That led him to believe she might be working with Coleman and the Treasury Department.

"Got a question for you, Coleman."

"Shoot," he said without a hint of irony.

"A couple of recently deceased drug suppliers, Martin and Benita Lozano, were laundering money through the Elysium Bank."

"Sounds more like a statement of fact than a question, Detective."

"Is it?"

Coleman took another bite of the apple. Holding it out, he said, "I'm gonna give you a bite of the apple, Santana, metaphorically speaking, of course. But that's all you get."

"Let's hear it."

"We have reason to believe that money laundering is occurring at the bank."

"You looking at Ashley Porter as a suspect?"

"I said one bite of the apple, Santana."

"How about her boyfriend, Derek Shelton?"

Coleman bit into his apple again and didn't reply.

"Thanks for the tip," Santana said, heading for the driver's-side door. "Enjoy your apple."

"Stay away from Ashley Porter," Coleman said in a more serious tone of voice. "I won't tell you again."

Santana opened the driver's-side door and peered at Coleman across the top of the unmarked. "And you stay out of my murder investigation."

"That a threat?"

"Take it any way you want, Agent Coleman."

*   *   *

Santana phoned Bobbi Chacon and had her meet him at a Subway, where they ordered two foot-long turkey sandwiches, Cokes, and potato chips and took the food to Como Park.

They sat at a picnic table by the lakeshore pavilion with its arches and columns, Palladian windows, and shiny white surfaces. Herring gulls screeched as they drifted over the water, looking for scraps of food along the asphalt walking paths and the patio beside the pavilion restaurant, their wings gilded in the bright sunlight and blue sky. The light breeze was warm and smelled of wet sand and fish.

"You still spending all your time on the Porter case?" Chacon asked in a tone laced with derision.

"I never was."

Chacon scoffed and took a bite of her sandwich.

"It would help if you were straight with me," Santana said.

"About what?"

"What you and Ryker were up to. Because whatever it was, it got him killed."

"So it's my fault Joel is dead," she said, her voice rising.

Santana shook his head. "It was Ryker's fault he's dead. He went into the Lozanos' house alone. No backup. What was he after?"

Chacon took another bite of her sandwich and set it on a napkin on the table. She chewed silently for a time before speaking.

"Six months ago Joel and I were searching the Internet for websites selling Desoxyn. We made a controlled buy from Midland Pharmacy, a mom-and-pop drugstore in St. Paul, using undercover names and a credit card."

Santana swallowed a bite of his sandwich and said, "What does this have to do with the Lozanos?"

"Hang on. I'm getting to it. We decided to dig a little deeper. So we sent a subpoena to FedEx asking for data on the shipping account used by Midland Pharmacy. What do you know? The shipping account had hundreds of entries, and not just shipments from the mom-and-pop pharmacy in St. Paul. Thirty-five other pharmacies were using the same national account to ship thousands of drug orders every week. The account was registered to and paid for by a company called Dependable RX. They have a website that looks like a legitimate online pharmacy. Visitors to the site can place an order for Desoxyn, or a number of other drugs, using a credit card. There's also a twenty-four-seven toll-free customer service line. The orders were sent to American doctors who wrote prescriptions that were then sent electronically to one of the thirty-five pharmacies to be filled."

"So what's the problem?"

"Even if the prescriptions were legal, doctors were prescribing drugs without ever having met their patients, a violation of the federal Food, Drug, and Cosmetics Act. And Dependable RX was selling thousands of prescriptions of Desoxyn. Someone was making a fortune."

"The Lozanos."

Chacon nodded.

"It makes sense now," Santana said.

"What does?"

"What we found on the Lozanos' computer and in the house. They were cutting ties with the Mexicans. Going into business selling Desoxyn. But where's the money?"

"What money?" she said, her tone unconvincing.

"You ever raided a stash house where there wasn't money? Lots of it."

She shook her head.

"The wall safe in their bedroom was open. There were drag marks in the pool of blood beside Ryker's body. Something was dragged through it. I think it was a bag of money."

Chacon didn't acknowledge what Santana figured she was thinking. So he said it for her.

"Ryker shot the Lozanos and was stealing the drug money."

Chacon's nostrils flared with anger. "You don't know that."

"Wrong," Santana said. "I know it. So do you. Why else was he at the stash house alone? Why didn't he let you know what he was doing? Where was his DEA ID, or any ID, for that matter?"

Chacon's eyes darted back and forth as if searching her brain for a logical answer.

"What do you know about Ryker's background?"

She shrugged. "I know he'd been with the DEA for ten years. Worked in Texas and Arizona before being transferred here."

"Any work problems in his background?"

"Not that I know of."

"Problems with drugs?"

She looked away before shaking her head.

Santana figured a drug habit might be why Ryker was behind on his credit card and loan payments.

"What about his personal life?"

Chacon stared at her half-eaten sandwich before her eyes slid over to him again. "What's that got to do with anything?"

Santana was about to answer when his cellphone vibrated. He recognized Janet Kendrick's number.

"I have to take this," he said, standing.

He walked a few paces away from the picnic table before answering.

"Where are you?" Kendrick asked.

"Having a quick bite to eat with Agent Chacon. What's up?"

"Dylan Walsh is dead."

"How?"

"We'll have to wait for the autopsy, but uniforms reported he'd been in a fight. Or drugs could be involved."

"I'm not surprised."

You better get over there and make sure the scene is secure. Forensics is on their way."

"What about Chacon?"

Kendrick let out a sigh. "We're partnering with the DEA on the Ryker murder. Take her along."

Chapter 30

Bobbi Chacon dropped her Mustang at the LEC and rode with Santana to Dylan Walsh's apartment, a feeling of dread hanging over her like black smoke. Walsh was alive when she'd left his place, though in a drugged state. If she'd hauled his ass in on another drug charge, he might still be alive. But could've or should've got her nowhere. Walsh had given her information that could lead to the perp who killed Joel Ryker. That carried more weight than the life of a shitbag like Walsh.

In her years with the DEA, she'd seen her share of senseless deaths, whether through overdoses or turf wars between gangs and cartels. In Dylan Walsh's case, it was only a matter of time before he met the same fate.

She was satisfied with her guilt-bending rationalization. She'd have to come up with another one if she withheld information from Santana.

Uniforms had cordoned off the area around Walsh's apartment with yellow crime scene tape. Santana spoke briefly with one of the uniforms, a black woman whose nametag ID'd her as Mitchell.

"Who found the body?" he asked.

"Neighbor." She checked the notebook in her hand. Gave Santana the neighbor's driver's license. "Guy's name is Jorge Rivera. No wants or warrants."

Santana scanned the license. "Where's Rivera now?"

She gestured toward a black-and-white parked at the curb. "Sitting in my squad. Thought it best to keep him away from everyone till the shields arrived."

Santana handed her the license. "Make sure he stays there till we come out."

"Copy that."

Chacon signed the entry log after Santana. Then she gloved up and slipped on a pair of booties.

Dylan Walsh lay slumped back on the living room couch, his head against the top cushion, his wide eyes focused on nothing. His face was red and badly swollen from apparent punches to his face. His bathrobe was opened at the waist, revealing a hairless chest and a pair of boxer briefs. A dead joint rested on the edge of an ashtray on the coffee table. What appeared to be crystal meth was scattered on a piece of tinfoil beside the ashtray.

Chacon's heart thumped in her chest. She hadn't beaten Walsh. But she had inadvertently scratched him. Things were suddenly going south on her, and she wasn't sure why.

"Looks like Walsh OD'd," she said, making the case for Walsh's death.

"Uh-huh," Santana said, bending over Walsh's body. "Right after he beat himself up." Santana leaned in closer. "Could get DNA off the scratch on his cheek," Santana said, looking back at Chacon.

"Maybe," she said with a half-smile. She could hear her blood rushing in her ears.

Santana examined Walsh's hands. "No evidence that Walsh fought back. If he did, he didn't land any heavy punches." He pointed to Walsh's red shins. "Look at this."

Chacon could only nod.

Santana felt along the edge of the coffee table.

"Maybe he banged his shins," Chacon said, trying to cover her tracks.

Santana straightened up. "Had to hit them awfully hard." He came around the coffee table and pushed it gently toward Walsh till the opposite edge aligned with the red marks on Walsh's shins. "More likely someone shoved the table against his shins."

Chacon felt the heat in her face. She looked away from Santana till her face cooled again.

"Let's do a quick search and then we'll talk with the neighbor," he said.

The SPPD's Forensic Services Unit was arriving as Chacon and Santana emerged from the house. They dropped their used gloves and booties in a waste container near the front door and headed for Officer Mitchell's black-and-white parked at the curb.

Santana opened the rear passenger-side door and asked Jorge Rivera to step out.

"Am I under arrest?"

"No, sir. We just want to ask you a few questions."

Rivera got out. He matched the photo on the license Mitchell had shown him. He was a short and pudgy twenty-two-year-old, dressed in faded jeans, sneakers, and a white T-shirt. He'd shaved his black hair close to his skull. A scraggily beard shaded his cheeks, chin, and the skin above his thin lips.

"Never been inside a police car," he said with a grin.

"Nothing to worry about," Santana said, shutting the car door. He took out his notebook, opened to a fresh page, and said, "How did you come to find the body?"

"I was walking my dog when I saw this fancy-looking Mustang pull up to the curb in back of the apartment."

"What do you mean by 'fancy,' Mr. Rivera?"

"It had stripes along the hood and roof."

"What color was the Mustang?"

"White with blue stripes."

Santana gave Chacon a long, hard stare and then turned his attention to Rivera again.

"You sure it was a Mustang?"

"Oh, yeah. I've done some bodywork on Mustangs. Never on a Shelby GT350 though."

"What happened after you saw the Mustang?"

"A woman got out and went into the house."

"Can you describe the woman?"

"Tall." Rivera gazed at Chacon. Then with a sheepish grin, he gestured at her and said, "Kind of looked like her."

"Why'd you decide to go into Walsh's house?"

"He invited me over earlier."

"Was the woman still there?"

"She'd already left."

"Did you see anyone else enter the house?"

Rivera shook his head.

"How long after the woman left did you go over to Walsh's house?"

"I'm not sure."

"Take a guess."

"Well, my girlfriend called. I talked to her for maybe twenty minutes. Then I went over."

"How did you get in if Walsh was dead?"

"I knew he was there 'cause he'd let the woman in. So when he didn't answer, I tried the door. It was unlocked."

"And he was on the couch when you entered."

"Yeah. At first I thought that he'd fallen asleep. Then I saw what somebody done to his face. And I saw his eyes." Rivera looked down as he said it, as if traumatized by his words.

"Ever do any drugs, Mr. Rivera?"

He lifted his chin and shrugged. "Sometimes."

"You touch anything besides the doorknob?"

He shook his head. "I called 911 as soon as I saw Walsh."

"You call me if you remember anything else," Santana said, handing him a business card. Then he turned to Bobbi Chacon and said, "Let's talk."

They walked over to Santana's unmarked. Chacon leaned her backside against the hood and crossed her arms.

"Now I know why you didn't want to drive here in the Mustang," Santana said as he stood in front of her. "Tell me the rest of it."

"Or what? You gonna arrest me?"

"The thought crossed my mind."

She shook her head in frustration. "I didn't kill Walsh."

"Try harder."

She looked off into the distance for a time before her eyes met his again. "What Rivera said is essentially true."

"So let me see if I've got this straight. You came here to brace Walsh. Things got a little rough. You bruised his shins with the table. Punched him in the face."

"No, no. I didn't hit him."

"What about the scratch?"

"Inadvertent."

"Forensics will match your DNA on file."

"Doesn't mean I hit him."

"No. Just that you could be in a world of hurt. What happened next?"

"I left."

"But not before you got the information you came for."

"Walsh gave me an address in Cathedral Hill. Woman named Dominique Lejeune lives there. She runs a modeling agency that's a front for high-class hookers."

Santana recalled what the Narco/Vice detective, Gabe Thornton, had told him about Dominique Lejeune, aka Carla Rossi.

"That's it?" he said to Chacon.

"No. After I got the info I needed, I beat the shit out of Walsh. Is that what you want to hear?"

"It's not what I want to hear. It's what the evidence tells me."

She held out her hands. Palms up and then turned them over. "See my knuckles? Whoever beat up Walsh would have marks on his knuckles and hands."

"Unless they used gloves."

"Come on, Santana. Why would I kill Walsh?"

She had a good point. Still, there were unanswered questions. "Why brace him in the first place?"

"I wouldn't have had to if you were doing your job."

Santana thought about it. "Someone came in between the time you left and the time Rivera got here. Someone looking for the missing money."

Chacon arched her eyebrows in alarm. "The cartel?" she said, stepping away from the unmarked.

"Whoever killed Walsh is going after Dominique Lejeune." He hurried toward the driver's side door. "You should've told me sooner, Chacon. We might be too late."

Her eyes held his for a moment as she opened the passenger-side door before she looked away, as if she had no excuse for her actions.

* * *

Gray clouds layered the sky as Santana and Bobbi Chacon sat in their unmarked parked along the curb in front of the three-story Italianate mansion where Dominique Lejeune lived. The mansion, originally designed in the 19th century for a rich businessman, was perched high on a bluff in the Cathedral Hill neighborhood overlooking the Mississippi River Valley and the St. Paul skyline, just off Summit Avenue, which was the longest stretch of Victorian mansions on a single road in the US.

Once known as St. Anthony Hill, many of the large houses, stone buildings, and churches in Cathedral Hill were first built in the 1870s, when the neighborhood became a fashionable location for the wealthy families of St. Paul. Artists and writers such as F. Scott Fitzgerald had lived and written at various homes and restaurants in the neighborhood.

Santana scanned the area, looking for anyone loitering in a car or van.

"Nothing," Chacon said.

Santana nodded in agreement. Realizing that he needed to ask Dominique Lejeune what she knew about Ana Soriano, it was time to come clean with Bobbi Chacon.

She unbuckled her seatbelt and reached for the door handle.

"Wait a minute," Santana said.

Chacon looked at him, her lips slightly parted and eyebrows raised in curiosity.

"I believe Ana Soriano was the fourth person at the Lozanos' the day Ryker was shot. She's an escort possibly working for Dominique Lejeune."

"And you just figured this out now?"

"A while ago."

"Holy shit! Soriano killed Joel."

"Martin Lozano killed Ryker."

"What makes you so sure?"

"Ballistics. The bullet that killed Ryker came from the Sig Sauer Lozano had in his safe. Lozano had GSR on his hands from the one shot he fired. Ana Soriano fired seven shots at Ryker with Lozano's Ruger, hitting him in the shoulder and hip. Neither of the wounds was fatal."

"Well, thank you very much for trusting your *partner* and keeping me in the loop, Santana."

"We need Ana Soriano alive."

Chacon smirked. "Yeah. Nothing but hired killers working for the DEA." She opened the passenger-side door and got out, slamming it behind her.

They walked up the long sidewalk leading to the mansion and rang the doorbell.

"Did you not see the NO SOLICITING sign beside the door?" The woman's voice emanated from the security camera attached to the wall above the front door.

Santana noted the irony of the sign as he held up his badge wallet toward the camera.

"What can I do for you, Detective?"

Santana slipped his badge wallet back into the inner pocket of his sport coat and said, "I'll let you know once we're inside." He looked up at the camera and offered an encouraging smile.

A few moments later the door buzzed. Santana and Chacon entered.

Santana could see that the expansive living room with a stone fireplace on the first floor had been converted into a photo studio. Scattered around the room were backdrops, cameras, lenses, LED lights, strobes, soft boxes, and umbrellas to soften and diffuse light.

He and Chacon climbed a long set of carpeted stairs leading to a landing outside Dominique Lejeune's apartment.

The mature woman leaning casually against the open door on the second floor held a long cigarette between the delicate fingers of her right hand. She wore a red sweatband and a red fitness jumpsuit with large black DYNAMITE labels stitched across both hips and thighs. The suit fit her like a second skin and accentuated her curvy figure.

"Sorry," she said, "but you caught me in the middle of my daily workout." She drew in a lungful of smoke, tilted her head back, and blew out a small cloud of smoke. Then, noticing the bemused look on Santana's face, she added, "We all have our contradictions. I'm sure you do, too, Detective . . .?"

"Santana."

Dominique Lejeune's eyes shifted from Santana to Chacon. "And you are?"

"Chacon."

Lejeune made a come-along gesture with her fingers and closed the heavy, thick door behind them.

Bobbi Chacon gave a low whistle as they walked into the luxurious apartment. "Nice digs," she said.

They followed Lejeune to a 40' by 40' room with mirrored walls that had been converted into a workout studio complete with a treadmill, elliptical, stationary bike, rowing machine, a Total Gym, adjustable weight bench, an A-Bench for sit ups, and a set of free weights and dumbbells.

Santana was envious.

Dominique Lejeune snuffed out her cigarette in an ashtray resting on a massage bench and climbed onto the treadmill. She dabbed her flushed cheeks with the long towel draped over the side rail, hit the pause button, and began walking.

"Go ahead with your questions," she said.

Santana reached over and pulled out the safety key, stopping the treadmill. "We're going to need your full attention, Ms. Lejeune."

"Well, aren't we rude."

"Hey, lady," Chacon said. "We're here to save your life."

Lejeune narrowed her eyes and looked at Santana again. "That's rather melodramatic, isn't it?"

"Why don't we sit down and talk about it."

Lejeune hesitated a moment. Then she grabbed the towel and headed for the living room. Santana and Chacon followed.

In the living room Santana and Chacon sat at opposite ends of the sectional. Lejeune sat in the middle.

"Why the concern about my life?" she asked.

"You're collateral," Chacon said.

Santana gave Chacon a look.

Momentarily chagrined, she shook her head and peered off into the distance as if she were no longer interested in the conversation.

Santana turned his attention back to Dominique Lejeune. "We're looking for a young woman named Ana Soriano."

Dominique Lejeune glanced away before her gaze came back to Santana. "Am I supposed to know this woman?"

"Do you?"

"I'm afraid not."

"What about a young man named Dylan Walsh?"

Her complexion lost some color as she shook her head. "What has Ms. Soriano done?"

"She may be involved in the recent murder of a DEA agent."

"My partner," Chacon said, lasering Lejeune with her eyes.

Lejeune tried a smile that didn't work. "I wish I could help."

"You might like to do more than *wish*," Santana said.

"Why's that?"

Santana leaned forward, rested both forearms on his thighs. "Money was taken from a safe the day the DEA agent was murdered. That money belonged to a Mexican cartel. Someone's come looking for it. Dylan Walsh was a casualty. But before he died, he likely gave that someone your name."

Now Dominique Lejeune's complexion lost all its color. She lowered her head.

"Tell us the truth," Santana said. "Your life could depend on it."

Lejeune lit another cigarette from the package of Virginia Slims Lights on the coffee table. As she let out a long, smoky breath, Santana could see her hand shaking.

"All right," she said. "I know who Dylan Walsh is . . . or was."

"How?"

"Through his father, Hal Langford."

"Where have I heard that name before?"

"Langford is James McGowan's campaign manager. Maybe you've heard of McGowan. He's running for the Senate."

Santana pictured the man standing beside McGowan at the Senate fundraiser.

"Why is the kid's name Walsh and the father's Langford?" he asked.

She shrugged. "Have to ask Langford."

"The mother still alive?"

"I heard she was killed in an auto accident a few years ago."

"What about Ana Soriano?" Chacon asked.

"I do know Ana. But I don't know where she is right now."

"Mind if we look around?"

"I do mind. So if you want to search my residence, come back with a warrant."

Santana knew if Ana Soriano *were* here, she'd be gone by the time he and Chacon returned with a warrant. They could search anyway, but that would lead to numerous legal problems that could sink the whole case.

"How do you know Ana Soriano?"

"She's one of the models at my agency."

"Models, huh?" Chacon said.

Lejeune nodded her head. "Yes," she said, glaring at Chacon. "A model."

"Are you in contact with her?" Santana asked.

"I have been."

"Does she have the missing money?"

Lejeune's face and eyes were expressionless as she stared silently at Santana.

"Whoever is looking for her is after the money," Santana said. "As long as she has it, her life is in danger. And if you know she has it, whoever killed Walsh will get the information out of you, Ms. Lejeune, one way or another. And they'll probably enjoy doing it."

"This house is impenetrable, Detective. You've seen the door. No one is going to break it down. There are bars on the windows and a state-of-the-art alarm system."

"Don't you ever go out?"

"Everything I need is right here."

"You have enough food to last till we find Walsh's killer?"

"Depends on how long it takes."

Santana considered asking Janet Kendrick for round-the-clock protection for Lejeune, but he knew with the tight funding, his request would likely be denied. Even when budgets were flush, he'd only gotten money to stash someone in a motel for a limited period of time—no more than a week or so. In the past he'd had a vacant squad parked in front of a house, hoping that the perp would think the cop was inside the house, but if anyone was really watching they would soon figure out it was a deception. He could have squads make multiple trips past the house, but again, it would be a tough sell for a determined perp.

Then there were the witnesses under protection who would call or visit people they knew, defeating his attempts to keep them safe. He could suggest moving Lejeune to someplace else, someplace safer and unknown to most people. Only he would know where she was, but he doubted Lejeune would move out of this place.

If this were a high-profile case involving someone famous, or someone with a friend or relative with real power to order 24/7 protection, like the governor or a senator, Santana might be able to get an okay for coverage. But Given Dominique Lejeune's profession, he had no real chance of success.

But the feds had more money at their disposal. Tying Dylan Walsh's death to the death of DEA agent Joel Ryker could be the way to go.

Santana looked at Chacon. "We need twenty-four-seven protection for Ms. Lejeune. I can't get the money from the SPPD budget, but you could get it from the DEA budget."

"No way," Chacon said.

"I don't think that's necessary, Detective," Lejeune said.

Chacon locked eyes with her. "Might cramp your business?"

"Are you always this obnoxious, Ms. Chacon?"

"That would be *Agent* Chacon to you. And, yes. When I'm looking for the perp who killed my partner, I get a little obnoxious."

"Something tells me it's more about your endearing personality."

"It's a mistake turning down the twenty-four-hour protection, Ms. Lejeune," Santana said, putting a stop to their squabble.

"Wouldn't be the first mistake I've made in my life," she said.

But it might be the last, Santana thought.

He handed her a business card. "Call me if you hear from Ana Soriano."

Dominique Lejeune looked at the business card in her hand before meeting Santana's gaze again. "If you think I really need around-the-clock protection, Detective Santana, I believe I can get it."

"And how is that?"

She paused for a short time before responding with a confident smile. "I have many important . . . friends who would offer to protect me if I asked for their help."

Santana wondered who these *important* friends were, and if he knew any of them. "Then I recommend that's exactly what you do."

She nodded and said, "If what you told me about Ana is true, that her life is in danger, then she's in danger from the police as well."

"Not the way to look at it," Santana said, wondering if there was an underlying message in Dominique Lejeune's words. "Ana could be innocent."

Lejeune tilted her head slightly and raised an eyebrow. "One would hope."

"We can protect Ana, Ms. Lejeune."

She offered a half smile. "Perhaps we all need to protect ourselves from whatever is coming."

"Or whatever is already here," Santana said.

*　　*　　*

Ana Soriano came out from her hiding place as soon as Santana and Chacon left the building. With the bedroom door ajar, she was able to hear the conversation they'd had with Dominique. When the detective had asked to search the mansion, a shot of adrenaline had rushed through her body, nearly causing her to scream. She'd cupped a hand over her mouth to muffle any sound.

Now, as Ana walked into the living room, she saw Dominique pacing in front of the couch, a lit cigarette in her hand.

When Dominique saw her, she stopped pacing and said, "You have to go. Now."

"I have nowhere to go."

"Your apartment."

"The police will look there."

"Ana Soriano doesn't exist in any database."

"I was fingerprinted when I came across the Mexican border."

"You're Ana Luna now. The police don't know where you live."

Stepping close to Dominique, Ana said, "You know what will happen if I'm arrested."

Cigarette ash fell like tiny dead leaves as Dominique jabbed an index finger at her. "Don't you dare threaten me, understand?"

"Then help me."

"I'm working on it. But it takes time."

"Time I don't have. I want the money that you put away for me. The money I worked for."

Dominique inhaled a lungful of smoke, tilted her head back, and blew out a small cloud. "I'll get it. In the meantime, there is someone I've been in contact with who can help you."

"Who?"

Dominique stubbed the cigarette out in the ashtray on the coffee table, opened a small wooden jewelry box beside the ashtray, and removed a business card.

"Here," she said, handing the card to Ana. "This man can help get you out of the country."

Chapter 31

After leaving Dominique Lejeune's place, Santana and Chacon headed for James McGowan's campaign office in downtown St. Paul, looking for Hal Langford.

"Quite the digs for a woman running a modeling agency," Chacon said, gazing out the passenger-side window.

Santana kept his eyes on the road and his thoughts to himself.

"You can't trust Dominique Lejeune," Chacon said. "I hope you know that."

"It's not about trust," he said. "It's about protection."

"We should surveil her. She knows where Ana Soriano is. If we watch her, I'll bet we find Soriano. Might even find the perp who killed Walsh."

"I haven't ruled that out. But first we need to notify Dylan Walsh's father, Hal, about his son's death. You ever done a death notification before?"

"Enough," Chacon said.

He considered calling Janet Kendrick and asking if Kacie Hawkins or another homicide detective could accompany him instead of Bobbi Chacon, but the chief, Tim Branigan, had ordered him to partner with Chacon. If it created a problem later, then it would be up to the department to fix it. Plus, whoever killed Walsh was still out there. He had no time to waste on bureaucratic turf wars.

"Death notifications aren't rush calls. Just follow my lead," he said, glancing at Chacon.

"No problem with that," she said.

McGowan's campaign headquarters was located near an I-94 overpass on St. Paul's East Side. Surrounded by asphalt and cement, the low-slung industrial building looked more like a bunker than a Senate campaign headquarters. A small sign in the parking lot was the only outward indication that a Senate campaign operation hummed away on the other side of the two glass doors.

The once-industrial space had been transformed by the addition of brown carpet and beige-painted sheetrock. Teams were working in small open pods made up of circular tables, where staff plunked away on their keyboards. One team sat around a TV showing a cable news channel. A whiteboard hanging on the sheetrock showed James McGowan's scheduled events, which included town halls, stump speeches, and media interviews.

A letter wall contained a sampling of mail sent to McGowan from supporters all over the state and country.

Santana saw a few push scooters that the mostly young staff used to speed from one part of the spread-out space to another.

A young, bright-eyed woman with brunette hair and a big smile approached them. "Can I help you?"

"We'd like to see Hal Langford," Santana said. "Is he here?"

"Yes, but he's very busy. My name is Donna. Perhaps I can assist you?"

Santana discreetly showed her his badge wallet. "It's important that we see him now."

Her smile dimmed. "Of course," she said. "Follow me."

Donna led them to a walled-in office at the end of a long aisle. Through the glass and open blinds, Santana recognized the man with the short chin and round face. Langford was seated at a large wooden desk. Behind a pair of rectangular glasses, his large eyes were focused on a sheet of paper he held in his right hand.

The door to the office was partially open. Donna knocked on it and leaned in. "Two police officers are here to see you, Mr. Langford."

"Well, show them in."

Langford stood as Santana and Chacon entered and closed the door behind them.

Santana held up his badge wallet.

"Ah, Detective Santana," Langford said. "I remember you from the fundraiser we held at soon-to-be-senator McGowan's home."

"You have a good memory for faces."

"A necessity in this business," he said. "It's all about people and contacts. I hate closed doors." He pointed at his office door. "Closed doors mean people are not . . . interacting. We think it's important for people to work together."

"This is Agent Chacon," Santana said, refocusing the conversation.

"FBI?" Langford said.

"DEA."

Langford's eyes narrowed, and he nodded his head slowly as if he suddenly understood their reason for being here. He sat down in the swivel chair behind his desk.

"Do you mind if we sit, Mr. Langford?" Santana asked.

He appeared to snap out of a trance-like state. "Be my guest."

Santana and Chacon pulled two metal chairs with plastic seats away from the wall and placed them in front of the desk.

As they sat down, Langford peered at Santana and said, "I know Dylan has a drug problem. If he's in trouble, I'd like to keep this quiet and out of the press if at all possible."

Santana believed it was best to get to the point quickly and to state the information simply and directly. If the facts about a victim's death were clear, it was better to leave no room for doubt or false hope. In Dylan Walsh's case, he suspected Walsh had died from a beating, but until he had the autopsy report, he couldn't be positive. Still, he didn't want to be brutally blunt or insensitive.

"We're sorry to have to bring you this terrible news, Mr. Langford. Dylan was found dead in his apartment this afternoon."

Langford released a long breath and sat back in his chair.

Santana remained quiet, allowing time for the news to sink in.

"I tried getting him off drugs, but it didn't work," Langford said. "After his mother's death, I lost contact with him. Even though he was my stepson, I cared about him and wanted to help."

That Dylan Walsh was Langford's stepson was new information, but it changed nothing. "We're not sure Dylan died of a drug overdose, Mr. Langford."

He acknowledged the statement with a nod. "You need to wait for the autopsy results. I understand."

Santana wanted to answer all of Langford's questions tactfully and truthfully without revealing more of the grim details than was necessary. His goal was to inform, not further traumatize. But Langford would need to ID his stepson's body at the morgue. That would raise more questions. It was better to raise them now.

"Dylan's face was red and swollen, Mr. Langford. We believe someone hit him."

"How red and swollen?"

Chacon shifted her position in the chair.

Santana glanced at her to make sure she was staying quiet. Then, looking at Langford, he said, "Enough so that he might've died from something other than drugs."

Langford leaned forward. "You think he was beaten to death?"

"We don't know for sure. We're actively pursuing leads."

"So he was murdered."

"We don't know that."

"What *do* you know?" he said, his voice rising in anger.

Chacon said, "We know that your stepson is dead. And now you know it, too."

Langford started to respond and then seemed to change his mind. Looking at Santana he said, "Do you have any suspects, Detective?"

While Santana suspected that the CJNG cartel was involved in Dylan Walsh's murder, he had no hard evidence and no suspects.

"Not at this time," he said. "Would you like us to make any phone calls to family, friends, or neighbors?"

"I can take care of that."

"Would you like someone to stay with you?"

"I'm fully capable of handling this," he said with a half smile.

Santana removed a printed card from his badge wallet and handed it across the desktop to Langford. "The names and telephone numbers of a victim advocate, medical examiner, and social services are on that card."

"When can I see Dylan's body?"

"The ME will contact you."

"About the news media."

"What about them?"

"James McGowan is ahead in the polls. He's going to be the next junior senator from Minnesota. I don't want anything interfering with the campaign."

"Like your stepson's death?" Chacon said.

Langford looked at her. "Your sarcasm is not appreciated. Dylan's death has nothing to do with the campaign. I'm merely asking you two to keep my name and any connection I had to Dylan's death out of the media and away from the campaign." He looked at Santana. "Can you do that?"

"No, I can't."

Langford frowned. "That's not the answer I expected to hear, Detective."

"The media will do what the media always does," Santana said. "I can't guarantee that they won't find the connection between you and your stepson."

"That's unfortunate," Langford said. He stood. "Please leave the door open on your way out."

*   *   *

Bobbi Chacon looked across the passenger seat at Santana as they drove away from the campaign headquarters. "Hal Langford is a complete asshole. He doesn't give a shit about his son."

"Stepson," Santana said.

"Like that's a reason not to give a shit."

"It isn't. But maybe it's a reason why Dylan Walsh was into the drug scene. Relationships—or in this case, a failed relationship—can impact life choices."

"So are you an armchair psychologist now or speaking from experience?"

"Maybe both."

Santana could feel the heat of her gaze as she sat silently for a time.

"That why you became a cop? 'Cause of a failed relationship?"

Santana wondered if there was a time when her voice wasn't laced with sarcasm. "No," he said. "Because of a dead one."

"Huh?"

"My mother's murder."

"Oh," Chacon said softly. "I didn't know. Sorry."

"Why'd you become a DEA agent?"

"What's this? True Confessions?" The sarcasm had returned.

"You never mentioned your father when I asked about your background."

"So what?"

"So where is he?"

"None of your business."

"You're right. It isn't."

"Where's your father?"

"He's dead, too. Killed by a drunk driver."

Bobbi Chacon sat quietly, staring out the passenger-side window. Then he felt her eyes on him again.

"Just 'cause you told me about your parents' deaths, doesn't mean I gotta tell you anything about my childhood."

"So don't."

"Okay, then."

A few minutes of silence followed as Santana drove toward the LEC.

"All right," Chacon said with a frustrated breath. "I don't know where he is now or what he's doing."

"Your father."

"No," she said. "Santa Claus."

"Let me guess. He ran out on you and your mother."

"Good one, Sherlock. Right after he left the Marine Corps."

"How old were you when he left?"

"Sixteen."

"Same age as me when my mother was murdered."

"That sucks."

"You ever look for him?"

She didn't answer.

"You did, didn't you?"

"Yeah. After I joined the DEA. He had a couple arrests for minor drug offenses and was living in Key West. Tending bar. I wasted some vacation time going to see him."

"It didn't go well."

"He'd married a Cuban *muchacha* my age, though he'd never divorced my mother. Had a couple of kids. Wasn't real interested in seeing his oldest daughter."

"You tell him what you did for a living?"

She laughed. "I did. That got him even less interested in me. I think he was dealing. Small-time shit. Thought maybe I'd arrest him. I should've."

"For a small-time offense?"

"Nope. For bigamy." She laughed again. "Anyway, that's the end of my sad story."

Santana doubted it. He'd never truly gotten over losing his parents while still in his teens. He was willing to bet Bobbi Chacon hadn't gotten over her estrangement from her father either. For all intents and purposes, he was dead to her, too.

"So what's the plan?" she asked.

"I drop you off at the LEC."

"What about the surveillance on Dominique Lejeune's place? It's the only lead we have."

"For now," Santana said.

Chacon thought for a moment. "You know, without a squad car in front of Lejeune's house, the guy who killed Walsh might show up."

"That would make it easier."

She smiled. "That's good thinking."

"I'm not sure it is," he said.

Chapter 32

It was a forty-five-minute drive north from the Law Enforcement Center to the Hazelden Betty Ford Foundation treatment and rehabilitation center, where Christine Hammond was being treated after leaving Regions Hospital. The drug and alcohol facility offered both residential and outpatient programs at the 500-acre lakeside retreat in Center City, Minnesota.

Visitors were permitted on Wednesday evenings from 6:30-8:00. Santana had spoken on the phone to the psychologist assigned to Christine Hammond's team and gotten permission to speak to her. Like all new patients, Hammond had spent the first 24 to 48 hours on a medical unit before being assigned to a treatment unit.

Before heading for Center City, Santana had checked the website for directions and noted the posted Prayer for the Day.

"I pray that I may welcome difficulties.
I pray that they may test my strength and build my character."

Though Santana had long ago lost his faith, he thought the words could easily be applied to cops as well as addicts.

When he arrived at the clinic, he was directed to the meditation center near the lake, where Christine Hammond met him outside the doors. He'd seen her once when she lay on the couch at Dylan Walsh's apartment after he and Bobbi Chacon had taken down Jamal Washburn and Dean Moody. The second time Santana had seen her was on the video recorded by Gordon Grant, where she lay naked and helpless on a stained mattress in his basement moments before being raped by an unidentified man.

Now she wore jeans, a pair of Nike sneakers, and a blue T-shirt with white lettering across the front that read:

RECOVERY IS A LIFESTYLE
NOT A DESTINATION

Her thick blond hair was piled atop her head as it had been on the two previous occasions, but she wore no make-up on her heart-shaped face, her clear complexion was no longer puffy, and her green eyes no longer glazed.

"Let's walk, if you don't mind," she said.

Though the evening was warm and humid, she strolled along the tree-shaded trail with her arms crossed as though she were cold. She was shorter than he remembered, maybe 5'6," and looking frail after going through detox upon arriving at the rehab center.

"How are you doing?" Santana asked.

When she didn't respond, he thought she hadn't heard him. But then she said in a whisper, "Better."

"I appreciate you talking with me."

"We haven't really said anything yet."

It was more a statement of fact than a rebuke.

They walked quietly for a time before Santana said, "I need your help."

"That's interesting," she said. "I'm the one usually seeking help."

"You have a good start here."

"My psychologist told me that addiction is giving up everything for one thing, but recovery is giving up one thing for everything."

"That's good advice."

"Best advice I've ever had."

"Is your family supportive?"

"My father left when I was five. My mother had mental health issues. I ran away when I was fifteen. Lived on the streets for a while till some creep tried to molest me. Then I lived mostly with friends and their families till I could support myself."

"How'd you get involved with Dylan Walsh?"

"I was working at a McDonald's. Dylan used to come in there once in a while. He invited me to a party at his place. We started dating."

"Did he introduce you to Dominique Lejeune?"

She stopped and peered up at him. "You know about her?"

"Not enough."

She nodded and began walking again. "We met Dominique for lunch about three months after Dylan and I started dating. She asked me if I'd like to do some modeling for her. Mostly catalogue photo shoots at her mansion. I thought it would be exciting. It was . . . for the first few months. Then she and Dylan asked if I'd like to make some *real* money."

"Doing what?" Santana asked, though he knew.

She let out a long breath, stopped, and stared off into the distance, her hands in the pockets of her jeans. "This is difficult to talk about."

"I understand. If it helps, I'm not here to judge."

She released another deep breath and paused before speaking again. "The men that did this to me . . ." Her voice trailed off, the emotional pain sharp in her eyes as she looked at him again.

"They'll pay for what they did to you. I promise."

She gave him a wan smile. "I hope so."

They walked once more as a fresh breeze rustled the leaves and sparrows chirped in the trees.

"Dylan started taking me to these parties."

"Where were the parties held?"

"I don't know. Whenever Dylan took me, I was blindfolded till we got there."

"Was it always at the same place?"

"Different places. But always expensive."

"Tell me about the men."

"Fat cats. They seemed nice. But the parties were always about sex."

"Could you identify any of these men?"

"They all wore these weird masks."

"What kind of masks?"

She looked at him. "Did you ever see the Tom Cruise movie *Eyes Wide Shut*?"

"I saw previews."

"Masks like that."

"Venetian masks," he said.

She shrugged. "If that's what you call them. After a few parties, I told Dylan I didn't want to go anymore. He convinced me to go one last time. I think someone put something in my drink that night. The next few weeks were all a blur. But I got really addicted to meth."

"Do you remember ever meeting a man named Gordon Grant?"

She shook her head and looked away.

Her reaction and body language indicated she might not be telling the truth. But Santana was reluctant to push her given her condition. He had a photo of her on Grant's bedroom wall and the video of her in Grant's basement, but he couldn't ID Grant or any other men in the videos themselves, at least not yet. And if the men wore hoods, Hammond wouldn't be able to ID anyone either. Still, the evidence he had against Grant was enough to put him back in prison for a long time.

"Did Dylan Walsh get you into drugs?"

"I'd like to blame him, but I'd smoked dope and snorted some coke before. But I don't know how I got so addicted to meth."

Santana figured Dylan Walsh had purposely hooked her on the meth.

"When you were modeling for Dominique Lejeune, do you recall meeting a young woman named Ana Soriano?"

Christine Hammond stopped abruptly as though she'd run into a wall. "Has something happened to her?"

"I don't know." Santana showed Hammond a photo. "Is this her?"

Hammond peered at the photo. "Sorta looks like her. But she looks a lot younger in that picture. And she goes by the name of Ana Luna now."

"I need to find her."

"Ask Dylan," she said, looking away. "He probably knows where she lives."

"Dylan's dead."

"What?" she said, her eyes wide with surprise and fear. "What happened?"

"He was killed, and whoever killed him is looking for Ana."

Christine Hammond crossed her arms across her chest again and shivered. "Oh, my God. It's about the money, isn't it?"

"Ana has it."

"Yes."

"Did she tell you how she acquired it?"

She shook her head. "Do you know?"

"I know that Ana is in great danger."

The trail they were walking had led them out of the woods to the lake. Christine Hammond stood quietly, staring at the water, her arms still crossed on her chest as though holding herself together.

"Hazelden is very expensive, Christine. Did Ana give you some money for treatment?"

She nodded. "The morning after the shooting, Ana came to my apartment asking for help. She had all this money in a back-pack. Said it was the ticket that would change our lives. She never told me where she got the money. I told her Dylan could help. We were waiting for her when the two men arrived."

"Washburn and Moody."

"I guess. Anyway, Ana never showed up. Next thing I know, I'm in the hospital. I tried calling her, but she didn't answer."

"Would anyone else know where Ana might be?"

Hammond thought about it. "If she was really desperate."

"Who?"

"There's this man who kept track of Ana. I saw him with Dylan a few times when he bought drugs. He's a pimp. Chico Caldera."

"Where does Caldera live?"

She shook her head. "Sorry."

"It's okay. You've been very helpful. Stick to the program. You're still young. You've got your whole life ahead of you."

She gave him a shy smile. "I hope you do, too, Detective Santana."

Santana cocked his head, looking for an explanation.

"This man Chico. He's very dangerous. You be careful."

Chapter 33

The banner headline and story in the St. Paul *Pioneer Press* the following morning was all about Dylan Walsh's murder and the ongoing investigation. Hal Langford and James McGowan's names were prominently displayed. Both men tried to distance themselves from Walsh's drug use and any political ramifications, though both made pleas to the police to find Walsh's killer. McGowan offered "heartfelt condolences" and a $25,000 reward for information leading to the perpetrator.

Janet Kendrick had left an early morning voicemail on Santana's department cell requesting that he be in her office first thing in the morning.

Now, as he sat in a chair on the opposite side of her desk, he could see the troubled look on her face and the concern in her dark brown eyes.

Leaning forward in her high-back chair, her forearms resting on the desktop, she said, "We've got a dead DEA agent and now the stepson of James McGowan's campaign manager. This has turned into a real shit storm. Tell me what you have."

"We believe—"

"You mean you and Agent Chacon."

"Yes. We believe Dylan Walsh was beaten to death by a Mexican *sicario*."

"Who's this *sicario*?"

"We don't know yet."

"So this is a drug deal gone bad."

"Walsh was a small-time distributor working with Martin Lozano. Lozano had a half-million dollars of drug money in his safe. After the Lozanos were killed, the money disappeared. The

CJNG cartel sent a *sicario* to collect the money. Walsh didn't have it, but he might've known who did."

"Do you know who has it?"

Santana decided to keep quiet about Ana Soriano till he had a bead on her location.

He said, "Ballistics showed that Ryker shot the Lozanos when they tried to stop him from taking the half-million dollars. Ryker thought Martin Lozano was dead, but Lozano was able to get to his Sig Sauer in the safe and kill Ryker before he died."

"Wait a minute." She rose in her chair. "You're saying a DEA agent murdered two people and tried to steal a half-million dollars?"

"That's the way I see it."

Kendrick rubbed her forehead with her fingers and then sat back down. "You're sure about this?"

"I am."

"So who took the money?"

"The same person the *sicario* is looking for."

"So there was a fourth person in the room?"

Santana nodded.

"Then you better find him first."

Or *her*, Santana thought.

*　　*　　*

After picking up Bobbi Chacon, Santana drove west along University Avenue—the southern border of Frogtown and the main artery between St. Paul and Minneapolis—past a slew of businesses and restaurants serving Cambodian, Thai, Laotian, Hmong, and Vietnamese. Once settled primarily by Germans, Scandinavians, and Irish in the last half of the 19th century, Frogtown was home to a new generation of immigrants—and to a string of gang murders.

Rain hammered the car's roof and sluiced across the windshield.

Santana had brought Chacon up to speed on his visit with Christine Hammond and her connection to Ana Soriano. He could tell Chacon was jacked up by the increase in her respiration rate.

"If Ana Soriano is at Hammond's apartment, we're taking her alive," he said, glancing at Chacon. The fingers of her gun hand caressed the grip of the Glock nestled in her waist holster.

"Yeah," she said, her eyes fixed on the windshield.

Turning off University Avenue onto Van Buren, Santana pulled to the curb in front of a six-story apartment building. "Hammond lives on the third floor. I've got the search warrant. I called the landlord. He'll buzz us in."

They hurried up the sidewalk and stood under an awning over the front door. Santana hit a buzzer in the lobby and waited for the landlord to let them in. After Santana showed him the warrant he'd secured, the landlord opened Hammond's apartment and asked them to lock the door when they left.

Once inside, Bobbi Chacon yanked her Glock out of her waist holster.

"Hold on," Santana said.

"I'm not letting Soriano get away," she said, raising her Glock as she strode into the living room.

"We don't know that she's here."

"Only one way to find out."

As Chacon started toward a hallway, Santana grabbed her by the arm.

She pulled away. "What the hell, Santana?"

"You follow me," he said.

She glared at him for a few seconds before she blew out a breath. "Fine."

Her belligerent tone indicated it wasn't.

They quickly cleared the bathroom and the two bedrooms, one on each side of the hallway.

"Shit," Chacon said when they came up empty. "Soriano's in the wind."

"We know she's been here," Santana said, holstering his Glock.

"That's a big help."

Santana nodded at the gun still in her hands.

Reluctantly, Chacon slid it in her waist holster.

"Glove up," he said, tossing her a pair of latex gloves he'd taken out of his coat pocket.

"Any idea what we're looking for?"

"Information that might tell us where Soriano is."

Chacon shrugged.

Santana gloved up. "We'll start here in the bedroom."

They searched through drawers, closets, and clothes, looking for anything that might lead them to Ana Soriano.

After thirty minutes of searching, Chacon said, "*Nada,*" her mouth twisted as though she'd tasted something bitter. "Now what?"

"I know one more place we can check."

"Thanks for letting me know."

"You're wound up enough," Santana said, just as his cellphone rang. He recognized Janet Kendrick's number.

"Are you with Bobbi Chacon?" Kendrick asked.

Santana glanced at Chacon, who was rummaging around Hammond's apartment as if there was a clue to Ana Soriano's whereabouts that they'd missed.

Something in Kendrick's voice cautioned Santana to be careful with his answer. So he went with a question of his own.

"Why?"

"The DNA forensics collected from Dylan Walsh's body turned out to be hers. I just gave the information to her boss, Scott Weston. You need to bring Chacon in."

"When I see her, I will," Santana said, disconnecting.

Chacon's cellphone rang. Santana figured it was Scott Weston.

He noted the distinct cellphone case as Chacon pulled her cell from a pants pocket. The case had a leopard design with a woman's full red lips in the background. He listened, hoping to get the gist of the conversation, but Chacon only nodded to herself and responded with, "Uh-huh."

When she clicked off, she stood with her hands on her hips, looking at Santana.

He could tell by the ashen look on her face that Weston had told her to come in.

"What's up?" he asked, offering her a chance to be straight with him.

"Nothing."

"Tell me."

"I don't need your help."

"Help for what?"

She shook her head and peered at Santana, her expression filled with disbelief. "Weston thinks I killed Dylan Walsh."

Chapter 34

Santana parked along the curb in front of a ramshackle single-story bungalow where Chico Caldera lived. The house had a raised roof and was located in St. Paul's North End.

"Thanks for cutting me some slack," Chacon said. "But Weston is gonna be pissed I didn't come in."

"We'll deal with that later. You're my backup—for now."

"So you need me to help you take down Caldera."

"Something wrong with that?"

She shook her head.

Santana also needed Chacon to keep the DEA off his back. As long as she was working the Ryker murder case with him, he had some control over it. Once Chacon was gone, Weston and the DEA could completely take it over.

"You don't believe I killed Dylan Walsh," she said.

"I believe you weren't honest with me about Joel Ryker."

"So I'm lying to you now?"

"You better not."

"That goes both ways, Santana."

He knew she was right. He hadn't been forthcoming about Ana Soriano's involvement in Ryker's murder.

"So we're even," he said.

Chacon sat quietly in the passenger seat for a time, peering out the windshield. "We can't see shit from here. All this rain reminds me of Miami. One reason why I hated the damn place."

"I'll knock on Caldera's front door. You cover the back."

"Don't trust me going in the front after the classic FUBAR at Walsh's, huh?" Chacon said. "I'll tell you this, Santana. That's the last time anyone sticks a gun in *my* back. No more 'fucked up beyond recognition.'"

He handed her an extra two-way radio and flipped up the hood on his SPPD poncho. "Let's go."

A chain-link fence surrounded the bungalow and the side yard. A small open porch with a railing ran along the front of the house.

Heeding Christine Hammond's warning regarding Caldera, Santana unsnapped the retention strap on his Glock, slipped the hood back on his poncho, and knocked on the door.

He knocked a second and then a third time. When he got no response he stood on the front porch, listening to the rain pounding on the roof and gushing out the downspouts. Then he used his two-way to contact Chacon.

"Where are you?"

"On the back porch staying dry," she said.

"Check the garage for a vehicle."

"Roger that."

A minute later Chacon radioed, "There's a vehicle in the garage."

"Stand by," Santana said, pounding on the front door. "Police! Open up!"

Santana waited for a time before knocking again and repeating his demand.

Twenty seconds later, he heard a latch slide back and saw the door open slightly. "Yeah?" a male voice said.

Santana held up his badge wallet. "Mr. Caldera?"

"That's right."

"St. Paul PD. Open up."

Caldera opened the door wider but kept his hand on the doorknob.

Santana recognized the man with the small mouth, curvy upper lip, and dark, heavy-lidded, close-set eyes from Caldera's DMV photo.

"What's this about?" Caldera asked.

"Ana Soriano."

Santana watched Caldera closely, looking for a reaction from the name, but all he got was a lazy shrug.

"Don't know her."

"She sometimes goes by the name of Ana Luna."

"Sorry," he said with another shrug, followed by a yawn. "I was sleeping when you knocked."

"Mind if I come in?"

"What for?"

"Look around."

"I told you I don't know this Ana woman."

"A woman told us you do."

"Then she's mistaken or lying."

"I could get a warrant."

"Why don't you do that," Caldera said, shutting the door and latching it.

"You in yet?" Chacon radioed.

"He won't let us in without a warrant."

"Then get one."

"On what grounds?"

"You're the hotshot detective. Think of something."

He needed an excuse to enter without Caldera's permission. A minute later he had one when a woman screamed.

"You hear that?" Chacon radioed.

"We're going in."

"Me first," she said.

Santana heard a crash from the rear of the building. Knowing he wasn't going through the heavy front door, he slid the Glock out of his holster and sprinted around back. The back door was open. Shattered glass was scattered on the porch and entryway.

He went in, hustling through the kitchen and into a small living room, where he found Chacon cuffing Caldera's wrists behind him. A young woman was seated on a worn fabric couch beside him. The young woman with the stringy blond hair, frail body, and hollow cheeks was wearing only a thin robe tied loosely around her waist. She had a deep bruise on her left cheek. Santana estimated she couldn't be more than sixteen.

"Said her name was Amber," Chacon said. She turned Caldera toward her and shoved him down on the couch.

Santana holstered his weapon. "Amber what?"

The young woman kept her eyes focused on the floor as she said, "Whitmore."

"How old are you?"

"Eighteen."

"Have an ID?"

She shook her head.

"What's your relationship to Caldera?"

"She's my girlfriend," Caldera said.

"That right."

"Yeah. That's right. Isn't it, Amber?" Caldera said, peering at her.

She nodded.

"Did he hit you?" Santana asked.

Amber's brown eyes flitted toward Caldera and then down at the floor again. "No."

"How'd you get that bruise?"

"I . . . fell," she said.

"What made you scream?"

She gave a sidelong glance at Caldera.

"He won't hurt you again," Santana said. He took a step toward Caldera and looked down at him. "Will you?"

Caldera kept his eyes focused on his shoes.

"Why'd you scream?" Santana asked her again.

"I didn't."

"Is there someone else here?"

"No," Caldera said.

"I'm asking her," Santana said. "Shut up till I tell you to speak."

A small smile crept across Amber's lips.

"Why'd you scream?" Santana asked once more.

"I saw a mouse. I don't like mice. That's all."

Santana looked at Chacon. They had entered the house after hearing a scream in order to prevent someone inside from being seriously injured or killed. He knew he had legal standing.

"I'll take a look around," he said.

"You can't do that," Caldera said.

"What did I just tell you?" Santana said. "Something wrong with your hearing?"

Caldera pointed his chin at Chacon and muttered, "She broke my back door."

"Take it up with the city," Chacon said.

Santana gloved up as he walked down a narrow hallway toward the back of the house and entered a bedroom on his right. Men's casual clothes were scattered on the floor and bed. A laptop computer sat on the top of a dresser. Opening a dresser drawer, he saw a loaded Smith and Wesson .38 revolver.

On the bathroom counter farther down the hallway were bottles of perfume, gift cards, and a pregnancy advice book.

In a second bedroom he found a variety of sex toys, a crack pipe, and plastic bins with women's clothes and lingerie in them. High-heeled shoes and boots lined the baseboards.

There were two closed doors in the bedroom. The door to Santana's right led into a small closet filled with dresses hanging on wire hangers.

When Santana opened the second door to his left, he saw a set of wooden stairs. Ten feet up, the stairs turned sharply to the right. He recalled that the house had a high raised roof.

Pulling the Glock from his holster, he climbed the first set of steps before pausing at the turn. He peered around the corner and saw a door at the top of the stairs. He started climbing again, following his Glock.

At the top of the stairs he pressed his back against the plasterboard wall to his left, turned the knob, and pushed open the door. It swung to his right. Then he peered around the corner to his left.

"*Hijo de puta*," Santana muttered.

Chapter 35

"**T**ell me about the two young girls locked in your attic," Santana said.

Chico Caldera slumped in a chair across the table from Santana in an interview room at the LEC. His heavy-lidded eyes were focused on the blank wall above Santana's head as if the answers to life's pressing questions were written there.

Caldera shifted his gaze to Santana's face. "They weren't locked in."

Santana had reported Caldera's address and the information about the two sex-trafficked girls at the residence to the FBI, but he and Chacon had left with Caldera after EMTs arrived, and before the feds had gotten to the house. He wanted to question Caldera before the FBI got their hands on him and cut Santana out of the loop.

He dropped Bobbi Chacon at her hotel after she promised she'd speak to her boss, Scott Weston, about how her DNA had ended up on Dylan Walsh. Then Santana had driven Chico Caldera to the LEC and taken him to an interview room.

The image of the two frail-looking girls in tattered clothes lying on the hard wood floor in the attic still burned in Santana's memory. They were from El Salvador and had told him and Bobbi Chacon the same story. They were fifteen years old and had taken *La Bestia* to the Mexican/US border in Nogales, Mexico, in search of asylum. After an interview with a US Citizenship and Immigration Services asylum officer named Raúl, they were placed in the Intensive Supervision Appearance Program and sent to separate homes across the border in the US. A few weeks later they were drugged and taken to Minnesota, where they were forced into sexual slavery.

"Cut the bullshit, Caldera," Santana said. "You're looking at twenty years and a fifty-thousand-dollar fine for sex trafficking. I'll check with ICE, too. See if you're here legally."

"What you want?"

"Ana Soriano."

Caldera shrugged. "Check your hearing. I told you I don't know the young woman."

"If you don't know her, how do you know she's young?"

Nonplussed, Caldera said, "Figure maybe she's like the girls in the attic."

"You're no help to me, Chico." Santana stood. "I'll let the FBI know you're here. See you in court."

"Hey, Detective. Maybe I have something for you."

"Like what?"

Caldera gestured casually with his handcuffed hands for Santana to be seated again.

"This better be good," Santana said as he sat down.

"Good for me, maybe. Not so good for you."

"Get to it."

A crooked smile creased Caldera's lips. "A policeman recruited girls for me. I can give you his name. But I want a deal."

* * *

Santana returned to the Homicide and Robbery Unit and sat down at his desk. The unit was deserted this late in the day. Janet Kendrick's office door was closed and the blinds drawn. Santana figured she'd gone home as well.

His thoughts and eyes shifted to the cold case murder board on the wall. Something had troubled him when he'd first reviewed the list of ten names recorded by previous cold case detectives. Now he knew what it was.

Ellis Taylor's name wasn't listed on the board.

That made no sense. The unsolved murder of an SPPD homicide detective should be at the top of the list.

In his career Santana believed he'd given equal weight to each and every murder he'd investigated, regardless of whether it involved a homeless person or a rich socialite. But he wasn't naïve. He knew there was more pressure on the department and the brass to solve high-profile killings, especially when the victim was well known. The same was true when a cop was murdered. The department took it personally, as did every officer.

So why wasn't Ellis Taylor's murder given the same attention?

Chico Caldera had fingered Taylor as the cop involved in procuring sex-trafficked young women. Caldera had offered no hard proof. Had Taylor's possible involvement with sex trafficking contributed to his death? But something about Taylor's death didn't fit, Santana thought. Neither did the lack of department follow-up.

He looked for Taylor's case file number in the SPPD's RMS, or Record Management System, but it wasn't there. He'd reviewed all the cold case files previously before choosing Madison Porter's. In hindsight, he didn't recall seeing Ellis Taylor's murder book.

He took an elevator up to the third floor, where the cold case files were stored in a small room not much larger than a closet. Rows of thick blue binders lined the shelves above a vacant desk. Santana quickly scanned each one, searching for the murder book containing information on Taylor's murder.

Ellis Taylor's murder book wasn't there.

He knew that all investigative units were allowed to maintain files of information. However, each commander was required to furnish the records unit manager and their deputy chief a list of the routine records and files kept within the unit that were not submitted through the usual process.

Santana couldn't recall what investigating officers had been assigned to Taylor's case. He called Kacie Hawkins.

"Do you remember who the IOs were on the Ellis Taylor case?"

"Why?"

"I'll explain later."

"I'll hold you to that," she said.

"Who were they?"

"Diana Lee was one."

"And the other?"

"Janet Kendrick."

Santana rode out a jolt of adrenaline.

"You still there, John?" Hawkins asked.

"Yeah. Thanks, Kacie. I'll be in touch."

From the desk chair in his cubicle, Santana stared at the closed door to Kendrick's office. Kendrick might have been the one who put the hold on Taylor's murder book. She could have pulled the file before assigning Santana to the cold case unit. Whether it was Kendrick, or someone else, Santana wanted to know the reason behind that decision.

Santana's cellphone buzzed. It was Kendrick.

"Commander," he said.

"What's going on?"

"What do you mean?"

"Don't play coy with me. The FBI is looking for Chico Caldera. The special agent in charge of the Minneapolis Field Office called me. According to him, you have Caldera in custody."

"He's in a holding cell."

"And why the hell is he there instead of with the feds?"

"I wanted to question Caldera before the feds got ahold of him."

"Regarding what?"

"Joel Ryker's murder. I thought he might know something."

"Well, did he?"

Santana considered asking Kendrick about Ellis Taylor's missing murder book and Taylor's possible involvement with sex trafficking young girls, but a voice in his head told him this wasn't the time. He and Chacon were the only ones who knew they were looking for Ana Soriano besides Tony Novak, who'd found her prints on the Ruger. Santana wanted to keep it that way for now.

"No," he said. "Caldera was a dead end."

"Then turn him over to the feds. And I understand Bobbi Chacon was with you at Caldera's after I told you she was a suspect in Dylan Walsh's murder. Where is she?"

"Turning herself in to the DEA."

"Why didn't you bring her in?"

"I was busy with Caldera."

"Well, I have some bad news for you, Detective. I spoke with Scott Weston right after the FBI called. Weston doesn't know where Chacon is either. So now I've got both government agencies crawling up my ass, thanks to you. I want you in my office first thing tomorrow morning."

"So you're not in your office now?"

"No. I have dinner plans. And you damn well better not mess those up," she said, disconnecting.

Santana doubted Bobbi Chacon had killed Dylan Walsh. But he had little doubt as to where he could find her.

His thoughts returned to Ellis Taylor's missing murder book. He could call Pete Romano, his former homicide commander, who'd been promoted. They still had a good relationship, but Romano belonged to the "good old boys club" and would protect the brass at all costs. A better choice would be Diana Lee, who'd worked in the Gang and Gun unit before transferring to Homicide and Robbery. If anyone would know why Taylor's book was pulled, Santana figured she would.

He called Kacie Hawkins again and requested Diana Lee's cellphone number.

"She's right here," Hawkins said. "You can talk to her on my phone."

A few moments later Diana Lee said, "What's up?"

"We need to meet."

"Regarding what?"

Santana didn't want to discuss Ellis Taylor's missing murder book on the phone. "A case I'm working," he said.

"That's a little vague."

"You have plans for dinner?"

"When and where?" Lee said.

"You name it."

"Six o'clock at the Little Asia Café."

*   *   *

Bobbi Chacon was sitting behind the steering wheel of a Nissan SUV, watching the building where Dominique Lejeune lived. Her cellphone was off so she wouldn't be bothered while she ate the cheeseburger and fries she'd picked up at a McDonald's drive-through near the Hertz lot where she'd rented the SUV. She'd conducted countless surveillances during her years with the DEA and had never gotten used to the boredom and fast food.

Turning off her cellphone so she could eat her dinner was a little lie she'd told herself. She knew Scott Weston would be trying to call her, wondering where the hell she was. Santana would be looking for her, too. She'd promised him that she'd talk to Weston, but she wasn't about to waste time defending herself against a bogus murder charge while Joel Ryker's murderer was still free. Not turning herself in would probably end her DEA career, but the hell with it. She'd find another line of work, preferably one that didn't require her to conduct hours of surveillance and to eat junk food, or deal with drug dealers and sex traffickers, the scum of the earth.

*   *   *

Eddie Machado had noticed the dark Nissan SUV when it had stopped along the curb two houses down from the Italian-ate mansion. The SUV had joined the long chain of homeowner vehicles lining the curb.

Eddie had been surveilling the mansion on and off since last night after leaving Dylan Walsh's house, hoping for an opportunity to enter it in search of El Mencho's half-million dollars. He'd felt comfortable parked here. There were so many cars his wouldn't stand out. He'd figured the driver in the Nissan SUV lived in one of the houses, but when no one exited the dark SUV, he scoped the vehicle with the long lens he carried in his satchel.

The driver was the same woman who'd gone to see Dylan Walsh, the woman driving the Mustang. The lanyard she'd worn around her neck with the badge holder had ID'd her as a cop or maybe a DEA agent.

Eddie had seen her two days ago at the Lozanos' house and then yesterday afternoon when she and the male cop had parked along the curb and entered the mansion, though they'd arrived in an unmarked squad car.

The license plate on the Nissan SUV was from Iowa. Eddie figured she'd chosen a plain-looking rental rather than the con-spicuous Mustang for surveillance.

When she and the cop had come here earlier, they'd spent nearly an hour inside. With his driver's-side window open, Eddie had heard the SPPD cop talking on an intercom with someone when they'd arrived. He couldn't make out all the words, but the cop had been speaking with a woman whose last name was Lejeune. She'd let the man and woman into the building earlier. So why was the woman agent sitting here now?

Eddie chewed on that thought for a time before he arrived at two possibilities.

She was likely waiting for someone other than Lejeune. Someone they'd come to ask Lejeune about. That left two possibilities. The agent could be waiting for him. Or, she could be waiting for the person who'd killed the DEA agent and taken the money from the Lozanos' house. Maybe he was closer to getting the money than he'd thought, closer to returning safely to Mexico and to El Mencho, his protector.

*   *   *

Santana was waiting in a booth along the wall when Diana Lee entered the Little Asia Café, a small restaurant located in the Sunrise Plaza on University Avenue. She was a petite woman with copper skin and shiny, shoulder-length black hair. Her detective badge was clipped to the front of her belt. Santana glimpsed her 9mm Glock in the belt holster underneath her blazer as she slid into the booth across from him.

"Eaten here before?" she asked with an expectant smile.

"Never. Have a recommendation?"

"I like the bok choy."

"Help me out."

"Stir fry with beef, chicken, or pork. But the Hmong sausage with sticky rice is good, too."

When the waiter appeared, Santana ordered the bok choy with beef and a Coke. Lee chose the pork with a glass of lychee.

"What's this all about?" she asked when the waiter left.

"Four years ago you worked the Ellis Taylor murder with Janet Kendrick."

Lee pushed a strand of black hair from the corner of an eye as recognition crept into her face. "Yes. I did. Why do you ask?"

"Because the murder book is missing."

"You're sure?"

"Positive."

"That's odd," she said, her eyes not quite meeting his.

Santana felt she knew something about the missing murder book but was reluctant to admit it, possibly because she feared retribution. He wondered now if Janet Kendrick had deliberately partnered Lee with Hawkins in order to keep tabs on what Santana was doing. Then he dismissed the thought since Lee and Hawkins had been partners before Santana returned from his leave. He went in a different direction.

"Tell me about the Ellis Taylor case."

Diana Lee thought about it, her eyes fixed momentarily on the empty space in front of her. "That evening Taylor and his partner, Darnell Robinson, went for drinks at a blues club after their shift. They left the club at closing, around one a.m. Taylor stopped at the Elysium ATM on the way home. The ATM was isolated. Had a poor line of sight from the street and parking lot. Taylor withdrew two hundred dollars. We checked both the ATM's and the bank's surveillance camera footage. After the withdrawal, the perp came up behind Taylor and stuck a gun in his back. Perp's head and face were covered by a hoodie and bandana. We figured he was waiting in the shadows for someone to come along and make a withdrawal."

"Did Taylor go for his gun?"

"No. He handed over the cash in his hand."

"And the perp just shot him?"

She shook her head. "I think Taylor was reaching for his wallet when he was shot. Maybe the perp asked him for it. Thought Taylor was reaching for the gun on his hip instead."

"Was that Kendrick's conclusion, too?"

Lee nodded. "We agreed."

Santana sat back in the booth as the waiter arrived with their drinks. Diana Lee sipped her lychee while he considered what she'd told him.

ATM robbers were usually male, under twenty-five years old. Many were likely intoxicated on alcohol or drugs. They usually worked alone, but sometimes used a partner for a lookout or getaway driver. They liked to hide near the ATM behind some obstruction until someone alone, preferably a woman, withdrew cash. They tried to avoid the video camera view and usually wore a hat, mask, bandanna, sunglasses, or hoodie to disguise their image. They often chose an ATM machine that wasn't busy and had some cover from the street. They approached from the blind side and victims, like Taylor, never saw them coming.

Santana said, "Any witnesses?"

"None."

"Any previous robberies at that ATM location?"

"None that were reported."

"You interview his KAs?" Santana asked, referencing Taylor's known associates.

"Taylor's parents were both deceased. He was a lifelong bachelor. Broke up with his last girlfriend six months before he was killed. We interviewed her plus two other women Taylor had seen in the past. None of them had anything negative to say about him and were saddened by his death."

"How long did you work with Kendrick?"

"About a year," she said hesitantly. "Till Kendrick transferred to Internal Affairs."

Santana nodded.

"So why are you looking into Taylor's death now?"

"I'm assigned to the cold case unit," he said.

Lee remained silent for a time, her eyes empty of anything he could read. Then she said, "I'm a little uncomfortable talking about Kendrick."

"Why is that?"

"She was my partner."

"And now she's your commander."

"She's yours, too."

"Anything else you can tell me about the Taylor case?"

"Why ask me about the missing murder book and not Kendrick?"

Santana looked at her but didn't respond.

"Is it because you think she has it?" Lee asked.

"Possibly."

"Why would she have taken it from the cold case unit?"

"Same question I'm asking," Santana said.

Chapter 36

Ana Soriano had taken a taxi to a large cottage-style house in a rural area just east of St. Paul near the town of Lake Elmo. The house sat on twenty acres of thick-forested land overlooking a lake and park reserve. In the bright moonlight Ana could see a barn and storage facility behind and to the right of the house.

As the taxi drove away, she let out a little laugh of relief. With visions of the police stopping the cab, she couldn't believe that she'd made it safely out of the city. She shuddered, knowing that if the Mexican assassin found her, things would be far worse than capture by the police.

Dominique Lejeune had told her that Diego Bianchi lived here and could provide her with a passport to get her out of the country.

Grabbing the backpack at her feet, she walked in the moonlight toward the front door of the house. Stars shimmered in the blackness overhead. Lamplight filtered through the blinds on the windows.

She rang the doorbell, the chimes unsettling the dark stillness surrounding her.

A slender man dressed in a crisp white shirt, unbuttoned at the collar, and neatly pressed wool pants cracked open the heavy wood door.

"Yes?" he said.

"I need your help."

"There's a service station in town."

As he started to close the door, Ana placed a hand against it. She'd never seen his tanned, mustachioed face before, but she recognized the Rioplatense dialect spoken in Buenos Aires and southern Italy from the languages she'd studied while "educating herself" as Dominique Lejeune had taught her to do.

"My car does not need help, Mr. Bianchi. I do."

"How do you know my name?"

"Dominique Lejeune sent me."

Bianchi's eyes narrowed as his expression shifted from annoyance to concern.

"My name is Ana Soriano."

Bianchi hesitated, unsure. "You were supposed to arrive tomorrow night."

"Things changed."

Bianchi waited a moment more before he let her in.

She followed him across the dark hardwood floor and into a living room that had a vaulted beamed ceiling, a heavy stone fireplace, and floor-to-ceiling windows.

Bianchi gestured for her to sit on a long leather couch.

She dropped the backpack beside her on the floor and sat down.

He stared at the backpack for a time, his tongue sliding across his thin lips.

His wide forehead seemed out of place with the rest of his narrow face, Ana thought.

"Would you care for a drink?" he asked. "I have extra *añejo* tequila. It's a vintage tequila aged between—"

"One and three years in small barrels," Ana said.

"Yes," Bianchi said with a little smile.

"Good that you can afford it," she said, letting her eyes scan the opulence. Dominique Lejeune had explained to her who Diego Bianchi was and how he'd become rich.

Supposedly a rug importer, Bianchi rinsed the dirt off money for the CJNG. In a classic real estate bait-and-switch scheme, he laundered the cash by placing the money made by the cartel in the US in offshore accounts and then used his percentage of the take to buy expensive real estate. Once he owned the properties, he used them as collateral to take out millions of dollars in loans from US banks. Since the money was in the form of loans rather than income, he paid no taxes on it.

Bianchi's method, also known as smurfing, involved breaking up large amounts of money into smaller, less-suspicious amounts below $10,000—the dollar amount at which US banks had to report the transaction to the government. Bianchi's money was then deposited into one or more bank accounts over an extended period of time.

Now Bianchi went to an elegant-looking granite-topped bar with a dark wood finish opposite the fireplace. He poured two ounces of tequila into a pair of snifters and brought one to Ana.

"I prefer a *caballito*," she said, using the Mexican term for shot glass. "*Con limón*."

"As you wish." He set one snifter on the coffee table in front of her and returned to the bar.

"Bring me the bottle," Ana said, recalling how she'd been drugged before. "I'll pour the tequila."

"You don't trust me?"

"No," she said.

"And yet you are here asking for my help."

"I don't have much choice."

"Perhaps not."

He placed a lemon wedge in a napkin, picked up the bottle of tequila and a shot glass, and placed them on the coffee table.

"That's the last of it. So take your time and enjoy it."

She watched as he sat in a heavy leather chair across from her, holding his snifter at the stem as he swirled the tequila gently to the left, creating a string of pearls effect as it clung to the walls of the glass.

"The dark gold color is perfect," he said with a satisfied smile. He tilted the tequila toward the lower rim and sniffed it before taking a small sip, which he held in his mouth.

"You should learn to drink it the Mexican way."

Ana poured the tequila in the shot glass, drank it in one quick swallow, and slammed the glass on the coffee table. Then she sucked the lemon slice.

"Perhaps I should," Bianchi said with a crooked smile.

"Do you have my passport?" Ana asked.

"I should have it tomorrow." Bianchi held up the snifter. "Perfection takes time. You cannot rush it."

"Time *is* the problem, *Señor* Bianchi. What am I supposed to do till then?"

He made a sweeping gesture with his hand. "You are welcome to stay here for the night. By tomorrow evening you shall have what you've come for."

*   *   *

During her three hours of surveillance of the Lejeune mansion, Bobbi Chacon had observed people coming and going in the neighborhood. But as dusk settled over the landscape and shadows grew long and hard, traffic had decreased and the neighborhood had grown quiet.

As Chacon opened her driver's-side window to let in some fresh air, she spotted someone walking along the sidewalk, heading in her direction. At first, she wasn't certain if it was a man or a woman because of the hoodie over the walker's head. But through endless hours of observation and experience, she knew men's movements tended to be straight and linear, and that men took longer strides and walked with their legs farther apart. Women tended to take shorter strides and to keep their legs closer together, which resulted in less side-to-side movement, even when walking swiftly.

Subconsciously, Chacon brushed the handle of the Glock on her hip, as if to confirm it was still in the holster, and fixed her eyes on the man moving toward her.

His hands were concealed inside the pockets of his hoodie. He walked with his head down, apparently comfortable in his environment.

Chacon watched as he passed by the thick trunk of a large oak tree and then the passenger side of the SUV. She picked him up again in her rearview mirror, her eyes focused on him as he continued walking north along the sidewalk till he turned left at the end of the block and headed west. False alarm.

She was still staring into the rearview mirror when she felt the gun barrel pressed against the back of her head. Instinctively, she reached for the Glock on her hip.

"Don't," the man said with a slight Spanish accent.

"My money is in my purse on the passenger seat," she said.

"I don't want your money."

She figured as much, though she'd held out some hope that this was merely a robbery. "Kill me and the DEA will be coming for your ass and for that sick fuck in Mexico you work for."

The man snickered. "Not if they are as stupid and as incompetent as you, *señorita*. Now slide your gun out of the holster with two fingers of your left hand and give it to me. If you make any sudden movements, I will put a bullet in your brain without thinking twice."

She did as told.

"Hand me your cellphone."

She gave it to him.

He dropped it on the asphalt and stepped on it hard. Then he brushed it under the SUV with a foot.

"Now we will walk together to the entrance of the building you have been watching. You will press the intercom. Again, if you make any unnecessary movements or try to attack me, it is over. *Estás terminada.* Understand?"

Chacon said nothing till he pressed the gun barrel harder against the back of her head. "I understand."

"Step out," he said. "Slowly. And keep your eyes focused ahead."

She did, closing the door behind her.

He pressed the gun against her spine and said, "Walk."

Chacon knew if she made a move, he would kill her. He was using her to get inside Dominique Lejeune's apartment and might kill her anyway once they were safely inside. She still had the gun in her ankle holster and the benefit of surprise. But it wouldn't be easy. This guy handled himself like a pro.

"When we get to the front door," he said, "you will ring the intercom and look up at the camera. You will tell the woman who answers that you need to talk with her again."

Chacon nodded, realizing now that the man had been watching Santana and her when they'd come to question Lejeune.

The man stood out of view of the camera, his back pressed against the building, and the gun barrel aimed at her chest.

Chacon wanted to get a look at his face, but he stood in the deep shadow of the building. She pressed the intercom.

"What is it, Agent Chacon?" Dominique Lejeune said after a twenty-second wait.

"I need to speak to you," Chacon said.

"About what?"

"We have reason to believe that the Mexican assassin is in the area."

The man waved the gun barrel at her.

"I'm safe in here," Lejeune said.

What a pain in the ass, Chacon thought. Going in another direction, she said, "I need to ask you some questions regarding new information that's come to light."

"Go ahead."

"Look, Ms. Lejeune. Perhaps we got off on the wrong foot last time. If you'd give me a few minutes, I'll be on my way. If you want to make a big deal out of this, I can come back with a warrant, and we can take it downtown."

"Where's Detective Santana?"

I wish I knew where the hell he was, too, Chacon thought, regretting now that she'd shut off her cellphone.

"He's running down a lead and asked me to talk to you."

"All right," Lejeune said. "But make it quick."

Chacon heard a buzz and then the door clicked open.

*   *   *

After leaving the Little Asia Café, Santana headed for Dominique Lejeune's mansion. He had a hunch that Bobbi Chacon had gone back there, hoping to spot Ana Soriano or the Mexican assassin who'd killed Dylan Walsh. It was what he would've done.

As he drove slowly along the street leading to Lejeune's, through pools of light from the streetlamps, he looked for Chacon's Mustang among the vehicles parked along the curb. He cruised past the mansion and drove another block before making a U-turn. He hadn't spotted the Mustang and realized now he wouldn't.

Chacon would use another vehicle for surveillance.

He started back in the opposite direction, his eyes scanning the vehicles on each side of the street, hoping to spot her. He'd passed the mansion once more when he saw an open driver's-side window on a dark SUV. Nothing unusual about that, except it was dark and leaving a window open in your vehicle in the city was asking for trouble, no matter what neighborhood you lived in. Still, people sometimes forgot.

Santana backed up so that his headlights illuminated the license plate.

IOWA.

Could be visitors from out of town. Or it could be a rental.

No vehicles were approaching in either direction. He killed the headlights, engine, and interior lights and got out, closing the door behind him.

Flicking on the mini-Maglite in his left hand, he approached the SUV, his right hand resting on his Glock. He beamed the interior, making sure no one was inside. McDonald's wrappers were scattered on the front seat. A cup half-filled with Coke sat in the cup holder.

As he leaned in, something crunched under his shoes.

He squatted and focused the beam on the asphalt.

Plastic.

Bending lower, Santana peered under the SUV and immediately recognized the leopard pattern case on Bobbi Chacon's shattered iPhone.

He shut off his Maglite and quickly looked around. Then, staying low, he returned to his SUV. He drove to the next corner, found a place to park on a side street, and headed back on foot toward Dominique Lejeune's residence. Bobbi Chacon was likely in there. And, Santana figured, so was the Mexican *sicario*.

Whether Chacon and Lejeune were still alive was anyone's guess—as was a way to get inside.

Chapter 37

Bobbi Chacon sat on her butt, her back pressed against a cool radiator, fuming that she'd let herself get taken by surprise again. Her hands had been tied behind her with plastic zip tie cuffs, and a blindfold had been affixed over her eyes. She still had the gun in her ankle holster but no way to get at it.

She sensed that Dominique Lejeune was seated on the couch across the room from her. She'd heard Lejeune's hands being bound behind her back and a yelp of pain as the *sicario* had tightened them. She wondered if he'd covered Lejeune's eyes as well. If he hadn't, it meant he didn't care if she'd seen his face, which meant Lejeune was as good as dead unless Chacon could get to her gun.

The zip tie cuffs weren't a problem. Whether her hands were tied in front of her or behind, she'd learned long ago how to break out of them. To snap the cuffs from behind, she only needed to bend and pull outward as she slammed her wrists hard against her tailbone. But if she tried it while the *sicario* was still in the room, she'd be dead, too.

He pulled the lanyard with her ID card out of her pocket. "DEA," he said calmly as he stood over her.

"That's right, douchebag. Or do you have another name?"

"Eddie," he said.

"Know what happens when you kill a DEA agent, Eddie?" She didn't wait for his response. "All hell rains down on you."

"Then we have something in common," he said, tossing the lanyard in her lap.

"Like what?"

"Help me find the woman who killed the DEA agent named Joel Ryker and stole the money from the Lozanos. Or hell will rain down on the two of you."

"If I knew where she was, I wouldn't be here," Chacon said.

"Ah, yes," he said. "We *are* searching for Ana Luna."

Chacon was about to say "Soriano," and then caught herself. Santana had told her that Ana Soriano had assumed the surname of Luna. That was the name Dylan Walsh knew her by. It might make it harder for the *sicario* to find her.

"You killed Dylan Walsh after he gave you her name," Chacon said.

Eddie didn't respond and Chacon thought he was about to kill her, too.

Then he said, "You don't know where Ana is, do you? On the other hand."

Chacon heard him walk away toward Dominique Lejeune on the other side of the room.

Lejeune whimpered.

"My partner is on his way here," Chacon said, hoping to bluff him and stall for time.

"He better hurry," Eddie said.

*　　*　　*

Santana knew he wasn't getting into the secure mansion through the front door or barred windows, so he worked his way in the dark around back, using his mini-Maglite to light the way.

He wasn't a big believer in burglar bars. They could hinder any attempt to get into the home, but they could also trap residents inside during an emergency. He knew of several fatal house fires where bars over the windows or doors had prevented occupants from escaping or hampered attempts to rescue them. Most local codes now required that window bars have a quick-release feature. More importantly, windows within the city limits of St. Paul could legally be equipped with bars—except for egress windows.

The back wall of the mansion had two such windows set in window wells made of corrugated galvanized metal. He figured the alarm had been deactivated to allow Chacon and the *sicario* to enter.

Using the solid end of his Maglite, Santana punched a hole in one of the windows large enough to reach his hand through and unlatch the window. It swung upward on hinges, barely giving him enough room to crawl through and drop to the basement floor five feet below.

He heard a skittering sound as he landed on his feet beside a set of three rusted cast iron laundry tubs. In the flashlight beam he saw a large cockroach crawl down one of the drains. Letting the beam play across the cement floor and walls, he located a wooden staircase directly ahead. The stairs led to a landing and then angled straight up to his right to a locked door.

Using his small tension wrench and feeler pick, Santana picked the lock. The door creaked as it swung slowly open on its hinges into a kitchen pantry stocked with canned and baking goods, boxes of pasta, and spices and oils.

Santana flicked off his Maglite, dropped it in his coat pocket, and drew his Glock. Then he opened a second door that led directly into a large open kitchen. Once he had his bearings, he found the staircase on the first floor off what was once the living room and was now a photo studio.

He climbed the carpeted steps to the second-floor landing outside the door to Dominique Lejeune's apartment. He knew from his previous visit that the heavy, thick door had a deadbolt. His only chance of getting in was if the door was unlocked. Carefully, he turned the doorknob and gave it a slight push.

It swung open.

Santana stood with his back against the wall and peered into the room.

No one.

His eyes scoped the area as he followed his Glock into the room. On the floor to his left he saw a set of broken flex cuffs and a blue bandana.

He headed down the hallway leading to the workout studio but stopped when he came to an open door on his right. Peering around the doorjamb, he realized it was the master bedroom.

Bobbi Chacon was standing beside a king-size round bed covered with satin sheets and a burgundy bedspread. A large round mirror was attached to the canopy over the bed. Chacon was holding her duty weapon along the side of her leg and looking down at Dominique Lejeune's body lying in a pool of blood on the hardwood floor.

"Chacon," Santana said softly, pointing his weapon at her.

She whirled toward him, bringing her weapon up.

"Easy," he said.

"Jesus, Santana! You scared the hell out of me." She holstered her duty weapon and gave him a relieved smile.

"What happened here?"

Chacon's smile vanished. "How about lowering *your* weapon."

Santana did but didn't holster it. "Is the place clear?"

Chacon nodded. "The *sicario* who killed her left five minutes before you arrived."

"Why did he let you live?"

"DEA has some advantages. Killing me just adds fuel to the cartel fire here and in Mexico."

"Can you ID him?"

"He blindfolded me. Never got a look at him. He made sure of that. Which is why he let me live."

"You get anything from him?"

"Said his name was Eddie. And I could tell by his accent that he was Mexican."

Santana holstered his weapon and crouched beside Dominique Lejeune's body. Keeping clear of the pool of blood behind her head, he saw that she'd been shot between her eyes and was no doubt instantly killed.

"Somebody loved to look at her naked self," Chacon said, staring at the mirror on the canopy bed, her hands fisted on her cocked hips, a wry smile on her face. "Bet she liked to look at whoever she was with, too."

Santana let the observation go.

"You think Lejeune told the *sicario* Ana's real name and where she is?" Chacon asked.

Santana stood and looked at her. He could smell the light, sweet fragrance of the pomade in Chacon's hair. "That's why he separated the two of you and took Lejeune into the bedroom. He didn't want you to hear what she told him."

"Maybe Lejeune didn't give up Soriano," Chacon said.

"With a gun pressed against her head? I doubt it. Like most people, she'd do anything to save her life."

"I wouldn't," Chacon said.

At first, Santana mentally dismissed Chacon's words as merely bluster. One look at her eyes, and he believed it.

"What about you?" Chacon asked.

"Depends on the situation."

"So you'd sacrifice someone else's life to save your own?"

"Lejeune saw Eddie's face. He would've killed Lejeune no matter what she'd said or done."

"I'm talking about you, Santana, not Lejeune."

"Anyone in that situation is already dead," he said. "So no, I wouldn't have given up Soriano."

Chacon grinned. "Despite all your obvious faults, Santana, I always hoped you had *cojones*."

Santana was about to ask her what exactly were his "faults" and then reconsidered.

"Eddie, the *sicario*, killed Dylan Walsh and Dominique Lejeune," she said. "That clears me of Walsh's murder."

Santana thought so, but he'd still have to convince Kendrick.

"So what's the next move?" Chacon asked.

"I get a warrant and forensics. Hope I can find something that points us in the right direction."

She skewered him with a glare. "What about me?"

"You make yourself scarce till I finish up here."

"And why should I do that?"

"Because I have to notify my commander, Janet Kendrick. If she shows up, she'll arrest you."

"You owe me one, Santana. Now's your chance to prove it."

*   *   *

One hour later the Cathedral Hill mansion was buzzing with Forensic Services unit and ME personnel. Yellow crime scene tape was strung across the doorway and was manned by a uniform with a clipboard holding the Crime Scene Attendance log. Outside, the media horde clamored for interviews.

Santana had notified Janet Kendrick. She would notify the deputy chief and Chief Tim Branigan of Lejeune's homicide. Branigan wouldn't want to be left in the dark once the media called. After speaking with Kendrick, Santana had called the Forensic Services Unit. Then he'd gotten his laptop out of his SUV and typed a computer affidavit. He'd e-mailed the affidavit to the Ramsey County attorney, who had forwarded it with an application for a search warrant to a judge.

Hands gloved with latex, shoes covered with booties, Santana and Chacon stood in Dominique Lejeune's living room waiting for the search warrant.

Martin and Benita Lozano, Dylan Walsh, and Dominique Lejeune, he thought. All four deaths related to the CJNG cartel and the missing half-million dollars. Who was next? Ana Soriano.

Santana's cellphone beeped. He scanned the text. The judge had approved the search warrant and was sending it to Santana's SPPD email address.

He needed a clue to Ana Soriano's location. He was betting that's where Eddie, the *sicario*, was headed.

Forensics had wheeled out Dominique Lejeune's body, so he and Chacon started their search in the master bedroom. The bedroom had the same boiserie walls and parqueted floors as the rest of the huge mansion. The decor reminded Santana of the Palace of Versailles, which he'd visited as a young teen with his sister and parents.

"Well, lookie here," Chacon said, paging through a medium-sized black notebook she'd found in a large manila envelope in the nightstand drawer.

Santana walked over to her. "What is it?"

"Black gold," she said, handing him the notebook.

As he turned the pages, Santana realized that no names were listed, only phone numbers.

"Harder to identify her clients," Chacon said, stating the obvious.

"We'll bag it as evidence," Santana said, thinking he'd like to crosscheck the phone numbers in Dominique Lejeune's black book with the list of names Gabe Thornton had given him using the reverse directory.

"Anything else in the envelope?" he asked.

Chacon removed a series of 8.5" by 11" sheets of paper.

"Looks like bank statements," she said, handing them to Santana.

He paged through them. "Individual accounts in women's names."

"For her escorts?"

Santana nodded. "Be my guess."

"Not real well hidden. Same with the black book."

"Lejeune figured the house was impregnable."

"Guess she figured wrong," Chacon said.

They spent twenty more minutes searching the master bedroom and then headed for the living room.

"Has to be something here that can tell us where Ana Soriano is," Santana said.

First thing he saw when they returned to the living room was Janet Kendrick. If looks could kill . . .

"Detective," she said.

It was more of a pejorative than a title.

"And this must be Agent Chacon," Kendrick added sarcastically, glaring at Chacon.

Chacon gave her a phony grin.

"What happened here?" Kendrick asked as her eyes locked on Santana.

He explained how he'd been surveilling Lejeune's home. How the *sicario* had kidnapped Chacon and used her to get inside. How he'd found Chacon's broken phone and entered through the basement window, only to find Dominique Lejeune dead.

"Want to hear my version?" Chacon asked Kendrick once Santana had finished.

"Not particularly." Kendrick removed the metal cuffs from the back of her belt. "I'm placing you under arrest."

"On what grounds?"

"Let's start with the murder of Dylan Walsh."

"That's bullshit."

"Hand over your weapon, Agent Chacon."

Chacon looked at Santana for support.

He said, "Chacon didn't kill Walsh."

"Frankly, Detective, I couldn't care less what you think."

Kendrick pushed back the flap of her blazer, revealing the holstered Glock on her right hip. "Your weapon," she said again to Chacon, the threat obvious in her voice.

Chacon smirked and handed Kendrick her weapon. "You going to cuff me, too?"

"Turn around," Kendrick said to her.

Chacon shook her head in disgust and turned around, her wrists behind her.

Kendrick cuffed her.

"Look, Commander," Santana said. "The *sicario* who killed Dominique Lejeune is the same guy who killed Dylan Walsh."

"And why would he do that?"

"Because he thought Walsh knew where Ana Soriano was."

"And who's Soriano?"

"She's the chief suspect in Joel Ryker's murder. The *sicario* is after the half-million dollars missing from Martin and Benita Lozanos' safe. Soriano has it. She worked as a high-price escort for Dominique Lejeune and likely came here for help."

"So why isn't Ana Soriano's name in any of your reports?"

Because I didn't want her being hunted down and killed by the DEA or SPPD before I could bring her in, Santana thought. But instead he said, "Chacon and I just figured it out."

"Is that so," Kendrick said, the skepticism obvious in her voice and the mild scowl on her face. "If all of this is true, then what's Chacon's DNA doing on Walsh?"

"She was after Soriano and wanted Walsh to tell her what he knew. It got a little rough. But she didn't kill him. The *sicario* did."

"And who's this *sicario*?"

"First name is Eddie," Santana said. "He's likely works for the CJNG cartel in Mexico. The DEA recently raided a number of their stash houses."

"Have you seen this *sicario*? Does he even exist?"

"He'll kill Ana Soriano unless we find her first."

"So you haven't seen him."

"He murdered Dominique Lejeune," Chacon said.

"What does he look like?" Kendrick asked.

"I was blindfolded. I couldn't *see* him."

"So you're no help." Kendrick directed a uniformed officer to take Chacon to his squad car. "I'll be down shortly."

"You're making a big mistake," Chacon said as she was led out the door.

"Seems to me you made a bigger one, Agent Chacon."

Kendrick faced Santana. "Go home and get some sack time and a shower. I'll see you in my office. Ten sharp, Detective."

"I don't have time to sleep and shower. I need to find Ana Soriano. Now."

Kendrick shook her head, but Santana could see the hesitancy in her body language.

He pressed his case. "If we try to pin Dylan Walsh's murder on Chacon, the DEA will eat our lunch."

"You mean they'll eat mine."

"That, too."

Kendrick looked at him for several long seconds before speaking. "Well, you could use a shower, but that can wait."

It was Kendrick's first attempt at humor. A good sign.

"But I need Chacon with me," he added.

"Why?"

"Because if we cut off Chacon, the DEA will cut us out. Remember, it was their agent, Joel Ryker, who was murdered."

"What are you looking for?"

"Somewhere Ana Soriano might've gone. I think Lejeune told the *sicario* before he killed her."

"All right," she said. "But you damn well better keep me informed."

"What about Chacon?"

Kendrick let out a breath. She crossed her arms as her gaze moved off Santana. "I'll send her up."

Santana's initial adrenaline rush had receded, replaced by a heightening sense of weariness. He needed to stay sharp and focused, and a good night's sleep would help. But he had to find Soriano before the *sicario* did.

He stood still in the room while the forensics team worked around him, his eyes searching for something, anything that might help him figure out where the young woman had gone.

Then his eyes settled on the open wooden jewelry box on the coffee table.

The box contained business cards, but not Dominique Lejeune's. The name on the cards was Diego Bianchi. Rug importer. The address was in Lake Elmo, east of St. Paul.

Someone, probably Lejeune, had likely given out one of Bianchi's cards with his address and phone number. Since the box was open, Santana figured it had happened recently and that Lejeune had neglected to close it. Might make sense to leave the box open permanently if it contained her business cards. Then again, it was all conjecture on his part. But he had nothing else to go on.

He considered calling Bianchi and then changed his mind. Intuition told him there could be something to this.

He looked at his watch. It was nearly midnight.

Santana decided to pay *Señor* Bianchi an unannounced visit.

Chapter 38

Eddie Machado counted four luxury rides parked in the long circular driveway in front of the large cottage-style house. He liked that the house was located in a rural area surrounded by a thick forest. Better to escape if it ever came to that. But he didn't like the cars parked in the circular drive. More people usually meant more problems. Dominique Lejeune had confessed that the woman he was searching for was Ana Soriano and not Ana Luna. If Soriano was here, Eddie wanted to get the money and get out as quickly as possible.

The house was well lit. Maybe a small party going on, Eddie thought. He wondered if Soriano was somehow connected to the place and if whoever lived here was armed.

Time to do some reconnaissance.

Eddie had parked fifty yards from the house near the tree line in the deep shadows of some pines. Now he retrieved his FN-7 from the glove compartment, made sure the overhead light was off, and got out of his rented Hyundai Santa Fe.

A stream of thin black clouds inked the sky. Eddie waited for one to cover the moon before heading for the house. Then he glimpsed a flicker of light out of the corner of his eye. He wasn't sure where the light had come from at first. He thought it had come from one of the windows near the back of the barn.

Not a bulb light. More like a lantern or a flame.

Now Eddie could hear solemn organ church music coming from the barn.

Eddie headed in that direction, seventy-five yards in the distance, moving swiftly across the shadowy grass, the gun held comfortably in his right hand, the scent of pine heavy in the cool night air.

He stayed low as he reached the gabled barn, ducking under each of the first two windows along the nearest wall till he reached the third and last window.

Eddie was sure this window was where he'd first glimpsed the light, but what appeared to be black silk covered the inside of the panes. Through a small gap along the edge of the silk, he was able to see a lit torch held in a sconce attached to a thick post. Standing near the torch he caught a side view of a figure dressed in a dark green hooded monk's robe with a waist cord.

His instincts told him it was a man dressed in the robe, but he couldn't be sure because a weird-looking mask covered the guy's face.

What the fuck?

He checked the two other windows, but both were totally blacked out.

Moving swiftly to the front of the barn, he saw that the sliding double doors were slightly apart. Through the slim opening, Eddie could see a long, wide room lit with torches and candles. The windows on both sides were covered with black silk and the floor with silver tiles. A line of mirrors ran the length of the room on both walls.

At the far end of the barn a hooded figure with a mask sat on a stool in front of a pipe organ. The music the figure played sounded like something from a horror movie.

It'd been a long time since Eddie had felt afraid, at least when he was awake. But this scene, this music sent a chill through him, as though someone had rubbed an ice cube along his spine.

Four figures in monk robes and masks were standing around a naked young woman in the center of the room. Her arms were tied behind her back. The rope securing her hands was connected to a tall wooden frame that held her upright. Her waist-length hair was as black as the silk covering the windows. The glazed look in her stunning eyes suggested she'd been drugged.

A figure to Eddie's right was filming with a video camera. Another was holding a boom mike above the wooden frame. A third man was seated on a chair behind a small table that held a laptop computer. The fourth man was reading from a script.

"This is Ana. As you can plainly see, she's a beautiful young woman. Her measurements are thirty-six, twenty-two, thirty-four. She's very experienced sexually, but is completely disease free. We guarantee it. She will make the buyer a very happy man. Bidding starts at fifteen thousand dollars."

Before he'd shot her, Dominique Lejeune had told Eddie what Ana Soriano looked like. To Lejeune's credit, she hadn't begged or pleaded. Eddie respected her for that and had killed her quickly.

The woman in the center of the room sure fit Lejeune's description. The guy had called her Ana. If the woman *was* Ana Soriano, then where was the half-million dollars? And what the hell was going on?

Eddie wasn't proud of much of what he'd done in the last four years, especially killing Isabella. But most of those he'd tortured and killed were members of other cartels El Mencho was at war with. Hell, their *sicarios* were doing the same things to El Mencho's *sicarios*.

But what he wasn't into was selling young women into sexual slavery. Besides, he needed Ana to tell him where the money was.

Eddie checked for security but saw none. Then he pushed the sliding barn doors open enough that he could slip through.

"Step back!" he yelled as he strode forward, his gun held in front of him in a two-handed grip.

The organ music stopped.

The figure at the organ reached for something under the bench.

Eddie shot him.

Then he waved the gun at the four figures. "On your knees! Hands on your head!"

The monk with the video camera and the one with the boom mike dropped the equipment on the floor and joined the other two figures on their knees.

Eddie moved to the left side of the wooden frame and looked into the eyes of the young woman. He saw Isabella now, not this young woman named Ana, and he shook his head and squeezed his own eyes shut for a moment, trying to erase the memory. One of the many ugly memories Eddie carried with him like a heavy weight.

Eddie palmed his switchblade and cut the rope holding Ana to the frame, and then the rope binding her wrists.

He wrapped an arm around her waist to keep her from collapsing. Eddie said to one of the kneeling hooded figures, "Stand up and take off your mask and robe."

The figure removed the mask. Eddie saw that it was a guy, like he'd thought. Probably mid-50s. Well groomed. Nice tux. The guy looked like money.

"Toss me the robe," Eddie said.

Eddie caught it with his free hand and slipped it over Ana.

"Back on your knees. Hands on your head. You three," he said. "Get rid of the masks and robes."

The others looked much like the first man. Dressed in tuxes. Distinguished. Manicured hands that had probably never done any hard labor.

One of the men started crying. "Don't shoot, please. We have money. We can pay you."

Eddie had never met a rich man who didn't think he could buy his way out of trouble, including politicians, businessmen, and the cartel *patrons* he'd known—but not this time.

Eddie shot him.

Looking at Ana, he said in Spanish, "I have been looking for you, Ana Soriano."

He smiled at her and stuck the gun barrel against the side of her head.

"Where is the money, *señorita*?"

Chapter 39

At one fifteen in the morning Santana and Chacon arrived at Diego Bianchi's estate and found the five bodies in the barn. All five men had been shot, one beside the pipe organ and four others to the right of a crudely constructed wooden frame. One of the four had been shot in the chest and three in the back of their heads. Based on the angle of the wounds, Santana figured all four were on their knees at the time they were shot.

Santana recognized only one of the dead men. He was Hal Langford, James McGowan's campaign manager.

A robe lay beside each body—except for the man who'd been shot in the chest.

Ana Soriano wore that robe.

She sat on the tile floor, her chin lolling on her chest, her left arm stretched above her head. A rope bound her left wrist to the T of the wooden frame.

Initially, Santana thought that she'd been shot, too, but upon closer inspection, he'd determined that she was unconscious or drugged.

Santana gloved up, loosened the rope binding her wrist, and knelt beside her.

"Ana," he whispered, attempting to rouse her.

"Leave her be," Bobbi Chacon said.

Santana peered up at her.

Chacon stood to his right, her hand resting on the grip of her holstered Glock.

"Move away from her," she said.

"What the hell are you doing?"

"She murdered my partner."

"No, she didn't."

"Quit protecting her, Santana."

"I told you before that Martin Lozano shot Ryker in the head with his Sig Sauer. Forensics matched the bullet in his brain with the gun."

"You're lying."

Chacon backed up two steps as Santana stood up.

"I'm not the one lying."

Chacon's cat-like eyes skittered as she processed his accusation.

"Maybe you and Ryker were working together. Maybe the two of you were after the money all along."

"You're full of shit, Santana."

"Am I? Ryker cut you out and went in alone after the money. You've been looking for it ever since."

"This is crazy."

"Planning to kill me?"

Ana gave a soft moan.

"I can show you the forensic reports, if you're still not convinced that Martin Lozano killed Ryker," Santana said. "In the meantime, I'm calling the EMTs and local sheriffs. We need to get Ana to a hospital."

Santana took out his cellphone and squatted in front of Ana as her eyelids fluttered open. "We'll get you some help," he said, brushing her cheek lightly with a hand.

Peering up at Chacon, Santana said, "Eddie has the money. He's probably on his way back to Mexico. But if you're still planning on shooting us, now's the time. Otherwise, give me a hand."

*   *   *

While EMTs checked Ana Soriano's vital signs, Santana and Chacon gave their statements to the local sheriff's department and to the state Bureau of Criminal Apprehension investigators who were assisting in the investigation.

Ana Soriano hadn't said much after her traumatic experience, but she'd confirmed what Santana had expected. The *sicario* had killed all the men. Inexplicably, he'd left her alive after locating the backpack with the half-million dollars of stolen cartel money in the house.

Using her federal status as a DEA agent, Chacon had big-footed the local deputies and BCA investigators and had taken Soriano into custody.

Santana gathered from the conversations between the BCA investigators and the local sheriff's deputies that Diego Bianchi, as well as Hal Langford and the other dead men, were prominent members of Twin Cities society.

Now Santana and Chacon stood outside a private room at Regions Hospital. After getting an okay from the EMTs, they had driven Ana Soriano to the emergency room, where she was examined. Having found no life-threatening injuries, but wanting to err on the side of caution, a doctor had advised that she remain in the hospital overnight.

"I'll take the lead on this," Chacon said.

Santana shook his head. "I don't think so."

"You want me to haul Soriano's ass to DEA headquarters, I'm happy to do it."

"You owe *me*, now," he said.

She chuckled. "How do you figure that?"

"If it wasn't for me, you'd still be sitting in a squad car or in one of the LEC interview rooms, telling your story about Dylan Walsh's murder to Kendrick. Or worse yet, you would've killed an innocent woman and be charged with murder. If I didn't kill you first."

"Is that right?"

"You know it is."

Chacon stared at him for a time before acknowledging with a shrug that Santana was right.

"If you're wrong about Joel's murder," she said, her hands fisted on her hips, "I want a confession from Soriano."

"Let's listen to her story before pronouncing judgment."

They went into the hospital room. Santana pulled up a chair beside Ana's bed. Chacon sat in a chair on the opposite side.

"Would you like water?" Santana asked.

Soriano's blue eyes were focused on her left hand that was shackled to a siderail. She shook her head slowly. Despite the hospital gown and horrific trauma she'd been through, he could see that she was a beautiful young woman. But it was the gaunt, haunted look in her eyes that held his interest. He'd seen that look before in victims of abuse.

Santana spoke to her in Spanish, figuring she'd be more comfortable speaking in her native tongue and knowing Bobbi Chacon was fluent in the language.

"I know you're from El Salvador. How old are you?"

"Nineteen," she said as her gaze shifted downward.

Santana thought she was lying, but he let it go for now. "How did you end up here in St. Paul?"

She lifted her eyes and looked at him, at Chacon, and back at Santana again.

Then she told them her story, speaking in a monotone voice, about fleeing from her country on the train known as *la Bestia*. How a man named Raúl had placed her in the Intensive Supervision Appearance Program and allowed her to stay at his sister's house in Nogales, Arizona, while she waited for her court hearing. She lowered her gaze once more as she spoke of her experiences of being drugged, and how she'd ended up with sex traffickers and eventually with Dominique Lejeune.

"Tell us how you got the money the *sicario* wanted," Santana said.

Chacon leaned forward in her chair.

"I took a taxi to the Lozanos' house the night before."

"Had you been there previously?"

She nodded. "Two times. I am not bisexual. Benita Lozano liked to watch Martin have sex with me."

"What happened early the next morning?"

"A man came into the bedroom with a gun. He told Martin to open the safe. Martin said he didn't have a safe, but the man knew there was a safe behind a picture on the wall."

Santana looked at Chacon and then turned his attention back to Soriano.

"Then what happened?"

"Martin opened the safe. The man told him to put the money in a backpack. But Martin pulled a gun out of the safe and the man shot him. Then, for no reason, he shot Benita."

"Why didn't he shoot you?" Chacon asked.

"I thought he was going to shoot me, too," Ana said. "He told me to put the money from the safe in the backpack. Then he put the gun to my head and asked me why he shouldn't shoot me. I told him I wouldn't tell. He said he thought I was probably illegal and needed to get out of here before the police came."

She paused and stared blankly into the distance.

"Go on," Santana said.

"I saw a chance to change my life," she said, gazing at Santana, her eyes filling with tears. "When the man headed for the door, I made a grab for Martin's gun and told him to leave the money and go."

"But he didn't," Santana said.

"No. He dropped the backpack on the floor and reached for his gun. I heard a shot as I closed my eyes and pulled the trigger."

"So he spared your life, and you killed him," Chacon said in Spanish, making no attempt to disguise the bitterness in her voice.

"Agent Chacon," Santana said as a warning.

She raised her palms in a surrender gesture and leaned back in her chair.

Ana's description fit the scenario and the ballistics evidence. Santana looked at her again.

"You said you heard a shot before you pulled the trigger. Who fired the shot?"

"I don't know. It happened so fast. When I opened my eyes, the man was dead."

"How do you know?"

She pointed toward the side of her head. "He had a bullet wound here."

"What did you do then?"

"I took the backpack and walked to my friend's house."

"Why didn't you take a gun with you?" Chacon asked.

Ana looked at Chacon. "Because I am not a killer."

Chacon stared at her for a time, but didn't reply.

"You went to Christine Hammond's apartment," Santana said.

Ana looked at him again. "Yes. Christine told me her boyfriend Dylan Walsh could help me if I paid him some of the money."

"Help you do what?"

She shrugged. "I wasn't sure at the time. But when I went to see Walsh, I saw two men enter his place. I did not like the way they looked and left."

That would be Washburn and Moody, Santana thought.

"So then you went to Dominique Lejeune for help," he said.

"Yes. I decided I wanted to go to France. She sent me to Diego Bianchi's house for a passport. But he must've slipped a drug in the bottle of tequila he gave me. I thought if I poured the tequila, I'd be safe. It was stupid of me. When I woke up, I was naked and tied to the wood frame. The hooded men were going to sell me. The *sicario* saved me."

Her tone of voice suggested she still didn't believe it.

"Did you see his face?"

She nodded. "Even though I was very groggy."

"Could you describe the *sicario* to a sketch artist?"

She looked blankly at Santana. "His eyes."

"What about them?"

"They were as dead as a snake's."

"Anything else you recall?"

"There was no feeling in his smile. It was thin and tight-lipped. Like a scar."

"The *sicario* shot everyone?"

"*Sí*. They were on their knees. The *sicario* asked them where the half-million dollars was. Bianchi said he'd tell him, but only if the *sicario* wouldn't kill him. The *sicario* promised he would let him live if he told the truth. If Bianchi lied, the *sicario* would kill him. Bianchi told him where the backpack with the money was. But the *sicario* lied."

She looked into Santana's eyes. "Why didn't he kill me?"

"I don't know."

"He covered me with one of the robes. Had me sit on the floor. He tied my wrist to the frame. And then . . ."

"Then what?"

"I saw a glint of . . . *emotion* in his eyes. Like he actually cared. It was very strange."

Santana could see the confusion in her own eyes.

"Had you ever seen Bianchi before?"

"No."

"How about any of the other men?"

She shook her head.

"Tell me about Dominique Lejeune."

Ana pointed to the side table. "Can I have some water, please?"

Santana filled a Styrofoam cup half-full and handed it to her.

"More?" he asked when she'd finished.

"No. Thank you."

She set the Styrofoam cup on the side table. Then she told them how she'd come to meet Dominique Lejeune through Chico Caldera.

"Dominique told me I could go back with Caldera or learn how to become a high-priced escort like the other young women at the party. She promised me that someday she would let me go. It was my choice."

"You mean you had *no* choice," Santana said.

"Not really," she said. "But Dominique was good to me and the other girls. She taught me manners and French. A percentage of the money I made she put aside, so I would have what she called a 'nest egg.' Usually once a month there were parties held at expensive homes in and around the cities."

"Do you know who any of these men are or where they live?"

"No. All the girls were blindfolded when we were taken to the parties. And when I had sex, it was always in a very dark room except when we were videotaped. But then we were blindfolded."

"What happened to the videotapes?"

"I don't know. But Dominique said that if we ever ran away and tried to start a new life without her permission, the videotapes would be released on the Internet. We would never be able to start a new life or get a job. And Chico Caldera threatened to hurt my mother in El Salvador if I didn't cooperate or to have me deported. If I go back to my country, the MS-13 will kill me like they did my brother."

"Did all the men videotape you and the others?"

"Some men did and some didn't."

"But you don't know who any of them are?"

She hesitated. "None except Martin."

"You're sure?"

"Of course."

"Did Martin Lozano attend the parties?"

"No. But he liked to videotape me having sex with him. That's why he had the hidden camera."

Santana straightened up. "In his house?"

"Yes."

"Where?"

"Somewhere in his bedroom."

Chapter 40

An SPPD sketch artist drew a composite of Eddie, the *sicario*, based on Ana Soriano's description, and the department issued a BOLO. Santana wrote a search warrant for the Lozanos' bedroom on his laptop computer and emailed it to a judge. While he waited for a response, he drove home for a quick shower, a shave, and a change of clothes. Back at his desk in the Homicide and Robbery unit, and fueled by a hot breakfast of eggs, chorizos, and cups of hot chocolate, he was working on reports when his personal cellphone rang.

He recognized the number belonging to Kelly Quinn, the *Pioneer Press* crime reporter, and a contact he'd used in the past. He let it ring a few times before answering.

"Santana."

"What went on in the barn in Lake Elmo?" she asked, sounding out of breath.

He could hear the hum of voices and the whirling blades of a circling helicopter in the background and gathered that she was on-site with the media horde.

"Can't give you that information," he said, "till the families of the victims are notified."

"Come on, Detective. My gut tells me this'll be a big story. Give me something."

"Okay. It'll be a big story. Call me later," he said, disconnecting.

It was early evening when Santana parked his department ride in the Lozanos' driveway. He and Chacon got out. As they headed for the front door, Santana veered off the sidewalk toward the corner of the house.

"Where you going?" she asked.

Santana flicked on his large Maglite. "I need to check something."

Chacon followed.

Santana stood in front of a flowerbed along the side of the house and held the beam on a large plant.

"They're black dahlias," Chacon said.

"I know."

"So?"

"Might be important," he said, making for the front door.

In the Lozanos' bedroom, they checked the books and bookshelves, the lamps, electrical outlets and wall sockets, a tissue box, the digital TV box, picture frames and the wall behind them, looking for the hidden camera Ana Soriano had told them about. There were no cushions or stuffed toys in the room that might have concealed a camera.

"Soriano was bullshitting us," Chacon said.

Santana gestured at her with a hand. "Close the blinds."

They each took one of the windows.

"Now what?" Chacon asked.

"Turn off the light switch."

"How the hell we gonna find anything with the lights off?"

"Do it," Santana said.

Chacon hit the light switch, plunging the room into darkness.

Santana took out his cellphone and put it in camera mode.

"What're you doing?"

"Surveillance cameras usually use infrared light for night surveillance," he said. "IR is only visible by a camera. You can see the same thing using a television remote. Just press the buttons while pointing it at your smartphone's camera. You'll see the infrared light emitted by the IR LED on the remote."

"Who taught you that?"

"A sociopath named Reyna Tran."

"How did—"

"Don't ask," he said.

Santana pointed his smartphone camera around the room. "Look for any bright or dim red or purple lights."

After a few seconds Chacon said, "There! On the wall! I see the infrared light."

"Of course," Santana said. "A fake smoke detector."

*   *   *

Later that evening Santana and Chacon sat in chairs on either side of Lynn Pierce at the SPPD forensics lab. She was working overtime on a Friday evening and had agreed to help them view the video on the camera they'd found in the Lozanos' bedroom.

Following the chain of command, and before processing the audio and video evidence, Lynn Pierce had removed the SD memory card from the camera and made a working copy, assuring that the original evidence would always be available in its unaltered state and for comparison to the processed copy.

"We never change the recorded data," she'd said. "Just enhance what's already present."

Once the SD memory card copy was inserted into a USB-C hub reader plugged into Pierce's computer, Santana said, "Go back to the night a week ago last Wednesday."

"That shouldn't be a problem," Pierce said. "This memory card can store up to one hundred twenty terabytes."

One minute later they were watching Martin Lozano and Ana Soriano have sex on the Lozanos' king-size bed. Benita Lozano was sitting on the edge of the bed, watching and masturbating.

"Should've brought some popcorn," Chacon said.

Santana rolled his eyes at her and said to Lynn Pierce, "Skip ahead."

At 5:47 a.m. on the time stamp, Joel Ryker entered the bedroom.

"Stop there," Santana said.

He leaned forward in his chair. Chacon did the same.

"Play it," he said.

What they saw on the screen matched the description of events provided by Ana Soriano. The kill shot had come from Martin Lozano's Sig Sauer. He'd struggled to his feet and to the safe and the second gun as Ryker headed for the bedroom door. When Ryker turned around to face Ana and saw the gun in her hand, his entire focus had been on her. He'd never seen the fatal shot coming.

It was also clear that with her eyes closed, Ana Soriano had no idea where she was shooting, other than in the general direction of Ryker. She managed to hit him in the shoulder and then his hip as he slid down the wall, already dead from the bullet in his brain.

Martin Lozano had collapsed and died after firing the fatal shot.

*   *   *

It was nearing midnight when Santana drove Chacon back to her hotel, following the red taillights along I-94 that streamed through the darkness.

The adrenaline rush that had galvanized him since yesterday had burned out. He needed another shower and a good night's sleep.

"You'll talk to Scott Weston?" he asked Chacon.

"First thing Monday."

"No question now about who killed Ryker?"

"You were right," she said.

"Not about everything."

She looked at him, her body tilted toward him in the passenger seat. "What do you mean?"

"How did Ryker know where the Lozanos' safe was?"

Chacon shrugged. "Suppose he figured it was on the wall. That's where most safes are hidden."

Santana shook his head. "You watched the video. There was no hesitation. He knew exactly where the safe was behind the Frida Kahlo picture."

"Lucky guess."

"I don't think so."

"Where're you going with this?"

"Did you and Ryker ever surveil the Lozanos' home?"

"Sure, because of the upcoming raid."

"You were working on the illegal meth pill distribution."

"That involved mostly pharmacies."

"You'd come across the Lozanos' names during your investigation."

"We did," she said.

"So how else could Ryker have known where the safe was —and how much was in it?"

"What're you getting at?"

Santana didn't want to hurt her, but she needed to know the truth. "When I searched Ryker's apartment, I saw a 'Thank You' card next to a vase of black dahlias."

Chacon thought for a moment. "Like the ones we saw in the flowerbed at the Lozanos'?"

"The same."

"So?"

"So the message on the note was a thank you for a 'quickie' Ryker had with a woman. She signed the note 'B' at the end. I thought it stood for you, Bobbi. But it didn't. It stood for Benita Lozano. Ryker was sleeping with her."

"Shit," Chacon muttered.

"You never wrote that note or gave him black dahlias?"

She shook her head.

"Looks like Ryker loved himself and the money. My guess is Benita Lozano planned to have him murder her husband, take the half-million, and frame Ana Soriano for it."

"What about the video?"

"Benita probably planned to destroy it. But Ryker decided to cut her out and take the money himself. According to the credit cards and bank statements in his apartment, he was up to his eyeballs in debt."

Chacon sat silently in the passenger seat for a time as Santana drove through the night.

He continued. "You watch that video carefully again, you'll see Benita Lozano's eyebrows raised and her jaw drop in surprise when Ryker points his gun at her. A split second later, her look turns to fear when she realizes Ryker plans to kill her. Remember, Ana Soriano said he shot Benita Lozano for no reason. Now we know what the reason was."

"But Soriano saw Ryker's face."

"But she couldn't very well admit it. That would open up a whole can of worms."

"My *partner*," Chacon said bitterly. "That son-of-a-bitch. I never was any good at picking men."

Chapter 41

When the BCA released the names of the dead men in the Lake Elmo barn on Saturday afternoon, it set off a feeding frenzy among Twin Cities media. Santana had spoken by phone with Kelly Quinn late Friday evening after dropping off Bobbi Chacon, and the *Pioneer Press* featured her byline prominently on the front page above the fold. Her headline story linked the dead men to the After Dark Club and the sex trafficking of young women.

James McGowan had released a short statement denying any knowledge of Hal Langford's involvement in sex trafficking and had temporarily suspended his Senate campaign.

Quinn had also written a feature story about Ana Soriano based on the information Santana provided. As promised, Quinn had described Soriano as a victim who'd first been trafficked and then forced into escorting for her own survival. Soriano had now become a key witness in the upcoming trials of those involved.

On orders from Janet Kendrick, Santana had told Quinn nothing about Ana Soriano's connection to Joel Ryker's death, the Lozanos' murder, the missing half-million dollars, and Eddie Machado.

On Saturday evening, Santana took Rita Gamboni out for dinner at the newly renovated Lexington Restaurant on the corner of Lexington Parkway and Grand Avenue. The restaurant had been in operation on and off since 1935 and was a gathering spot for local politicians and celebrities. The latest restoration had added a rooftop bar, but the two of them sat at a round table covered with a white linen tablecloth in the elegant dining room.

Rita looked stunning in a burgundy sheath column, knee-length chiffon dress. The scoop neck and three-quarter-length sleeves were made with lace sequins. She wore a slim sterling silver necklace with a garnet teardrop pendant and matching drop earrings.

Rita ordered the seared sea scallops and Santana ordered the salmon Oscar. They shared a bottle of an oak-aged Chardonnay and a walleye cakes appetizer.

"Rumor has it the deputy chief's announcement will come next week," Santana said.

"Possible," Rita said with a hint of a smile.

"Good luck."

"You really mean that?"

"If it's what you want, then, yes, I do."

"That's not exactly a ringing endorsement."

"You're walking in with your eyes wide open. You know the risks."

"And the rewards," she said.

Santana took a bite of walleye cake and thought about his next comment. "You have political ambitions, Rita?"

"Only ambition I have right now is deputy chief of major crimes."

Santana thought the words "right now" were prescient.

"I saw the story in the paper about the young El Salvadorian woman," Rita said, changing the subject. "What's going to happen to her?"

"The DA has placed her in Freedom House now, where she'll get some help and support to get out of the life."

"And she'll testify for the prosecution," Rita said.

"Ana Soriano isn't a murderer. Martin Lozano killed Joel Ryker, the DEA agent, after Ryker tried to rip off a half-million in drug money."

Rita was about to take a sip of her wine but paused. "You know this for certain?"

"Lozano had a hidden camera in the bedroom. We've got the video."

"I didn't see anything about it in the paper."

"The DEA and department will bury it or come up with another story."

"You don't care?"

"As long as Ana Soriano isn't charged with murder, I'm good."

Rita sipped the wine and set her glass gently on the table. "Sensational case like Ryker's would be hard for the DA to walk away from," Rita said. "Especially if he has political aspirations."

"You think he does?"

"Never met one who didn't."

"Always the political angle."

"You've found ways to get around it before."

"Having you as deputy chief won't change my commitment to the truth, Rita."

"I never expected it would."

Santana finished his walleye cake and drank some wine. Then he said, "Sex trafficking might be connected to Ellis Taylor's murder. Haven't put all the pieces together yet. Maybe you can help me."

Rita cocked her head. "How?"

"When you were commander, did you assign Taylor and Robinson to Madison Porter's murder case, or did they request the assignment?"

Rita considered the question for a time before answering. "I believe they requested the assignment."

"Both of them?"

"I can't say for certain, but it might've been Robinson."

Santana nodded. "Janet Kendrick and Diana Lee worked Taylor's murder."

"And?"

"Taylor's case file number isn't in the RMS," Santana said, referencing the SPPD's Record Management System. "And Taylor's murder book isn't with the rest of the cold case files."

"You think Kendrick pulled it?"

"I do."

"Well, all investigative units are allowed to maintain files of information."

"But isn't each commander required to furnish the records unit manager and their deputy chief a list of the routine records and files kept within the unit?"

"If they weren't submitted through the usual process."

"So why would Kendrick pull Taylor's murder book?"

"Only one way to know."

"Thought you might say that," he said.

*   *   *

After arriving home late that evening, Santana sat in a soft leather chair in the living room, nursing a glass of aguardiente, an anise-flavored Colombian liqueur derived from sugar cane. Gitana lay curled on the floor at his feet.

The dinner with Rita had rekindled the spark between them, despite obvious pitfalls. They'd both felt it, especially after a long and passionate goodnight kiss. But rather than succumb to the heat of the moment, they'd both agreed to proceed slowly. Perhaps because each knew that if their relationship failed for a second time, there would be no attempt at a third.

Santana was still amped up from the evening as thoughts of his current cases and his previous Dalínian dream drifted into his consciousness. An idea emerged.

Salvador Dalí wrote of "the taut and invisible wire that separates sleeping from waking." During this short period of hypnagogia, our sense of here and now transitions from the real world to the dream world, often causing out-of-body experiences and lucid dreaming states that were unreachable during waking consciousness and in deeper sleep. Dalí used a napping technique he called the "slumber with a key" to unlock this state of mind and to release the radical ideas of his subconscious.

In that brief hypnagogic state between sleeping and waking, Dalí momentarily entered a state similar to REM sleep where his mind was fluid and hyper-associative, allowing creative connections to form between seemingly remote concepts unrecognizable to him in waking thought.

Santana had begun experimenting with this technique while he was on leave from the SPPD and visiting his sister, Natalia, in Spain. Like Dalí, this "sleeping without sleeping" had helped open his mind to the meaning of his dreams and to his subconscious, without what Dalí called the "heaviness" of a longer *siesta*.

To achieve this state that allowed him to dip into his subconscious, Santana set his drink on the coffee table and took his house key out of his pocket. Holding the key in his left hand, lightly pressed between his thumb and forefinger, he tilted his head back and let his arms hang over the arms of the chair. Then he closed his eyes and relaxed.

Dalí always placed an upside-down plate under the key so that he would hear it when it fell from his hand. From experience, Santana knew that his house key falling on the hardwood floor would bring him quickly back to consciousness.

He'd also experimented at work with a simpler and quieter spontaneous nap procedure in which he sat perfectly upright with his neck unsupported. The muscle paralysis that occurred at the onset of sleep would cause his head to nod off.

Now, as Dalí had instructed, Santana let his mind be "progressively invaded by a serene sleep, like the spiritual drop of anisette of your soul rising in the cube of sugar of your body."

As Santana descends into the depths of his subconscious, his body freezes as if he were in a block of ice. For a moment he's in a grove of twenty-foot higueras, *or fig trees. He reaches for one of the brownish-purple fruits hanging from the twisted branches and the deeply lobed, wide leaves, but the fruit is just inches beyond his outstretched hand.*

Then he's startled by the sound of the key hitting the hardwood floor.

The sleep paralysis gradually lifted, like a heavy blanket removed from his body.

Santana sat up in the chair and saw Gitana staring at him, a look of concern in her eyes and on her face.

"I'm fine, girl," he said as his mind continued searching for the symbolic meaning.

He felt the images of the fig trees were related to the cases he was working. Knew that he was close to making the connection. As close as his outstretched hand was to the low-hanging fruit.

*   *   *

After a long Sunday morning run with Gitana, a cool shower, and a hearty breakfast, Santana sat down at his dining room table and began comparing the SEXTO list of thirty men Narco/Vice Detective Gabe Thornton had provided with the list of phone numbers in the black book Bobbi Chacon had found in Dominique Lejeune's nightstand.

Santana found a dozen matching numbers, indicating that some of the men on Thornton's list belonged to both SEXTO and the After Dark Club Ana Soriano had told him about.

The rest of the numbers from Dominique Lejeune's black book either had nothing to do with SEXTO, or these particular men hadn't been caught up in the sting operation led by Narco/Vice.

Santana found no match for some of the remaining phone numbers in the reverse directory. He figured those numbers either belonged to burner phones or burner phone apps that concealed the user's call history from anyone gaining access to their phone bill.

Burner phone apps didn't show whom you called or who called you on your monthly billing statement. But, no matter how efficient the burner app was, the service provider could still trace it. The provider could identify your location as well by using the data from cell phone towers. If he had to, Santana could get a warrant that would force the company behind the burner app to disclose the information used when signing up.

He hoped he wouldn't have to go that route.

There were nearly seventy phone numbers in Dominique Lejeune's black book. Santana would turn over the information to Gabe Thornton in Narco/Vice. But he could find no connection that would lead him to the person who had murdered Madison Porter.

Before returning the black book to the evidence envelope, Santana made copies of all the pages. Then he drove to the Freedom House women's shelter to see Ana Soriano.

* * *

When Santana arrived at the shelter, he discovered that Ana had slipped out sometime during the morning hours. The staff had no clue where she might've gone.

Santana thought he might.

He found her in Dominique Lejeune's mansion, ransacking the bedroom. Since forensics had finished processing the crime scene, no uniformed officer was guarding the front door.

"You won't find what you're looking for," Santana said, startling her.

She whirled around, her hand on her heart.

She'd changed into a pair of faded jeans and a black halter top that revealed a bit of her toned belly.

"We found the bank statements when we searched the place."

"One of those accounts is mine."

"I suspected it was."

"The money," she said, tearing up. "It's all I have. I *earned* it."

"I'm sure you did."

"What am I supposed to do now?"

"Let someone help you."

"I want to go back to my apartment, not the shelter."

"With no money?"

She dropped down on the edge of the bed, put her face in her hands.

"If the DA finds out you left the shelter, he'll put you in jail."

"I'm dead if I'm sent back to El Salvador."

Santana sat down beside her and handed her a wad of Kleenex from the box on the nightstand. "If you testify for the prosecution, the DA will work to keep you here."

She rubbed her eyes and blew her nose. Then she looked at him with a coy smile and put her hand on his thigh. "I can be good to you if you help me."

He shook his head. "It isn't like that, Ana. It doesn't have to be like that ever again."

She quickly withdrew her hand as her face flushed with embarrassment. Looking away she said, "It's all I know. It's who I am now."

"No," Santana said. "You can be whoever you want to be."

She sat still for a time as her breathing slowed.

Santana saw the tension release from her body.

"Why do you want to help me?" she asked, her eyes empty of anything he could read.

"I was sixteen when I came to this country alone. But I had a support system here. A couple that helped me. Without them, I don't know where I'd be today."

He stood. "I have to take you back to the shelter. I need you to promise me you'll stay there till I can speak to the DA and find a better situation."

She peered up at him. "Promise me you'll get me out of there."

"I will," he said.

She searched his face with her eyes, looking, he imagined, for reassurance that he was telling the truth.

"Okay," she said.

He smiled. "Good decision."

She looked away. "There is something I didn't tell you."

"Oh?"

"All the young women I met."

"What about them?"

She peered up at him, a confused look on her face. "When they got a little older, they disappeared."

"How do you mean?"

"We'd all attend the parties, and then one night one or two of the girls wouldn't be there. I'd never see them again. Usually another younger girl or two would attend in their place. Dominique said the older girls had fulfilled their contracts and collected the money she'd put aside for them. But I never believed it. Something happened to them."

Santana was putting it together now. The men in the barn who'd attempted to sell Ana Soriano. Christine Hammond drugged and videotaped. The young woman he'd seen tied to a wooden frame on the SEXTO website on Martin Lozano's computer. He remembered her name was Serena.

"You found Dominique's black book?" Ana asked.

"Yes."

"I have one, too. But mine has the names of many of the men and some phone numbers."

"You told me you never saw their faces."

"I didn't. But when I used their bathrooms, I always checked the medicine cabinets. Many were taking medications. Their names and phone numbers were on the pill bottles. And when they used the bathroom or went into another room, I would find their wallets in their pants pockets. I have a list in my apartment."

Santana's heartbeat kicked up a notch. "Do you give me permission to search your apartment?"

"Yes."

"I'll make good use of the list."

"You'd better," she said.

* * *

Once Eddie Machado had collected the money and taken out the sick fucks that were about to sell the young El Salvadorian woman, he'd driven to Wichita, Kansas, approximately halfway between the Twin Cities and El Paso, Texas.

As he drove, his thoughts kept shifting to Ana Soriano. She was nothing to him. And she'd taken the cartel money that didn't belong to her and already spent some of it. She was as guilty as the men that had tried to steal it from her.

So why had he let her live?

Because she reminded him of Isabella, the only woman he'd ever cared about. He was hesitant to use the word "love," as he had no idea what the word meant now. He'd loved his parents. But that was so long ago that he'd forgotten the feeling. He only remembered the joy that he'd felt when he was with Isabella, and the gut-wrenching emptiness and tearful sorrow he'd felt when he'd shot her.

He wondered if he'd ever love anything or anyone again.

He'd rented a room in a La Quinta Inn and slept in fits and starts because behind his eyes he saw the faces of others he'd killed, like a movie playing in his head. Then he saw Isabella's face, and it jolted him awake.

Tears ran down his cheeks. He'd cried when he shot Isabella. He'd cried when his relatives asked him to leave the house, and he'd spent his first night alone on the streets of Mexico City.

Maybe he'd cried the first time a man had used him for pleasure, and he was left with searing pain and self-loathing that had dulled over time like the blade of a cheap knife.

Letting Ana Soriano live made him feel good. Sure, she'd reminded him of Isabella. Could've passed for her twin, maybe. But he told himself now that he would've let her live no matter who or what she looked like. He was tired of the killing, especially innocents that were caught in crossfires or those, like Isabella, who were in the wrong place at the wrong time.

At sunrise, Eddie showered, ate a decent buffet-style breakfast, and hit the road again, stopping only for gas and fast food before checking into a Holiday Inn Express fourteen hours later, where he slept for a solid, dreamless eight hours. Given the problems he'd encountered with the Sinaloa Cartel and the CBP agent, crossing the Arizona border was too risky.

In a phone call with his CJNG contact, Eddie had been told to cross the border in El Paso, where it would be safer. The CJNG had a presence across the border in Ciudad Juárez, strengthened by its alliance with the Nuevo Cartel de Juárez, or New Juárez Cartel. But presence didn't equal dominance. Like other large cartels, the CJNG had found it increasingly difficult to control strategic territories the more it expanded.

Eddie knew that the CJNG had less influence in Ciudad Juárez than rivals such as Los Salazar, a powerful cell of the Sinaloa Cartel, and La Línea, an increasingly powerful faction of the Juárez Cartel. Then there were the numerous smaller street gangs, which controlled much of the micro trafficking.

So, yeah, he'd cross the border in El Paso because that's what he'd been told to do, but nothing was truly safe.

Eddie stayed in Album Park, one of El Paso's safest neighborhoods. Having spent some time running shipments across the border, he'd learned that neighborhoods like Album Park, Zack White, and Mission Hills were the safest places to stay. He steered clear of higher-crime areas like Borderland, Central, and

Las Tierras. He didn't want to shoot some crackhead or meth freak trying to rob him of the nearly half-million dollars he was carrying and then be forced to spend the rest of his life in a US prison.

He dropped the Hyundai Santa Fe at an Alamo agency and took a taxi back to the hotel, where he waited for another CJNG *sicario* to leave him a car for the trip across the border.

Chapter 42

On Monday morning Santana stopped by Janet Kendrick's office. She was seated behind her desk, reading a report on her desktop. She looked up and waved him in. "I'm reading your summary report on the Ryker killing."

Santana sat down in a chair in front of her desk.

"Just got off the phone with Scott Weston at the DEA," she said.

Santana waited.

"Impressive work, Detective."

"Ryker murdered Benita and Martin Lozano and tried to steal a half-million dollars in drug money."

"I saw the video and sent a copy to Weston."

"How's the DEA going to spin it?"

"However they want. But Weston will owe us," she said. "I'll have him in my pocket. You have a problem with that, Detective?"

"Not if they keep Ana Soriano out of it."

Kendrick sat back in her chair and tapped the tip of her pen on the desktop. "She shot a DEA agent."

"It was clearly self-defense. And Martin Lozano fired the fatal bullet."

"What about the money she attempted to steal?"

"The drug money was her ticket out of the sex trade. Don't see how a jury would ever convict her, given that Ryker was crooked. The DA knows that would all come out in a trial. Something the DEA wouldn't appreciate."

Kendrick gave him a thin smile. "Have this all figured out, huh?"

"Wasn't hard."

"Why so much interest in the girl?"

"She needs a break," Santana said.

Kendrick quit tapping her pen. "I suppose something can be arranged. She's been through a lot."

"There's something else," he said.

"Related to the Ryker killing?"

He shook his head. "Ellis Taylor's murder."

Kendrick's pale complexion flushed.

"Where's Taylor's murder book?"

Her eyes stayed locked on his, but they had a glazed look as if she were seeing something else. Then she said, "I worked the case. It was never solved. I'm still trying to solve it."

"That the only reason you have the murder book?"

"Be careful, Detective."

Of what? Santana thought. "You could've had me look into Taylor's murder when you assigned me to the cold case unit."

"I let you choose the case you wanted."

"So I'm choosing."

"Why are you looking into Taylor's case now?"

"Because I think Taylor was involved in sex trafficking."

Kendrick's eyes narrowed. "Can you prove it?"

"I have an eyewitness and sex trafficker named Chico Caldera."

"And you believe him?"

"I do. And I need to see Ellis Taylor's murder book."

Kendrick hesitated before responding. "This is between you and me. You discover something, you come to me with it and no one else."

He nodded, but he wasn't going to let the department or Kendrick bury this one.

*　　*　　*

Santana decided he'd read Ellis Taylor's murder book that night after dinner. For now he switched gears and reviewed the list of names he'd recovered from Ana Soriano's apartment. He'd located the list inside a picture frame hanging on the wall, where she'd told him it was hidden.

Now, as Santana looked at the list of names and phone numbers, he smiled to himself. A blackmailer would have a field day with the prominent men who used the services Lejeune provided. It didn't surprise him. The assholes thought they were untouchable.

He made a phone call and then headed for The Nook to meet James McGowan.

The Nook, a popular St. Paul neighborhood bar and restaurant, first opened in 1938. Known for its Juicy Lucy burgers and featured on the *Diners, Drive-ins, and Dives* program, legend had it the location was once a horse barn and a gas station.

Santana sat with McGowan at a table in an old train car in the basement bar, where over sixteen thousand one-dollar bills dangled from the ceiling. Many of the bills were pinned by toothpicks and signed by the donator. Customers not seated in a booth or at a table sat on bar stools that ran the length of the long bar. Through the glass windows opposite the bar, Santana could see the Ram-Ham Bowling Center, a classic old bowling alley with open ball returns and wood lanes that smelled of smoke, beer, and oil.

"Try the bacon cheeseburger with onion rings," McGowan said. "I'm buying."

He was dressed in a burgundy polo shirt and khaki pants. His hair was perfectly coiffed and his nails neatly trimmed. A gold Rolex glistened on his wrist.

Santana smiled and said, "Thanks, but I'll pass. This isn't a social call."

"Didn't think it was. But you might as well enjoy yourself while we're here."

"Maybe another time."

"Suit yourself. So I imagine you're here about Hal Langford. Truly an ugly situation." Not waiting for Santana's reply, McGowan said, "And something I know nothing about." He offered a politician's smile that was full of bright white teeth but lacking in any warmth.

"Tell me about the After Dark Club," Santana said.

McGowan raised his eyebrows in a questioning look. "Never heard of it."

Santana took a sheet of paper from the inner pocket of his sport coat, unfolded it, and slid it across the table.

McGowan scanned the paper. "What's this?"

"A list of phone numbers and names given to me by an escort. All the men on that list belonged to the club run by a woman named Dominique Lejeune."

"The recently murdered madam."

"That's right. Hal Langford's name is on the list."

McGowan shook his head. "He made a big a mistake."

"Belonging to the club certainly was. But here's the rub. Many of the women used by the men in the club were victims of sex trafficking. You know any other men on the list?"

"Wait a minute now, Detective," McGowan said, raising a hand in a stopping gesture. "I sure as hell never belonged to any sex club involved in trafficking."

Santana kept his eyes on McGowan's face, looking for any tells indicating that he was lying. Either McGowan was a practiced liar—not out of the question for a politician—or he was telling the truth.

"Did you know about Langford's involvement?"

"Of course not. If I had, I would've fired him on the spot."

"Who hired Gordon Grant?" Santana asked.

"I told you before, it was an agency."

"I need the name."

McGowan gave it to him. Then he looked down at his half-eaten burger and then at Santana again. "You ever read any Henry David Thoreau?"

"In high school."

McGowan nodded and leaned back in his chair. "Thoreau wrote that 'The price of anything is the amount of life you exchange for it.'"

"An odd man to quote considering the fortune you've built, isn't it?"

"I'm using my money to help build a better world. Thoreau was an environmentalist, as am I. We both believe in the power of the individual. I can't accomplish what I need to accomplish, Detective, if the people who work for me are continually involved in scandal. After Gordon Grant . . ." He paused and shrugged, as though the answer were obvious.

"I go where the case takes me."

"No matter who gets hurt in the process?"

"Tell that to the women victims," Santana said.

Chapter 43

Four bridges spanned the border between El Paso and Ciudad Juárez, Mexico. One was the Stanton Street Bridge. It had three southbound vehicular lanes and one vehicular northbound dedicated computer lane for SENTRI holders. The Secure Electronic Network for Travelers Rapid Inspection was a US Customs and Border Protection program that allowed expedited clearance for pre-approved, low-risk travelers entering the United States at Southern land borders.

Eddie figured he'd use the Stanton Street Bridge, which usually had less traffic and security. All he had to pay was a three-dollar toll and he'd be home free.

After a shower and a shave, he tossed the briefcase with the money in the trunk of the late model white Honda Accord a *sicario* had left for him in the Holiday Inn Express parking lot and headed for the bridge.

* * *

Danny Valdez still felt a twinge of pain from the bruise on his chest as he stretched his arms above his head and got up from his chair at the SENTRI processing facility adjacent to the Stanton Street Bridge. If it hadn't been for the Kevlar vest, the bullet that had struck him in the chest would surely have been fatal. As he tumbled backwards down the hill near Nogales, Arizona, that day, he remembered a saying he'd learned in training.

"If dispatch doesn't know where you are, then only God can help you."

Fortunately, a passerby had seen his unmanned SUV parked at the side of the road. Curious, he'd stopped and seen Danny at the bottom of the hill. EMTs had taken Danny to the emergency room, where he'd been released after an examination.

Despite Danny's protests, his wife had insisted he transfer to a safer and more secure location. One week later his supervisor had transferred him to El Paso and the Stanton Street Bridge facility, where he was more likely to die of boredom than a gunshot.

The facility was staffed by the DHS and CBP. Danny had no problems with his new colleagues. Everybody had welcomed him. But he missed Arizona and wanted to be where the action was. His wife and kids were still there, packing up before the move. So he was living in a hotel and looking for a house to rent between shifts.

Today the temperature in El Paso had hit 102°. By 8:15 in the evening, as twilight veiled the city, it had cooled to a balmy 85°. He was used to the Arizona heat, but the air here felt muggy.

Danny adjusted his duty belt and stepped out of the facility, surveying the short line of cars creeping forward toward the bridge leading into Mexico. Many, he knew, were Mexican workers returning home. The northbound SENTRI lane was quiet at this time of night. Most Americans had left Ciudad Juarez long before dusk, fearful of being in the city after dark.

Danny couldn't blame them.

*   *   *

Eddie Machado fiddled with the radio on the Honda's dashboard as he waited in line to pay the toll and cross the Stanton Street Bridge. The *sicario* who owned the car had set the channels to mostly *ranchera* music. Eddie hated it. He was more into *banda* and ballads.

His left arm rested on the open driver's-side window as he turned the radio down low, not wanting to draw any attention.

As he looked up from the dashboard and out the windshield, his eyes locked on the CBP agent standing outside the

SENTRI facility. At first, Eddie didn't know why the Mexican looked familiar.

Then he knew.

It was the guy he'd shot outside Nogales, Arizona. Valdez was his name.

What the fuck was he doing here?

Eddie glanced in the rearview. No way to back up with a car directly behind him. No way he could move forward. He was boxed in.

He reached into the glove compartment for his FN-7 and slipped it in the waistband under his shirt. He kept his head down and eased the car forward. There were three cars ahead of him before he'd be on the bridge and across the border.

Eddie tried not to look at Valdez, but when he did, he saw the agent staring at him.

Shit!

Valdez was walking toward the Accord now. Maybe not sure he was looking at the guy who'd shot him.

Eddie eased the Accord forward. Only two cars were ahead of him.

Then it all went to hell.

The agent was holding up his hand in a stopping gesture and speaking into the mic clipped to his vest.

Reinforcements. Decision time.

Eddie unlatched his seat belt, opened the driver's-side door, and rolled out, using the car as a shield as he drew his weapon.

He stood and laid his forearms across the top of the car, his gun aimed at Valdez.

"Stop!" he called. "Or this time I will shoot you in the head."

Valdez stopped and moved his hand away from his holstered gun.

Behind Valdez Eddie could see two agents hurrying out of the building, their guns drawn.

Eddie backtracked quickly, keeping the gun pointed at Valdez till he got to the last car in line, an older model Chevy sedan. He yanked open the door and pulled out a frightened, heavy-set Mexican woman from behind the wheel.

Then he fired two quick rounds in the general direction of the agents moving toward him, hoping to warn them off, before he jumped behind the steering wheel and slammed the door.

Shoving the gearshift in reverse, he jammed the gas pedal to the floor. Screeching tires against hot pavement sent a plume of gray smoke in the air as the car shot backward. Eddie counted to three in his head, making sure he had enough speed, and swung the steering wheel hard right, spinning the car into a 180 J-turn.

He could hear guns go off and bullets thudding into the trunk. Thrusting the gearshift into DRIVE, he heard the rear window shatter. Bullets zinged past his head.

Then the Chevy died.

Eddie tried the key, the engine whining with effort.

Fuck it.

He swung open the driver's-side door, knelt behind it, and fired four quick shots in a left to right pattern through the open window. The charging agents scattered, but a round caught one in the leg and he went down.

Eddie was up and running now, past a Silva's Supermarket on his right, sprinting away from the bridge along the sidewalk on Stanton Street. He ran by an immigration office and Nicky's bar, people fleeing in front of him and the shouts of CBP agents behind him. Sirens wailed in the near distance.

He took cover behind the trunk of a thick tree in front of a communications store to catch his breath and surveil the landscape behind him.

Eddie counted four CBP agents and another three DHS agents moving cautiously in his direction, led by Valdez.

Should've made sure he was dead back near Nogales, Eddie thought.

Running again, he got to the corner of Seventh and Stanton, where he tried to carjack a pickup driven by a thick-bodied Latino, but the man ran the stoplight and Eddie was left standing in the middle of the street.

Cop cars were coming at him from all directions now.

Shit.

Eddie made a decision. Then he began walking back toward the approaching agents, carrying the FN-7 down along his leg.

"Drop the weapon and get on the ground!" Valdez yelled. "Now!"

Eddie kept coming.

"Drop your weapon!" Valdez yelled again.

Eddie stopped and smiled at Valdez. Then he lifted his arm, the gun hanging loose in his hand.

A volley of shots rang out and Eddie went down, choking on the blood pooling in his chest.

As he took his final breath, Eddie Machado thought of the beautiful face of his Isabella and of the three Mexican deaths his mother had told him about.

Who, he wondered, would speak his name for the last time?

Chapter 44

That same evening, a cup of hot chocolate in front of him and Gitana resting under the dining room table at his feet, Santana opened Ellis Taylor's murder book. He started with the callout —the first entry in the Chronological Record. Janet Kendrick and Diana Lee were alerted that patrol officers had been called to the scene at the Elysium Bank ATM, where a late-night customer had come across Ellis Taylor's body. Kendrick and Lee had responded along with teams from the Forensic Services Unit and the ME's office.

Once Taylor had been ID'd, Rita Gamboni, the Homicide Commander at the time, had been notified, along with the chief.

Because it was a high-profile case, the lead detective, Janet Kendrick, had composed all of the first entries, initialing each one. She wrote clearly and precisely, giving Santana a clear picture of the investigation.

Both Kendrick and Lee believed that Taylor had been murdered for the two hundred dollars he'd withdrawn from the ATM, and whatever money he'd had in his wallet. The detectives found no indication or evidence suggesting this was a targeted murder.

According to the autopsy report written by Reiko Tanabe, the Ramsey County medical examiner, Ellis Taylor had been shot at close range in the heart and had died at the scene before patrol officers and the detectives had arrived. The ME had removed a mostly intact .38 caliber bullet from Taylor's chest. The rifling twist on the round identified it as having come from a Colt revolver.

Santana moved on from the chrono to the Victim section of the murder book and Ellis Taylor's bio, authored by Lee and drawn from interviews with friends, known associates, and department documents. Lee's notes matched what she'd previously told him at the Little Asia Café.

Santana recalled that Taylor had been well liked by his colleagues in the department. He'd risen up the ranks from patrol officer to detective in the Crimes Against Property Division, where he'd worked primarily in arson and fraud and forgery before making the move to Homicide and Robbery. Santana wondered if Taylor had worked sex crimes, figuring that was where he might have become involved with young girls and Chico Caldera, who'd said Taylor was the cop that had been recruiting underage girls for sex trafficking. Unless Caldera had a beef with Taylor, which he could've had, it made no sense for him to lie. Perhaps, Santana thought, Caldera had been mistaken.

Kendrick and Lee had traced Ellis Taylor's movements the last night of his life. He'd worked the day shift and then had met his partner, Darnell Robinson, at a blues saloon on Rice Street for dinner and drinks. They'd stayed till closing and left in separate vehicles.

Robinson said he'd driven straight home. Given the time stamp on Ellis Taylor's withdrawal slip, he'd driven straight to the bank after leaving the club.

Santana considered his options. Nothing in Taylor's bio or background connected him with sex trafficking. That didn't mean Taylor wasn't involved. But something just didn't fit. Santana needed to figure out what it was—and soon.

* * *

He spent the following morning writing reports and re-reading Ellis Taylor's murder book. Then he got up from his desk and went to the Property Room to look through the evidence recovered from the ATM crime scene and to cross-check it with the evidence inventory in the murder book. Taylor's pants, socks, shirt, shoes, underwear, and belt were there, along with his wallet, driver's license, credit cards, an admission stub from the blues saloon, the last place he was seen alive, and his cellphone.

Returning to his desk, Santana flipped open the Property and Evidence Report tab in the murder book. From past experience he knew that the length of time wireless providers kept call records varied. Ellis Taylor's personal phone wireless provider, AT&T, kept call detail records for five to seven years for postpaid bills and had been keeping cellphone tower records since 2008. Kendrick and Lee had obtained those records and had matched them with Taylor's locations.

On a hunch, Santana searched the cellphone tower records for the evening Madison Porter was murdered. Based on the cellphone tower records, Ellis Taylor had not been near Battle Creek Park or Pig's Eye Regional Park that evening four years ago. Didn't mean Taylor hadn't killed her. Maybe he hadn't carried his personal cellphone with him that night. Still, it raised more questions in Santana's mind.

He turned to the Summary Reports, looking for something he'd missed, something that could point him in the right direction, but nothing clicked.

As he sat back in his chair, his eyes were drawn once again to the whiteboard listing the unsolved murder cases. Ellis Taylor's name was still missing, not surprising given that Kendrick hadn't added it. As Santana's gaze lingered on the board, he had a thought.

All photos from the time a rookie officer was hired till the time of their retirement photo were kept in their SPPD personnel file, along with letters of commendation, thank you letters from citizens, and education records. Officers had a new photo taken with every promotion and with every new chief. SPPD personnel records were part of the public record and could be viewed —but not copied or taken away—by non-police personnel. Anyone retiring in the last few years would have a fairly current photo in the file available to any detective. Santana could access the files, but he knew it would be more advantageous if he kept Kendrick in the loop, especially if a photo became part of a criminal investigation of a detective.

He knocked on her open door.

She stopped typing on her computer and waved him in.

He sat down in the chair in front of her desk. "I emailed you my report on the shootings at the Lake Elmo estate and Hal Langford's death."

Kendrick clasped her hands on the desktop as if she were about to pray. "What about James McGowan?"

"Far as I can tell, he isn't involved in the sex trafficking."

"You know the chief supports McGowan's Senate candidacy."

"I heard rumors," Santana said.

"Even if McGowan wasn't involved, his campaign is in flames."

"Guilt by association."

"Exactly."

Santana paused a moment before he spoke again. "There's more. It involves Taylor's murder. Give me another day."

Kendrick hesitated before giving a reluctant nod.

"And I need a photo of Darnell Robinson from his personnel file. And four other black officers chosen at random."

"What for?"

"Like I said, give me another day."

Once Santana had Darnell Robinson's retiree photo, and the photos of four random black officers, Santana returned to his desk. Using his computer, he accessed the SPPD Officer Down Memorial Page and downloaded a photo of Ellis Taylor.

Then he walked over to the LEC to re-interview Chico Caldera.

With his heavy-lidded eyes focused on empty space and his slumped posture, Caldera affected the casual "I could give a shit" attitude of a practiced felon.

"Figure you'd want to help yourself, Chico," Santana said.

"Already told you about the crooked cop. Still waiting for the DA's offer."

"I'll talk to him."

"You do that."

"In the meantime, I need you to look at some photos."

Santana opened a file folder, took out a mug shot of Gordon Grant, and set it on the table in front of Caldera.

"Do you know this man?"

Caldera glanced at the photo. "Yeah."

"How do you know him?"

"We met online through a website."

"SEXTO?"

Caldera nodded. "Grant liked to film men having sex with women."

"You mean raping underage girls."

"I don't know about that," Caldera said with a shrug.

"Sure you do, Chico. You provided Grant with young women like the two girls held captive in your attic."

"That a question?"

Santana opened the folder again and removed four photos of random black officers he'd gotten from Janet Kendrick, along with the photos of Darnell Robinson and Ellis Taylor, and placed them on the table in the interview room in two rows facing Caldera, three in each row.

Caldera took a moment before he worked up the energy to look at them.

"Any of these cops Ellis Taylor?"

"This some kind of trick, Santana?"

"Not at all. Just asking you to identify Taylor."

Caldera managed to sit up in the chair and scan the photos. Then he pointed at the second photo in the middle of the first row. "That's him," he said, identifying the photo of Darnell Robinson.

"See anyone else here you know?"

"This cop," he said, pointing to the photo of Ellis Taylor. "Came by the house one day. Showed me an ID. Said he was Ellis Taylor. Didn't know what to believe. Didn't matter much."

"Why not?"

"Guy was shot dead a month or so later."

Santana leaned forward. "This is important, Chico." Pointing at the photo of Darnell Robinson, Santana said, "Did you tell this officer that a man calling himself Ellis Taylor had come by to talk to you?"

Caldera sat silently for a time, staring at Santana, his face an expressionless mask, his cuffed hands resting on the table. "Seems like somebody's been gaslighting me," he said at last.

"I need to know, Chico."

Caldera chewed on his cheek. Then he nodded. "Yeah, I told this guy," he said, pointing at the photo of Darnell Robinson.

Chapter 45

Santana gathered up the photos and drove to the women's shelter where Ana Soriano was staying. They sat at a round table in the lounge.

"How are you doing?" he asked.

"Okay," she said. "The people are nice here. But I still don't want to stay."

"Be patient. Let me work something out."

She shrugged as if she had no choice.

"I'd like you to look at some photos." Santana opened the folder he'd brought with him and spread the six photos in front of her on the table in two rows of three. "Do you recognize any of these men?"

She stared at the photos for a time, her eyes narrowing as she appeared to zero in on one photo.

"This man," she said, pointing to the photo of Darnell Robinson.

"How do you know him?"

"When I was first forced into trafficking, he came to the house where I was kept."

"Were you there alone?"

She shook her head. "There were other girls."

"How many?"

"Maybe eight or ten. They came and went."

"Did you have sex with this man?"

As she looked at him, her eyes seemed to fill with dark and disturbing memories.

"Yes," she said. "More than once."

"How about the other girls?"

She nodded.

"Did he tell you his name?"

"No. But I saw his badge wallet once. His name was Robinson. I never forgot it."

"Why is that?"

"Because I knew then that I could never go to the police in this country for help. They were all just like the police in El Salvador."

"Not all of them," Santana said.

*   *   *

Back at his desk in Homicide and Robbery, Santana knew he needed more evidence of Darnell Robinson's involvement in sex trafficking and the possible murder of his own partner for the DA and for his own satisfaction. He'd known Robinson for years. Like Ellis Taylor, Robinson had been a respected cop. On the witness stand, a good defense attorney might be able to poke holes in Chico Caldera's and Ana Soriano's testimony as well as their credibility. And beyond their testimony, Santana thought, how could he prove Robinson's guilt or innocence?

There were other unanswered questions as well. Why had Ellis Taylor begun investigating his partner? What had tipped him off? Did Taylor suspect Robinson had also been involved in Madison Porter's murder?

Santana recalled the photo he'd taken of the evidence box sign-out sheet in the Property Room. He opened his cellphone and photo app and scrolled through till he found the photo in question. Taylor had looked at Madison Porter's evidence box three weeks before his murder. What was he looking for?

Santana opened Madison Porter's murder book and turned to the Summary section.

Darnell Robinson had interviewed Gordon Grant. Neither detective had looked at Grant's background and record. If that were Robinson's responsibility, then Taylor would have relied on his partner to run the check. And if Robinson knew Grant through the SEXTO website and was trafficking young girls like Madison Porter, then Robinson would have made sure Grant never became a suspect in Porter's murder.

Robinson also lived in Highwood Hills near Battle Creek Park and the kill site.

A flyer protruding from underneath a pile of reports on Santana's desk caught his eye. The flyer was from a seminar he'd attended prior to taking his leave from the department to visit his sister in Spain. The workshop involved the use of reverse location warrants.

A reverse location search warrant, sometimes called a "geofence" warrant, differed from a traditional search warrant in that it didn't identify a suspect and establish probable cause to ask for evidence of a suspect's crimes. Instead, it asked Google for information about anyone with a cellphone who passed through a designated area during a certain period of time. Santana could then work backwards to identify a possible suspect.

Location warrants assured privacy would be preserved through a two-step process. Google would first anonymously assign an identification number linked with each device's serial number when turning over the records. If a device's location, movement, or timing established probable cause, Santana could go back to the judge and get a second warrant ordering Google to reveal the name of the cellphone's owner.

Santana wrote up the warrant for the evening of July 16, four years ago. In order to narrow the scope and increase his chances of approval, he included a map of Battle Creek Park. He took it to Janet Kendrick for approval.

She read it and then, as her eyes locked on Santana, she laid the warrant on her desktop.

"You asked me to keep you in the loop," he said.

She nodded but didn't reply.

"Darnell Robinson was involved with sex trafficking, posing as Ellis Taylor," he continued. "I've got two eyewitnesses."

Kendrick let out a long breath and fiddled with the paper-clip in her hand. "This isn't good."

"Not for Robinson," he said, knowing full well that she meant not "good" for the department.

"Who's the other witness you have besides Chico Caldera?"

"Ana Soriano."

"The escort?"

Santana nodded.

"Not the most reliable witnesses."

"Robinson raped her."

Kendrick dropped the paperclip on the desktop and sat back, her forearms and hands planted on the armrests, her right index finger rhythmically tapping it as though she were silently counting the beats of her heart.

Santana wanted to raise a question that had been bothering him ever since he'd noticed Ellis Taylor's name was missing from the whiteboard listing unsolved cases.

He said, "You suspected Darnell Robinson killed Taylor all along. That's why you kept Taylor's murder book, isn't it?"

Kendrick nodded her head—slowly.

"Why?" he asked.

She let out another breath. "The .38 caliber bullet the ME pulled out of Taylor's chest. Robinson used to talk about his love of the Detective Special. Had one in the military before joining the SPPD. Hated it when we switched to Glocks."

"Lots of Detective Specials around."

"True. But it went out of production in '86. Not a weapon typically used by gangbangers who like the firepower of the nine millimeters."

Santana recalled that when he'd first joined the SPPD, the senior plainclothes detectives used to talk with reverence about the easily concealable, snub-nosed, six-shot Colt Detective Special. It was the first revolver produced with a swing-out frame and was chambered for higher-powdered cartridges like the .38

Special, the standard service cartridge for most US police departments from the 1920s to the 1990s.

"You ever confront Robinson?"

"I didn't have enough to go on."

"You could've gone after the gun."

"And if Robinson got rid of it," she said, "I would've had zip."

"We've got more than that now."

She handed him the reverse location warrant. "That's up to you."

*   *   *

Santana wrote up a warrant to search Darnell Robinson's cabin and then took it and the reverse location warrant to a judge. Once the reverse location warrant was signed, he emailed a copy to Google. Since this was a murder case possibly involving the sex trafficking of minors and narrow in scope, Santana hoped the company would respond more quickly when the Google screener received it.

On the way back from the courthouse, he picked up a couple of tacos and a Coke at the Rusty Taco. While he ate at his desk in the Homicide and Robbery Unit, he thought about how Ellis Taylor might have made the connection between Gordon Grant and Chico Caldera.

He remembered that Grant had once been charged with fifth-degree criminal sexual contact. If Taylor had discovered the charge, he might have talked to Grant. Would Grant have told Taylor about Caldera? Santana doubted it. But what if Taylor had talked to the victim? Could she have told Taylor about Caldera? Would she have even known about him?

Santana accessed the state Bureau of Criminal Apprehension portal on his computer, searching for the original police reports pertaining to Gordon Grant's arrest.

When he pulled up Gordon Grant's arrest report and read through it, he was surprised to learn that the young fifteen-year-old victim Grant had molested was Christine Hammond. It made sense. Grant had taped Hammond's photo to his bedroom wall, and Hammond had told Santana that some "creep" had molested her when she was fifteen and living on the streets. So Hammond had known Gordon Grant and Chico Caldera. If Ellis Taylor had questioned her about Grant, she could've led him to Chico Caldera. Caldera had admitted telling Darnell Robinson that Taylor had come around asking questions.

Those questions, Santana suspected, had gotten Ellis Taylor killed.

Santana dialed the Hazelden Rehabilitation Center. After identifying himself, he asked to speak to Christine Hammond. He was told she was in a group meeting. Santana left his phone number and a message to please call him back as soon as possible.

*　　*　　*

Early that evening, when Santana still hadn't heard from Christine Hammond, he was thinking that he'd have to make another trip to Hazelden. But then his cellphone rang.

"Detective Santana?"

"Hi, Christine. Thanks for getting back to me."

"Sorry it took so long. After the group meeting, I met with my psychologist and then had dinner. They didn't give me your message till then."

"No problem."

"I'm going home soon," she said in a voice that held both excitement and apprehension.

Santana wondered where "home" would be.

"I'll be living with a former Hazelden counselor till I get a job and can get back on my feet."

343

"Good for you," he said, thinking about Ana Soriano now, and what he could do to get her out of the shelter and into a safe and secure place where she could heal.

"How's Ana?" she asked as though reading his thoughts.

"She's fine. Living temporarily in a women's shelter."

"Thank God. I was so worried about her. I hope she won't be sent to jail and back to El Salvador. She doesn't deserve that after all she's been through."

"I'm going to do what I can to make sure that doesn't happen."

"What is it you wanted to talk to me about?"

"I apologize for having to bring this up, but it may be part of a case I'm working."

"It's okay. We talk about pretty much everything in our group sessions."

"Gordon Grant," he said.

He heard a quick intake of breath.

"I need to know, Christine, if a detective named Ellis Taylor ever came to you asking about Grant. It's important."

She was silent for a few moments longer before she replied. "I don't remember his name. Was he black?"

"Yes."

"I spoke to him about Grant."

"Was this before or after you met Dylan Walsh?"

"After," she said.

"Do you recall your conversation?"

"The detective asked if I knew Madison Porter or if Grant had ever mentioned her name. I told him I'd only known Grant briefly and had never known or met Madison Porter, though I'd heard she'd been murdered. I remember I got really frightened when I thought Grant might've killed Madison Porter."

"Did Dylan Walsh know Grant?"

"Dylan sold him drugs. But he never let Grant come around when I was with him. That was nice of Dylan."

"You told Walsh that Grant had sexually molested you."

344

"Yes."

"Do you recall what drugs he sold Grant?"

"Sorry. I don't remember."

Santana figured Dylan Walsh was selling Grant Rohypnol, or roofies. The drug found in the video room in Grant's basement. The same drug Walsh gave Christine Hammond so that Grant and others could rape and videotape her, Santana thought. Mr. "Nice Guy."

"You said Dylan Walsh introduced you to Chico Caldera."

"I don't remember it ever being that formal. Caldera just came around when he wanted a new supply of drugs."

"Did you know that Caldera was involved with sex trafficking?"

"Not at first. But when I started working for Dominique Lejeune, I saw Caldera around. And Ana told me all about him. He was very scary."

"When you spoke to Detective Taylor, did you talk to him about Chico Caldera?"

"Yes."

"Did you tell anyone else you'd talked to Taylor?"

"I told Dylan."

There it was.

Walsh, Grant, and Caldera all knew each other. Walsh would've told Grant and Caldera about Christine's conversation with Ellis Taylor. Caldera then told Robinson.

"Did Grant or Caldera kill Madison Porter?"

"No," Santana said.

"Do you know who did?"

"I believe so."

"That's good to know."

"You've been a big help, Christine. Take care of yourself."

"I will. Is it okay if I send you my address and phone number when I get out? I'd love to see Ana."

"Please do," Santana said.

Chapter 46

The following morning Bobbi Chacon was waiting by Santana's desk in the Homicide and Robbery Unit when he arrived.

"You're up early."

"Good news," she said with a grin. "The *sicario* we were looking for was killed at the El Paso border crossing. Name was Eddie Machado. He was a top assassin for El Mencho and the CJNG cartel. Agents found the money in the trunk of his car."

Santana dropped the signed search warrant for Darnell Robinson's cabin on his desktop. "They all go down the hard way eventually."

She nodded. "I'll sleep better."

"So what now?"

"I've applied for a transfer back to Texas and a possible promotion. I've got some juice with Weston."

"Because you're keeping your mouth shut about Joel Ryker."

"That, and because we solved his murder."

"Good for you."

Her eyes narrowed. "You don't like it?"

He shook his head. "Kendrick is using Ryker's complicity as leverage over Weston, too."

"The way of the world," she said.

"When are you leaving for Texas?"

"Any day now. Soon as the paperwork is completed."

"Good luck to you, Bobbi."

Her complexion flushed and she looked away for a second. "Not 'Chacon' anymore?"

Santana smiled.

"Well, that's progress. Speaking of which, how's your cold case coming?"

"Moving in the right direction. Got to drive up north and serve a search warrant."

"Someone involved with the murder?"

"Possibly."

She slipped her hands in her jean pockets. "Want some company? Shouldn't go without backup."

Santana thought about it. "I'll fill you in on the way."

*   *   *

Darnell Robinson lived three hours from the LEC in a two-story A-frame cabin on a northern lake outside Grand Rapids, Minnesota. The log cabin was set back on a green lawn in a clearing about thirty yards off a dead-end dirt road. Sunlight reflected off the large windows like a yellow flame and spread onto the first-floor wrap-around deck. A late-model black Ford-150 pickup was parked in the gravel drive.

As Santana and Chacon exited the car, he immediately felt the drop in temperature. While the temp was a hot and humid 85° in the cities, the air here felt dryer and a good ten degrees cooler among the birch and tall pines that reached for the blue sky.

"Quite a place for a retired cop," Chacon said.

Santana led the way up the steps and onto the deck to the front door.

Since it was a "Knock and Announce" warrant, Santana knocked on the door and called out loudly, "Police! Search warrant! Open the door!" He waited a few moments and then knocked and announced again.

Then he peered through the glass.

"Maybe he's down by the lake," Chacon said, pointing toward the thick forest blocking the water from view.

They spread out and walked toward the back of the cabin till they reached a narrow footpath that wound through the trees toward the lake. A minute later they came out of the woods and into a clearing at the edge of the water.

Darnell Robinson, clad in flip-flops, khaki shorts, and a sweat-stained, sleeveless blue shirt, was unloading fishing gear from a good-sized pontoon onto a dock.

Bobbi Chacon released the strap on the Glock holstered on her hip and stood on the sandy beach while Santana walked onto the dock.

Startled by the footsteps, Robinson looked up, his jaw dropping and his eyebrows arching momentarily in surprise.

"Santana," Robinson said with a smile. "What gives?"

Santana held up the warrant. "We have a search warrant. How about walking up to the cabin with us?"

Robinson noticed Chacon.

Chacon offered a little wave.

"Who's that?" Robinson asked, directing his question to Santana.

"Bobbi Chacon," she said. "DEA."

"What the hell?"

Santana waited.

"I don't get it," Robinson said. "What're you looking for?"

Santana was close enough to see Robinson's dark brown eyes jittering as he thought through his options. He figured Robinson knew why he and Chacon were there, so he ignored Robinson's question.

"You can make this easier and faster, Darnell, if you'll just cooperate."

"You're not gonna tell me why you're here?"

"You were a detective once. Figure it out."

Robinson looked at each of them for a long beat. "Okay," he said with a shrug. "Come on up to the house."

Inside the spacious cabin with the light oak flooring, Chacon stood beside a fireplace whose stone rose from the hearth to the high-beamed ceiling. Santana flanked Robinson by standing on the opposite side of the room by a door along the glass wall facing the deck. Robinson stopped in front of a counter separating the living and dining room from the kitchen and the shiny stainless steel appliances. He was facing Santana while reading the copy of the warrant Santana had given him.

Bobbi Chacon repositioned herself beside the two wood-and-glass gun cases on the wall to Robinson's left. One case held a Winchester Model 94 rifle and a Remington 870 shotgun. The second case displayed a series of handguns. Santana recognized a .357 Colt Python Magnum, a German made Walther P38, and a Colt single action Army revolver, also known as the Peacemaker. He couldn't see the other guns because Chacon was standing in front of the case now.

The artwork and dream catcher hanging on the walls was mostly Native American. But on the rustic coffee table in front of a red leather couch, Santana saw a familiar piece. It was a sculptured replica of a melted watch, one of Salvador Dalí's most well-known pieces. The sculpture looked like the tongue of a shoe mounted on a square bronze stand. The melted watch had a green background with gold numbers and edging.

"Well, hell," Robinson said, walking behind the counter. "Take the load off your feet and have a beer."

"Keep your hands where we can see them," Santana said.

"Hey, chill out, John," Robinson said. He dropped the warrant on the counter, opened the refrigerator, took out a can of Budweiser, and pulled the pop-top. Then he leaned his elbows on the counter and sipped the beer.

"Fan of Salvador Dalí?" Santana asked.

Robinson's eyes caught Santana's hard stare before he averted them. "Not particularly. Wife liked him. Picked up a few items when we were in Spain years ago."

Santana recalled the fig trees he'd seen while in a hypnogogic state. Now he understood the meaning.

"Your wife, Regina, was born in Figueres, Spain, in Catalonia, near the French border."

"That's right."

"Same place Salvador Dalí was born."

"Yeah."

"Big Dalí museum there."

Robinson nodded.

"In Spanish *higueras* means fig trees, but in Catalan the trees are called *figueres*."

"Interesting bit of information, I guess, but so what?"

"Ever read any books about Dalí and his work?"

"Not me," Robinson said with a little shake of his head. "Might be some books about him around here. Haven't cleaned things out since my wife passed away."

"Funny thing about time," Santana said. "It's a human notion. Dalí considered it constricting but important in memory."

"That so?" Robinson said, drinking more beer.

"Time is fluid and universal," Santana said. "Has no limits and stops for no one. What do you think, Darnell?"

"Haven't given that much thought."

"Maybe you should."

"Why don't you get to it, Santana?"

"Okay. Let's start with your dead partner."

Robinson straightened up and laid his palms on the counter. "What about Ellis?"

"He was on to you. A few weeks before he was murdered, he checked out Madison Porter's evidence box. He was reworking the case. Discovered that Gordon Grant had been convicted of criminal sexual conduct. Taylor interviewed the young girl Grant had molested and then tried to interview Chico Caldera. Grant and Caldera were involved with sex trafficking young girls. Caldera told you about Taylor's visit."

Robinson licked his lips. "I don't know any Caldera. And I wasn't involved with sex trafficking."

"Caldera picked you out of a six pack," Santana said, referring to the six photos he'd shown Caldera. "Thought you were Ellis Taylor. Picked Taylor's photo out too. ID'd him as the cop that came by his house asking about you a couple weeks before he was shot to death. Young girl who was sex trafficked and who you raped ID'd you as well."

"You know me, John. I ain't no killer."

"People can change their addresses, Darnell, but they can't change who they are. And then there's Madison Porter."

Robinson paused a beat. "You think I killed that girl?"

"She liked to jog in Battle Creek Park every evening before dark. You lived near there. She was young and pretty. A perfect candidate for the SEXTO website. Grant knew her because he lived in the neighborhood. Likely convinced her to let him take the photo of her he kept in his bedroom. Maybe you two talked about kidnapping her. But things went haywire when you tried to abduct her, and you killed her. Then you tried to mislead Kendrick and Lee by staging the crime scene to look like something from a Salvador Dalí Alice in Wonderland drawing. Got the idea out of one of your wife's books. You were worried Taylor had gotten on to you. That's why you killed him, too."

"You're a crazy son-of-a-bitch."

"Where's your Detective Special, Darnell? Bet the bullet the ME pulled out of Taylor will match that gun."

Robinson stood silent for a time, his eyes moving from Santana to Chacon and then back again. "Lost that gun in the Northwoods."

"Convenient," Santana said.

"Probably was here," Chacon said, pointing toward the missing gun in the second row of the case.

"Have to get a replacement," Robinson said, stepping behind her. Then, in one quick motion, he grabbed a fistful of her hair, pulled a long knife from the butcher block on the kitchen counter, and held the blade against her throat.

Santana drew his Glock and held it steady at Robinson.

"Goddammit!" Chacon said.

"Take your gun out of the holster and toss it aside," Robinson hissed in Chacon's ear.

She kept her eyes on Santana as she slid her duty weapon out of the waist holster.

"Easy now," Robinson said.

Chacon tossed the Glock onto a couch cushion.

Robinson's eyes were wide with excitement as he glared at Santana. "Your turn. Drop the gun, Santana, or I swear I'll kill her."

"Don't do it, John!" Chacon yelled.

"Shut up!" Robinson said to her, pressing the knife tighter against her throat.

"Kendrick knows where we are and why we're here," Santana said. "Killing Chacon won't change anything."

"Not for you, maybe, but it'll sure as hell change for her."

Chacon held her eyes on Santana and then looked down toward her left ankle, sending him a message.

"Time's growing short, Darnell."

"Thought you said it never stops."

"That's Dalí's idea. Time stops for those who are dead."

"You keep talking, that's exactly what'll happen to Chacon. Now drop the gun."

Santana shook his head. "Not a chance."

"You think I won't kill her?"

"You said you weren't a killer, Darnell. Prove it."

Robinson stood perfectly still, his eyes looking at some distant point. "Didn't mean to kill that Porter girl, Santana. Things just got out of hand."

"Drop the knife, Darnell."

Robinson looked at Chacon for a moment. Then he shoved her hard away from him and came at Santana, the knife raised in a stabbing position above his head.

Santana stepped back. "Freeze, Darnell!"

Robinson kept coming, a blank expression on his face.

Those were the last words Robinson ever heard.

Chacon pulled the Glock out of her ankle holster and shot Robinson in the back of the head.

Epilogue

The outgoing SPPD Chief of Police, Tim Branigan, dealt with the initial blowback from the department's conclusion that Darnell Robinson had murdered both Madison Porter and his former partner, Ellis Taylor. Branigan then retired and left for "Blue Heaven" in Idaho and his new chief position.

Santana helped Jamal Washburn work out a plea deal with the DA for a shorter sentence provided he testified against Dean Moody. Same with Chico Caldera, though he'd be spending years in prison on sex trafficking charges. Gordon Grant's trial was scheduled for later in the year, but Santana had little doubt that Grant would be a very old man before he ever finished his time behind bars, if he even lived that long.

Raúl Torres and his sister, Luciana, were arrested by Customs and Border Patrol agents and charged with sex trafficking.

A search of Hal Langford's apartment turned up checks he'd illegally written from James McGowan's campaign fund to the expensive law firm representing Gordon Grant.

McGowan lost his Senate bid but vowed to run again.

Kelly Quinn, the *Pioneer Press* crime reporter, wrote an exposé about the prominent local men involved in the After Dark Club, based on information provided to her by Santana and Gabe Thornton, the SPPD Narco/Vice detective.

Kenny Coleman and the Treasury Department arrested Derek Shelton, who was accused of laundering drug money at the Elysium Bank, primarily from accounts established by Martin Lozano. After admitting that she knew about Shelton's involvement, Ashley Porter had been working for Coleman and collecting information for the Treasury Department.

Before Bobbi Chacon left town for a new position with the DEA in El Paso, Texas, Santana took her out for dinner at Mancini's steak house.

Gone were the T-shirt, jeans, boots, and pomade hair. In their place were a black silk blouse and slacks, open-toed sandals, understated makeup and lipstick, and tousled hair.

Santana hardly recognized her.

"A dress would be too much," she said when he picked her up.

Over wine and fried calamari, she said, "Where'd you learn all that stuff about Dalí?"

"Been into surrealism ever since I was young."

"And the figs? That connection was weird."

Santana considered bringing up the subject of his dreams and Dalí's "slumber with a key" technique but rejected the idea. Bobbi Chacon, he knew, was more grounded in the here and now.

"You weren't gonna give up your gun to Robinson," she said, not waiting for his reply.

"That wasn't the plan."

"Oh, so you had a plan."

"I was counting on you."

She smiled. "Well, I won't miss having a gun stuck in my back or knife at my throat. But I will miss working with you, though that's not easy for me to say."

"Why?"

"Not a lot of trust in men right now. But you might be an exception."

It was Santana's turn to smile. "I'll take that as a compliment."

"Good, because it'll probably be the only one you get."

"Well, here's one for you. You saved my life."

"Nah," she said with a dismissive wave. "Robinson would've never stabbed you."

355

"You think?"

She sipped some wine and nodded. "More likely suicide by cop. I think he was just working up the nerve to do it."

"That's a little cold, isn't it?"

"Right," she said. "I'm sure you were thinking how cold-hearted it would be to kill Robinson as he came at you with a butcher knife."

"You ever kill someone before?"

"Nope."

"How do you feel about it now?"

She set the wine glass on the table and looked at Santana, her amber eyes glowing like the candlelight on the table. "The asshole murdered an innocent young girl and his own partner. I'm not losing any sleep over the fact that I killed him. How about you?"

Santana shook his head.

*   *   *

Later that same week, Rita Gamboni was named Deputy Chief of Major Crimes. Santana wasn't sure how the two of them would untangle the bureaucratic web her new job and his role as a homicide detective had created.

June lived up to its reputation as Minnesota's rainiest month, limiting the time Santana spent on his boat, the *Alibi*. But with the ongoing gang violence and the city's rising murder rate, he figured he wouldn't have much time for recreation and relaxation anyway.

A judge appointed Santana temporary guardian of Ana Soriano after learning she was just seventeen. She moved into a spare bedroom in his house and made an instant connection with Gitana.

She reminded Santana of his sister, Natalia. He'd had to leave her behind when he'd fled Colombia at sixteen after killing the men who'd murdered his mother. Though he felt both the killings and fleeing were justified, and Natalia had been safely hidden and protected, he'd never totally forgiven himself for leaving her. Left alone, she could very well have ended up a victim of sex trafficking like Ana Soriano. Now, he thought, he'd been given a second chance at saving a young girl. He saw it as part of his mission and also something beyond it. He had to do all he could for her.

They planned an outing with Christine Hammond, but two weeks after being released from the Hazelden Rehabilitation Center, she overdosed on meth mixed with fentanyl.

Santana and a tearful Ana Soriano were two of a dozen people, mostly from Hazelden, who attended her funeral. No one had been able to locate Christine's mother.

In his eulogy the minister spoke about the poet Robert Frost, who said, "The best way out is always through."

The minister ended the eulogy with another Frost quote. Asked what he thought was the most important thing he'd learned about life, Frost said that he could sum up everything he'd learned in three words.

"It goes on."

It was a message Santana had taken to heart. He hoped Ana Soriano would as well.

Reward

I offer you, the reader, the opportunity to redeem a cash award for introducing this novel, or another of the author's novels, to any producer who offers an acceptable contract [to the author] for his work. The reward offered is 10% of any initial option contract for film up to a maximum of $10,000.00.

Our mutual goal is to introduce this work to producers. Many of you are familiar with the term "six degrees of separation," the theory that anyone on the planet can be connected to any other person on the planet through a chain of acquaintances that has no more than five intermediaries. This is what I aim to accomplish here with your help.

- Think about whom you know and whom they might know.
- Think about whom you know that reads and would enjoy this book.

Send any leads, opportunities, or introductions via email to www.christophervalen.com

Thank you in advance for your help.

Afterword

Human Trafficking is a criminal activity that is characterized by the exploitation of adults and children for profit. The two most common types of trafficking are labor and sexual slavery. Each year, according to the US Department of Justice, an estimated 14,500 to 17,500 foreign nationals are trafficked into the United States. The number of US citizens trafficked within the country each year is even higher, with an estimated 200,000 American children at risk for trafficking into the sex industry.

The National Human Trafficking Resource Center (NHTRC) is a national, toll-free hotline for the human trafficking field in the United States and is reached by calling **1-888-373-7888** or e-mailing NHTRC@PolarisProject.org

Report missing children or child pornography to the National Center for Missing and Exploited Children (NCMEC) at **1-800-THE-LOST (843-5678)** or through the Cybertipline or **Text the National Human Trafficking Hotline at 233733.**

Acknowledgments

The following resources have been helpful in my research: *50 Secrets of Magic Craftsmanship* by Salvador Dalí. *The Surrealist Manifesto* by André Breton. *The Dali Legacy: How an Eccentric Genius Changed the Art World and Created a Lasting Legacy* by Dr. Christopher Heath Brown and Dr. Jean-Pierre Isbouts. *The Espace Dalí*, Paris, France.

The author wishes to thank the following people for their help with this novel.

Abigail Davis, Linda Donaldson, Lorrie Holmgren, Jenifer LeClair, Chuck Logan, Peg Wangensteen, and Jennifer Adkins, my editor, for your time, insightful reads, edits, and suggestions of the work in progress. Thanks also to Rebecca Treadway for another great cover.

Special thanks to Tim Lynch, Homicide Commander, St. Paul Police Department (Ret.), for once again sharing his knowledge and expertise.

And, as always, thanks to my wonderfully supportive wife, Martha, without whose inspiration and experiences John Santana would not exist.

Made in the USA
Middletown, DE
17 January 2022